Paths of Exile

Carla Nayland

Published by Quaestor2000 Ltd
Cheshire, 2009

Quaestor2000 Ltd, 15 Turner Close CW1 3WZ
Website: http://www.quaestor2000.com
British Library Cataloguing in Publication Data
Data Available

ISBN: 978-1-906836-09-2 (paperback)
ISBN: 978-1-906836-10-8 (large print)

Printed and bound in Great Britain by
Lightning Source UK Ltd, Milton Keynes
and in the United States by
Lightning Source Inc., La Vergne, Tennessee

geond lagu lade longe sceolde hreran

mid hondum hrim cealde sæ

wadan wræclastas

wyrd bið ful aræd

(he must for a long time

travel the waterways, the ice-cold sea

tread the paths of exile.

Fate goes as it must)

From *The Wanderer*, tenth-century Old English poem

PICTS

DAL RIADA

50 Miles

STRAT CLUT

GODODDIN

BERNICIA

RHEGED

DEIRA

ELMET

LINDSEY

GWYNEDD

POWYS

EAST ANGLES

DEMETIA

GEWISSAE

KENT

SOUTH SAXONS

DUMNONIA

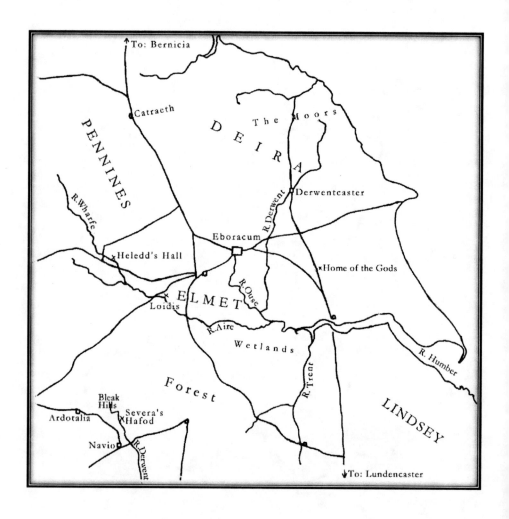

Chapter 1

Eadwine sprinted up the crumbling steps and ran round the ramparts to a point where he could see the southward road.

It was empty.

So sure had he been that he would see it filled by his brother's approaching army that at first he thought his eyesight must have failed. With an impatient gesture he rubbed the stinging sweat out of his eyes with his torn and bloodstained sleeve and looked again.

The road was still empty.

His stomach knotted into the hollow pain of fear. He had no need to look over the northern rampart to see the smear of dust on the horizon that marked the position of the invading army he had been harrying for the last two days and nights of ambush, snare and murder. He had delayed them. He had left half of them dead. He had made the survivors curse the day they came to Deira. He had made their leader, one Black Dudda, into a bitter personal enemy who had sworn to see him dead. And it had all been for nothing, if Eadric was not here with the main army.

The old fort was half derelict and wholly indefensible. There was no garrison of any kind. The local population would be no help in any fighting, accustomed as they were to an easy and peaceful life here on the rich plain of Derwent Vale. The warden of the northern march was supposed to protect them from border raids, and no enemy had got this far in Eadwine's three years of tenure.

Until now.

The smear of dust on the northern horizon was perceptibly closer. An hour away, Eadwine estimated, or a little more. A hundred warriors with fallen comrades to avenge, thirsting for blood. And nothing stood between them and the heart of Deira, except Eadwine and the battered handful of weary survivors with him.

**

Snatches of talk floated up to him, as men shoved to slake their thirst at the fort well.

"– I told him his high and mighty brother wouldn't bother coming, too busy chasing skirt in Eboracum, I said –"

"And you know he won't hear a word against his brother, so you might as well save your breath –"

"Reckon he's going to fight them here?"

"What, in this dump? Piss on these walls and they'd fall down."

"There's nowhere better, not til you get all the way to Eboracum. He'll have to fight here."

"A dozen of us, against a hundred of them?"

"We fight bravely and make an end worthy of a song!"

"A bloody short song –"

"You got a better idea? If he runs home they'll call him a coward. Could you face that?"

"I'd rather be dead!"

"No problem there. Sup up, lads, we'll all dine in Woden's hall tonight."

"First one there gets the beer in –"

"Last one gets the pick of the girls —"

***

Eadwine stopped listening. Icy sweat prickled down his spine. There was no more scope for hit-and-run fighting now they were out of the moors and marshes and onto the plain. If he did not fight here, he would have to flee ahead of the invaders and bear the shame of being called a coward. If he made a stand here, outnumbered many times over and with no useful defences, he and the men with him would die. A stark choice, shame or death. Yet he could not see it as simply as that. Already men had died at his command, men he had known and counted as friends, men who had families who would mourn their loss and perhaps curse him for it. If he was going to order men to die, he wanted to have something practical to show for it. What could a stand against overwhelming odds achieve? At best, they could hope to take a dozen of the enemy with them and delay the rest for an hour or two. If Eadric was on his way with the army, that hour or two would give Eadric time to get here and crush the invaders before they could plunder Deira. That would be worth the cost. Eadric would be proud of him.

He peered over the wall again. Still no sign of movement on the broad pale ribbon of the southward road. Eadric was not coming.

"Why?" Eadwine muttered. "Why, why, why? Eadric, where are you?"

To which, of course, there was no answer but a nameless, gnawing fear. Surely nothing but some terrible disaster could have prevented Eadric from answering his urgent summons? Eadric, the golden hero of Deira, would not have abandoned even the insignificant youngest brother to fight outnumbered ten to one, except in some dire need. What was that need? What was happening? What would Eadric want him to do?

***

"Lord?"

Eadwine whipped round, startled out of his thoughts. Lilla, the youngest warrior in the warband and the closest to a friend, had come noiselessly up the steps and was holding out a pitcher. Clear water dripped down the sides, and Eadwine was suddenly aware that his throat was parched dry as the dusty road. He drank in greedy gulps, spilling water over his face and chest, forgetting to breathe until he choked on it. How long since he had last drunk? This morning at least. Twelve hours of fighting on a hot day, wearing metal armour. With the partial slaking of his thirst came more unwelcome physical sensations, ignored until then. Hunger, aching fatigue, the crushing weight of his mail shirt, the small pains of minor wounds, a dull throb behind his eyes. And over it all the sick dread of anxiety. Why had Eadric not come? What to do for the best?

"Wulfgar says it's just a raid," Lilla said, sounding doubtful. "He says they'll loot the hall here, burn a few unimportant villages and go home."

Eadwine winced. That was typical of Wulfgar, who was good at fights and better at starting them. Talking of 'burning unimportant villages' in front of Lilla, who had joined the warband after his family and home were destroyed in a raid, was tactless even by Wulfgar's clodhopping standards.

Lilla grinned, and pushed his mop of chestnut hair back from his face. "I didn't fight him. I thought you wouldn't thank me for it. Anyway, it's boring. I always win."

"Almost always," Eadwine said dryly. Lilla was small and lithe and fast, like a stoat to Wulfgar's bullock, but brawn had been known to triumph over speed.

2

"And in answer to your next question, of course he's wrong. A raiding party is a dozen or a score. Two hundred is an army."

"They look in a hurry to get somewhere, too," Lilla added. "Where?"

"It can only be Eboracum." Eadwine gestured at the southward road. "That's where that army-path goes. It's the heart of Deira. If they take Eboracum they take the kingdom."

"But –" Lilla began, and broke off uneasily.

"Go on."

"Well – I've never seen Eboracum. But you say it's a great city. A fortress. Bigger than my whole village and all the fields around. Even if they still had the two hundred they started with, that wouldn't go far against Eboracum, would it?"

Eadwine sighed. He had been puzzling over that himself for two days without mentioning his doubts to anyone, but he should have known Lilla would be bright enough to work out the problem for himself. "They might as well try to fell a tree with a spoon," he agreed.

"So what are they really after?"

"If I knew that," Eadwine said wearily, dragging his hand through his filthy dark hair, "I'd know how best to stop them getting it."

Movement below forestalled Lilla's reply. A stocky fair-haired warrior was shepherding a fussy little man in through one of the cart-sized breaches in the fort wall.

"Ah!" Eadwine exclaimed. "Ashhere's found the steward. About time!"

In theory he should stand on his dignity as the king's son and wait for the steward to come to him, but he had never cared much for protocol. He raced down the steps two at a time, careless of the loose stonework. Lilla paused to retrieve the pitcher and followed at a rather more sensible pace.

**

"Message? What message?" said the steward blankly, when he was finally convinced that the smoke-blackened and bloodstained scarecrow in front of him was indeed the king's youngest son. "No, Garulf never came here. Know him anywhere, I would. Was it important?"

"You're about to be invaded by Black Dudda and a Bernician army," Lilla informed him. "In about an hour, I'd say."

The steward paled. Evidently Black Dudda's reputation was known even this far south. "The Butcher of Eden Vale?" He flapped his hands as if trying to swat a wasp. "Why aren't you fighting them? You're supposed to guard the border! You're supposed to protect us!"

Deornoth, headman of the village at Beacon Bay and leader of what was left of its militia, spat. "A bit of help wouldn't go amiss," he said, with a sour glance at the steward's immaculate clothes and comfortable paunch. "Where are you when we get raided, eh?"

"Oh, well, if you can't put up with raids you shouldn't live on the border," said the steward, with a shrug.

"Leave it, Deornoth," Eadwine warned. "And you too, Fulla." He swung round to confront a bearded barrel of a man in malodorous sheepskins who subsided with a sulky muttering, then turned back to the steward. "You're certain Garulf never passed here? So Eadric would never have got my message?"

"Looks that way," agreed the steward. "Any road, Lord Eadric's got his hands full already. Rumour says he's fighting Aethelferth of Bernicia way out

3

west." A complacent wave of the hand indicated somewhere comfortably far off. "Eboracum or Dere Street or somewhere."

The news struck Eadwine like a blow to the stomach. Eadric under attack! His instinctive reaction was to race to his brother's side with all possible speed and give his own life to save him. Then, hard on its heels, came rational thought. Black Dudda's purpose became clear in a flash of insight, like sunshine breaking through fog. A surprise double attack, worthy of the clever and deceitful Aethelferth. One army to march down Dere Street on the traditional invasion route from the north and draw Eadric into battle on the plain. A second, under Black Dudda, to appear on this back route out of the moors and stab Eadric in the back.

So Eadric needed Black Dudda's army stopped. For a moment the prospect of making a stand here and dying gloriously in the attempt beckoned to Eadwine as sweetly as a girl in a summer hayfield. No-one could scorn him as a coward if he did that. It was the warrior's way, the hero's way. But the glory would be empty. A few deaths here, however noble, would not stop Black Dudda and would not help Eadric. A warning might save Eadric's life. Put like that, it was no choice at all.

Eadwine looked round wildly. "Get me a horse!"

The steward spread his hands. "We don't keep any horses here –"

"Then we march," Eadwine said grimly. "Now. We're an hour ahead of them. If we march all night we might yet warn Eadric in time. Tell your folk here to scatter and take their animals with them. Black Dudda is very angry and he'll take it out on this estate, but he's in a hurry. He won't go far from the road."

The steward gaped. "What? But you can't –"

Eadwine turned to Deornoth and Fulla and the other men of the militia. "You'd best go home now. Look after your folk and your families. You've done your duty and more besides."

Deornoth hesitated, looking half relieved and half disappointed, then offered, "We'll stay if you ask us to."

"Just take note I've already done my seven days for this month," rumbled Fulla. "I know my rights."

"Believe me, I know you do," Eadwine said dryly. His stern face softened. "I thank you for your offer, but your families need you more than I do now. Someone needs to keep order on the March until I return."

"Aye," Deornoth agreed, unhappily. "You'll come back?"

"I am still the Warden of the March, until the king says otherwise or until I die. Don't fear. Aethelferth and Black Dudda will break on Eboracum's walls like a ship on your cliffs. Unless the Three Ladies choose otherwise, I will be back before winter." He looked round for the five remaining warriors of his warband, who were already picking up weapons and filling water skins. "Got everything? Come on then –"

"Well!" declared the steward to the world in general. "I never thought I'd see the day when a king's son ran away like a coward without a blow struck, leaving us defenceless in the path of an army –"

Eadwine turned on him like a stooping falcon. "*Half* an army. Thanks to us! Don't tell me you didn't see the beacons summoning men to fight. And what did you do? Nothing! You left the Marchmen to do the fighting while you dozed behind our shields. You in the south think because you never see a raider that means there aren't any. Well, you're about to find out what it's like, and it's your responsibility to get the people of this estate through it with the least possible

4

harm. So get off your lazy arse and herd your sheep out of danger. Earn your keep." He turned on his heel without waiting for a response and strode back to his weary companions. "Come on. One more march. You can rest in Eboracum."

***

On and on, mile after mile, the pale ribbon of the army-path unrolled through field and copse and pasture. Following it in the faint starlight made few demands on weary minds and bodies. None of them spoke. No-one had the energy for the marching songs or ribald banter that would normally pass the time.

Half-stupefied with fatigue, Eadwine seemed to see the ghosts of all the other soldiers who had marched this road in the past and would march it in times yet to come, striding out to conquer new lands, or fleeing in shame from bloody defeat, or hastening to the aid of comrades in some beleaguered outpost. He thought with gratitude of the men who made the road, so long ago that no-one now remembered who they were, or even whether they were men or giants or gods. The builders were gone now, but their roads and their fortresses still remained, still guarding the rich plains of Deira, if only men had the wit and the courage to use them.

***

"Open up!" Eadwine hammered again on Eboracum's north gate. "Open up!"

A pale worried face appeared on the ramparts above the gatehouse. "Who's there? Stand back so I can see you."

"I am Eadwine son of Aelle," Eadwine shouted up, stepping back onto the causeway so that the morning light would shine on his face and armour. "Open up!"

The sentry was still wary. "Give the password."

"I've been away for half a year, how would I know today's password?" Eadwine snapped back, losing patience. "But I know you, Ceolred. You hold land from Aldhere of Eoforwic, your ginger sow got into your storeroom last Yule and drank all the beer you'd brewed for your sister's wedding, your children are called Eadgyth and Ceolferth and your wife was expecting another this Midsummer just gone. Now get down here and open this gate!"

Running footsteps pattered in the gatehouse, the locking bar rattled in its socket, and the gate creaked open to reveal two suspicious spearmen.

"Can't be too careful," mumbled the older of the two, reluctantly standing aside. "Raiders and thieves all over the place, they've already burned the wharves and all the boats on the river, and folk say there's an army coming –"

"Two armies," Eadwine corrected grimly. "Or rather, one and a half. Where can I find my brother?"

"Lord Cynewulf's with the King –"

"No, no, my *brother*. Lord Eadric. The heir to Deira. Where is he?"

The guards exchanged awkward glances. Eadwine's voice grew sharp with anxiety. "What's happened? *Tell me!*"

The older sentry put a hand on his arm with rough kindness. "Easy, lad."

Eadwine went very still. What little colour was left in his face drained away and his voice dropped to a whisper. "Is he hurt?"

The sentry swallowed, shuffled, and finally spoke.

"Lord Eadric is dead."

5

Chapter 2

Eadwine stumbled to his knees beside the remains of the pyre. So it was true. Eadric was dead, and it seemed the sun had fallen out of the sky.

He found he was clutching a handful of ashes, as if trying to reach out to his beloved brother. Sighing, he opened his hand and let the grey fragments drift away on the wind. He should have formed a shield-wall and offered battle at Derwentcaster fort after all. A world without Eadric in it was a world not worth living in.

A slight sound penetrated his misery. He looked up, and for a moment his heart leaped in wild joy. Some mistake! Eadric was here, alive and well –!

He reached out and the illusion faded. Not Eadric. Eadric's son, Hereric. The boy had his father's blond colouring and muscular build, and the deceiving eye of hope had done the rest. Hereric's face was puffy from crying, his blue eyes bewildered. He recognised his young uncle and crept out from the willows fringing the river.

"My father's dead," he said, in a flat, dead tone that failed to stop his voice from quivering..

Eadwine's heart went out to him. Here was someone in greater need than himself.

"Yes," he answered, not trusting himself to say more.

"He died in battle." Hereric sniffed, unable to stop himself, and paused until he thought he had his voice under control again. "He was very brave –"

The sentence terminated in something between a snort and a sob, and the boy turned round hastily to hide his face.

"We'll avenge him, Hereric," Eadwine said quietly. "All those who killed him will die."

"But it won't bring him back!" That was a howl of pure misery, as Hereric gave way to his grief. "He's *dead!* Oh, he's dead, he's dead, and I'll never see him again –!"

The tears came in a scalding flood, and Eadwine put his arms around the boy and held him until the storm passed and Hereric's racking sobs died away into a series of sniffles and gulps and long shaking breaths. He said nothing, because he knew that if he spoke he would break down himself.

After a while, Hereric pulled away, averting his face and scrubbing at his eyes. Eadwine looked tactfully in the opposite direction until a tug at his sleeve indicated that Hereric considered himself presentable again.

"Don't tell anyone I was crying," he said, in a small and shaky voice, and then began to cry again, quietly and hopelessly. "I don't want to leave him," he wept, "it's all cold and grey and lonely here –"

"But he isn't here any more," Eadwine said softly, striving for something that might ease the boy's grief. "He isn't lying in the cold ashes. His spirit has flown away on the smoke and gone straight to the gods. So you and I are here missing a father and a brother, and your mother is missing her husband, but Eadric isn't missing us. Tonight is his great night. Tonight he enters Woden's hall. Don't think of him as he was when he was laid on the pyre, but as he is now. The limp that troubled him since his fall two winters ago has gone. The wounds that killed him have all vanished. His hair is thick and gold and gleaming, even where he was going bald on top. He is as strong and handsome and merry as when he was a young man and carried you around on his shoulders, but he has the wisdom and the experience of his years. He is dressed in his best clothes – green trousers, a blue tunic, a scarlet cloak. A slave girl is arraying him for war. She settles his mail shirt on his shoulders. Girds his sword at his waist. Standing on a stool – for he was a tall man – she sets his boar-crested helmet on his head. In his left hand he takes his shield. In his right he grips his spear."

A quick glance sideways confirmed that he had Hereric's rapt attention.

"Now see him entering Woden's hall. It is a magnificent building, a hundred times bigger than the palace at Eboracum, built not from stone but from massive timbers hewn by the giants at Thunor's command. Tapestries worked by Frija and her maidens adorn the walls, showing how Woden hung upon the World Tree to win the mead of poetry, how Thunor fought the serpent and defeated the giants. All are so richly ablaze with gold and colours that the pictures seem alive. A great fire burns in the centre, built from whole trees, and the light of it flows over the land for miles around. Over it hangs a huge cauldron, big enough to cook two whole oxen at once. Woden's handmaids, each as fair as the fairest princess, carry mead and meat and bread to the warriors. A skald sings the Lay of Beowulf. All the great warriors are there, at feast after a day in the field. Look along the mead-benches at all the famous faces. There is Offa, who was king in Angeln over the sea. Osferth, who first brought the men of Deira across the sea to serve the Emperors in Britannia. Westerfalca, who kept faith with the kings of Eboracum when the Jutes rebelled and was recognised as the first king of Deira in consequence – your great-great-great-great grandfather, Hereric. And at his side sits Eadhelm, your uncle who fell at the battle of Caer Greu and who your father avenged on the field. Every man there is a king or an atheling.

"Now the door swings wide. The flames flicker and out of the swirling smoke strides your father. His mail coat glitters. The grey blade of the spear in his hand glints. The red eyes of the boar upon his helmet glow as if alive, defying anyone to harm the man under its protection. On his shield the fire-drakes writhe, blue and red and green. The hilt of his sword, gold and jewelled, flashes in the firelight so that it hurts the eye to look upon it. At his shoulder the brooch on his cloak sparkles. Beside him the slave girl, though a strapping lass, can barely stagger under the weight of gold and silver plate in her arms.

"The skald ceases in his song. All along the mead-benches the warriors stop their talk, fall silent and turn to gaze. Woden's handmaids pause in their serving and stare, nudge one another and whisper. There are great names among the drinkers in that hall, men who were kings here on earth, yet none came there more richly provisioned, nor more noble in his bearing. All eyes follow him as he strides through the hall. Who is he, this tall and handsome man, bearing gifts of such splendour? Surely a king, king of the greatest kingdom on earth.

"He approaches the top table where the gods sit at meat, the three sons of Tiw Allfather who rule the world of the gods. Woden in the centre, an awesome figure more than man-high, his face shrouded, his one eye burning like a coal. Lord Frey on the left, the foster-son, his golden hair bright as the sun. Thunor on the right, his shoulders three times broader than a big man, his red beard flowing over his mighty chest. On the table before him lies his hammer, that forged the earth and has shattered many a giant's skull, and in his hand he holds the whetstone that makes the lightning flash in the skies. You and I, Hereric, would fall in fear before them, but your father has passed the dread gates of death and they hold no terror for him. He stands before Woden as a thane before his king, respectful, admiring, but not servile, a free man among his equals. At his gesture, the slave girl spreads her burden on the table before the gods. They are pleased with the gifts, for though they have many rare and beautiful things, they have nothing finer.

7

"Woden rises, cloaked in shadow. He is tall, taller than the tallest man, and his head brushes the rafters of that lofty hall. His voice is like the roar of flame in a forest, like the thunder of waves upon a shore. Woden speaks."

Eadwine pitched his own voice as deep as it would go. "Welcome to my hall, Eadric son of Aelle, Atheling of Deira. Long you have been in the coming. There is one here who has waited for you."

He reverted to his normal tones with a certain amount of relief. "And from the mead-benches rises his brother Eadhelm who fell alongside the kings of Eboracum at Caer Greu more than twenty years ago. They embrace, for they were close here on earth and long kept one another's backs against the foe, and it was to avenge Eadhelm that Eadric slew the Bernician prince. He takes his place on the mead-benches, between Eadhelm and Westerfalca. Mead is brought to him, and boiled meat, and fine white bread. And at a word from Woden the skald sings again, but this time it is a new lay, the Lay of Eadric of Deira, the scourge of Bernicia, the helmet of his people.

"And at the end of the evening, when men are beginning to think not of talk and song but of sleep, Lady Frija, Queen of the gods, enters the hall. More lovely is she than any human lady, adorned with gold and jewels of rare beauty. She bears a great golden cup filled with rich red wine, and after Woden and Thunor and Frey have drunk she carries the cup to your father, first among all Woden's thanes. Her eyes are bright like the stars at evening, and her voice is like the sparkling of clear water."

He considered trying to imitate a goddess' falsetto and decided against it. If he succeeded he would never hear the last of it. "She welcomes your father to her lord's hall, and says that she will never again fear the attacks of the giants. And so your father enters Woden's service, not the least among his housecarls, and there he will fight for Woden and Thunor against the giants until you go to join him and are welcomed to Woden's hall in your turn."

Hereric sniffed again, but his face had relaxed and when he spoke his voice was more normal. "I wish somebody had told me all that before."

"Surely you knew about Woden's hall?"

"Sort of," agreed Hereric, wiping his nose on his sleeve. "But nobody tells it like you do. I missed you when you went up north." He peered up at the sky. "Is Dad really up there somewhere looking down on us?"

"Yes," Eadwine said firmly. Consoling the boy had brought him some comfort too. "So we have to make him proud of us. You'll grow into a fine young man in a few years, and people will look at you and see your father in you. You're his immortality, Hereric, as much as any of the poetry his skalds will sing about him. As long as men remember him as the great hero he was, he will never really die." He took Hereric's arm. "Come along. The sun is well into the west and we ought to be getting back to the city before they bar the gates. This is no time to be outside the walls. Look at the smoke in the north! The Bernicians can't be more than a few miles away."

"Why aren't you fighting them?"

Eadwine managed not to flinch at the question. "I have been."

"Did you win?"

"Not exactly."

Hereric looked doubtful, not being aware that the question could have any answer other than yes or no. He liked his young uncle, who was undeniably odd and whose interest in Brittonic poetry and devotion to his betrothed made him a frequent target of mockery, but who was kind and funny and always had time for

8

him. Hereric did not want to think Eadwine was a coward and have to despise him. He swallowed. "You didn't –" he hesitated over the shameful words "– you didn't run away?"

"Not exactly."

Hereric swallowed again. "Did you kill lots of Bernicians?"

"Yes."

Hereric looked a little happier with that answer, though still puzzled. "Why aren't you pleased about it?"

Eadwine ran his free hand wearily through his hair. "Because it doesn't seem important any more."

"Why are they attacking us? King Aethelferth's supposed to be our ally, isn't he? Since Aunt Acha went to Bernicia to marry him. It's not fair!"

"Because Aethelferth never keeps his promises," Eadwine said bitterly. "His Brittonic nickname is Aethelferth Flesaurs, which means Aethelferth the Twister in our language. You know his banner is a double-headed serpent? Think of it as a two-faced snake. It suits him."

"Why –" Hereric began, and broke off, shrinking close to Eadwine's side in sudden fear. The riverside path was barred by a huge warrior, towering half a head taller than Eadwine (who was himself a tall man), broad in proportion, and bristling with red hair and red beard. He could have been the god Thunor come to earth, except that instead of a whetstone and a hammer he carried a wicked-looking spear and a small round shield of unmistakable design.

Hereric planted himself shoulder-to-shoulder with his uncle and drew his small eating knife from his belt, determined to sell their lives dearly.

"It's all right, Hereric," Eadwine said, "this is Drust. He belongs to my warband."

Hereric's eyes were as round as the shield. "But he – he – he's –" his voice dropped to a shocked whisper "– he's a *Pict!*"

"Son of the Goddess," chorused Eadwine and Drust in unison.

Drust grinned. "Ye're learning." He looked down on Hereric like a kindly giant. "Ye can put the knife away, laddie. Ye're safe enough. We only eat boys at the full moon."

Hereric gulped, and then realised he was being teased. His expression changed from one of terror to one of fascination.

"I keep my tail in my trews and my cloven hooves in my boots," remarked Drust, after some minutes under Hereric's unblinking stare.

Hereric blushed and stammered an apology.

"Och, dinna fret, laddie. Ye're no the first to look at me like that here."

"You ought not to be wandering around on your own down here," Eadwine said. "Didn't I tell you to go to the King's hall for food and rest? Big square stone building in the middle of the city, go through the courtyard and the hall's opposite the main gate, you can't miss it." He ran a hand through his hair in a distracted gesture. "I meant to –"

"Ye did, and I didna mind ye. I dinna care tae leave my lord outwith the walls, and with the enemy so close. Yon guard tried tae stop me, but I can take care of myself."

Eadwine sighed. "I'm sure you can, but I don't want you beating up all our soldiers. Here." He unfastened the brooch from his cloak, turning it so the incised bull design caught the light. "My word doesn't count for much here, but the badge of my father's house does. Wear that and no-one will challenge you."

9

"How come you're working for Uncle Eadwine?" Hereric interrupted, his curiosity overcoming his alarm.

"We agreed –" Eadwine began.

"He beat me," said Drust, admitting the disgrace with the air of one who won't shirk an unpleasant duty but wants to get it over with as soon as possible.

Hereric looked at his uncle with new respect. He had beaten this mighty warrior?

"So you're his slave? But you've got weapons and everything –"

"I swore to serve him if he let my men go free. Ye could call me a hostage."

Hereric frowned. "So your men left you and ran away? That's disgusting! They should have died for you!"

"Aye, weel. And they would ha' done, in a fair fight, if they thought it would ha' saved me. But as it was –" he cast Eadwine a glance of grudging admiration "– as it was, none of us was going to get home alive. So I made a bargain."

"They should still have died for you! You had a right to expect them to!"

Drust fixed him with a disconcerting stare. "Ye think so, laddie? Ye dinna think they had a right tae expect me tae spot the trap? I was the fool. 'Tis right I should pay the price. 'Tis a cruel thing tae have other men die for ye, laddie. Ye mind that, when ye're old enough tae lead."

"But – you're the important one – they don't matter –"

"Hereric, I'm surprised at you," Eadwine said, a sharp edge in his tone. "Where did you get that idea from? Everything works both ways. You expect your men to obey you, and that means you have to take as much care of their lives and their honour as you do of your own. More, if anything. You expect the people of your lands to feed and clothe and maintain you and your warband, so they expect you to protect them. Rights on both sides. That's what makes it fair." He looked at the smoke smearing the northern horizon and his hands clenched and unclenched like a man in pain. "And the Twister is burning Eboracum Vale, and I can't stop him! I couldn't even keep Black Dudda out of my own March –!"

"Och, they'll be away home soon," Drust said comfortably. "The Twister canna take yon city. Ye could hold it with a parcel of weans and women. I'm thinking yon auld Romans canna ha' been much for fighting, or they wouldna ha' needed tae build such a thing."

"Cynewulf says that," Hereric put in, excited to be discussing warfare with this exotic new acquaintance. "He says walls are for cowards and we should march out and fight on the honest earth like men!"

"Cynewulf is the biggest fool on the Council, and that's a hotly contested title," Eadwine said. "All mouth and prick, as – as –"

He broke off. That had been Eadric's epithet for his illegitimate rival, and the sudden reminder of his loss took his breath away.

"But lots of people say the same," argued Hereric. "Treowin agrees with him." He only just refrained from adding "So there!" Treowin was Eadwine's oldest and closest friend, so Hereric expected Eadwine to concede the point immediately. Instead, Eadwine merely shook his head and sighed.

Drust grinned. "Och, 'tis all true that ye Sassenach sheep havena the sense of a babe. Aethelferth canna take yon city, but on the field he'll eat ye, laddie. He's thrashed every king in the North who's ever fought him."

"But they were only Brittonic, or Irish, or something," Hereric protested. "Not proper warriors like us. Everyone says we'll beat him in battle easy enough."

Drust's grin turned into incredulous laughter. "Och, if I'd ha' known, I'd ha' led my men down Dere Street and never bothered with yon cliffy coast, and I'd be King of the North in Eboracum now. Ye seem determined tae lose." He sobered up, and turned to Eadwine. "'Twould be funnier if I wasna in the middle of it. Can ye make them see sense?"

"I never have yet," Eadwine said wearily, "but I can try."

Hereric looked uncertainly from one to the other. He was looking forward to the excitement of a battle that would avenge his beloved father. The prevailing wisdom at court considered Eadwine a dreamer with a head full of moonshine, and as Drust had lost to him he must be even less of a warrior, so their opinions should be of little account. But they sounded very *certain*. And his father's death had shaken his belief in Deiran invincibility.

"So what do you think we should do, then?"

"Stand a siege," Eadwine answered instantly. "Look at the walls, Hereric! Imagine you're an enemy soldier trying to attack. Could you climb them? No. Could you batter them down? No. Could you break open the gates? Not with us on the towers and the gallery hurling stones and spears and arrows at you. So you sit down outside and try to starve us out. But you're a long way from home, you've no shelter, it's past the end of summer and in a few weeks it's going to be wet and cold, you've burnt all the harvest on your way here, and after a few weeks of bad food and bad water and sleeping in the mud your soldiers start falling sick with camp fever. And then we sally out from the city, where we've been warm and dry all this time, and Aethelferth will think himself lucky if he gets home alive. That's what cities are for. That's why Coel the Old made the giants build Eboracum for him, a long, long time ago."

They hurried in through the river gate, almost a short tunnel since the walls were so thick, and Hereric felt almost sorry for the attackers.

"Can I –?" he began, but was interrupted by a disapproving voice.

"Eadwine! I was just about to send a search party! Where have you been?"

"Visiting my brother's grave," Eadwine said sharply. "By the Hammer, Treowin, why so many people? It looks as if you've come to arrest me!"

"Don't joke about it!" Treowin exclaimed. He was about Eadwine's age, the son of Deira's most aristocratic family, a thin, dark young man with an intense manner. He jerked his head in the direction of the smoke in the north. "I hope you've got a good reason for that."

An attractive dark-haired woman, no longer quite young, pushed her way through the crowd, calling Hereric's name in a strong Brittonic accent. Hereric scowled, recognising her as Rhonwen, one of his mother's ladies, and tried to hide behind Drust. But he was too late. Rhonwen had seen him, and swept down as inexorably as the incoming tide.

"Hereric! You bad boy! Your mother was so worried – Why, Eadwine! They told me you were back." She stood on tiptoe, put her arms round Eadwine's neck, kissed him very deliberately, whispered something in his ear that made him start and stare at her, and then took Hereric's reluctant hand and led the boy away, throwing a suggestive smile over her shoulder.

"Old flame still burning for you, eh?" Treowin smirked, joining in the ribald laughter. "Nice-looking piece. You take her up on it. No call for you to be faithful to your wife after you're married, never mind before."

11

Eadwine was still gazing after the woman, not listening, his mind in a whirl. Those whispered words had not been an amorous invitation after all. Rhonwen had said, *Princess Heledd fears for the boy's life. Come to her chambers after dark.*

Treowin shook him by the shoulder. "You've work to do first." He looked at his friend sympathetically. "You look terrible. I'm sorry, I'd make excuses for you if I could, but the Council said *now* and they said it more than an hour ago. I hope your story's a good one. They're not pleased with you."

***

"And what the hell have you been doing?" Aethelferth of Bernicia slammed his fist into his palm and every man within earshot jumped. "You got here in twice the time with half the men. What are you, an old woman?"

Black Dudda stumbled through his sorry tale. The harbour mouth blocked by a burning ship so he had to land on the wrong side of the river. The ford spiked with Roman thorns, turning it into a killing ground of crippled and floundering men under a stinging rain of arrows. The deliberately set moorland wildfire that engulfed his camp and roasted those who could not run. The scouts and forage parties who set out and never returned. The sudden assault from forest or reed-bed that came without warning and vanished without trace, save for the wounded and dead.

The scar on Aethelferth's face stood out livid against his tanned skin as he listened, never a good sign, and the other captains and warlords exchanged wry glances. Black Dudda had been the subject of much envy when Aethelferth selected him for command, but now it looked like a very short straw indeed. More than one put a hand to an amulet or good-luck charm and offered silent thanks to their favourite god or saint.

"I told you they'd got a competent marchwarden for once," commented one of the captains, speaking Anglian but with the lilting accent that betrayed a Brittonic origin. "There's a reason why I've given up raiding that coast."

Aethelferth gave him a level stare. "You know him? Who is he?"

"Eadwine son of Aelle. Your new wife's youngest brother. Half-brother, I should say. Lord King," he remembered, as an afterthought.

Aethelferth frowned. "Acha doesn't think much of him. He's a stripling."

"He's a weasel bastard and I'm going to break his neck!" snarled Black Dudda, who did not take defeat well.

The Brittonic captain eyed him with dislike and not a little satisfaction. Even in the fierce company of Aethelferth's captains Black Dudda was regarded with a mixture of disgust and fear. He turned back to Aethelferth.

"Eadwine is young, yes, but he's sharp. And he's his mother's son. Or perhaps I should say his grandfather's grandson. Your fathers slew Peredur King of Eboracum and his brother over twenty years ago at Caer Greu, and Peredur's son ran away, yes. But Peredur left a daughter too, and she married Aelle and made herself Queen of both Eboracum and Deira. This Eadwine is the result. He is the heir of Coel the Old, King of all the North, and this is Coel's city. Blood like that tells, Lord King."

An uneasy muttering broke out, and the captains looked unhappily across the newly-deserted fields to Eboracum, glowing gold in the setting sun. The ancient fortress was rectangular and immensely strong, sitting on a natural defensive site between two rivers. The broad River Ouse flowed past the south-west walls, spanned by a single imposing stone bridge that linked the fortress with the civilian city on the opposite bank. On the east side of the fortress was the River Foss, smaller but still a notable barrier, and the two rivers joined at an oblique angle some half a mile south of the fortress, protecting that flank. If any enemy made it across the natural defences, he was faced with a deep ditch to cross, full of clinging brambles. Then an earth rampart topped by thirty feet of vertical limestone walls jointed without ledge or crack. The massive gates in each wall were flanked by projecting towers and topped by a fighting gallery, from which the defenders could rain missiles down onto the attackers. Two huge many-angled towers on the corners fronting the Ouse, and more towers at the other two corners and at intervals round the rest of the circuit, completed the picture.

Aethelferth's captains, hardened fighters to a man, paled. The emperor who had rebuilt the city's forbidding defences three centuries before had intended it to overawe barbarian warriors. It was still working.

Aethelferth spat. His original intention had been thoroughly wrecked, partly by Black Dudda's delay and partly because the Deirans had bolted into their city like mice into a hole at his approach, rather than marching out to stop the burning of Eboracum Vale as they were supposed to. But he was rarely at a loss for long. He already had a new plan for the impregnable city.

"Remember, lads," he said, "it ain't the walls that fight. You think Aethelferth the Twister can't outwit Aelle Ox-brains?" He drew his sword and held it up, the blade glowing red in the dying light. "Hear me, Woden! Hear me, O Masked One, Lord of Hosts, Master of the Gallows, Giver of Victory! Put fear into the hearts of our enemies, shackle them in the war-fetters, drive them witless and terrified before us! Give us victory, and I will give to you Aelle and his son Eadwine, King and Atheling, as a gift to your power! This I swear on my sword and call all the gods as witness! Hear me, O Terrible One! Hear me!"

A large black crow, startled by the shouting, flapped out of the trees and flew away looking for a more peaceful place to roost.

"A raven!" someone cried. "The bird of Woden! See, it flies over the city! An omen! He has given them into our hands!"

Chapter 3

Rhonwen was watching for Eadwine at the entrance to Heledd's apartments, a warren of rooms that had once been the offices of the legionary headquarters. She swung the door closed behind him.

"Here," she said, pushing a cup of wine into his hand. "Sit down. I'll go for Princess Heledd."

"I'll go to her. I know she finds it painful to walk."

He had known his brother's wife – his brother's widow – ever since she had first come to Deira as a bride to seal the alliance with the neighbouring Brittonic kingdom of Elmet. Heledd had never been robust, and thirteen years of largely unsuccessful childbearing had left her with unspecified but persistent health problems. Now she was thirty but looked forty, her beauty faded and her smile tired. She did not rise as they entered. Eadwine greeted her in the Brittonic fashion, with a kiss on both cheeks, and took her hands.

"My poor Heledd," he said softly, speaking Brittonic. "What can I say? But he died a hero. That will be a comfort to you, in time."

Heledd lowered her eyes. She had seen the grief etched on his face, and could not hurt him by letting him see that her greatest regret over her husband's death was that it had occurred just at the point when she was trapped in a besieged city with no way of getting back to her homeland. Eadric had bestridden his household like a golden god come to earth, and had treated both his pretty and bewildered foreign bride and his recently-motherless little half-brother with the same careless kindness that he extended to any vaguely appealing creature that did not annoy him. Both had been equally dazzled at first. For Heledd, who even at seventeen had known that men who truly respect their wives do not shame them by flaunting a succession of mistresses, the fascination had quickly worn off. For Eadwine it never had.

"We must bear it as best we can," she said, wishing she could comfort him rather than burden him with another problem. "Mother of God, but you look terrible! You need a good meal, a bath, and a good night's sleep, in that order. The second I have no doubt Rhonwen will be delighted to help with. The first I can provide." She indicated a table set for two and laden with food. "You will dine with me? I do not think you will wish to go into hall tonight?"

"You heard about the Council?"

"Some of it. Rhonwen was chased away before the end. Eat. Don't start talking or you won't stop. You can have peace and quiet here. I owe you that, at least."

She remembered what a Godsend he had been to a frightened bride adrift in a strange country, unable to speak the language and all but abandoned by her husband as soon as she was safely pregnant. A bright, curious, lively seven-year-old, equally at home in both languages, who had translated for her, helped her to learn Anglian, found her a Christian priest from the Brittonic monastery on the other side of the river, and talked incessantly on every subject under the sun – except the father he was never able to please. Now the boy had grown into this wary, intelligent young man, weary from over three years of command on the dangerous and thankless northern border. She noted the pallor of his skin, the dark smudges under his eyes, the tenseness in every movement, a muscle that occasionally twitched in his cheek. It was hard to believe that he was not yet quite twenty.

"Tell me about the Council," she said, when he pushed away his plate and tilted back his chair.

Eadwine shrugged, staring moodily into his wine cup. "Much as you'd expect. The King blamed me for not preventing them landing, for not defending Derwentcaster, for not giving battle on the plain, for raising the March militia without proper authority, for disbanding them without permission, for not fighting hard enough and for losing too many men."

"He's lost battle after battle all summer, he's been kicked from one end of Deira to the other, thrown out of every fortress except here at Caer Ebrawg, and he blames *you* for not beating Aethelferth the Twister with ten men?"

Eadwine shrugged again. "He has to blame someone. So – I am still Warden of the March, in so far as the March still exists. But here Cynewulf commands."

"Cynewulf? Mother of God!" There could be no greater insult to Eadwine than this blatant preferment of his slave-born half-brother.

"You didn't expect he'd give the command to me? The runt of the litter?" He slammed his fist against the table in a rare loss of control. "The King should have tied me in a sack and chucked me in the river at birth, like you do with unwanted kittens. It would have been better for all concerned."

"Not for me," Heledd said quietly, "nor I suspect for the folk of the March. And you have more support here than you think. Aelle may be soft in the head over that strutting stallion he fathered, but there are many who remember that you are the Queen's son."

14

"Including my father," Eadwine said bitterly. He drew a breath and ran his hand through his hair. "Sorry. I ought to be used to it by now. It won't matter who commands in any case. The Council had one more thing to do besides humiliating me. They have decided that tomorrow morning we march out and fight Aethelferth in open field."

"Mother of God! Why?"

Because he has lost all hope, Eadwine thought, not looking at her. *Because he is the leader, he chose wrongly, he has failed to defend his kingdom and all can see his shame, and a glorious death in battle means he can die a hero and he will not have to choose and fail again.* Aloud, he said, "Because we have had twenty years of peace and the old men who fought at Caer Greu are mostly gone and the young men are eager for battle to show their prowess and have not thought that we could lose. Because defending a city under siege is tiresome and tedious work, and there are many who will grow bored and cry shame on him for shirking a battle, as there were those who cried shame on me at the Council. And because he is old and fat and sick, and he fears to die in his bed. A charge to glory, a bloodied blade, a swift pain soon over, and then the everlasting feast in Woden's hall. When Cynewulf and Treowin and their kind shout for battle, who can blame him for being convinced?"

"Perhaps all the other men – and women – who will die and suffer for his selfish whim," Heledd said sourly.

"Do you think I did not try to make him see that?" He drained his wine cup. "Is there much of this left?"

Heledd blinked, surprised. He had changed more than she thought. "Of course. I suppose you have a right to get drunk."

"No, no. I was thinking of you. Tomorrow. If you barricade yourselves in here and put all the wine, mead and beer in the outer room, the looters will find that first, drink themselves senseless on it and leave you alone. They'll find you eventually, but by then they'll have sobered up and you'll be able to argue with the commanders. Aethelferth won't ill-treat a Princess of Elmet. He isn't stupid. It should be possible for your servants to get Hereric out in the confusion, or you might get away with disguising him as a slave. Aethelferth will know he exists – he will have learned the entire family tree from Acha – but he's never met any of us. He won't recognise Hereric."

"Or you, either," Rhonwen interrupted. "Don't throw your life away just because the King's a fool! Stay here with us! Please!"

She was almost sobbing, remembering the shy boy of four years ago who had told her she was beautiful, who had responded to her tutoring with such awed gentleness, who had said *Teach me what to do, Rhona. Some day I shall have a wife, and I cannot expect her to love me for my looks.*

"Ah, Rhona, the finest warrior on earth couldn't defend you alone against an army. Your best bet is to hide in the ruins and hope to escape notice. They're not likely to find our courtyard –"

He broke off, and Rhonwen knew he was remembering the same summer, the ruined courtyard filled with roses.

"I didn't mean that," she sobbed. "I meant you should get away – somewhere safe –"

"My place is at my father's side, whether he wants me there or not. Heledd – was this of the battle what you feared? I am sorry I can think of nothing better. I have been racking my brains all the way here."

"No," Heledd said slowly, "though it may change things. Rhonwen, watch the door." She leaned forward, speaking now in Latin. It was a rare language in Britannia now, two centuries after the departure of the Empire, but the Brittonic royal families still taught it to their children and Heledd in turn had taught it to Eadwine, as a joke that if she was going to have to learn Anglian he was going to have to learn something too. And it gave a guarantee against eavesdroppers.

"I believe," she said, "that Eadric was murdered."

There was a long pause, and Heledd wondered if he had not understood.

"Murdered?" he whispered eventually, in the same language. "But – they told me he died in battle. Caught by a Bernician patrol, with only a few of his men. They died honourably, fighting to the end."

"He may have died in a battle, but it was not battle that killed him," she said cryptically. "When they brought him home, I laid out his body. It is a wife's duty. He had wounds, yes, but they were superficial. Almost as if done for show. The wound that killed him was made by a knife, long of blade but very narrow, no more than half an inch wide. It had pierced between the rings of his mail shirt and gone straight to the heart. Your brother was stabbed in the back."

Eadwine shivered, trying to absorb this new shock. "Who could do such a thing?"

"The heir to the kingdom is bound to have enemies." She paused. "I am not so concerned with *who*, Eadwine, as *who next*? I fear that whoever sought the death of the father will also seek the death of the son. You do understand? Hereric is all I have left. I need your help. Eadwine, you must save him!"

He still seemed dazed. "Treachery, on top of everything else," he said, his voice slow and hopeless. "Perhaps my father is right, and the gods have turned against us."

***

Rhonwen had not understood the conversation, but she saw Eadwine put his head in his hands and saw the flicker of disappointment cross Heledd's face. She understood that the Princess had asked something of him, something that he could not do.

"My lady," she said in Brittonic, "you expect too much. One man cannot turn back the tide." She left the door and came to stand behind Eadwine's chair, resting one hand lightly on his shoulder. Although he looked as limp as a worn-out rag, the muscles were tense and knotted like a heap of badly-spun wool. "You should get some sleep, my dear," she said softly. "You look terrible."

He raised his head and ran a hand wearily through his hair. "I'm getting very tired of people telling me that."

"It's true," Heledd said, her voice full of sympathy. "You look like a walking corpse. When did you last sleep?"

Eadwine shrugged. "Two nights, three, I don't know. What does it matter? There'll be all the time in the world for sleep after tomorrow. I only wish there was something I could do for you."

"I am sorry. I should not have asked. What could you do? Rhonwen is right, one man cannot turn back the tide."

"The tide!" He sprang to his feet, knocking the chair over. "The tide, the tide!" He smote his forehead. "Oh, what's happened to my brain? High water is in about an hour, isn't it?"

"Ye-es," Rhonwen said, eyeing him dubiously. "But –"

16

"Heledd, Hereric *must* get out of the city tonight. You cannot trust anyone in Deira now. Eadric's enemy, or enemies, will certainly betray Hereric to Aethelferth. What easier way than to let someone else do their killing for them? Hereric's life depends on getting out of Deira before tomorrow. And you're his passport to the court of Elmet. King Ceretic can hardly deny refuge to his aunt and her son. You must go too."

The two women exchanged doubtful glances. "The bridge and the gates are all watched," Heledd said carefully, "and in any case I cannot walk or ride far or fast —"

Eadwine was pacing back and forth, his eyes alight with purpose. "You can sit in a boat. I think I know where one might have survived. Collect all the gold and all the jewellery you can wear or carry. I'd rather you took it than the Twister. Be ready here with Hereric in an hour. I'll send one of my men to guide you if I can't come myself. Rhona, I'm sorry, you'll have to take your own chances."

"I don't see —" Heledd began.

"Trust me. Have I ever let you down?" He grinned, suddenly alive again, as a candle flares brightest just before it burns out. "If this is going to be my last night on earth, I'll damn well do something useful with it! Be ready."

***

Half an hour later, three figures plodded, dripping, through the ruins of the civilian half of the city on the opposite bank of the river. It was a cheerless place, especially in the middle of the night, with shabby clay and timber huts squatting in what had once been gracious gardens and the gravel streets potholed and choked with weeds.

"I don't know what you see in this place," Ashhere grumbled, stubbing a toe on a broken roof tile. "And I don't think much of midnight swimming."

"We could hardly fight Aethelferth's guards on the bridge," Eadwine whispered back. "You should try swimming the river at half-tide when the current's running fast. Then it's really hard work."

"How do you find your way around?" Lilla asked. "This city goes on for ever in all directions!"

"Don't you know every tree and every stone around Deornoth's village, where you grew up? Well, I grew up here. I used to come here a lot at one time. This place —" Eadwine stopped beside a paling fence and rapped hard on the gate, "— is full of interesting people."

A small loophole in the gate jerked open and a man's head popped out, with all the hair shaved off forward of a line joining the ears over the crown. Lilla jumped back, startled.

"God be with you, Brother," Eadwine said to the apparition, in perfect Brittonic. "I am Eadwine son of Aelle. I am known here. I would speak with Father Ysgafnell, if you please."

***

Father Ysgafnell was an elderly Brittonic priest, bald as an egg and with one eye and one hand missing. He greeted Eadwine like a long-lost son, apparently not at all surprised at his arrival in the middle of the night, half-dressed and dripping wet.

"My boy! Have you realised the error of your heathen ways at last and come to pray?"

***

Ashhere and Lilla watched suspiciously from their seats by the fire, hands clutched around amulets for protection against any heathen magic. Lilla had not come across the Christian religion before, but Ashhere had heard blood-curdling rumours of vile cannibalistic rites, involving the ritual murder of a prophet and feasting on his flesh and blood. He wondered if the old priest's missing hand and eye were something to do with their foul rituals, and shivered. The less he had to do with people who followed such a cruel and violent god, the better as far as he was concerned.

Eadwine seemed unconcerned, returning the greeting with every appearance of delight and carrying on a vigorous conversation in Brittonic. Lilla clearly understood not a word, and although Ashhere knew some Brittonic, chiefly to make it easier to give orders to the peasants on his father's recently-acquired estate, they were talking far too fast for him to catch more than a few words here and there. The best he could say was that it didn't look threatening, and that nobody had been turned into a toad – yet.

***

"Yes, I've still got the boat," Father Ysgafnell was saying to Eadwine, "but whatever do you want it for, lad? A siege is no time to take up fishing. You can't be short of food yet, they've only just arrived. A *battle*? Against Aethelferth the Twister? In open field? Holy Mary Mother of God!" He crossed himself.

Ashhere, seeing the gesture, took a tighter hold of his hammer amulet and muttered a prayer to Thunor to protect them.

"Truly, Saxons carry their brains between their legs!" Ysgafnell continued. "And you want to make yourself scarce before tomorrow, eh? Sensible lad."

"Not me," Eadwine managed to get in, "it's for Princess Heledd and her son –"

"Ah, down the Ouse on the ebb tide and up the Aire on the flood to Loidis, eh? Well, in my opinion any sensible man would go with them, but I won't argue. What are your friends so frightened of, by the way? Huddled together like a pair of wet hens. What, me? Do they think I want their eyes to replace the one I lost to a Saxon spear at Caer Greu? Worry not, little chickens, yours are blue and I want a matched pair –"

"Don't tease, Father," Eadwine said, laughing. "Will you show us to the boat? There's not much of the night left."

"If you need somewhere to hide tomorrow, lad," Ysgafnell said in a low voice, as they made their way across the enclosure scattered with little beehive-shaped cells, "you come to us. I know they say it's a disgrace to survive if your king is killed, but between you and me, whoever said that knew nothing about pig-headed kings and had probably never been in a battle. *I* have, and I'm telling you, lad, don't throw your life away."

"I don't intend to run away," Eadwine said stubbornly. "And I don't want to live in exile, thank you."

"Believe me, lad, a heroic death isn't all it's cracked up to be."

"*You* never tried it."

"That was uncalled for, boy, and in my days as a spearman I'd have had your balls for it, but I am above such things now and will let it pass in the spirit of Christian forgiveness, amen." He paused for breath and went on, in a changed voice, "I heard about your brother. I'm sorry. But I still say you shouldn't rush to join him. Splendid life with the gods and all that, but I recommend keeping the one you've got for as long as possible."

18

"They say Aethelferth doesn't like Christians," Eadwine began cautiously. "You may want to take yourself out of the way tomorrow –"

"My dear boy, nothing would brighten my last hours more than watching one Saxon king trying to kill another."

"I suppose I asked for that," Eadwine said, after a pause.

Ysgafnell put a fatherly hand on his shoulder. "Sorry. You're so much your mother's son I forget that you're your father's as well."

He pushed beneath a weeping willow, and pointed to a small skin boat drawn up to the bank under its branches, invisible to the world. Ashhere and Lilla looked at it doubtfully. They were used to proper boats, clinker-built from good solid timber, not these fragile cockleshells.

"It'll float," Eadwine reassured them, switching back to Anglian. "Sit in the middle and take an oar each. You'll have to get across the river quickly. Wait for me under the willow by the south tower, where we came just now."

"Aren't you coming with us?"

"I think it would help if the guards on the bridge were all looking the other way for a bit. Wait until you hear a commotion from upstream, then hurry across as fast as you can. It should be just about slack water by now, it'll be easy."

He ducked back under the willows, and they saw him vault the fence, climb up onto a ruined wall and vanish along the bank. A few minutes later, the silent night erupted in a furious quacking and splashing and clapping of wings as a couple of hundred panicked waterfowl fled from their roost and flapped into the night.

"Off you go, lads, and good luck to you," said the old priest, in execrable Anglian. "I shall pray for you tomorrow, heathen Saxon imbeciles that you are. I think you're going to need all the help you can get."

***

"I don't know, Lady," Treowin said for the fifth time, sounding distinctly aggrieved. He was very conscious of his position as the heir to Deira's noblest family and rather resented running errands, even to oblige his best friend. "Eadwine asked me to bring you and the atheling here. He didn't favour me with an explanation."

"Where does that hole go?" Hereric wanted to know, staring in appalled fascination at the black maw of the shaft disappearing down into the middle of the street. They were gathered in the shadow of a partly-collapsed archway in a part of the ruined city he had never visited before, where a rotting timber cover had been pushed aside to reveal the shaft. It was a manhole leading down into the main drain of the old city, but none of them knew that.

"I don't know," Treowin answered crossly.

"Why are all those ducks on the river quacking like that?"

"I don't know."

"What's happening?"

"I don't know."

"Where's Uncle Eadwine?"

"I don't know."

"Why –?"

"Oh, by the Hammer, boy, will you be quiet? He told these two –" pointing at the hulking shadows that were Wulfgar and Wulfraed "– to collect food and then wait here, and he took two others with him and said they were going swimming."

"Why swimming?"

"How the hell do I know?" Treowin snapped, and went back to biting his nails.

"Relax," advised Wulfgar, or possibly it was Wulfraed. Although the brothers came from one of his father's estates, Treowin could never remember which was which. "His schemes sound crack-brained, but they work."

A light flickered at the base of the hole. Hereric held tighter to his mother's hand and took a step back. Everyone said the old city was full of ghosts, evil creatures that came out at night and drank blood.

Now they could hear something breathing in the shaft, and the scrape and creak of something creeping upwards. A dark shadow formed at the mouth of the hole, and drew itself up over the lip. Hereric squeaked in fear. Treowin stepped forward, ostentatiously pushing Heledd and Hereric behind him, and in one swift movement seized the shadow and held his drawn sword to its throat.

"I might have known I should have sent Ashhere up first," Eadwine's voice said in a whisper. "Put me down, Treowin. Is the lady here?"

"Yes!" said Hereric eagerly. "We're here! Are you taking us on an adventure – Ugh, you're all wet! Where have you been?"

"In the river, twice."

"Why?"

"To get to the other side."

"Do we have to swim too? Mam can't, you know –"

"She doesn't have to, you're going by boat. To Loidis, where your cousin is the King –"

Hereric jerked his hand out of his mother's grasp. "I'm not running away! Running away is for girlies and cowards! I want to stay and fight in the battle!"

"Hereric," Eadwine said, in a stern voice his nephew had never heard before, "you cannot always do what you want. You can't fight tomorrow, you are too young. It will be a full three years before you take the spear. You can help us best by living safe at your cousin's court, where you will grow to manhood and learn the arts of war, and one day come back to avenge us. And make your great father proud."

**

Heledd found that a wooden ladder led down the shaft into a dank, malodorous stone-lined tunnel, its floor puddled with filthy water. Eadwine was waiting at the bottom, a lamp balanced in a recess in the wall. He held out his arms to her.

"I'll carry you," he said. "The floor is slimy and treacherous. I'm used to it. Ashhere will help Hereric. You carry the lamp for me."

He was stronger than she had expected, lifting her with apparent ease. She hooked one arm round his shoulders, and held the lamp up with the other. The whole floor of the tunnel seemed to shift and slither away into the shadows ahead, and oily ripples came lapping back. The smell got worse, if that were possible.

"Rats," Eadwine said. "Don't be afraid, they won't come near the light."

Behind them they heard Hereric yelp in disgust, quickly cut off, and the heavy sloshing sound as first Wulfgar and then Wulfraed descended the ladder. Then a scraping sound as the trapdoor was pulled across.

Heledd repressed a shiver. "How do you know about this disgusting place?"

"From when I was Hereric's age, or a bit younger. Treowin found the trapdoor under a heap of leaves and brambles. We hauled it up, and he bet me I wouldn't dare go down and follow the tunnel to its end. I was terrified, but I was damned if I was going to lose a dare. And then later it was a convenient way out of the city when the gates were all barred."

"Ah. I thought you knew Rhonwen before she joined my ladies."

"It was useful for visiting Father Ysgafnell, too. Ah – here we are. Leave the lamp here. I can't risk a light being seen on the bank."

He waited for the others to catch up, spoke a few quiet words of command, and moved cautiously forward again, feeling for each step. The remains of the lantern light faded behind, and a dim grey glimmer showed ahead. Starlight on the river. Heledd felt strands of ivy brush her face, a bramble tugged at her cloak as Eadwine lifted her over the lip of the ditch, and they were out.

A solid-looking shadow moved on the bank, and she made out a large coracle bobbing on the swell. A strange way for a Princess of Elmet to return to her homeland, but better than being taken as a prize of war.

"No time for farewells," Eadwine whispered. "They won't chase wild geese for ever, and you must be away before they start looking this way again. Wulfgar, Wulfraed, take the oars. You are in the Lady Heledd's service now. I release you from mine and from all obligations to me. Guard the lady and the Atheling with your lives. Heledd – fare you well. May your Christian God hold his hand over you. Hereric, make your father proud of you. Go now, quickly!"

The cockleshell boat, laden to its limits with four occupants, slipped soundlessly out onto the black water, turned like a leaf spinning on the ebbing tide, and was gone.

***

Eadwine tugged at Lilla's and Ashhere's sleeves to indicate they should make their way back though the tunnel. They had hardly taken a step when a sentry's voice roared out from above.

"Halt! Who goes there?"

They dropped into the ditch and lay rigid among the brambles, waiting for the expected hail of spears and arrows. Stupid way to die, skewered by their own sentries under the walls of their own city..... But no missiles came. The sentries were not concerned with them after all, but with something else moving in the ditch nearer to the river gate. Something that was far too heavy to be a rat, something that had not had three years' practice ambushing raiders on the March and did not know how to move silently through undergrowth. Someone creeping in the pre-dawn dark from the enemy camp to the river gate. And they had left their weapons in the city.

Eadwine froze, heart pounding, trying to judge whether it was really men moving in the ditch or merely his overwrought nerves making an enemy attack out of a foraging hedgehog. If it was men, it was not many, no more than two or three. Not enough for an attempted attack. A reconnaissance party, perhaps, trying to judge the state of the ditch? Whatever it was, it was moving away.

He released a breath he had not known he was holding, feeling his strength draining away along with the tension that had kept him going for the last few crowded hours. He shivered, suddenly cold in his wet clothes. Back to the city, barricade this drain just in case, and then there was no more for him to do. He might get an hour's sleep before sunrise.

***

"Bugger," Aethelferth muttered, standing on the edge of the Bernician camp and watching the dawn lighten over the city and its still-shut gate. "Bugger, bugger, *bugger!*"

Chapter 4

"Assemble in the courtyard!" bawled the herald, doing the rounds of Eboracum's ramparts. "Assemble in the courtyard!" He saw Ashhere, Drust and Lilla sitting in a row on the wall above the north-west gate, sharing bread and cheese and beer and apparently leaning on a bundle of rags. "You lot! Who's your lord?"

Lilla, whose peasant forebears had generations of experience in dealing with unwelcome royal officials, saluted smartly. "Lord Eadwine, sir!"

"Where is he? I've been looking for him since dawn!"

"He went that way, sir!"

The herald looked down at the coloured threads on his tally stick. "You're to fight with Lord Eadric's hearth-troop. On the left, next to Lord Treowin's men. Get going."

"Yes, sir!" cried Lilla, not moving. "Right away, sir!"

The herald glared, but he was in a hurry and had better things to do than chivvy three unimportant housecarls. He scurried off.

***

"I think they mean it this time," Ashhere said. "We'd better wake him."

"Shame," sighed Lilla. "When he's asleep he doesn't know his brother's dead." He shook the rags gently. "Lord?"

The bundle stirred, rolled over, and was revealed to be Eadwine, rolled in his cloak and covered by Ashhere's. He sat up, his face still grey and drawn from grief and weariness.

"What is it?"

"Battle," said Lilla, succinctly. "They still haven't seen sense."

Eadwine rubbed his eyes. "Not our decision." He yawned. "Have you got your gear?"

Ashhere pointed to a stack of weapons and a mail shirt against the wall. "And we collected yours too."

"And we got you dry clothes," added Lilla, handing over a bundle of cloth. "Treowin told us where to look."

"And breakfast," said Ashhere, proffering a plate and a flagon. "It's beer, not mead."

"You have been busy," Eadwine said, dressing with his customary speed and handing Ashhere his cloak back. "What have I done to deserve all this attention? Don't answer that." He broke off a chunk of bread and peered out of the nearest embrasure at the Bernician camp, pitched just out of spear range below. "How odd."

"What?"

Eadwine pointed. "They're all armed and ready, but they're sitting in rows and eating. As if they were all lined up for battle and then stood down for some reason. Looks like they were planning a dawn attack and it was called off. But they're only just starting to fetch timber to make ladders, look. Wonder how they were expecting to get in without ladders?" He yawned again, exhausted, and dismissed the problem as not immediately relevant.

Some of the Bernicians had noticed the movement on the walls and were pointing and jeering. One of the captains, a big fair-haired man in bright mail, stalked to the edge of the camp.

"Cowards!" he taunted. "Come out and fight!"

"Little does he know," Ashhere grumbled miserably.

Eadwine shot him a sharp glance. Since they must fight, it was his responsibility to see that his men fought in good heart, whatever the depth of his own despair. He leaned over the wall as if to take a good look at the man below.

"Well, well. If it isn't our friend from three days ago. Four days ago now." He cupped his hands to his mouth. "Black Dudda!"

The man in mail started. "Who wants him?"

Eadwine stood up in the embrasure and shouted, as he had shouted four days ago across the fords of Esk, "I am Eadwine son of Aelle, Warden of the North March, and you are not welcome in my land!"

"This is not the North March," jeered another voice from the camp, with a strong Brittonic accent. "Saxon pigs!"

"I am also Eadwine son of Elen daughter of Peredur, heir of Coel Godebawg, Protector of the North," Eadwine called back. "Get back beyond the Wall, bog-trotter!"

Black Dudda jabbed his spear in their direction, but it was much too far to throw, especially as he would also have to throw upwards, and he sensibly did not make a fool of himself by trying. He hurled a stream of insults instead.

Eadwine scorned him with a laugh. "Fine words! But words are cheap, and you have many fewer men than when we last met! Have you brought the rest to die on the walls of Eboracum?"

"I'll see you dead, boy!"

"When?" Eadwine jeered back. "It was your men did the dying! Take a good look, men of Bernicia! Here's the man who lost half an army fighting ten Deiran warriors!"

Black Dudda's face went crimson and he ran a few paces forward. "Cowards' tricks! Weasel's tricks!"

"Too clever for you, bollock-brain!" Eadwine mocked, and added in an undertone, "Pass me a spear, out of sight. If I can annoy him enough he'll come within range, and he hasn't got a helmet on."

But Black Dudda was not stupid. He shouted a final insult, and stalked back into his camp. Eadwine cast a last look over the wall and jumped down from the embrasure. "Oh, well, it was worth a try – Ash! Get down!"

Ashhere, who had been leaning with his back against one of the other embrasures, obediently threw himself flat just as a spear flew over his head and rattled against the nearby tower, accompanied by a stream of derisory Brittonic from below.

"By the Hammer," Lilla chided, retrieving the weapon, "Thunor must have his work cut out looking after you!"

Ashhere got up, shaken. "What the –?"

"That Brittonic fellow was creeping through the bushes," Eadwine explained. "I was watching him. It seems you weren't."

"They haven't got tails after all," Lilla said, taking a cautious look over the wall. The Brittonic spearman had run back out of range and was now capering at the edge of the Bernician camp, shouting Brittonic abuse and occasionally emphasising a point by turning his back, lowering his trousers and flashing his bare backside at the walls. "What's he saying?"

Eadwine listened for a moment. "Well, if you really want a translation, we're creeping toads who lack male swords, we fornicate with pigs – I wonder how that's supposed to work without the proper equipment? – and we're all bum-boys and arse-prickers." He leaned forward and shouted something in Brittonic over the walls. He had a clear, carrying voice, and the Bernician camp erupted into a howl of laughter. The spearman whipped round, brick-red with fury, ran forward, dropped his trousers to his ankles and waggled his genitals obscenely at the watchers on the walls.

Drust looked at Eadwine in admiration. "What did ye say?"

"I told him if he hoped to get lucky, darling, he'd better wash his arse. Now he's demonstrating what he and his friends are going to do to our women. Which is really not intelligent when you've come within range and have just given the enemy a free spear. Ash? We could all hit him from here, but you owe him one, I think."

Ashhere grinned, the spear flew back, and a scream echoed up from below.

"Good shot, Ash," Lilla said, as they clattered down the rampart stairs at a run. "He'll be your slave when you get to Woden's hall."

"Do foreigners go to Woden's hall?"

"He should," Eadwine joked. "He died with his sword in his hand."

***

They were still laughing as they ran into the palace courtyard. No-one else was. The yard was a milling mass of men and horses in no particular order. It seemed that Aelle wanted to lead a grand procession out from the city, with the mounted leaders riding at its head. They would dismount to fight, of course, for cavalry fighting was a Brittonic tactic that most of the Anglians regarded with profound suspicion, but riding rather than walking to war was a symbol of prestige that Aelle was not prepared to give up. A heated argument over who was going to ride in front of whom was developing among the great lords, and looked about to come to blows. It took an outstanding leader to weld all the individuals together into a greater whole. Aethelferth of Bernicia was such a one. Eadric, at least according to Eadwine, was another. Aelle of Deira was not, or not any more. He was past sixty now, not in the best of health, and cut a somewhat pathetic figure in his splendid armour, grey-bearded, balding and fat, shouting querulously in his wheezy voice at the quarrelling lords.

Eadwine threaded his way through the press to where a big, fair man with a scarred face was haranguing a slightly less indisciplined-looking knot of men.

"– and you'll make Lord Eadric's name live for ever in song – Ah, here's the little brother!" He wrung Eadwine's hand. "We fight with you today. For Lord Eadric's memory!"

"For Eadric's memory," Eadwine agreed, suddenly sober. "Ashhere, Lilla, Drust, this is Beortred. Captain of my brother's hearth-troop. Whatever happens, stick with Beortred today. You can trust him with your lives. My brother did." He clapped them each on the shoulder in turn. "I'll have to ride at the front, but I'll join you in the line. If I don't get another chance to say this, you're the best. And you've got my permission to get as drunk as lords tonight. May the Three Ladies be kind to you."

Ashhere shivered, watching Eadwine push through the crowd to the King's side. The Three Ladies of Fate, the implacable weavers of destiny who were

24

impervious to pleas and petitions, who would raise a man high at one moment and dash him into the dust on a whim, whose dominion extended even over the gods. If there was a bleaker power to put your faith in before a battle, he couldn't think of one.

"That sounded like a farewell," he said sadly. His spirits had risen after the incident on the walls, but the sullen chaos in the courtyard had punctured his confidence again.

"I don't suppose he cares if it is or not," Lilla answered. "When you've just lost the most important person in your life you don't have much heart for going on without them."

"I care," growled Drust. "Yon stupid king can kill himself if he likes, but he isna taking my guid lord with him. Not if I have anything tae do with it."

"Right!" rumbled Beortred, at Ashhere's elbow. "Hear that, lads? Protect young Eadwine with your lives today! Until Hereric's of age, he's the nearest we've got to Lord Eadric."

***

Eadwine sat his horse a little distance from the rest of the lords, having tried to suggest something to his father and been rebuffed. He was armed for battle, except for the heavy helmet which he would not put on until the last minute. He rarely wore it on the March, where the grubby routine was more akin to hunting than battle and its eye-catching splendour would be a liability. The helmet, even more than his mail and decorated sword, marked him out as a prince or a lord, a man to be killed.

He smiled grimly to himself. Good. He had attached his last three followers to Beortred, who would see them right if anyone could, and if he himself was fated to die it would be a relief. At least it would ease this unbearable ache of loneliness. How was it possible that the world could continue without Eadric alive in it? Eadric, the golden and glorious hero, treacherously stabbed in the back by some unknown assassin. *Why?* Violent death at the hands of a rival was never far away, if you were considered at all important. But the conventional method was for the rival to pick a fight in public, or to gather his followers and march openly on your hall. Once the victim was dead, the murderer would announce who he was, who he had just killed and why, and would brag about the deed at every opportunity. It was up to the victim's kin to take revenge, and if they could not, or would not, or tried and failed, that was taken as a sign that the gods approved of the new status quo. The murderer gained wealth, or a woman, or prestige, or recognition of his superior power. What possible point could there be in a murder that was not claimed? It had a hint of madness about it.

Eadwine tried to make his weary mind think. The murderer was probably in this courtyard, and if he could only work out who it was, today would be his opportunity to avenge Eadric. That would ensure his brother would be pleased to see him in Woden's hall, that would mean he need not feel ashamed in that glorious company. But it had to be the right man, and there was no shortage of possible candidates.

One of the other athelings? Unlike property, the kingship did not pass automatically to the eldest son but was elected by the Council from the adult males of the royal family, and if the King was seen to be failing the jockeying for position would often start long before his actual death. With Eadric gone and Hereric under-age, the most obvious contenders for heir were Eadwine himself, Osric and Aethelric who were the sons of Aelle's brother Aelfric, or some more distant cousins descended from Aelle's grandfather. It could be any of them. It

25

could even be Cynewulf, Aelle's beloved illegitimate son by a pretty farm girl. Cynewulf was in his early twenties, a repeat edition of Aelle in his magnificent prime, and already had much support on the Council. With Eadric gone, enough of the Council might be prepared to overlook Cynewulf's low birth on his mother's side and back him as the heir.

Or someone from one of the other aristocratic dynasties, like Treowin's family? Aelle's ancestors were no more noble than the other adventurers who had led groups of warriors to serve one Emperor or another over a period spanning half a century. Arguably less than some. All the warrior families claimed descent from Woden, as the god had a notorious sexual appetite and was prone to visiting the ravishingly beautiful wives of early chieftains and leaving superhuman hero-sons who went on to found the family fortunes. But in Treowin's family the errant wife had been a daughter of Offa the King of Angeln, and Aelle could not match that. What better way to achieve a change of dynasty than by getting rid of the leading member of the existing one?

Or it could be some other motive, nothing to do with the kingship, some personal revenge for a real or imagined slight. Eadric must have made a great many enemies in his time, not least from his tireless pursuit of other men's wives. Or some traitor or agent of Aethelferth, removing the most effective enemy leader on the eve of battle? But any of them would surely have gained more from claiming the murder than from keeping it secret. It made no sense at all.

Eadwine gave up, too tired and too despairing to think. He looked across at his father with cool compassion. Was this how Aelle felt, hedged about with impossible demands in a world that was grey and tired and bereft? And how bright and simple the vision of Woden's hall, with all the trappings of a warrior's life and none of the tiresome responsibilities. One step across a battlefield, one enemy blade faced without flinching, and a failure became a hero. So simple. So easy.

***

A clatter of hooves under the arch announced Treowin's arrival, wheeling to a stop before the King in a showy display of horsemanship. He held his spear aloft, getting the morning sunlight to glint off the blade.

"The priests say –" he paused for dramatic effect, "the priests say – Woden has accepted the sacrifice! We shall have victory!"

Amid the cheering, Ashhere fingered his hammer amulet uneasily. Despite his father's status as a landholder, he found it hard to revere the terrible and deceitful war god. Woden was just as likely to accept sacrifices from both sides and cruelly break faith with one or both, like serving some arrogant and tyrannical lord. Ashhere preferred to rely on Thunor, who might be less powerful in the sphere of warfare but was certainly more trustworthy. Lilla and Drust seemed equally unimpressed. Lilla gave his allegiance to Frey Lord of the Vanir, god of peace, fertility, good harvests and farmers, the exact opposite of Woden's violent chaos. Ashhere was unsure of Drust's faith, if he had one, except that a goddess presumably featured somewhere prominent. It occurred to him that he had no idea which of the gods Eadwine put his faith in. He looked to see if Eadwine was cheered by the promise of the war god's favour, but although his horse was still there and a servant was holding his spear, Eadwine himself had vanished.

Lilla nudged him, pointing to where a group of richly-dressed women had emerged onto the steps of the palace. Aelle's wife and her ladies, bringing the cup of good health. One of the women, a beauty with flowing golden hair and a face like a flower, had separated from the group, and Eadwine was hurrying through the crowd towards her.

"Is that his girl?" Lilla asked. Eadwine rarely spoke of his betrothed, as if he considered the subject too sacred for discussion, but from the little he had said Lilla had envisaged someone resembling the goddess Frija descended to earth – at the very least.

Ashhere followed his glance, and grinned. "Yes, that's her. Aethelind daughter of Aldhere of Eoforwic. What do you think of her?"

"Nice tits," said Drust approvingly.

"Er – very pretty," Lilla said, with rather less certainty. It was none of his business, of course, but he had expected his mercurial captain to have chosen someone more – unusual. Still, perhaps it was some great marriage of state.

"Oh, no," Ashhere said, in response to his tentative question. "It's a respectable enough family but they're not real nobs, not like Treowin. Like Pa, the father was one of Aelle's thanes who was in the right place at the right time and got given some Brittonic nob's lands after Caer Greu. They've got a hall and a village at Eoforwic, just south of Eboracum, between the two rivers and near the burial mounds. Aethelind was helping with the family washing one sunny day, Eadwine happened to be passing, and he fell for her as if he'd been struck by lightning. The family couldn't believe their luck – rumour has it the father told her to insist on at least another ten hides of land before she lost her cherry – and then Eadwine asked to marry her, and the father went to the temple of Frija and gave the goddess *two whole cows* by way of thanks. The King said he didn't care who Eadwine married as long as he kept out of his sight – this was getting on for three years ago, and he still had four older sons then – so Aethelind's father invited half the kingdom to a huge feast and got them trothplighted before anyone could change their minds. Good party, that was. Not often you can get drunk for a week."

Lilla could only conclude that there must be more to Aethelind than met the eye. Fragments of the conversation drifted across the courtyard, heard through gaps in the general noise. Aethelind's voice was sweet, but a little reproachful.

"– they told me you came back yesterday morning and you never came near me *all day* – yes, I know about the Council, but did you have to go to your slave girl – well, whatever she is, then – I wish you'd leave those grubby peasants to look after themselves and then we could get married – Darling, how can you ask such a thing? Of course I still love you. I can't wait to get married. I finished all the embroidery *months* ago, and Papa says he'll give us a hall if the King won't. Darling, of course you're going to win today. You must protect us from the wicked Bernicians – have you heard what they do to captured women? You mustn't let me down. There, the Queen's calling me. Kiss me. May the gods be with you. Protect me today. Don't fail me."

She skipped away after the other ladies. Eadwine stood for a moment gazing after her, looking utterly wretched. Then, with rather more force than was necessary, he slammed on the helmet that would mark him for death and strode back to his horse.

Ashhere watched Eadwine vault into the saddle with the ease of a born horseman, and retrieve his spear from the servant. Treowin offered a flask of mead and he waved it away, earning a burst of derisory laughter from Cynewulf.

"Drink deep, die happy, little brother!" Cynewulf bellowed, appropriating the flask, taking a long swig and hurling it away over the crowd. He had obviously been following his own advice for some considerable time. Eadwine's response, whatever it was, provoked another mocking laugh, and a sidelong kick from

Cynewulf's stallion. Eadwine's horse shied and reared, and only superb horsemanship kept him in the saddle.

"I'll give you your orders, little brother," Cynewulf roared, as Eadwine struggled to soothe his frightened horse and bring it back under control. "Here *I* command, and don't forget it!" He held his spear high. "Hail to Woden, Lord of Battle! We march to victory!"

"Victory!" the cry was taken up, and the crowd surged forward out of the courtyard.

Ashhere, Lilla and Drust sighed, finished the beer, and followed.

***

Aethelferth scowled at the walled city. It had never fallen by storm, so the legends said. Well, there had to be a first time for everything. He had not made himself overlord of Britannia from the Forth to Elmet by crying over spoilt plans. His captains were eagerly discussing scaling ladders and grappling ropes and speculating on the possibility of setting fire to the massive gates with a big pile of brushwood and newly-killed fat pigs. Lying north of the Great Wall, for most of its history Bernicia had been outside the Empire, and to the Brittonic component of its aristocracy Eboracum was the symbol of an alien occupying power. Burning it down, however impractical, was a prospect to be relished.

Aethelferth was not particularly interested in avenging wrongs, real or imagined, that went back half a millennium or more. The Brittonic propensity to bear grudges until the end of time was not something he shared, although he regularly made use of it. He wanted Deira because it was rich, fertile and populous, and he wanted Eboracum because it was the capital of the North. He had destroyed the armies of mighty Rheged, the Pennine kingdoms and Dal Riada, forced Strat Clut to pay tribute, his first wife had been one of the Pictish line of Queen-Goddesses, and *still* people dismissed him as a jumped-up warlord enjoying a run of good luck. Eboracum would change all that. Eboracum would prove that Aethelferth of Bernicia – Aethelferth of *Britannia* – had come to stay. He was going to take Eboracum, or die in the attempt.

***

The blare of war horns from the city roused their attention. Aethelferth snapped a few commands, but his Anglian veterans were already forming smoothly into a shield-wall and his Brittonic cavalry taking position on the flanks. It was only a precaution, for he was expecting a parley rather than a fight. Even Aelle Ox-brains wouldn't throw away the advantage of the greatest fortress in Britannia.

The gate opened. A forest of banners appeared, over a seething mass of horsemen in no particular order. It was going to be an impressive parley, Aethelferth thought, counting the number of showy helmets and mail shirts on display. Beard of Woden, but Aelle himself was there! The royal standard-bearers had managed to get to the front, one carrying the standard wreathed with oak leaves, one flying the banner of the red bull. Aethelferth grinned. He had no great respect for his father-in-law, considering him a feeble old has-been. Black Dudda pointed out one of the other riders as the last son, the one whom Aethelferth had pledged to Woden if the god gave them victory.

And then, behind the horsemen, appeared a river of men carrying spears and shields.

"Their army's coming out!" someone exclaimed.

"Will you look at all that loot?" someone else said, as the front row of the shield-wall started eyeing up targets among the enemy leadership. This looked like a good day to get rich.

"Holy Mary, Mother of God!" said the Brittonic captain who had spoken the night before. "All our prayers are answered!"

The enemy riders dismounted and the horses were led away. The enemy priests came forward to shout incantations and ritual insults. Behind them, the spearmen shuffled and squirmed into a deep but uneven-looking shield-wall. Gaps and lumps formed as men edged nearer to comrades they knew and away from strangers who followed a different lord. The whole line began to creep right as each man tried to get further behind his neighbour's shield.

The Bernician cavalry licked their lips, anticipating the collapse and the pursuit. No pleasure in the world could compare with riding down a broken enemy over level ground.

Aethelferth stepped forward, spear in hand. Truly, Woden was fighting at their side today. Already the god had put madness into their enemies. Nothing else could explain their behaviour. His oath, and the promise of King and Atheling as sacrifice to the god's power, had been accepted. Woden was keeping his side of the bargain, and now it was for Aethelferth to keep his. He flung the spear over the Deiran host and cried in a great voice,

"Now I give you to Woden!"

The Bernician shields locked together, as solid as Roman masonry. The spears came up, all at the same moment, like a monster displaying a row of steel teeth. These men had followed Aethelferth for twelve years, and they had never been beaten in battle.

They charged.

**

"Woden promised us victory," mumbled Treowin, to no-one in particular. "We'll beat them easy enough."

**

Aethelferth prodded disdainfully at Aelle's corpse and spat on it for good measure. The dead king's armour and weapons were stacked nearby, under guard to protect them from looters. They would be taken back to be displayed in the temple of Woden in the Bernician capital of Bebbanburgh. Who had looted the clothes Aethelferth neither knew nor cared. All across the battlefield his men were busy getting rich. The Brittonic cavalry were in their savage element, flushing out petrified fugitives from hiding and driving them into the river, or hunting them across the human wreckage before tiring of their sport and slashing them down with sword or spear. Their whoops mingled with the groans of the wounded and dying. A stray dog ran past with something red and dripping in its mouth. Two more snarled and snapped over a corpse. Gulls shrieked over the unexpected feast.

In the middle of the field, as near to the original centre of the Deiran line as could be judged, two sets of three stakes had been raised. The central stake of one set held Aelle's head, its grey beard dripping blood. The others each held an arm, impaled through the palm of the hand. Woden's ravens would come to feed on these grisly relics and carry the news to their master. Half of Aethelferth's pledge was fulfilled.

But the second set of stakes was still empty. And the terrible war god was not one to accept half-measures.

**

"Eadwine was here," panted one of Aethelferth's thanes, turning a body over with his foot. "He was trying to reach their King when Hrothgar felled him. And here's Hrothgar, look, with somebody's spear in his guts –"

"May he feast for ever in Woden's hall –" someone said

"– so Eadwine must be around here – er – somewhere –"

Aethelferth glared at them. "Find him! Find him quickly!"

"Er – what does he look like?"

Nobody knew. They were looking for a young man wearing an ornate helmet, a jewelled sword and an oversized mail shirt. But any of those items would probably have been looted already, and how were they to tell one stripped corpse from another?

"Into the city!" Aethelferth snapped. "Find someone who knew Eadwine! Now!"

***

Black Dudda, abandoning the looting, came to join the search and contributed the information that Eadwine was tall, thin and dark-haired. This reduced the number of candidates considerably, but it was not enough to be certain they had found him. And Woden's wrath if he was fobbed off with the wrong man was too terrifying to imagine.

Aethelferth was staring doubtfully at a lanky youth who looked to have been about sixteen, although it was difficult to tell because his head was split in half, when a shout from the direction of the city announced success.

"Here, Lord King! Found one! They say she was his mistress once –"

Two burly soldiers were dragging a woman between them, not so much because she was putting up any resistance as because she seemed too dazed to walk without assistance. She stared at Aethelferth with vague, unfocused eyes. Then she caught sight of Aelle's three stakes, and the set of three more stakes waiting empty, and screamed and screamed.

***

Rhonwen hardly felt the slap, or the rough hands shaking her, and she was only dimly aware of the harsh voice insisting, "Eadwine! Eadwine son of Aelle. Which is he? Show me, you bitch! You were his whore, you know him. Find him! Find him!"

They were forcing her past the heaps of corpses, some already naked, some half-stripped, turning them over, forcing her to look into the dead faces. Tall men, short men, fat men, thin men, old men, young men, boys, blond- dark- or brown-haired, with limbs missing or heads shattered or bellies ripped open like a gutted fish. She stumbled over spilled intestines, slipped in blood, she was sick, she wept, dazed by so much horror, and they slapped her and forced her on. And all the while the constant refrain, "Which is Eadwine? Is this him? This one? Find him, you useless bitch, find him!"

She peered through her tears and shook her head, and they grew angrier and angrier. But still he was not there.

"You slut, if you're lying to me –"

Rhonwen found enough courage from somewhere to glare back at him, this hulking bear of a man who had destroyed all the world she had ever known.

"He is not here!" she taunted him in Brittonic. "You fool, you miserable worm, you've failed! He's not here, and he's going to come back one day and kill you! Kill you!"

30

She saw that he understood, saw the fury in his face, saw her approaching death, and she did not care. Because she also saw a flicker of fear cross the scarred face.

"My Lord King!" A breathless rider, covered in mud and foam, reined in beside them. "Lord Owain sent me – fugitives – mounted – fled into the marshes – headed south – he pursues them, but 'tis hopeless country – he says, set guards on the fords of Aire – Eadwine is among them, but they must cross the river – you will take him there –"

Aethelferth pushed Rhonwen from him, cursing. "Woden's breath, who let him slip away? What do I feed you for? Guard every bridge, every ford, every harbour, every road out of this wretched country. I'll give its weight in gold to the man who brings me his head! And you, slut –" he turned suddenly on Rhonwen, "I'll want you again. Don't think your lover has escaped. I have pledged him to Woden, and nowhere in this world or the next will he be safe from me."

Chapter 5

Aethelind stood trembling in the deserted family hall. All the servants had fled to hide somewhere. She supposed she should hide too. She could hear the shouting and whooping from the city, mixed with the shrieks of women. How could the army have collapsed like that? Like a sandcastle swept away by a single wave. Her father had been in the shield-wall, but she had not seen what had happened to him, or to Eadwine. The first reaction of the Queen and her women had been disbelief, the second horror, and the third panic. Aethelind had fled through the city, made a group of panicked servants help her unbar the south gate, and bolted for home. She had had no idea what she would do when she got here, except possibly put her head under the blankets and hide. She didn't think that would help much.

The shouting was getting closer. She looked round frantically. The hall was a simple building, not unlike a barn in construction and shape. There were a few trestle tables, a few benches, her father's great carved chair and a side table holding the stacks of wooden bowls and platters, cups, jugs and the great gold friendship cup. Nowhere to hide. She scuttled through the door into the family chamber, which occupied one end of the hall and was walled off by a thin wooden partition. Her bed, neatly made and standing against one wall. Her father's big bed, a muddle of disordered blankets and grubby sheets, with the coverlet trailing on the floor. She could hide under the bed – though she had better empty the chamber pot first – but that would be the first place anyone would look. The wooden chests holding the spare sheets and blankets and her clothes – her father's clothes tended to live on the floor – were ranged along one wall. Could she hide in one of them? But they were not big enough, and anyway they would be the second place someone would look.

She ran outside into the yard. The barn! She could hide there! She fled inside just as the first loud raucous voices arrived.

Unfortunately, the barn was the third place they looked. Aethelind cowered behind part of an old cart, listening to the sound of splintering wood and quarrelling voices from the hall, squealing pigs and cackling chickens from the yard, and two or three men grunting and kicking things around in the barn. They were searching systematically, starting by the big door and working up to her end. She crouched lower. There was no way out. She tried not to breathe. Dust and cobwebs tickled her neck and her nose. Frija, protect me, don't let me sneeze, don't let them find me – Something heavy thumped against the cart and the rotting timber shook from top to bottom. Aethelind tried to back away and found the wall of the barn behind her. The cart crashed to the ground, and Aethelind found herself looking through a cloud of dust at two very large, very savage-looking men, covered in blood and with spears in their hands.

It was at this point that it occurred to her that it might have been a good idea to bring a knife.

***

"Ashhere! Ash! How many fingers am I holding up? Ash!"

"Twelve," Ashhere muttered groggily, and flopped back against whoever was holding him. His face and neck were unpleasantly wet and cold, he ached all over, and he had a pounding headache. It must have been quite a party –

"Ash!" the voice insisted. More cold water sloshed into his face, and a hand slapped his cheek. "Wake up!"

Ashhere surfaced reluctantly, to find that the pest was Lilla. He put a hand up to his aching head, and encountered a jagged cut and a lump the size of a hen's egg.

He groaned. "What hit me?"

"A troll in ring mail," Lilla answered. "At least, that's what he looked like. I thought you were dead, but Drust wouldn't believe me. Your old helmet did its job one last time after all."

Ashhere remembered. He remembered charging to meet the Bernician line, then somehow he and Lilla and Drust had been fighting in one of the splintered fragments of the Deiran shield-wall, trying to cut a path through to Eadwine in another fragment. Then he remembered dodging a spear only to see the great iron sword descending, and a vague thought that his next sight would be the queue for Woden's hall. He struggled to sit up against Drust's strong arm, expecting to see the familiar sight of the walls of Eboracum rising above the Ouse.

What he actually saw was a desolate expanse of salt marsh and a wide river swirling in muddy channels between hummocks of weed. A dead tree stuck up out of the mud like a picked skeleton, and a pair of oystercatchers skimmed above the water, calling their eerie cry as they disappeared downstream. There was an all-pervading smell of dead fish, rotting vegetation and salt water.

"Where are we?"

"The end of the world," Lilla said, shivering.

"Down the river ye call the Ouse, near the sea," Drust said. "Hiding from yon demons on horseback."

Which meant that Lilla was as near right as made no difference. The marshy wasteland where the Derwent, the Ouse and the Aire all met and flowed into the Humber formed the southern boundary of Deira. Ashhere knew vaguely that the world probably carried on beyond Deira's borders, but he had never given it much thought. There were tales of enchanted forests where you could enter but never find your way out again, and of barren wildernesses that went on for ever and were inhabited by trolls and dragons and other monsters. Ashhere shivered at the thought. He believed he had seen a troll once, on the moors of the North March, a huge vague shape looming out of the mist. Drust had jeered at him and said it was a rock, and in the morning there was indeed a giant boulder there, but Ashhere remained convinced that he had had a narrow escape from being a troll's supper. He certainly had no desire ever to see another one.

Then a worse thought occurred to him. 'Hiding', Drust had said.

32

"We didn't – " his voice faltered, "– we didn't run away –?"

"No, no, it's all right," Lilla reassured him. "Eadwine's here too."

That made it all right. If you stayed with your own lord, it didn't count as running away, whoever else you abandoned. Your lord might have disgraced himself by flight, but the disgrace did not extend to you. Loyalty to your own lord was paramount, even if his behaviour was dishonourable. It was the one absolute certainty in an unreliable world.

Ashhere looked around. He could see maybe twenty filthy and bedraggled men, all looking exhausted and many wounded to a greater or lesser degree, and about the same number of tired-looking horses miserably trying to graze the rank grass. Very few of the men had spears or shields. Some had swords, more had fighting knives, and a few had no weapon left except ordinary eating knives.

"Where is everybody?"

"This is everybody," Lilla answered sombrely.

Ashhere gaped, struggling to comprehend the scale of the disaster. His father and elder brother had been in the battle too, in the centre of the line among the King's hearth-troop. He could see neither of them among the battered survivors. Clutching his hammer amulet, he murmured a prayer for them. Thunor would see their spirits safely into Woden's hall.

Arguing voices were coming from somewhere behind him. He recognised one of them as Beortred's, the captain of Eadric's hearth-troop, because he had heard it yelling orders before the shield-wall wavered and then broke. It was clipped and assured, accustomed to command.

"– I'm telling you, we'll stay here tonight and cross at low tide tomorrow –"

Eadwine's voice, harsh with pain and anger. "And I'm telling *you*, that'll be too bloody late. Woden's breath! A broken shoulder won't kill me. Being overtaken by Aethelferth's soldiers will. If you insist on using me as an excuse for deserting your King, bloody well do the bloody job properly!"

"*Deserting?!*" A sword rang as it was drawn. Eadwine laughed, a demonic sound.

"Go on, kill me. You think I care? Makes it a bit pointless though, doesn't it, scraping me off a battlefield only to dump me in the river?"

"I wish we hadn't bothered!"

"So do I! So don't bother any more, understand? Every man for himself. You were all in my father's service, or my brother's. They're both dead, so you're all free to go. Got that? You owe me nothing. You can all go home."

"You're being bloody ungrateful," came Treowin's voice, crossly, "considering we saved your life."

"For what, exactly? A few hours or a few days while the Twister hunts me down?"

"Oh, nonsense. I know it's been a close call so far, but we've lost them now. We'll get to Lindsey soon and they're our allies. You're the king of Deira now –"

"The King of Deira is dead. If you didn't see it, I did."

The bleak misery in Eadwine's tone made Ashhere's flesh creep. Aelle's end must have been terrible.

"I'm sorry," Treowin said gently. "Really I am. But Aelle's dead, and you're his eldest legitimate son, and as far as I'm concerned that makes you King unless the Council decides otherwise. So Caedbaed of Lindsey will help you –"

"You're being unusually stupid today. Haven't you understood yet? The kingdom of Deira – no – longer – exists. The Twister is king now. Got it?

Caedbaed of Lindsey will change his play to match the board as it is *now*, not as it was yesterday. If we still held Eboracum, that would be different –"

"You were right about that," Treowin said miserably. "We should have listened to you. I never imagined they'd walk all over us like that –"

"Too late," Eadwine interrupted. "Aethelferth won and we lost. Get that into your head and stop snivelling over dreams of winning the kingdom back."

"There's still hope, as long as you live."

"So he can't afford to let me escape, can't you see that? Anyone who is a friend to me is an enemy of the Twister. *Anyone*, understand? Including you. So take your men, and anyone else who'll follow you, and clear off. Whatever the Ladies have in store for me I don't expect anyone else to share it."

"I'm not leaving you!"

"Why not?" Eadwine said cruelly. "You've abandoned one king today, you can abandon another. Now bugger off. I don't want to see you again."

***

Eadwine came limping along the river bank to where Ashhere sat with Lilla and Drust. His cloak was slashed to ribbons, the tarnished mail was scored where blades had struck home, and his helmet was dented and missing some of its decorative panels. The gold ring-brooch fastening the cloak on his right shoulder had been shattered almost in half and some of the mail rings were bent and broken. A sword-stroke with that much force behind it could easily have broken the collar-bone, even though the mail had successfully turned the edge. He had switched his blood-crusted sword to hang from his left shoulder, and jammed his right hand into the sword-belt as a crude sling.

He stood looking down at them, his face unreadable behind the mask of the helmet, a menacing stranger from the fringes of nightmare.

"Not dead after all, Ash? And I thought you were one of the lucky ones."

"I was," Ashhere said, missing the sarcasm. "Was it you told them to get me out?"

"No," Eadwine snarled. "Nobody asked my opinion on anything." He plucked the fragments of the ring-brooch from his cloak and tossed one half to Ashhere and the other to Lilla. "Here. Not much reward for three years' service, but that's all I can do for you. Drust, you're released from your oath. Now get lost, all of you."

"I don't understand –?" Ashhere began.

Eadwine swore. "I know you're thick, but what *exactly* do you not understand? Get lost. Go away. Bugger off."

Ashhere was hurt and bewildered. Eadwine had never spoken to him like that before. "B-but – where to?"

"How should I know? Go home. Go and find another lord to serve. Go and jump in the river for all I care." He glared round at them. "Go on, bugger off!"

"No," Lilla said flatly. "You are my lord and I go where you go."

"Not now, you don't. Can't you get it into your thick head? The Twister's not interested in you lot. You're not worth spit to him. But *my* head was worth its weight in gold as soon as he realised he wouldn't find it on the field. I'll be hunted for the rest of my life, which isn't likely to be long. So bugger off, all of you."

"No."

He swore savagely at them. "Deira's finished. *I'm* finished. You're better off without me."

"No. Never."

"You can't do this to us," Ashhere pleaded. He could imagine nothing worse than wandering through the world bereft of a lord to look after him and make his decisions for him. That was the deal; you obeyed your lord and he provided for you. It might amuse the Three Ladies to torment one or both of you by preventing you fulfilling your obligation, but you had to try to the very limits of your ability. On both sides.

"You can't desert us," he insisted. "We're lost without you."

"Oh, by all the gods –!" Eadwine clenched and unclenched his fist, the muscles in his throat working. "What the hell did I do to deserve you lot?"

They exchanged glances, not sure if this was a blessing or a curse.

"Very well," he said, his voice a little more normal. "Never let it be said that I failed you as well. On your own heads be it. You'll regret it, I warn you."

Ashhere found himself grinning inanely from sheer relief. "Where are we going?"

"Lundencaster. Aethelbert of Kent rules there, and he is overlord in the South. If anyone can defy the Twister it's him. Well, come on then! If we're going we might as well get there."

"Right." They looked about uncertainly. Dusk was already beginning to fall. "What do we do?"

"Cross the Ouse. Here. Now."

"How?" Lilla gasped, looking at the river swirling through the mud flats. The tide had dropped since they had first halted here, but there was still an awful lot of water in the river and it was flowing fast. "You can't swim with a broken shoulder. You'll drown."

"That'd solve everybody's problems," Eadwine snapped bitterly. "But horses can swim. Kick them into the water, don't let them turn back, and all you have to do is hang on."

This proved to be the case. By the time they were all gathered, soaking wet, muddy and exhausted, some considerable way downstream on the opposite bank, they found that another dozen men had copied the idea and followed them. Among the newcomers were Treowin and Beortred.

"What are you lot doing here?" Eadwine demanded curtly.

"Coming with you," Treowin said, "and don't argue about it, because you're not going to change our minds."

But it seemed that Eadwine was past arguing with anyone. "Suit yourselves," he said indifferently. "It's your funeral."

***

They spent a cold and miserable night in the marshes on the south bank of the river. A few men found scraps of food in pouches or saddlebags, but for most of them there was nothing to eat. Nobody dared light a fire to dry their wet clothes, even if they could have found anything in the salt marshes that was dry enough to burn, but as it turned out that mattered very little, for they were all drenched again crossing the Aire in a similar way as soon as it got light the next morning. There was a perfectly good ford across the Aire about ten miles inland, where an army-path crossed the river, but Eadwine was adamant that Aethelferth would be guarding it by now and nobody had the nerve to find out if he was wrong. Capture would mean execution or sale as slaves. A dismal day floundering through more marshes and wading or swimming muddy rivers was succeeded by an equally dismal night.

***

It was a sullen and dejected little group that faced a bleary dawn on the second day. After the third or fourth river they had found their way up onto slightly higher and drier ground, but it had rained most of the night and put paid both to Beortred's attempts to light a fire and to anyone's attempts to sleep. There were no farmsteads to steal food from, and Eadwine had refused to stop to try to fish or hunt – in any case none of them had hunting gear and only Drust and Beortred even had a spear – so all they had eaten since the defeat was a few elderberries and some sloes. Hunger was becoming unpleasantly insistent. Bruises, cuts and other injuries from the battle were stiff and painful, and saddle-soreness added insult to injury for everyone except Eadwine and Treowin, who were the only two really capable riders in the group. Eadwine remained indifferent at best, hostile at worst, and that added considerably to their misery. If he was deliberately trying to drive them away, it was certainly working. Several men had already given up and left to try their luck elsewhere, reckoning that anything was better than starving to death in the company of a man who hadn't a civilised word for anyone. Seven remained besides Eadwine and his three companions, and their patience was visibly running out.

***

"This is getting stupid," Beortred growled, as they were preparing to depart in the early morning chill. It had stopped raining and the sun was slowly creeping out of the mist over the marshes, but a cold and searching wind was blowing from the east and making them all shiver. They had almost forgotten what it was like to be warm, dry and fed, and Beortred was developing a cold, which added to his ill-temper. He sneezed, and glared at Eadwine. "Are you listening to me? I'm fed up with this. Dragging us through one marsh after another, mile after bloody mile. I say we go back to the nearest army-path, now."

Eadwine was adjusting his horse's saddle and did not pay him the courtesy of looking round. "Go where you like. I didn't ask you to follow me."

"Come back to the road with us," Treowin argued. "We've lost them, I tell you. We haven't seen anyone since we crossed the Ouse."

"That," said Eadwine with exaggerated patience, as if he were addressing a particularly slow-witted child, "is the point of keeping to the wasteland."

"They've given up," Treowin insisted, keeping his temper with obvious difficulty.

"If they were ever after us in the first place," grumbled Beortred. "I bet this is all in your head. The Twister's not the slightest bit interested in you."

"You're running from shadows," Treowin insisted.

"And I'm buggered if I'm swimming the Trent," Beortred declared.

"I'm not intending to swim the Trent –"

"Some sense at last!"

"– because I'm not intending to cross it."

"What?"

"You're mad!"

"But Lindsey's just on the other side," Treowin protested, above the general chorus of complaint. "We'll be safe there. We've ridden quite far enough."

"I agree with that," muttered Ashhere under his breath. "Next time I want to see this wretched horse is in a stew."

36

"I told you, you might be safe in Lindsey, but I won't be. How many times have I got to say it before it sinks into your thick skull?"

"Why do you have to be so bloody obstinate?" Treowin demanded, beginning to get angry. "Caedbaed of Lindsey is Deira's ally."

"*Was*. Past tense."

"Oh, come on –"

"Treowin, has it escaped your notice that I am obliged to take vengeance on Aethelferth for my father's death? In the unlikely event that I survive, that is. Giving shelter to me is inviting the wrath of the Twister. Caedbaed *might* choose to use me to pick a fight with Aethelferth, but I'd put more faith in a Jute's promise. If he has any brains at all he'll cash in my head. I'm no blood-kin to him, remember." He swung painfully into the saddle, trying not to jar his broken shoulder. "You go and ask Caedbaed for refuge in Lindsey if you like. I'm going south."

***

Treowin scowled blackly at Eadwine's back as they rode on. He was reluctant to abandon his friend, partly from long affection, and partly because he had only the haziest idea of geography beyond Deira's borders and had very little idea where they were. But he was getting very tired of this – to his way of thinking – unnecessarily tortuous journey to an unknown destination. He had no idea where Lundencaster was, except that it was a long way away, and if Eadwine continued to insist on avoiding the army-paths it was probably going to take them all winter to get there. Whereas Lindsey offered the prospect of food, fire, rest and women within a few hours' ride. He disagreed with Eadwine's assessment of Caedbaed's likely attitude. Kings sheltered royal exiles all the time. When an atheling ended up on the wrong side of a dynastic dispute, he fled over the border to the neighbouring kingdom, where he lived in comfortable exile at his host's court, treated as a member of the king's household. When a suitable opportunity arose, the host king would raise his army and restore the exiled atheling to his kingdom, on the understanding that the restored king paid substantial tribute thereafter to show his gratitude to his benefactor. The rival would either have been killed or would have fled to a different kingdom, where *he* lived in exile until he could persuade *his* host to invade. And so it went on, back and forth without end, like the ebb and flow of the tides. The Brittonic kingdoms to the north and west of Deira did it all the time – indeed this was one reason why the aristocracy in both Bernicia and Deira was getting steadily more and more Anglian as time went on, as Brittonic kings and nobles obligingly fought one another and left widows, daughters and sisters who were only too glad to marry powerful protectors of any background.

Treowin could see no reason why Caedbaed of Lindsey should be an exception. His outlook on the world was entirely Anglian and centred on his father's hereditary lands on the Deiran Wolds. He knew vaguely that Strat Clut, Pictland and Dal Riada were 'up north' beyond Bernicia, and that Rheged and the Pennines were 'out west' beyond Eboracum Vale, but he had no real idea of the vast expanse of Aethelferth's tributary dominions. Whereas he knew Lindsey to be a fair-sized kingdom, nearly as big as Deira and if anything more populous, ruled by a fellow Anglo-Brittonic royal dynasty. Indeed, he considered Caedbaed's family to be distant kin to his own, since they also claimed a tenuous descent from the great Offa of Angeln. Eadwine, he thought, was being unreasonably cautious – he hesitated to use the word 'cowardly' of a friend.

***

Treowin realised he had fallen behind and kicked his tired horse into a canter. The others were gathered in the shade of a cluster of thorn trees, but it soon became apparent that they were not waiting for him.

"– and I've bloody had enough of you," Beortred was saying. "There's no danger, I tell you."

"It's your funeral," Eadwine said indifferently. "But you can see there are soldiers on the bridge."

The hawthorn thicket was at the top of a pasture sloping gently down to a great slow river, much wider than the Ouse, meandering idly through vast scrubby cattle-dotted water meadows. The Trent, ancient boundary of the domains of Coel the Old, dividing North Britannia from South. In this part of its course the river formed the border of the kingdom of Lindsey, and ahead of the thicket it was crossed by an army-path and a substantial stone bridge. Above the bridge, on the west side, sat a small walled fort, its defences in remarkably good repair. At the west end of the bridge, spanning the army-path from ditch to ditch, a company of men was drawn up. The fort garrison, probably with other additions, at least twenty strong.

"Collecting tolls," Beortred said curtly. "Anyone can see that. I've done duty myself, at Catraeth on Dere Street and at Calcacaster on the way to Loidis."

"So have I," chimed in several other voices.

"I don't like it," Eadwine insisted. "Why so many of them?"

"Because it's an important road," Treowin said impatiently.

"More likely they're looking for us," Eadwine said. "For me. Aethelferth could easily have sent messengers to Lindsey by now."

"*Could* have!"

"When Aethelferth realised he'd lost us, he'd send men to watch the roads and guard the bridges. To capture us when we try to cross. It's what anyone with any brains would do. Why do you think I've been avoiding the roads?"

"Beard of Woden!" Beortred bellowed. "Your brother would be ashamed of you! Skulking and hiding like some thieving slave! If Aethelferth wants your head, he's bloody welcome to it! *I* am going to ride down there and across that bridge, and ask for service with the King of Lindsey. Who's coming with me?"

"I am!" cried Treowin, hoping this would force Eadwine's hand.

"And me!"

"And me!"

Everybody was, apparently, except Eadwine and therefore also Lilla, Ashhere and Drust. Ashhere looked longingly at the bridge, but loyalty held him back. Besides, he was reminded of numerous times on the March when Eadwine's seemingly absurd notions had turned out to be right.

"Please yourselves," Eadwine said. "I didn't ask you to come with me. Go where you like. And," he added unexpectedly, "good luck to you."

***

Ashhere had expected they would ride on, but instead Eadwine stayed watching as Beortred's party rode cheerfully down to the bridge. He was moving restlessly along the edge of the thicket and back again. The sun glittered off his helmet, and Ashhere was alarmed to see that some of the men on the bridge were pointing in their direction. It was not like Eadwine to give away a position in this slipshod manner. He thought about warning him to be more careful, but was afraid of getting his head bitten off.

Drust had no such concerns. "Can ye no keep still?" he said bluntly. "Yon fancy armour attracts attention."

"Shut up," Eadwine answered, but without anger. The bitter hostility they had come to dread had gone and his voice was thoughtful, much as on the March when he had a problem to solve. He unfastened what was left of his cloak, which was knotted together by two of its torn ends, and tossed it to Drust. "Here. Fix that on the end of your spear."

"What for?"

"To keep the blade warm," Eadwine said acidly. "To look like a banner, what do you think? Now go to the other end of this line of trees, and keep out of sight until I tell you. Lilla, Ashhere, over here."

***

Beortred's group was almost up to the line of soldiers. They dismounted gratefully, Treowin and Beortred leading, waving and calling cheerful greetings. The soldiers did not wave back.

"Not very friend –" Ashhere muttered, just at the moment when the soldiers levelled their spears and closed in like a pack of wolves on their quarry.

Eadwine was already kicking his horse into a gallop. "Drust, wave that banner and make enough noise for an army! You two, gallop after me and shout for all you're worth!"

They burst out from the cover of the thicket and pounded across the pasture. Ashhere clung on to the reins, the saddle, handfuls of the horse's mane and anything else he could get hold of, terrified at the appalling speed. He heard Drust's mighty voice bellowing from the thicket and remembered he was supposed to shout too.

"Deira!" he roared. "Eadwine for Deira!"

He wondered if he ought to draw his sword, but decided he had better hang on to the horse with both hands in case he fell off. Ahead, Eadwine had no such difficulty. He had long mastered the Brittonic cavalry skill of controlling a horse with the pressure of his thighs, leaving both hands free for weapons. His right arm was useless because of his broken shoulder, but his left brandished his sword to great effect.

"Caer Ebrawg!" he cried, his voice high and clear. "Caer Ebrawg!"

The soldiers wavered. They had already seen the tell-tale flashes of armour spread widely along the thicket and betraying the presence of a large warband. Now they saw a banner appear and horsemen charging down upon them, led by a mighty warlord in glittering armour, whirling a terrifying sword and shouting a war cry. A *Brittonic* war cry, moreover. It was a century since Arthur's heyday, but a healthy respect for Brittonic cavalry was hard-wired into the brain of every foot-soldier in South Britannia. The weight of a man's head in gold wasn't much use if you didn't survive to cash in the prize.

They fled in the direction of their fort. Treowin and Beortred gave chase.

"Don't fight, you bloody fools!" Eadwine screamed. "Run!"

Treowin heard and understood. He threw his sword at his opponent, caught one of the panicked horses, vaulted up and hauled one of the other men up in front of him. Beortred managed to follow suit, on the second or third clumsy attempt. Two of the others were luckily still mounted, and the last man managed to grab one of his colleagues and leap aboard as they hurtled away down the army-path.

39

By this time the soldiers had counted their attackers and were advancing again. Eadwine wheeled his horse and brandished the sword in a sweeping gesture that encompassed the entire length of the thicket.

"Drust! To me! To me, men, to me!"

The soldiers saw the banner and another horseman emerge from the thicket, and froze. It was only a few seconds before they realised they had been had – but by this time Eadwine had thirty yards' start.

"Ride!" he yelled at the rest of the group. "Ride for your lives!"

A spear clattered onto the metalling and convinced even the most reluctant rider that a headlong gallop was the lesser of two evils. They obeyed. A second spear fell harmlessly a few yards behind.

"Back to the marshes, lord?" someone called.

"No!" Eadwine shouted back. "Stick to the army-path – outrun them –!"

"Bastards," Treowin gasped. "Murdering bastards! Never gave us a chance to explain – just turned on us – and they're supposed to be our allies – !"

"I told you, losers have no allies. We're walking loot, Treowin, like a pig is walking bacon. Get used to it."

***

They rounded a bend and saw they were coming to another river, much smaller than the mighty Trent. There was no bridge nor any sign of the remains of one, and the road continued clearly on the opposite bank, indicating the likely presence of a paved ford. And then they saw the soldiers. Seven or eight men with spears, lined up across the road and barring access to the crossing.

"Shit!" cried Treowin.

"Dismount and fight!" bellowed Beortred.

"No!" Eadwine shouted. "Keep riding!"

An hour ago most of them would have laughed at this extraordinary order, or ignored it. But after their experience at the bridge, if Eadwine had ordered them to walk through fire they would have tried to obey.

"Get close together!" Eadwine called, drawing his sword again. "Gallop straight for them! They're facing the wrong way. They won't stand!"

The soldiers were indeed facing the wrong way. They were drawn up at the lip of the bank on the east side of the river, just where anyone attempting to cross from the west could be cut down with ease as they clambered up from the ford. But this meant that against an attack from the *east* the soldiers would be trying to hold a precarious footing where a single step back would send them sprawling down the bank into the river.

One soldier glanced over his shoulder at the drum of approaching hooves, did a horrified double-take when he saw that they weren't going to stop, grabbed his neighbour's arm and shouted something to his companions.

The line did a reasonably adept about-face, and eight wicked spear points came into the attack position. They were not going to give up easily.

Lilla found his gaze irresistibly drawn to the spear tips, and his mouth went dry with fear. The prospect of floundering through a ford at a gallop was bad enough – what if he lost his balance and was thrown, what if the horse stumbled on something – but he also realised how very vulnerable he was to those steel blades. He had no body armour of any kind and no shield for protection, although in any case he needed both hands to cling on to the horse. Somebody else was riding at his right, but his left side was open, and a big powerful-looking man was hefting his spear threateningly just where Lilla would have to pass. He saw the blade poised, saw the big spearman draw his arm back for the killing blow – and then another horse swept up on his left, and Eadwine's sword slashed down in a spray of blood. Lilla saw Eadwine jerk in the saddle, but there was no cry and he thought the jerk must have been part of the sword-stroke. The big spearman fell away and rolled down the bank into the river, blood pouring between his fingers as he clutched at his face.

Lilla's horse slithered down the bank, stumbled, righted itself, and plunged through the ford after the others in a wall of spray that drenched them almost as thoroughly as if they had swum the river again. He felt the heave of muscles as the horse climbed up the opposite bank, and then they were pounding on along the army-path. He risked a glance around and saw that they all appeared to have made it safely across and they were all laughing fiercely or grinning like children at a fair.

"Beard of Woden!" Treowin panted. "Madness! Lunacy! We should all have been killed! But what a way to go!"

They slowed to a trot, the horses now getting very tired, especially those with double burdens. To their right, the sun gleamed on the wetlands they had crossed so painfully the previous day. To their left, scrub and heathland graded into denser woodland, with a ridge of forested hills rising beyond. The edge of the great dark forest that blanketed large parts of inland Britannia.

"What now, lord?" Beortred called breathlessly to Eadwine. "We can't gallop much further."

Eadwine was fiddling with something at his left side. He looked over his shoulder, scanned the country around, and looked over his shoulder again. There was no sign of pursuit. They seemed to be alone on the road.

He gestured at the woods.

"Off the road," he gasped, his voice ragged. "Go to ground –"

Eadwine set his horse to jump the roadside ditch, and Lilla noticed that he reeled in the saddle, as if drunk or overcome with weariness. He shut his eyes as his own horse jumped, hung on to its mane for dear life, and hoped it would have the sense to follow its companions. The land was uncultivated scrub, a mixture of hazel, willow, hawthorn and gorse, rank grass, weeds, thistles and nettles. Reedy grass or, occasionally, brilliant moss revealed the existence of wet patches, and small sluggish streams appeared with little warning. Lilla let his horse do the steering and clung on as best he might, deeply grateful that at least they were not trying to do this at a gallop.

The woods began to close around them, mostly oak and ash with an understorey of hazel and brambles. They were going slowly now, following a thin track that twisted and turned under the trees. Some had dismounted, partly to ease stiff limbs and aching backsides and partly to avoid low branches. Eadwine was slumped low over his horse's neck. No-one spoke. The light was filtered and dim green, reminiscent of swimming underwater in a silty river. Small birds flitted and chirped in the branches, never visible. A blackbird shrilled its alarm call. High in the canopy, a couple of wood pigeons rose into clapping flight. A squirrel skittered up a tree and chattered crossly at the intruders. By common consent, when they came to a small clearing they stopped. They could see nothing except the surrounding trees and each other. It was as if the world outside had ceased to exist. They were safe.

"How did you know?" Ashhere asked, leaving his horse and coming to look up at Eadwine. "Fighting from horseback, and them not standing at the ford, and everything?"

Eadwine was swaying slightly, his head drooping.

"It's all in the poetry," he said in a tired voice, "if you listen."

"What now –?" Treowin began, and broke off, staring in horror at Eadwine's left hand, which was trying to clamp the bunched skirt of his tunic against his waist.

Blood was trickling slowly between the fingers.

"Catch him!" Beortred yelled, as Eadwine folded up and sagged sideways into Ashhere's arms.

Chapter 6

Aethelind screamed as the two looters dragged her out from behind the cart. They laughed, and two more broke off from looting the hall and came to join in the fun. Her terror seemed to amuse them, and they formed a ring around her, jeering and prodding at her with their spears. She wept and begged for mercy and shrieked for help, and they laughed some more and boasted to each other of the things they were going to do to her. Then they fell to quarrelling over who was going to be first, and Aethelind tried to run away.

This proved to be a bad idea. One of them tripped her with his spear and she fell heavily into the scattered straw. They gathered round, much uglier now and angry. One stooped and ripped off the brooches fastening her gown on each shoulder. The festoon of beads draped between the brooches broke, and beads flew in all directions. Harsh hands tugged at her girdle and pawed at her skirts. Aethelind screamed again and again. And again.

The panting weight was suddenly hauled off her, and the looters' raucous cheering ceased abruptly, but Aethelind's hopes of a miraculous rescue were swiftly dashed. A dozen more equally savage-looking spearmen came crowding into the barn, led by a fearsome warlord in filthy mail and battered helmet. They circled like a pack of stray dogs about to fight over a bone.

The warlord gestured towards the door with his bloodstained sword.

"Bugger off," he growled at the looters. "This is ours."

One of the looters, probably the one with the largest amount of portable booty, already had. The one who had been pawing Aethelind glared at the warlord in impotent rage.

"Who says so?"

"Hereward of Tweed Vale."

Aethelind had never heard the name, but the looters obviously had. The man paled, but he wasn't prepared to yield his prize easily.

He hefted his spear menacingly in Hereward's direction. "We got here first!"

"And there are more of us, so bugger off."

The man lunged with his spear. The warlord flung up his shield, his sword flashed, and the man staggered backwards with his belly slit open like a paunched hare. The sword flashed again, and he crumpled soundlessly to the ground in a spreading pool of blood from his cut throat.

Aethelind was too shocked to scream.

"Now bugger off," Hereward snarled at the remaining looters, "before I gut you too."

They did not need to be told twice.

"Get up, girl," Hereward growled at Aethelind, and two of his spearmen hauled her to her feet, clutching her gown in one hand. Without her brooches the top half of the dress was unsupported, and she was very grateful that her under-dress was of thick linen, with a high neck and long sleeves.

Hereward took his helmet off, revealing a head of shaggy fair hair matted with sweat and dirt, an unkempt beard and a broad, weatherbeaten face. He was heavy-built but not tall, probably around thirty-five or forty.

"You live here, girl?" he said, somewhat indistinctly.

Aethelind nodded, then realised he was talking to her breasts. Men tended to do that. That was something familiar amid the ruin of her world.

"Y-yes."

"Whose hall is this?"

"My father's," Aethelind faltered, and began to cry quietly. "Where's my father? What happened to him?"

"If he was in the battle he's dead," said the warlord curtly. "They're all dead, except the atheling, and he won't escape for long." He appraised the barn in a sweeping glance. "Nice place you got here. How much land?"

"Sixty – sixty hides – I think –" Aethelind stammered. She felt numb. All dead. She was all alone with nobody to protect her.

Hereward grinned, displaying stained and broken teeth. "Right, lads. We'll have this place. It's time we settled down." He gestured at the corpse. "Chuck that in the river, and if any more of his kind come sniffing round, fillet them and chuck them after him. I'll collar the King before anyone else does. You stay here. Make yourselves at home." His eyes went back to Aethelind. "Keep that girl for me."

He strode out. Aethelind drew a long shaky breath. The semicircle of spearmen eyed her hungrily, like dogs whipped off a juicy bone. But she was sure they would not dare disobey their master. The body on the floor was eloquent testimony to the consequences. Besides, they were men. Aethelind was an expert on men.

"You heard your lord," she said, and was relieved to find that her voice was only a little tremulous. "This is his home now. He'll want it ready for him when he comes back. So we'd best make a start."

***

"Stop it, Lilla –" Ashhere begged, "it wasn't your fault -"

Lilla was pacing up and down, twisting his hands together in his distress. "That spear thrust was meant for me, and – and Eadwine took it instead –"

"You'd have done the same for him."

"That's *different* – and now he's *dying* –"

"It's very bad manners," said a faint voice, "to talk about someone as if he wasn't there."

Eadwine was still stretched on his back where they had laid him down after his collapse, but his eyes were open and regarding them with a concerned expression.

Lilla threw himself on his knees and seized his hand.

"Lord! We thought – we thought –"

"So did I, but it seems the Three Ladies haven't finished with me yet. Lilla – it was nothing to do with you. That fellow was aiming for anyone he could hit, and so was I. And he got the worst of the exchange. You couldn't even have hit him back, not without falling off your horse."

"I know you're right," Lilla said, with something that might have been a sniff, "but I owe you one."

"You're not keeping count, are you? I ran out of fingers ages ago." He tried to sit up, winced, and thought better of it. "Did everyone make it? How long have we been here? We have to move –"

"You're in no fit state to be going anywhere," Ashhere said, his voice still shaking a little from shock. The spear had pierced Eadwine's mail shirt and inflicted a deep gash in his left side. Beortred and Treowin had made no attempt to investigate – what, after all, could they hope to see at the bottom of a dark hole persistently filling with blood? They had simply stuffed handfuls of Eadwine's linen undershirt into the wound and pressed down hard until, after a heart-stopping few minutes, the red stain at last stopped spreading. The rest of the undershirt was ripped into bandages and used to bind the crude dressing in place. It seemed to have worked, and the fact that Eadwine was conscious and able to talk was a hopeful sign, but Ashhere was afraid that the terrifying bleeding would start again. Nor was the puncture Eadwine's only injury. Stripped of armour and tunic, his upper body was a mass of heavy bruising, lacerated where mail rings had been driven into the flesh, and his right shoulder was horribly swollen and discoloured around the damaged bone. It must hurt to move, even to breathe. No further explanation was required for his foul temper. It was astonishing to Ashhere that he had managed to keep going at all, especially considering that he must have been close to exhaustion before the battle even started. He knew from their time on the March that Eadwine was capable of extraordinary endurance – having recognised at an early age that he was not built for brute power and so devoted his attention to developing stamina instead – but even so, there had to be a limit somewhere.

"I'm not dead yet," Eadwine announced, and proved it by sitting up, successfully this time – although he went very pale and his face glistened with sweat. Drust reached out an unobtrusive hand to steady him, surprisingly gentle for so large and powerful a man.

Eadwine looked round at the ring of anxious faces. Very nice of them to be so concerned, but why couldn't one of them do some thinking for a change? He wanted nothing more than to lie down and never wake up, but it seemed that if he did not come up with a decision nobody else would. They would simply stay here like a flock of sheep waiting to be slaughtered. He wondered irrelevantly if sheep had a mythical afterlife, full of endless grass and – well, whatever else sheep dreamed about – and if that explained their willingness to queue up to be killed. His imagination skipped ahead to visualise an ovine Woden – a wolf in sheep's clothing if ever there was one – and he had to fight down a burst of insane laughter. He cursed his inventive mind for its irritating tendency to wander down side tracks when he was overburdened with problems, just when coherent thought was most necessary.

"We can't stay here," he insisted, "a blind worm could follow our tracks, we can't have covered more than a mile or two from the ford, and that wasn't very far from the bridge. Those fellows have at least one fallen comrade to avenge, not counting the prospect of getting rich. They'll be here soon, so we'd better not be."

"We'll defend you to the death," Ashhere said stoutly, hoping he sounded braver than he felt. He was cold, wet, hungry, weary, sore and now very frightened. It was bad enough being out of his own country, disoriented and lost, and now it seemed that every man's hand would be raised against them into the bargain.

44

"Apart from keeping Woden's doorwardens busy, what does that achieve?" Eadwine said sharply. "*One* death is what they're after. If you're not going to give it them, we might as well at least make them work for it."

"So what do we do?" Treowin asked. "You can't ride."

"No," Eadwine agreed ruefully, "I've just proved that, haven't I? I haven't fallen off a horse since I was about six."

Even sitting still he was dizzy, and he had discovered that any sudden movement of the head made the world spin alarmingly. Loss of blood, he supposed. He might be able to stay on a horse at a very gentle walk, but at a gallop or even a trot he would inevitably be thrown.

"I might be able to hold you in front of me – " Treowin began doubtfully.

"All the way to Lundencaster?"

"How far is it?"

"About two hundred miles."

Shocked silence. Most of them probably would not have estimated that the world was that big.

"A horse litter?" Lilla suggested. "We could probably rig up something."

"Too slow, too clumsy. Next time we're chased we wouldn't have a chance." Eadwine took a deep breath. "I can walk, I think, if somebody will steady me. It's much harder to track men on foot than horses. This is a very big forest. So we turn the horses loose and disappear into it."

"I could track eleven men through a forest," Lilla objected.

"They probably haven't got a tracker as good as you."

Lilla looked pleased at the praise, but still doubtful – as well he might.

"I've got a better idea," Treowin announced. "They're looking for Eadwine of Deira, right? So if they're chasing him on the army-paths, they won't waste time searching this forest and the rest of you will be safe."

"But we've just said he can't ride to Lun – what's-its-name," Beortred protested, puzzled.

"How do they recognise Eadwine?" Treowin demanded. He picked up Eadwine's discarded mail shirt and pulled it over his head. "They've only seen him in battle. In armour. In *this* armour." He pulled on the helmet and buckled on Eadwine's sword. "How do I look?"

The resemblance, at least at a superficial level, was remarkable. Treowin had the same tall slender build, the same dark hair and short sparse dark beard. The mail shirt was as bad a fit on him as it had been on Eadwine, and the helmet obscured most of his face.

"Treowin, you can't do this –" Eadwine began.

Treowin turned on him passionately. "You risked your life to save mine at the bridge. Why should I not do as much for you?"

"There's a difference between a risk and a certainty. If Aethelferth thinks you're me, do you know what he'll do to you?"

"Yes," said Treowin, and blanched. He drew the sword and went dramatically down on one knee. "I would gladly die for my King!"

The others promptly followed suit. Eadwine's unhelpful mind conjured up another image of sheep, and again he had to fight down hysterical laughter. Well, he had been wishing someone would do some thinking. Be careful what you wish for. It was a good plan, better than anything he had thought of. But it had the appalling flaw that his oldest friend would be courting danger that was meant for him.

"You can't do this," he said again.

"You can't stop me."

Which was quite true. Once an idea had captured Treowin's sense of the dramatic it was never any use trying to talk him out of it. Except by offering him a better role.

"If you're going to fool them," he suggested, "you might as well lead them as merry a dance as possible. Don't get caught."

"What?"

"The longer Aethelferth chases you, the more chance we have." *And the more chance you have*, he thought to himself. "All the way to Kent if you can manage it. And then you can take service with Aethelbert."

Treowin paused, clearly not having considered that escape was a possibility and that he might not be required to die after all. His retainers, who would be obliged to go with him, exchanged glances and brightened up noticeably.

"How do we get to Lundencaster?"

Yes! Eadwine thought. He traced a J shape in the leaf litter with his finger. "This is the River Trent." He drew a horizontal line across the top of the J. "This is the Humber. We're about here." He pointed to a spot on the left side of the J near the top of the long arm. "You go south, staying on the west bank and keeping away from the actual shore. It's border country, wooded , sparsely settled. Most likely you won't see anyone. In the middle part of its course the Trent bends east-west, see?" He indicated the curve of the J. "So you'll eventually find it lying across your path. It's not such a big river there. Easier to cross. Fords and bridges. Once across, head south, and a bit east depending how far west you had to go to find a crossing-place, and all the army-paths lead to Lundencaster. The Brittones call it Caer Lundein."

"Whose lands do we pass through?"

"All sorts. Mercians, Middle Angles, East Angles, some Brittonic odds and ends, and more Saxon and Jutish kings than maggots in a corpse. None of them amount to anything much. South of the Trent was Arthur's empire, and it all fell apart after Camlann, so you'll find an upstart king on every hilltop. But they're all subject to Aethelbert of Kent. Insist you're on your way to him and they won't dare challenge you."

Treowin grinned and counted the horses swiftly. "Eight. That makes us a fair-sized warband. A match for any southern nobody!" He glanced round the men. Five of them were his retainers. "You'll come with me, obviously. You three –" this was addressed to Ashhere, Lilla and Drust, "I assume will stay with Eadwine? So that's seven of us and one spare horse –"

"Two," said Beortred, gruffly. "I'm staying." He came to kneel beside Eadwine. "I served Lord Eadric twenty years. I'd be honoured to serve you."

The mention of Eadric's name and the reminder of his loss stabbed Eadwine as surely as the spear, except that this wound was not likely to heal so easily. The woods blurred in a haze of tears. But he must not break down, must not, *must not…..*

"Thank you," he said, and if his voice was unsteady it was no more than might be attributed to his injury. "My brother was a great man."

"Do not measure yourself by him," Beortred said, and his voice seemed slow and sad, as if his world too had a great hole in it.

46

"If I could be one-tenth the man Eadric was," Eadwine answered, "I would be content."

He struggled to stand up, the woods tilted like the deck of a ship rushing down a roller in a storm, and a grey mist swirled across his vision, but Drust's strong arm saved him from an undignified crumple to the floor.

Through the rushing in his ears, he heard Treowin bidding him farewell and his own voice answering. They clasped arms, probably for the last time, and then Treowin sprang lightly into the saddle, wearing the armour with far more panache than Eadwine felt he had ever managed.

"Death to the Twister!" he cried, and thundered away down the path, his retainers following with rather more effort and rather less style.

It seemed very quiet and very lonely when they had all gone. Another loss, Eadwine thought, another face never to be seen again. Of all the many imminent deaths he could foresee, somehow Aethelferth's seemed to be the least likely. Pity that soldier at the ford hadn't had a better aim, and then the whole mess would be somebody else's problem. He ran a hand through his tangled hair. Even that small action tugged at the torn muscles in his side and made him flinch. He looked around for his tunic, already wondering how he was going to solve the problem of stooping to pick it up and then straightening up again without falling over, but Lilla had anticipated this and handed him the garment. Whoever had stripped it off had had the sense to rip neatly up all the seams on the right side, so he could pull it on without having to move his broken shoulder. The woollen cloth felt strange against his skin. His belt held it approximately closed around his waist, and a couple of large thorns fastened the front and back together at the shoulder, like a brooch clasping a woman's dress. Another strip was ripped off his cloak – there was not much of it left now – and tied into a sling.

"It doesn't seem right that you don't have a sword," Lilla said, and indeed it did feel strange without the familiar weight at his shoulder and hip. He had worn the sword since he was fourteen, ever since Eadric had presented it to him. It should have been his father presiding over the ceremony, of course, but he had been almost glad of the insult, for Eadric had made of the ritual something warm and affectionate as well as stern and formal, welcoming him to his new status as a prince of Deira. And now the sword was gone, another link to his beloved brother broken, and one of bitter significance, for he was no longer a prince.

"I still have a dagger," he reassured Lilla, and was relieved to hear that his voice sounded almost normal. At least he could control *something*. "Which will be enough, for I don't think we're going to do any fighting."

They looked more anxious, if that were possible, for fighting was something they understood, something familiar in a world that was suddenly very big and very alien. They would, Eadwine thought, have been much happier being slaughtered by an enemy warband than embarking on an unknown journey into the enchanted forest. So would he, for that matter, and he cursed the stubborn pride that impelled him to play the game to its last move, as long as there was any move to make.

He looked up at the sky. He could not see the sun, but he could estimate its position from the shadows on the trees. It was a long way down towards the west. Two or three hours of daylight remained.

"We go north-west," he told them. "To Elmet. Princess Heledd will give us refuge."

If she ever got there, he thought, but it was no time to voice doubts.

47

They cheered up visibly, as they always did as long as someone seemed to have a firm plan. A sketchy deer path led out of the clearing in approximately the right direction and they followed it, Beortred and Drust beating down brambles and holding overhanging branches aside, and Lilla supporting Eadwine. Ashhere, still sore from his head wound, hovered helpfully.

"Isn't this Elmet already?" Lilla asked.

"Too far south, I think," Eadwine answered, in a faint voice.

"Where is it then?"

"I'm not quite sure. Either Middle Britain or whatever's left of the South Pennines, I suppose."

He felt, rather than saw, Ashhere and Lilla exchange an anxious glance, and added hastily, "I know where we are. I just don't know who rules here, if anyone does. The South Pennines is a mess. Half a dozen brothers and cousins were fighting over it for years, it got divided and recombined and redivided, and I don't know who was the last man standing. Or even if Ceretic of Elmet managed to make them all tributary to him He started trying as soon as he became King, but the one thing they could all agree on was that they hated him worse than each other, so he was having a hard time."

"So we're walking into a war zone?" said Ashhere, cheerfully. "Nice. I thought you said we weren't going to fight?"

"We aren't."

"What *are* we going to do?"

"Hide," Eadwine said grimly. "Try to find a way through the forests to Elmet before we're caught. Hope that the Three Ladies lose interest in us *very* soon. And hope that Ceretic is more inclined to honour alliances than Caedbaed of Lindsey."

***

"What else could I do?" Ceretic of Elmet snapped at his advisors. "The wretched woman turns up out of the blue in my hall, brat in tow, and throws herself on my protection in front of the whole court! You expect me to turn her away and lose face in front of everybody? She knew that, damn her. So she and the boy and those two tame trolls she brought with her are under my protection now, part of my household, and nobody lays a finger on them without making an enemy of me. Understood? So go and tell Aethelferth's envoy that."

"Aethelferth won't like that as an answer –"

"That's his problem. It was him that let them escape. I don't see why I should be expected to wipe his arse for him."

"Lord King, you dare not anger Aethelferth."

"*Dare?*"

"Er – it would not be wise –"

"I am not Aethelferth's lackey! He gets a free hand in Deira, I get a free hand in the South Pennines, that was the bargain. I've kept my half. Princess Heledd is my father's sister, and that makes the boy my cousin. Aethelferth can't expect me to betray a blood-tie. What does he really want?"

The advisors exchanged glances.

"What of the other atheling, Lord King?"

"Eadwine? He's no relation. Half-brother of my aunt's husband? Aethelferth can have him for all I care. How much was he offering for his head?"

***

Travelling through the forest was slow and arduous. At first the ground dipped to a low-lying wet area, with great stretches of swamp and stagnant water surrounded by willow and alder, and they made an unpleasantly damp and fly-plagued camp. On the next day, the ground began to rise slowly but steadily and the forest giants of oak, ash and holly dominated again, with a dense understorey of hazel and thorn. There were few paths, and these were only animal tracks that as often as not petered out or went in the wrong direction. Much of the time they had to find a way through the tangled undergrowth, an obstacle course of fallen trees, clinging brambles, impenetrable thickets, and waist-high bracken. Without the mighty strength of Drust and Beortred they would never have forced a way through. Several times they had to cross sluggish rivers, one of which was large enough to require a considerable detour upstream before they found a place shallow enough to wade across, which put them far out of their intended course. At least, though, the rivers did confirm that they were not actually going in circles, however much it felt like it. Ashhere was convinced that the trees moved when he wasn't looking, deliberately blocking their path, but whether the forest was enchanted or not it was hopelessly confusing. An occasional glimpse of the sun or a star through a gap in the canopy was their only navigational aid. There was little light and less air. Animals – at least, Ashhere hoped they were animals – rustled in the leaf-litter or snuffled through the undergrowth, but they never saw more than a flitting shadow. In the nights, they sometimes heard wolves howling in the distance. It was autumn, so there were nuts and berries to eat, but it takes a lot of hazelnuts to fill the stomach of an active man. Lilla was invaluable here, for his family had taken the other route to advancement that had opened up after Caer Greu and had left the overcrowded Deiran homelands to clear uninhabited land on the March and the moors, land that their heirs would hold in perpetuity under folk-right rather than at the gift of the king. The March consisted of thirty-odd miles of virtually untouched forest and even on the moors the valleys were heavily wooded, so the settlers in their clearings relied as much on the surrounding forests for their food as on their embryonic farmsteads. Lilla could recognise edible fungi, and unearth wild roots, and find herbs to eat, but still there was never anything like enough. Drust tried to kill a squirrel, but it whisked away to safety in the canopy and it took so much trouble to retrieve his spear that he did not try again. After several days of this they were filthy, ragged, tired, hungry, limping on blistered feet, and despairing of ever getting out of the forest, and to make matters worse it became clear that Eadwine was beginning to fall ill.

He did not complain, in fact he hardly spoke at all – which was a worrying sign in itself. He staggered on through the day apparently in a stupor, and as soon as they stopped for the night he slumped to the ground and lay like a dead thing until someone roused him and forced him to eat whatever dubious food they had managed to find. To expect him to share in the watches was out of the question, but after the first night his sleep was broken and troubled by dreams. There were no decisions to make or problems to solve, but instead of switching off his mind seemed to have decided to root among his troubles. He muttered and moaned in his nightmares, imagining that his father and brother were reproaching him for their deaths, scorning him for failure, sneering at him for the loss of Deira, even mocking him for allowing Treowin to take his place. He imagined Treowin captured and executed, and pleaded desperately with the Twister to take him instead. He relived the skirmishes at the bridge and the ford, except that this time his stratagems did not work and he saw his companions butchered despite his pleas for their lives. Worst of all were the dreams where he saw Aethelind captured, beaten, raped, enslaved and brutalised by Aethelferth's soldiery, where he struggled and failed to reach her, where he begged her forgiveness and she cursed him for a coward and a fool. Lilla, who happened to be on watch, heard his rising distress when this dream came on the third night and could not bear to listen. It was a great risk to wake someone from a nightmare, for the wandering spirit might not have time to find its way back to the body, but Eadwine's anguished whisperings wrung his heart. He shook Eadwine tentatively by the shoulder – and recoiled in shock. The heat was palpable even through clothing. Not a nightmare. Fever.

***

In the morning, however, Eadwine's temperature was almost back to normal and there was little sign of illness beyond an unnatural-looking flush to his face and his obvious exhaustion. Lilla feared they might have to carry him, but he managed to stagger to his feet with Drust's help and stumble on, his shoulders sagging and his head drooping. Mercifully, the forest was now less dense. The land had started rising again after the last river, as one would expect, but it had kept rising and now the oaks and ashes were giving way to more open woodland of birches and rowan trees brilliant with berries. They felt a breeze, and for the first time in days they could see the sky clearly. It was overcast and dreary, with shredded veils of low cloud moving in the wind, but in comparison to the green gloom of the forest it seemed almost cheerful. The sparse woodland gave way to scrub, and then to a wide moor carpeted with heather, coarse grass and dwarf juniper, dotted with the occasional twisted rowan or stunted hawthorn. Behind them the forest rolled away into the distance like a green sea. Ahead, the moor continued to rise gently, literally until it met the sky. Low, damp cloud swirled down almost to the treeline, so that everything beyond a hundred yards or so faded into obscurity. A fine drizzly rain was partly falling, partly being carried on the wind. It was cold after the closeness of the forest. A buzzard soared overhead, circled as if to examine them, and then with a disdainful flick of a wingtip peeled away over the moor. Ashhere shivered, and thought that perhaps the forest was not quite so bad after all. This was a bit like the moors of the North March, but somehow bigger, wilder, emptier and more threatening, the kind of place the gods would choose to banish giants and trolls and terrible monsters.

An eldritch screech and a man's yell froze his blood and he whirled round, grabbing for his sword with one hand and his hammer amulet with the other. Beside him, Beortred's rugged face was ashen under its tan and his spear was shaking in his hand. Lilla was clinging to Eadwine, and it was not entirely clear who was holding up who. Drust was bounding across the moor, chasing a sliding shadow that ducked and dived among the low plants. He hurled his spear, a squeal of pain tore the air, he stooped and the squealing stopped abruptly. He came back, grinning in triumph, his spear in one hand and the limp body of a mountain hare dangling from the other.

"Dinner," he said.

***

"They belong to the Great Mother," Drust explained, propping the hare's head reverently in the branches of a rowan tree and wedging the mouth open with a stick. "Ye let the spirit escape into the rowan, which is Her tree, and give Her the skin and the feet, too, and at the next full moon She will make him run again. Always She sends the hare when the Children of the Goddess are in great need."

"Right," said Ashhere uncertainly, prodding the fire. "Er – that's very nice of her. Very helpful."

He cast a pleading glance at Eadwine, who would normally have been fascinated by this rare glimpse into Drust's theology and could have been relied on to rescue Ashhere from the conversation, but Eadwine was huddled shivering against the trunk of the rowan with his face resting against his knees.

"How did you hit it from that distance?" Beortred wanted to know, threading chunks of hare onto his knife and holding it over the flames. "I could hardly even see it."

"Ye're a blind Sassenach sheep," said Drust, grinning. "We hunt hares at home." He looked around at the desolate, soaking moorland. "This reminds me of home. A bit tame, though."

"This is *tame*?" Lilla exclaimed, edging nearer the fire. "I wouldn't like to live where you come from."

"Ye wouldna last five minutes, laddie."

The friendly bickering floated over Eadwine, along with the scent of toasting meat, but he was not really aware of any of it. He was cold, a gnawing sort of cold that made his bones ache and seemed impervious to the fire, and the wound in his side was growing insistently more painful, like a great throbbing ball of flame. He tried to doze, which was a mistake, for he succeeded and was immediately assailed by another feverish dream, in which Eadric was standing over him, taunting him for being too late, again. *I came as soon as I could*, Eadwine tried to tell him. *I did not know you were in danger. I would have died for you!* It was no good. Eadric had never been much inclined to listen in life, and he was not much inclined to listen now. Eadwine tried to reach out to him, to catch his hand and *make* him listen, but Eadric's form shimmered and faded away into a heap of ashes and a faint smell of smoke.

***

"Wake up, lad." A rough but kindly voice, and a big hand shaking his shoulder. "Come on, wake up. Real food for once!"

Eadwine lifted his head and found Beortred leaning over him, holding out half a dozen lumps of roast meat skewered on a long eating knife.

"Hare," he was informed. "From your hairy friend. It's hot, take the knife. You need a hand, lad?"

Eadwine shook his head and reached out his left hand. The smell of the meat made his stomach turn over, but they would worry and fuss if he refused. He nibbled at the meat, slowly so they would not insist on giving him any more. It was not a very big hare, probably one of this year's youngsters, and it would not go far between five. Better that it should be shared between the four who were most likely to survive. He had not mentioned his growing fears to the others, but he was sure that his wound was not healing as it ought. It should not hurt so much, and it was beginning to swell. Something was wrong, and he had an idea what it might be. Was that why Eadric was so insistent, he wondered? Summoning him? But he would not go to join his beloved brother, for a death by illness rather than by violence would not qualify him for entry to Woden's hall. And in any case he would be ashamed in that company, with his father and brother unavenged.

He slid the last piece of meat off the knife with his teeth, and swallowed it. Useful for camp-cooking, a knife with such an unusually long, narrow blade – His heart skipped a beat and then began to race to make up for lost time. He stared at the blade, turning it over and over in his hands. *A knife, long of blade but very narrow, no more than half an inch wide...it had gone straight to the heart...your brother was stabbed in the back.....stabbed in the back....stabbed in the back.*

"Whose knife is this?" he asked, but he already knew the answer.

"Mine," answered Beortred, turning and holding out his hand. Beortred. Captain of Eadric's hearth-troop. The man who should stay at Eadric's side to the last, to keep his back against the foe – or stab him in it.

Eadwine did not relinquish the knife. His hands were trembling. He met Beortred's eye and held it, the knife gleaming dully between them.

"How did my brother die?"

Beortred did not answer immediately. There was nothing necessarily sinister in that, for he was not an articulate man. But it seemed more than merely being stuck for words.

"He was caught by a Bernician patrol. Only a few men with him," he mumbled at last. "They were overcome."

"Were you there?"

Beortred shook his head, lowering his gaze. "I was – separated. A – a fall from my horse." Well, that embarrassing confession of clumsiness might have been enough to explain his hesitancy. Possibly. Eadwine said nothing. Most people were uncomfortable with silences and tried to fill them, especially if they had something to hide.

Beortred was no exception. "I came upon them afterwards," he continued. "It – it was too late. Had already happened. I – I could not believe it." He lifted his eyes suddenly and met Eadwine's glance. "I would have died for him!" he said passionately. The pain in his voice was raw, heartfelt. Eadwine would have sworn an oath that it was not faked.

"A pity," he said, very low and very even, not taking his eyes from Beortred's face, "that you were not at his side when he died."

Beortred looked down, but not before Eadwine had seen something flicker across his face. Deceit? Certainly. Guilt? That as well, and something more.

"Here," he said, handing the knife back. "Use it well, Beortred. A most – distinctive – weapon."

Beortred's normally ruddy face was pale and he was sweating as if he too was in the grip of fever. The brief glance he flicked at Eadwine could only be described as furtive. A man with a guilty secret, a man in deadly fear that he had been found out.

He jumped to his feet and stamped out the fire with startling violence. "Come on then!" he shouted roughly. "Can't sit here all day!"

***

The rain fell all afternoon, a persistent soaking drizzle, and if anything the mist got thicker. It was as disorienting as the forest and a good deal more eerie. The going was no easier either, for the moorland flattened out into a great wide plateau and conditions underfoot got wetter. And wetter. Soon they were floundering in a peaty morass, each man trying to pick his own way between infrequent – and frequently illusory – spots of firm ground. The bare peat had the consistency of thick black porridge, too soft to stand on but too dense to wade through, and apparently without any firm bottom, as Beortred found when one bog-hole swallowed his leg to mid-thigh and then retained his shoe with a triumphant slurp when he managed to haul himself out. Tussocks of grass provided some support, but often would emit a squirt of foul-smelling peaty water when trodden on. The fluffy white heads of bog-cotton and the glowing colours of sphagnum moss they learnt to avoid, after Ashhere blundered into a deep quagmire up to his waist and it took the combined efforts of Drust and Beortred, using their cloaks to spread their weight, to drag him out. Lilla

52

supported Eadwine, on the grounds that they were the lightest combination, but even with all their experience of bog-trotting on the moors of the March progress was unimaginably slow and filthy. There were no landmarks close at hand, and the mist made it impossible to aim for any distant mark. They were hopelessly lost, and once they even crossed their own trail and realised despondently that they had gone around in a circle.

It was getting on for dusk when they finally won out of the bogs and onto drier and firmer ground. They had lost all sense of direction, and the failing light was little help, although they tried to guess the position of the sunset from the relative brightness of the sky and set off in the direction that three out of five believed to be north-west. Three out of four might be more accurate, for Eadwine seemed to be only half-conscious.

The firmer ground was due to a line of rock outcrops and boulders, formed of some curiously harsh and abrasive rock that they had never encountered before. If you stumbled against a boulder, it seemed it would take the skin off your hands, if you stubbed a toe you looked for a hole in your shoe. Sometimes the rock lay in great flat slabs, easy to walk on – provided that you had not lost a shoe – but riven with deep cracks and chasms falling away into darkness. Some of the chasms were big enough to trap a foot and break an ankle, and in the gathering dark they were treacherous and difficult to see.

Ashhere collided with a boulder that he could have sworn had not been there a second earlier, put out a hand to save himself, found that the boulder was apparently not there any more, and fell heavily. His shoulder bounced off the edge of a rock slab, and he felt himself falling backwards and downwards, with the great boulder spinning above him. He screamed, knowing it was about to crush him – and then he was lying on his back in springy heather and Drust was trying to make him stand up.

"It jumped out at me!" he gasped. "It was trying to crush me!"

"Ye tripped," Drust said. "Ye're asleep on your feet."

"I tell you, it jumped out at me!" He whipped round, catching another movement out of the corner of his eye. A great towering figure, striding through the mist, following their trail. He screamed again.

"A troll! It's a troll!"

He pointed, hand shaking, but the giant figure had disappeared, hidden by a swirl of fog.

"I tell ye," Drust insisted patiently, "it's a rock."

"They're trolls!" Ashhere wailed, sobbing with pain and fright. He clutched for his hammer amulet and found to his horror that it was gone. "The gods have deserted us – trolls all around us – no help – they're coming to get us – they'll kill us all –!"

He clutched at Lilla in his panic, and found he was trembling too.

"It's c-c-coming," Lilla choked out, "c-c-can't you hear it –?"

A low moaning, sighing sound came drifting along the trail.

"Wind in the rocks," Drust protested, but his voice was also shaking and he had gone very pale. He was not thinking of trolls, which did not figure in his bestiary, but of the White Fairy whose wailing cry summoned men to their deaths.

Beortred strode forward, jaw thrust out, spear in hand.

"Troll or whatever it is, it's got me to get past first! Stay here!"

"Wait!" Eadwine cried, roused from his daze. "Not one man alone!"

Beortred half-turned, looking back over his shoulder. His face was pale, the mouth contorted, the eyes glassy with terror.

"I couldn't save your brother," he said, with surprising intensity, "but by the Hammer I'll save you!"

Drawing his sword in his other hand, he leaped away into the mist. They heard the low moan again, this time something between a sigh and a hiss, like a heavy beast drawing its breath before a spring. Beortred shouted a war-cry, his voice defiant but ragged with fear. They heard the ring of metal on stone, then the moaning sigh again, and then they heard Beortred scream, a long-drawn cry that faded into silence.

"It got him!"

It was never clear who said that, nor who spoke next. Indeed, it may not have been spoken at all, but simply the same idea filling all their minds.

"Run!"

Chapter 7

Ashhere came slowly out of stupor. A cold wind was blowing over the moor and a thin chill rain was falling on his upturned face. It was the rain that had roused him, although it must have taken a long time about it because his clothes were wet through. He shivered, sneezed, shivered again and sat up. Memory came creeping back like a whipped dog.

He had run until his strength failed. How far? He had no idea. Where were his friends? He had no idea about that either. He bit his lip. How could he have been such a coward? To run away, leaving his lord behind in danger – there was no greater shame. No excuse, not even if a whole herd of trolls were after them.

A grey dawn was creeping over the moors. He must have been lying here – wherever here was – all night. He peered into the ever-widening circle of gloomy light around him. Tussocky grass, heather turning from purple to biscuit-coloured, fluffy heads of bog cotton. He tried standing up, and discovered that he was still apparently in one piece, with only some more bruises and a stiff back to show for the night's flight. He had been lucky, far luckier than he deserved.

His horizon now widened but all it showed him was flat moorland in all directions, disappearing into a damp greyness that was a hybrid between mist and drizzle. He stared around, hopelessly. How could he even begin to search for the others? Which direction to start? A movement caught his eye and he whirled round, hand on sword-hilt even though he knew trolls could not move in daylight, but it was only a miserable-looking sheep with a sullen teenage lamb at its side. They stared at Ashhere for a moment and then galloped away into the gloom, their hooves beating a tattoo long after they had vanished from sight.

That gave Ashhere an idea. Perhaps sound travelled further than sight in this miserable wilderness.

"Halloooo –!" he hailed, with all his might.

Nothing but the sigh of the wind through the grass.

"Halloooo –!"

His heart leaped. Just at the instant he had called, he was sure there had been an answer that was not an echo. He waited. Nothing, no – yes! There it came again! He shouted in answer, running over the moor in the direction of the voice, until he slithered down over the lip of a peat hag and met Drust doing the same from the opposite direction.

"The others –?" he gasped.

Drust had found them, but Ashhere's relief was short-lived. They were in far worse shape than he was. Lilla had stumbled into a bog hole in the dark and wrenched his knee so badly that he could hardly walk. Eadwine was with him – it was a measure of their panic that Eadwine had managed to run at all – and his fever had risen again, far worse than before. He lay shuddering and shaking, sometimes conscious of their presence but more often lost in some terrifying delirium. Now he thought he was dead and languishing in the dread realm of Hel, where the cowards suffer for ever in terrible cold with fell beasts gnawing on their rotting flesh, while his father and brother caroused in Woden's hall and laughed at him.

Ashhere reached for his hammer amulet, shuddering at the thought of this terrible fate, and shuddered again when he realised he had lost it among the troll-haunted rocks the night before. He was certainly not going back there to look for it, though the prospect of struggling through this monster-haunted wilderness without Thunor's protection was too fearful to contemplate.

They looked at each other, feeling how acute was their reliance on Eadwine. Without him they were hopelessly lost, in more than just geography. If it occurred to any of them that if they had followed his orders at the Ouse they would not have been here to get lost, they did not say it.

"Oh, bugger," Ashhere muttered.

The others did not disagree.

"We canna stop here," Drust declared.

Nobody disagreed with that either, but like many uncontroversial statements it was not very helpful. Eadwine had told them to go to Elmet, which was north-west. But how far? And was it still north-west from here? And which direction was which? And where was here anyway?

Ashhere took hold of Eadwine's hand and brushed his matted hair back from his face. "Lord," he whispered. "Please wake up."

Eadwine's eyes flickered open. "I told you – you'd – regret it," he muttered. "Poor Beortred – what a way –"

The sentence terminated in a hiss of pain, although he had not moved and nobody had touched him. His face was a ghastly greenish-white, beaded with great drops of sweat.

"Where must we take you?" Ashhere begged. "Please tell us."

"Nowhere – idiot –" With an effort Eadwine drew a quivering finger across his throat. "I'm dying – give me – the kindness cut –"

"No!" Lilla cried. "No, no –!"

Eadwine gasped, and there was a desperation in his face that froze Ashhere's heart. "That spear – it ripped the gut – can't you smell it?"

Ashhere swallowed. He had caught the stench of putrefaction from the wound and had begun to fear the same thing himself. A pierced gut was inevitably a death sentence.

"Nonsense," he said firmly, hoping that if he ignored the problem it would go away. This philosophy had worked for most of his life, and he saw no reason to change it now. "It – er – it probably needs clean bandages. That's all. Drust and I can carry you. Lilla can lean on a spear, or hop, or something."

"Without food?" Drust said quietly.

And there was the problem. It was days since they had last eaten properly, and their strength was visibly ebbing away. Even the short distance Ashhere had covered to meet Drust had come near to exhausting him. Unless they could find something to eat, he and Drust would soon be unable to do any more than sit down and starve beside their friends. And they could hardly hunt while trying to carry a sick man. What Eadwine was asking was the most – the only – sensible thing to do. But that did not mean Ashhere could steel himself to do it.

"We're not leaving you," he said flatly. "We'll stay with you til the end."

A ghastly laugh. "Remember – to cash in – my head –"

"Oh, dear Lord!" Lilla wailed, and it was not at all clear whether this was addressed to Eadwine or to Lilla's god, Frey Lord of the Vanir, protector of farmers.

It was then that Ashhere remembered the sheep. Trolls do not keep sheep. And just as he worked out what the sheep must mean, carried on the wind there came a faint sound of hope. A late-rising rooster crowed to the sky. Somewhere down there was a farm.

***

"Saxons! Saxons!"

The cry ran ahead of Ashhere as he slithered down the last of the steep and awkward path that had taken him down through the woods. How did they know, he wondered, when he hadn't even opened his mouth yet? He supposed it was his blond hair, or his beard, since Brittonic men generally followed the peculiar custom of leaving the moustache but shaving the rest of the face. He was alone and unarmed, not at all a pleasant situation for him. But they had agreed that they would have trouble fighting a farm full of determined peasants, so their best hope was to beg – which meant that whoever went should look as unthreatening as possible so as not to be mistaken for a bandit. They could not all go, since Lilla and Eadwine would be unable to run if the inhabitants turned nasty, and as Ashhere spoke some of the language the task had fallen to him. He had followed the approximate direction they had heard the cockerel, and found that the moorland was cut abruptly by a steep-sided glen, full of tangled woods and with an unseen stream rushing in the bottom. He had followed the top edge of the wood, come across some sheep tracks, and followed them until he could see that the glen opened out into a much larger valley filled with oak forest. All the sheep tracks converged at the head of a muddy path that wound down through the woods into this large valley, obviously leading to the farm where the sheep and the rooster lived.

The path ended in a large clearing. The stream from the glen chattered down to meet a much larger river, and around the confluence on both sides of the stream was a large open field dotted with a dozen or so cows. A little above the field, on a flat area beside the stream, a rather tumbledown drystone wall enclosed a large area, a cross between a yard and a paddock, with a midden on the side furthest from the stream and a cluster of rectangular wooden buildings in various stages of decay at the other. One had a thin stream of smoke rising from the thatched roof, and was therefore presumably the house. It looked in rather better repair than the others. Chickens scratched around the buildings. A couple of ponderous sows and a busy herd of well-grown piglets rooted in the yard and in the fringes of the surrounding woods. A fenced vegetable plot occupied one end of the yard, mostly empty apart from weeds, but still sporting some spinach, a few cabbages and a row of turnips.

Ashhere stopped at the end of the track, where a gate stood open. He held up his hands, palm outwards to show he had no weapon, and composed his face into what he hoped was an ingratiating smile.

Four women were clustered by the doorway of the house. A pale child aged about fourteen, nervously clutching a shovel, a statuesque middle-aged matron wielding a wood-chopping axe, and two young women, one holding a kitchen knife and one with a cleaver. The one with the cleaver was extremely pretty, with sparkling brown eyes and a cloud of curly dark hair with a ribbon tied in it. She looked Ashhere up and down, and gave him a flirtatious smile. The matron elbowed her crossly.

"Er – ladies," Ashhere began, groping for words in Brittonic and elevating them in rank because he could not remember the word for 'goodwife', if there was one. "I am traveller. I have hunger." He patted his stomach, which obligingly growled for effect. The pretty woman laughed, and was elbowed again. "Give me food." A rarely-used word surfaced, just in time. "Please."

He had addressed himself to the large matron, partly because she was the eldest and partly because she was tapping the axe against her meaty palm in a decidedly menacing way. But it was the young woman with the kitchen knife who answered. She was a striking-looking creature, slender and small-boned, with honey-coloured skin, straight glossy black hair pulled back in a braid, and cool watchful green eyes that reminded him of a cat's.

He failed to understand a word she was saying, and shook his head unhappily.

"Lady. I do not understand. Talk slow. Please."

She obliged, pronouncing each word slowly and clearly as if to a slow-witted child. This, Ashhere thought, furrowing his brow in concentration, is a bit better. The dialect was somewhat different to the Brittonic spoken in Eboracum Vale, more rounded and flowing. It was reminiscent of Drust's Pictish, and he remembered that Pictish was supposed to be a hybrid of the language of the Attacotti – who lived in stone towers at the end of the world in the north and ate raw fish – and a form of Brittonic. Presumably this form of Brittonic. He should have sent Drust down, but too late now. At least he understood most of it. She was saying her name was Severa – an outlandish name if ever there was one – and asking him who he was, where he was from, what he was doing and where he was going.

He tried to reply, but his Brittonic was not good enough for him to begin to explain, and anyway he was very tired and very hungry.

"Food," he repeated, more urgently. "Eat. Food. Please."

The exotic girl – Severa – said something to the pretty one, who hurried into the house and came back with a steaming bowl and a spoon. Ashhere took it gratefully, thanked her, and turned to go. It was not much between four, but they probably had nothing to spare and it was a great deal better than he might have expected.

They shouted angrily after him, pointing at a bench, and he understood that he was supposed to eat here.

He shook his head. "No, lady. I go. I have friend."

Severa said something in a sharp tone, reverting to her rapid speech again, but he guessed from her glance around and her sweeping gesture that she was saying his friend should come out of hiding and join him.

He shook his head again. "My friend is sick. He cannot come. I go."

Another torrent of words, out of which he gathered that he was to bring his sick friend to the farm. He shook his head again. The experiences at the bridge and the ford had been salutary ones. Everyone was a probable enemy, even four

57

farm women. He was not going to risk bringing Eadwine into a trap from which there might be no escape.

"No, no, no, no, no, *no!*" he insisted vehemently, shaking his head until he felt dizzy. "We do not come. We have danger. I go. Please."

Severa tut-tutted impatiently, gave him a withering look, took the bowl and the spoon from him, and disappeared into the house.

Ashhere watched miserably. Had he just lost any prospect of a meal? He thought about using violence, but the large matron was still hefting the axe and in his present weakened state he was not entirely sure of his chances unarmed even against four women.

Severa re-emerged, this time carrying a heavy-looking cooking pot. She emptied the bowl back into it, inverted the bowl to act as a lid, hung the spoon from the handle, and handed it all to Ashhere.

He blinked. The pot was reassuringly heavy and smelled appetisingly of garlic and onions.

"Thank you!"

She smiled, a brilliant smile that lit up her remarkable face and striking eyes, and shooed him in the direction of the track as if he had been a stray chicken. As he passed through the gate, he heard the matron take a deep breath and begin a vigorous scolding.

***

"Oh, do be quiet, Blodwen," Severa said, after about five minutes. "Until Samhain Eve what I say goes, and in any case it's done now, so you might as well save your breath. Luned, lass, he's gone, you can put the shovel down now."

Blodwen was still in full spate.

"– giving our dinner to some stinking tramp –"

Severa shrugged. "Surely we can spare a dish of pottage for a couple of starving travellers. Anyway, you were complaining this morning that I'd put too much garlic in it. So look on it as an opportunity to make another batch to your own taste. Gwen can finish the butter." She cast a despairing glance at the pretty dark girl. "*Gwen.* Is there anything you won't flirt with?"

"Did you see the shoulders on him?" sighed Gwen, gazing dreamily up the path. "D'you suppose all Saxons are that big?"

"He couldn't've been a proper Saxon," Luned protested shyly, "because he didn't have any horns. Uncle says they have horns on their heads. Like this." She put the shovel down and demonstrated.

Severa snorted. She had a low opinion of Luned's uncle. "Perhaps they shed them, like stags do in the spring," she said flippantly, and immediately wished she hadn't. Luned did not understand sarcasm.

Gwen heaved another sigh.

"Didn't he have *lovely* blue eyes –"

"*Gwen,*" reproved Severa in passing, "at least do some work while you drool."

***

It rained on and off most of the day, and the mist never lifted off the moors. Gruffuyd, Blodwen's half-witted son who in theory was the shepherd – although privately Severa thought that the sheep probably herded him rather than the other way around – brought the flock down earlier than usual, wet through, cold and despondent even though he had successfully found the missing ewe. Even the sheepdog, normally impervious to weather, looked miserable. Severa thought of the tramp and his sick friend up on the hills, and bit her lip.

58

Another flurry of rain decided her, and she picked up her cloak as soon as it stopped.

"I'm going out for a walk."

***

It proved very easy to follow the tramp's footprints in the damp ground. When the track emerged from the woods, the sheep hooves all went one way and his went another, his prints clear and obvious in the peat. In a hollow below a peat hag she found her cooking pot, bowl and spoon, all scraped clean. No sign of the tramp.

"Ungrateful fellow," she muttered crossly. "You could have brought them back!"

But there was no sign of the sick friend either, and more prints – more than one set – led away from the hollow, going roughly north through the bogs. She knew for a fact that there was no habitation for at least a day's journey in that direction. The tramp and his sick friend were in for another uncomfortable night on the moor.

"Stupid man," she said to herself, following the prints. "Stupid, stupid man! Serves him right!"

She had gone only a few yards when she was seized from behind and her wrists pinioned in a powerful grasp. She lashed out with elbow and knee, and was rewarded with a muffled grunt, but her captor did not seem to be seriously inconvenienced. A foot tripped her neatly so that she stumbled, and her arms were twisted painfully behind her back.

"Come quiet," rumbled a deep voice in broken Brittonic, "or I wring your neck like chicken, yes?"

***

Severa was half-dragged, half-pushed a few yards further to a couple of large boulders, where to her astonishment – and a certain amount of relief – the blond tramp who had come begging for food emerged. Behind him she could see that a ragged cloak had been rigged across the gap between the boulders and another had been secured across the top to form a crude shelter. A feeble fire sputtered reluctantly in the middle, and to her surprise she saw a third tramp huddled over it, apparently trying to coax the flames into life. He too stood up, and she saw he was limping heavily. Presumably he was the sick friend. The tramp hadn't seen fit to mention a third man, though, let alone one with the strength of two. She craned her neck to look at her captor, a huge bear-like man with a red beard mingling with his chest hair. All three of them were bare-chested, despite the damp chill, and she felt a cold twist of fear in the pit of her stomach. What were they going to do with her?

"Let go of me, you oaf!" She stamped on the Red Bear's foot, but he didn't seem to notice. "You," this to the blond one who had begged for food, "you think this is a fair way to repay me? I give you food and you assault me? Tell this great lummox to unhand me, now! I came to help you!"

They conferred anxiously in a guttural language that she took to be Saxon.

"We want you not here, lady," the blond one said, after a while. "But do not want to kill you. You go away."

"Kill me –!" Severa repeated, dumbfounded, angry and more than a little frightened. "You half-wits! Can't you understand anything I say? I came to help you!"

Exchange of blank looks and shrugs.

"Listen to me, you idiots! I want to help you!"

59

"Why?"

They all started at the question, and Severa realised that what she had taken for a heap of blankets lying by the fire was in fact another man. Mother of God, how many more of them were there? The voice had sounded weak, as if articulating a single word was a great deal of effort. *This* must be the sick friend. She tried to go towards him, but the Red Bear held her back.

"Because if I was cold and sick and hungry I hope some kind stranger would help *me*!" she retorted, since although sick at least he appeared to understand Brittonic. "Tell this oaf to let go of me. I came to help!"

He spoke a few words in the barbarous language, and the effect was miraculous. The Red Bear released her and stepped back, though they still looked suspicious.

She knelt beside the sick man. He was lying on two tunics, with a third folded under his head, and covered by a cloak and some rags. One glance told her that he was seriously ill. He seemed quite young, but he was thin, haggard, his eyes glittering with fever, his face unhealthily flushed, his breathing ragged. He was soaked in sweat and shivering violently. When she felt for the pulse in his wrist it was a racing, thready beat, and the skin was burning hot.

"Mother of God! You need a doctor."

"Too late," he gasped out. "But please – help – my friends –"

He lapsed into the foreign language, and she shook her head at him.

"Brittonic, speak Brittonic! What happened to you?"

"Spear – in the – guts –"

"May I see?"

Severa pulled aside the cloak covering him and saw the lower left side of his tunic was stiff with dried blood. She turned back the cloth, gently, and came close to retching at the sight. A crusted bandage, saturated with pus and dried blood, was welded to an ugly swelling of inflamed, discoloured flesh. The stench of corruption was overwhelming. Severa laid her hand on the swelling to confirm that it was hot, and even though she barely brushed the skin the sick man gasped and flung back his head. He did not scream, which surprised her, but the arched back and the cords standing out in his neck confirmed his agony. Severa shuddered, but even as she fought down her nausea, she had an instinct that something was wrong. She sniffed at the wound again. It made her gag, but, yes, something was missing. She leaned over his face and sniffed again. Then she turned back the cloak over his feet. One shoe was missing and the foot was covered in raw, red blisters under the dirt.

She sat back on her heels. She was sure now.

"I believe I can help you," she said quietly.

***

Ashhere watched tensely, hand on sword-hilt. He had never killed a woman and did not want to start now, but if she did Eadwine any harm –! Eadwine had said *She's a friend. Do as she says*, but the intervals of lucidity were getting shorter and less frequent, and he was not entirely sure whether Eadwine had really understood. He had lapsed back into the Hel dream again now, though this time he was entreating Frija, Woden's queen, to intercede for him, much as an unsuccessful supplicant thrown out on his ear by the thane will often creep round to the women's chamber to try his luck at convincing the thane's lady.

The woman obviously understood none of it, and was arguing with Eadwine in a torrent of impatient Brittonic. Probably she was annoyed that he had drifted back into delirium and was no longer comprehending her. Ashhere wished she would not speak so fast. He could understand Brittonic quite well when it was spoken slowly and deliberately, and he was even beginning to get used to the strange local accent, but when she spoke fast all the words seemed to come out at once and he got hopelessly lost. She leaned over Eadwine again, this time speaking very slowly and carefully as one might to a recalcitrant child. It was lost on Eadwine, but Ashhere caught a word he understood. Doctor, wise woman, herbwife, witch – it could mean any or all of them, but it always meant one who knew the craft of healing.

"What are we waiting for?" asked Drust, who had understood the same thing.

Ashhere hesitated. "We – we don't know who's down there – there might be enemies – "

"It wouldna matter if the Twister himself was waiting for us," Drust retorted brusquely. "If we stay here he'll be deid for sure."

He stooped, folded the cloak over Eadwine, and lifted him bodily into his arms.

"Lead on, lady."

***

"Be quiet, Blodwen!" Severa snapped, before the tirade could get going. "I want fire, lots of hot water, the ragbag, an old bowl, the honey, and my birthing bag. In here."

She led the way into the vegetable and fodder store. The roof did not leak – well, not much – and as it had once been the house it had a hearth. She ducked under the hanging strings of onions and began spreading bracken to make a bed. The limping tramp and the blond one came to help. Severa hoped the sick tramp was unconscious, but as the Red Bear laid him gently down he drew in a sharp gasping breath and mumbled something in the foreign language. Even without being able to understand a word she could recognise his pain.

It was Gwen who brought the things she asked for, and took an unconscionable time over lighting a fire. It would be, of course. Gwen would ogle anything in trousers, and there was no denying the Red Bear was a magnificent specimen. She hovered in the doorway like a dog eyeing a bone.

"Out!" Severa barked, and she fled.

The sick tramp was painfully thin and covered in ripening bruises and partly-healed lacerations. His right shoulder was horribly bruised and swollen from the internal bleeding from a broken bone, but as far as she could tell the bone was beginning to mend, was more or less straight, and required no immediate attention from her.

The abdominal wound was a different matter. She soaked the revolting bandage repeatedly in boiled water until she could peel it away. The flesh beneath was livid, coloured a disgusting greenish-purple. Pus dribbled from the open lips of a deep gash. It stank. Severa stared at the wound, half-wishing she had never started this. Yet she was certain, *certain* that she was right. And there was the grim comfort that the most incompetent doctor in the world could hardly make this any worse.

She put her hand to the cross hanging at her neck and said a silent prayer to the Father, the Son and the Holy Spirit, then added others to the Blessed Lady Mary, to Arawn Lord of the Dead, to the Great Mother and to the local water-goddess for good measure. *Surely* one of them might be listening. She reached into the pouch at her waist for the roll holding her grandfather's medical instruments, selected the large scalpel and held the blade briefly to the flames.

The three tramps gazed at her wide-eyed and fearful, but with a terrible hope.

"Hold him down," she said, and set to work.

***

"Lord King! Lord King! We found him!"

The tumult of talk and laughter on the mead-benches died away. Aethelferth stopped with a hunk of meat halfway to his mouth. One atheling was in prison back in Eboracum, another was believed to have escaped by sea, and the boy was under Ceretic's protection in Elmet, but they did not matter. Aethelferth had not pledged them to Woden.

The mud-stained, blood-spattered guard captain paused for effect, revelling in his moment of glory.

"Eadwine of Deira!"

An expectant hush fell as the prisoner was shoved forward into the firelight in the midst of the hall. He stood proudly, despite having his hands tied behind his back, and held his head high. All the Bernician warriors recognised him instantly – the tall thin figure, the mail shirt made for a broader and shorter man, the elaborate gilded helmet, the jewelled sword. The captain cut the helmet's chin strap and lifted it off, revealing a head of tousled dark hair and a handsome, chiselled face wearing an expression of intense and implacable hatred.

"Caught him on the Great South Road," announced the captain. "Running for his worthless life like a thief!"

Aethelferth was satisfied. The ex-mistress had disappeared on the night after the battle so he had not brought her with him on this punitive raid beyond the Derwent, but this haughty prisoner was clearly the prince he had pledged to Woden.

"You are Eadwine son of Aelle?" he demanded, though he had no doubt of the answer.

Treowin held his head higher. How dare these scum feast in his father's hall? One day there would be a reckoning! One day Eadwine would return to Deira at the head of an army and sweep them into the sea with fire and sword! And by dying in his place Treowin would make that day come, even though he would not himself live to see it. It was a death that would earn him everlasting fame. He glared into Aethelferth's eyes.

"I am Eadwine son of Aelle son of Yffi, by right of blood the King of Deira, and I will be your downfall!"

Aethelferth was unimpressed. He belched and took a long swig of mead.

"How did Aelle Ox-brains produce this strutting cockerel?"

He leaned forward across the table, ignoring the raucous laughter, and fixed the prisoner with a stare of cold triumph.

"I have pledged you to the Masked One, cockerel." He beckoned the guard captain forward. "Take him to the Home of the Gods."

The shock almost felled Treowin. He had expected to be executed, possibly there and then in the feasting hall. He had not, in his wildest nightmares, envisaged a ritual slaughter. The Home of the Gods was the oldest and most prestigious temple in Deira, founded by Treowin's own ancestors as their first act after being granted their lands by the Emperor and maintained by them ever since. Treowin had trodden the familiar path from his father's hall to the sacred oak grove many times, for festival and funeral, wedding and birth, to thank or propitiate or petition the gods. But never as a condemned man, never in the certain knowledge that he would never return.

***

The three temple women were already waiting at the entrance to the grove, and the door to the House of the Dead stood open. Treowin came close to falling down in terror when his guards released him. No living man entered the House of the Dead. It was where a body was brought after death, and there handed over to the temple women to be prepared for burial or burning.

The women closed around him, ghostlike in their white robes and veils, took him by his shaking hands and led him through the portal. There, they removed their veils. A young girl, a grown woman, and a crone. No living man was permitted to see their faces, but Treowin had been dedicated to the gods and therefore for all intents and purposes he was already dead. Like a corpse, they stripped him of armour and clothing. Like a corpse, they washed him from head to foot, trimmed his beard and combed his hair. Like a corpse, they laid him down on a soft couch by the fire, and chanted slow, sad songs over him. They laid wheat bread, cooked meats, smoked ham, fruit and mead by his head, as would be done on a funeral pyre, except that Treowin was clearly expected to eat and drink, and did. In one other departure from the usual ritual – at least, Treowin hoped it was a departure – the girl removed her own clothing and lay beside him on the couch, fondling him. But the other two remained looking on, and in any case Treowin was too unnerved by the whole eerie business. He signalled for more mead instead, and drank himself into insensibility.

***

He was still half-dazed with drink and terror when morning came. The women replaced their veils and tied a blindfold over his eyes. He heard the door creak open. Two of the women took him by the hands and led him outside and up the winding path to the sanctuary. He felt the warmth of the sun on his skin. Leaves and twigs rustled under his bare feet. High above, the breeze sighed in the branches.

Treowin felt the sun grow stronger as they emerged into an open space. This must be the central clearing. A rhythmic drumming started up and was joined by other drums in a throbbing, pulsing beat. A man's voice – presumably that of the priest, although Treowin did not recognise it – was raised in a sonorous praise-chant, extolling Woden's power and asking him to accept this gift. When the responses were made, the volume of sound took Treowin's breath away. The crowd must be enormous. Aethelferth must have turned out most of the district to witness his triumph. This was a great gift to the gods indeed, the gift of royal blood. Probably the sanctuary had seen nothing like it in all its long history.

There was grass under his feet now instead of the earth and leaves of the path. The women stopped and turned him to face the crowd, still keeping hold of his hands. Oddly, Treowin's overwhelming feeling was a sense of shame at standing naked except for a blindfold in front of so many people.

The priest's chant ended in a high ululating yell. The drumming reached a crescendo and then ceased. Utter silence fell. Treowin steeled himself for the slash of a knife across his throat, as was done for the sacrifice of animals. But instead he felt a noose of coarse rope looped around his neck, and a cold steel point pressed against the right side of his belly, under the ribcage.

The women released his hands. The blindfold was whipped from his face. Dazzled by the light, he glimpsed an unfamiliar priest using all his weight to keep a sapling bent in a taut curve, the other end of the noose tied to the top of the sapling, and Aethelferth drawing back his spear to deliver the killing blow, and he understood. Aethelferth would drive home the spear, at the same moment the priest would release the sapling, and Treowin would be jerked high into the canopy to die, strangled and pierced, among the oak leaves.

Then the numinous tension was shattered by a woman's shriek.

"Treowin! It's Treowin! Oh, my brother, my brother! Treowin!"

Aethelferth's eyes blazed. He drew back the spear – but instead of a killing blow, he struck through the rope. The strands frayed and parted. The sapling sprang back harmlessly into the air.

He seized Treowin by the throat and shook him as a terrier shakes a rat. His voice was a hiss of pure rage.

"If you are not Eadwine, *where is he?*"

Chapter 8

It was long after dawn when Ashhere woke, feeling utterly drained and somehow rather beaten up, as if he had lost a wrestling match. Something was digging uncomfortably into his neck. Closer inspection revealed it to be the hilt of Drust's sword. He sat up, squinting in the strong sunlight pouring in through the open door, wondering why he could possibly have gone to sleep in Drust's lap in an onion shed, and then his memory tardily provided him with the answer. He shivered. He was frightened of witchcraft, and frightened of the green-eyed, black-haired witch, who looked at him as if she thought someone had already turned him into a toad. She had said, as far as he could understand, that she had to open Eadwine's wound to remove the evil that was killing him, and Ashhere had believed her. But he had not expected it to be so harrowing an experience. Had she gone? He crept tentatively to Eadwine's side. No sign of the witch, but in the exact place where he had last seen her, kneeling beside Eadwine's shoulder, a cat sat upright with its tail curled neatly around its toes. A very trim, very supercilious, very elegant pure black cat. With green eyes.

Ashhere clutched for the amulet that wasn't there. The cat twitched its tail and stared at him with unblinking contempt. Ashhere glared back. The cat won.

When he looked up, the cat had gone. He clenched his hands until they stopped trembling, then reached out and touched Eadwine's face, very gently. It was still too hot, but the fever was not as high and his colour looked a little – a very little – healthier. Eadwine stirred at the touch and his eyes opened drowsily.

"Ash –?"

Ashhere could have wept for joy, and promptly forgave the witch everything and more. She could have turned him into a toad then and there and he would still have been grateful.

"You're alive, you're alive –!" And then, anticipating Eadwine's next question. "We're all safe, we're all here, you're not to worry about anything!"

Eadwine smiled, rather vaguely, as if he was not fully awake. "Frija promised me," he murmured dreamily, already beginning to slide back into sleep, "Frija promised –"

His voice drifted away. Ashhere had no idea what he was talking about, but that was not an unheard-of occurrence, and it was about time Eadwine's dreams were visited by something pleasant for a change.

Ashhere jumped as a shadow cut off the light and Severa came briskly in through the open doorway. He looked for any sign of a cat's tail under her swirling skirts, but was disappointed. Or possibly relieved.

She handed him a large bowl of porridge – did they live on nothing else? – and a jug of milk, and stooped briefly over Eadwine. Drust and Lilla had woken at her entrance and now sat up, blinking owlishly. She included them all in a disapproving look and said something in a sharp tone that Ashhere did not understand, until she made a face and held her nose. He exchanged a sheepish glance with Lilla. She had a point there. The atmosphere in the hut was distinctly pungent, and it had nothing to do with the onions.

Severa thrust a bowl of soft soap into Lilla's hand, and pointed out of the door and down the slope. "River," she said curtly. "You wash." She pointed to a bucket in the corner of the hut, then to Eadwine's slumbering form. "You bring water. You wash him. Understand?"

Without waiting for an answer, she swept out again as briskly as she had come. Ashhere had another furtive look for a tail.

***

"Are you out of your mind?" Blodwen scolded, scouring a cauldron in the dairy. "Four bandits –"

"One's half-dead," Severa said pacifically, "so he doesn't count. Anyway, they seem terrified of me. I'd be flattered except they seem equally terrified of the cat. Not like that, Luned, you really should have got the hang of skimming cream by now –"

"– tramps and thieves and I don't know what –" Blodwen continued.

Severa ignored her. "Gwen, pack the butter in *firmly* if it's to keep all winter."

"– you'll have them stealing the chickens from under our noses –"

"Oh, Luned, give it here. I can skim the cream and manage the cheese. You help Gwen with the butter. Never mind, lass, the cows are going dry and you're good with the pigs. It's about time you started taking them into the forest for the nuts – "

"– and burning the place down, I shouldn't wonder –"

"Gwen, not too much salt, we can't afford it –"

"– we'll all be raped in our beds!"

"Don't get your hopes up," Gwen muttered, loud enough to be heard. Luned tried to stifle a giggle and failed. Blodwen turned scarlet.

"Slut!"

Gwen gave her a sweet smile. "Ooo-ooh, listen to the pot calling the kettle black. Who was sneaking about trying to get a peep this morning?"

"I was not!"

"Yes you were, Blodwen," Severa said placidly. "I saw you. Your tongue was hanging out. The big one's quite something, isn't he? He's called Drust, by the way. Gwen, where do you think you're going?"

"To do the laundry. Being as it's stopped raining, you see."

"Nothing to do with the fact that I sent the tramps to bathe, of course. That hut stinks like a lord's hall the day after a feast."

Blodwen abandoned the half-scrubbed cauldron and made a grab for the laundry basket. "It's my turn!"

Gwen refused to relinquish it. "'Tisn't!"

"'Tis!"

They tugged the laundry basket back and forth between them.

"None of us is going *anywhere near* the river this morning," Severa said firmly. "Leave the poor men alone! Or at least wait until they're in a fit state to appreciate your attention. They look nearly dead on their feet."

"I was only trying to help," Gwen protested, the picture of injured innocence.

65

"Yes, and I'm the Empress of Rome. Back to work, both of you!"

***

Her patient's fever continued to abate, he appeared to be sleeping peacefully whenever she went to check on him and his wound showed no signs of festering again, so Severa left him alone and left his friends to look after him. She was pleased to have been proved right, and reckoned that now she should employ the doctor's most valuable skill, that of knowing when not to interfere while nature cured the disease. It was towards sunset on the next day when she took them their evening porridge and found that her patient was fully awake at last.

His gaze fastened on her as she approached, and she noticed he had remarkable blue-grey eyes, sharp and piercing. Her grandfather had always insisted that the best steel had a blue tint to it. His features were sharp-cut too, and not just because he was worn from illness. A young hawk, she thought, irrelevantly. With a broken wing.

"How do you feel?"

His mouth quirked slightly, as if he was trying not to laugh at the absurdity of the question.

"Terrible," he answered weakly. "I understand I have you to thank."

"For feeling terrible?"

"For being alive to complain about it." He paused, as if recovering his breath or gathering his strength. "Drust says you are a goddess. Ashhere says you are a witch."

So that explained the gratifying deference, and their terror of the cat.

"You speak their language, don't you? Will you do me a favour? Explain to your friends that the cat is just a cat? She catches mice and steals the cream when she thinks I'm not looking. She's not me in shape-changed form, she's not a familiar, she's not a demon or a spirit. She's just a cat, all right?"

What a relief it was not to have to try to communicate in single words and sign language!

"I don't pretend to have any idea what that was all about," he said, after translating, "but I've told them. They don't believe you, by the way. And I must say they have a point. How did you cure me of a ripped gut, if not by magic? Such wounds are always fatal."

"I didn't cure you of a ripped gut."

"Well, I don't seem to be dead." A flicker of laughter crossed his expressive face. "Unless every priest of every god I've ever heard of was spectacularly wrong, anyway."

"You didn't have a ripped gut."

"No? It had all the signs."

"Your feet were covered in fresh blisters from a long walk. You couldn't have walked that far with a hole in the gut, you'd have been dead within the first day or two."

He considered this thoughtfully. "Mmm. I remember thinking it was taking an inconveniently long and painful time to die. But surely you couldn't be certain just from that?"

"Ah, what made me certain is that I like garlic."

A narrow line of concentration appeared between his brows. "Forgive me for being stupid," he said at length, "but I don't see –"

Severa laughed. "Forgive me for being cryptic. It is a bad habit of mine. Garlic pottage, remember? I knew you must have eaten some because I could

66

smell it on your breath. But there was no smell of garlic from the wound. So no hole in the gut."

"Clever."

"Common sense."

"Maybe, but a rare skill to find on a remote country farm! How is that?"

"It was my grandfather's craft. He taught me. Keep a wound clean and that is half the battle. Some useful advice for the amateur who bandaged you up with scraps of metal and cloth still in the wound! No wonder it was festering. If I may –?"

At his nod, she turned the blanket back, a minimal amount to avoid embarrassing him, and examined the gash.

"It does well," she said, satisfied. "Which I have to say is more than I expected. What happened to you?"

He hesitated. "We were on the wrong end of a fight," he said, at last.

"I didn't think you fell out of a tree," she said dryly. "Who are you and where are you from and what are you doing here? It is a strange thing to see a Brittone travelling with Saxons."

"I am fortunate in my friends," was the guarded answer. "And in any case, Drust is a Pict, not a Saxon."

She was not to be diverted. "Whatever," she said impatiently. "Are you going to answer my question? What were you doing on the moors? Looking for sheep to steal?"

He was indignant. "Certainly not!"

"Then what?"

"Passing through."

"Over the moors? There's nothing on the other side except forest to the end of the world. Nothing comes from that direction except thieves."

"How many times do I have to say it? We are not thieves."

"Then what?"

"Travellers."

"Oh, yes, and I'm the Empress of Rome!"

"With a name like Severa you very well could be, or at least named for an Emperor. It is a Latin name, is it not?"

"I can't help my name," she said sullenly. "And stop trying to change the subject! If you claim you aren't thieves, what are you?"

Eadwine groaned to himself. He did not feel up to being interrogated, but he could hardly tell her to mind her own business. She was their hostess, she had saved his life, and until he was fit to travel they were dependent on her goodwill – unless he was prepared to turn the bandit she obviously thought him. He scrambled to think of an innocent explanation for the presence of four strangers. There weren't many. Most people never went more than a few miles from their homes in a lifetime.

"We are poor country men," he said, hoping that might elicit some sympathy. "Driven from our home, looking for new land to settle. We were attacked on the road, took refuge in the forest, and lost our way."

She did not look convinced, but shrugged and did not press the point. "Have you a name? Your friends told me theirs, but did not seem to understand when I asked yours."

Now he had to think again. This was becoming hard work. His real name was out of the question. Even a rumour of his presence would provoke Aethelferth to send a warband, and the consequences were likely to be as severe for the farm as for himself. No warband would willingly miss an opportunity to make a little profit when outside home territory. He had found that out as a green youth in his first season, when he had pursued raiders back over the border into Bernicia and the warband had cheerfully run amok. It had taken the execution of one of his own men to impose his authority, and he had fully expected to be lynched for it. The memory still made him shudder. But the incident had given him a name, and it could probably be translated –

"Steeleye," he said.

Severa arched one well-marked black eyebrow expressively. "If you say so."

"Am I allowed to ask you a question, Mistress?"

She laughed. "Fair exchange, I suppose."

"What place is this?"

He did not expect to be given a precise answer, for a country woman would only know her own village and its immediate neighbours, but he was hoping for something that would give him a clue to their location. Unfortunately, the river was called the Derwent, which was not much help as half the rivers in Britannia seemed to bear that name. There was even one in Deira. The half-dozen villages strung along the river and its tributaries were all subject to a lord who lived with his warband in a stone fort on one of the tributaries. Everyone called it simply 'the fort', but Severa said hesitantly that her grandfather had told her it used to be called Navio. This was not much help either, as Eadwine had never heard the name. He tried another tack.

"Who is king here?"

This was even less fruitful. The only king she knew by name was Arthur, who was thought of as a great and good king of somewhere far away and long ago. No doubt the great man – now more than seventy years dead – would have been highly gratified at this proof of his everlasting fame, but it was not of much practical use.

"Never mind," Eadwine said, when it was clear that her world extended no further than about a day's walk in any direction. "How long may we stay here, Mistress?"

"Until Samhain Eve."

He was puzzled to be given a fixed date and a little disappointed that it was so soon. He had lost track of time but it probably was not much more than a month away.

"I thank you, Mistress," he said politely. "I am sure I will be fit to travel by then."

She clicked her tongue impatiently. "What do you take me for? I wouldn't throw out a dog if it was still sick. I meant you can stay here until we leave."

This was really confusing. "Leave here? You don't live on this farm?"

"This isn't a farm, it's a hafod. A summer farm, yes? Cows in the meadow, pigs in the woods, sheep on the moors. Our village is Derwent Bridge, half a day's walk down the river. Most people stay there and work the fields and harvest the crops. A few of us drive most of the village's animals up here at Beltane and tend them all summer, making cheese and butter until the cows go dry and then fattening the pigs in the woods when the nuts start to fall. Then at Samhain we drive them back to the village for the winter. Until Samhain you may consider yourselves our guests here, provided you behave yourselves. But my authority only extends to the hafod. After we return you must either leave or ask the village headman, my husband's brother, for permission to stay longer."

"I understand. I am deeply grateful to you. We all are. May we earn our keep? I am afraid four strangers will be a great burden to you."

She cast a disapproving glance at the spear propped against the wall, and at the swords that Lilla, Drust and Ashhere were all wearing.

"What do fighters know about farming? Like as not you'll do one job and make two. All I ask of you and your friends is that you keep out of the way, don't eat too much, and don't steal anything."

***

These instructions were not too difficult to follow. In any case, they were all exhausted and glad of the opportunity to sleep as much as possible, although they made sure someone was always on watch. Gradually, their bruises mended and their strength came creeping back. They cleaned and sharpened their weapons. Eadwine begged needles and thread from Severa and they sacrificed the remains of his cloak to repair the rest of their ragged clothes. Ashhere chipped a billet of oak out of the firewood supply and laboriously whittled it into the shape of a hammer. It made him feel better, although the cat seemed unimpressed. Soon Eadwine was able to stagger out of the hut to sit on the bench by the door, where he could watch the hafod at work. Transhumance was not widely practised in Deira, so a summer farm was a new concept, and indeed any kind of farm was a new world to him. Farming was a constant feature in the background of his life, in the sense that one passed fields of crops or herds of cows, but he had never observed one in detail before.

The routine seemed fairly simple, and Severa would usually answer questions when she brought them food, although she seemed startled and sometimes exasperated by his ignorance. All the animals were corralled in the walled yard during the night. Each morning, the cows were milked and then turned out into the meadow, two of the women drove the pigs into the woods, and the sheepdog took the sheep up onto the moors, with the half-witted shepherd tagging along behind. The other two women, invariably Severa and one other, stayed on the hafod washing, carding and spinning wool – the sheep had been sheared earlier in the summer, and there was a whole shed stuffed full of raw fleeces – processing astonishing quantities of milk into butter and cheese, and working on a variety of other tasks such as collecting honey, brewing mead, doing laundry, digging the vegetable patch, mending and cooking. The main meal was eaten around sunset, when the animals and their herders had all returned, and was a simple – not to say monotonous – diet of rye or barley porridge flavoured with onions, garlic or other vegetables, milk, butter, soft cheese, a little honey and a few eggs. Sometimes the herders would bring back nuts, berries or mushrooms gathered from the moors or the woods. Meat, Severa informed him, only appeared if one of the chickens got sick. The people tending the animals took bread and hard cheese with them, since they would be out all day. For those who stayed on the farm there was more porridge, if anything. Bread required grinding grain, which was toilsome and wasteful, and so was made in batches every few days and kept strictly for the herders. They did not brew beer, since no grain was grown on the hafod and it was quite enough trouble to bring enough up in the spring to keep them in pottage for the summer, and although they brewed mead it was stored away and not drunk. The only drink was water from the stream, which fortunately was clear, bright and refreshing. The stream was the abode of a water-goddess, who kept watch over the hafod and guarded it from harm, and under no circumstances was she to be angered by throwing any dirt or rubbish into the water. Laundry, bathing and anything else that needed a large quantity of water was done by the river.

In many ways it was a pleasant time, for the world had suddenly shrunk to one farm, nine people and a dog, and it was easy to forget that they were on the run from war and murder. What spoiled it was a growing atmosphere of disquiet. The dog kept a stern and disapproving eye on them when it was not out with the sheep. The young girl viewed them in wide-eyed terror, as if she expected them to eat her alive. The pretty woman and the matron – labelled by Drust the Flirt and the Expert – were always stealing sly glances in their direction, but fled if approached. Only the shepherd seemed unworried by their presence, and he did not seem to have registered their existence. Severa herself seemed to grow less friendly and more anxious as they recovered, as if she expected them to assault her or steal the chickens. It was annoying, a little hurtful, and distinctly insulting.

**

Severa sometimes thought that if she had known they were warriors she would have left them on the moors to starve and good riddance. To be sure, they *seemed* harmless enough, and the young captain – Steeleye, if she believed the name – was quite polite. But Severa had been brought up on lurid tales of Saxon and Pictish raids, of villages torched, animals slaughtered or stolen, men massacred, women and children abused and taken as slaves. The High King Arthur had won his reputation fighting the Saxons, and as he was the greatest king Britannia had ever known, it followed that Saxon raiders must exceed all others in inhuman savagery, with the possible exception of the Picts. It was not much comfort that Steeleye was obviously Brittonic – despite his rather scruffy beard – for the district knew from frequent and bitter experience that Brittonic bandits were as plentiful as wolves and more destructive, and his unwillingness to tell her his name or business only confirmed they were up to no good. The only possible comfort was that they had obviously lost their last fight, which suggested they were not very competent thieves, although they would be more than a match for four women, a half-wit and a dog. Sometimes the three who were not hurt exercised with their weapons, and though Gwen and Blodwen thought this was very exciting as well as scary, to Severa the powerful muscles and glinting blades were merely chilling. Even the killing of a single sheep or pig, if they grew bored with porridge and decided to help themselves to a roast dinner, would be a serious loss to the village. And they could do much, much worse than that. What had possessed her to invite them in? She must have been mad.

**

Severa woke, as she always did, before dawn and reluctantly. Mother of God, but she was tired! You really needed more than four women and a half-wit to run a hafod, and it had been a long, hard summer. She rolled out of her blankets and into her clothes, making a mental list of all the things that had to be done that day. Too much to do, as usual. So she had better make a start. The village depended on the hafod for a large part of its food supply, and if she shirked the work here the whole village would be hungry this winter.

Outside, it was just getting light. She let the chickens out of their shed, and noticed that the door to the fodder store was standing open. She peered in. The tramps, and all their weapons, had gone. Sneaking off into the night like the thieves they were –

The sound of splintering wood made her spin around, to see with horror that three bulky dark figures were climbing in over the smashed gate. The pigs squealed and the sheep bleated, all scrambling on top of each other to get to the far end of the yard. The dog flew at the intruders, barking and snarling.

"Saxons!" she screamed. "Saxons!"

More bulky figures were visible behind the first three, and she had a terrifying glimpse of heavy clubs and glinting blades. This was what every farmer prayed would never happen, the sudden eruption of brutal violence into their unremarkable lives. Gruffuyd came bounding out of the house, seized the wood-chopping axe and rushed at the intruders, roaring with inarticulate rage. Severa thought of the knives and sprinted into the dairy. She tripped over an empty pail, fell against a table, and snatched up the biggest kitchen knife, the one she used for jointing chickens. She ought to be able to do some damage with that.

A bulky figure appeared in the doorway, silhouetted against the growing light. She stepped forward, knife in hand.

"Come on, you bastard –"

How could anyone so big move so fast? He pounced like a cat on a mouse, she stabbed the knife into empty air, and a burly arm went round her neck and a hand clamped over her mouth. She bit it, hard. Her assailant yelled and slammed her back against the wall with a force that half-stunned her, but she still had hold of the knife. She twisted in his grasp and stabbed him in the chest with all the strength she could muster.

He didn't die. Instead, he bellowed like a furious ox, thumped her in the stomach, smacked her hard around the head and wrenched her wrist until she thought she would faint with the pain. The knife clattered to the floor. She cried out, and the man hit her, more than once. Outside, she could hear shouts and shrieks, above the noise of panicked livestock and furious barking.

"Bitch!" snarled the robber, in Brittonic, and slapped her again.

"Need a hand here, mate?" a familiar voice asked from the doorway.

The tramp she knew as Steeleye was standing there, with a long dagger in his left hand. There was blood on the blade.

"No!" growled the bandit. "Who the hell are you and what do you want?"

"Same as you, but you beat us to it." He came in, cautiously.

The bandit backed behind the table, dragging Severa with him, and drew a sword. "Drop the knife."

Steeleye obliged. "Whatever you say. You're the boss." He took another step into the house. His face had a hard, calculating look.

The robber flailed the sword. "Keep back!"

Steeleye's expression became ingratiating. He held up his left hand. The right was clearly visible in the sling and both were empty.

"Calm down, mate. Your lads are rounding up outside. Not a bad haul for a fleapit like this. How about we help you drive the beasts, split the profits and share the women?"

Severa glared at him. All her worst fears were confirmed. He ignored her, keeping his eyes fixed on the bandit's face, and came a little further in.

"You can't drive them all on your own and neither can we. So we join forces and there'll be more to go round. Six to four, fair and square. Or two to one if you like, you're better than we are."

The bandit was not good at arithmetic. His brow creased. Severa took the opportunity to grab for a cleaver hanging on the wall, but he was much too quick for her and jerked her arm until she screamed.

"Here," Steeleye said, alarmed, "don't break her! She's worth money. I know a slaver who'll give you gold for her, mate. You want a hand with her? She's a lively bitch." He was edging closer. "Here, tell you what. I'll hold her for you, and then you hold her for me."

"Judas!" Severa was sobbing with pain and impotent fury. "I cure you, I give you food and shelter, and this is how you repay me! Thieves! Murderers! I hope you rot in hell for all eternity –"

She was aware of a sudden blur of movement, then she was thrown sideways and fell to the floor amid a cascade of empty bowls and settling pans. There was a crash, a bubbling yell, something warm and sticky sprayed across her face, and a heavy body thudded down on top of her.

She lay still until the world stopped spinning, then decided she was probably not dead and struggled to lever herself up. The thief was sprawled on his back across her, with Steeleye's small eating knife embedded in his throat. He was very dead. The table was lying on its side and the floor was apparently swimming in blood. Steeleye was crouched on hands and knees, very pale and swearing under his breath.

Severa tried to imagine how much it must have hurt to throw his whole weight across the table with a broken shoulder and a half-healed wound, and failed.

"Why –?" she choked out.

"Because," he said, between gasps, "I can't throw a knife left-handed to be sure of hitting him and not you. So I had to get close enough to jump him."

He rocked back on his haunches, put a hand to his shoulder, and swore again. "Should have practised more – "

He retrieved his knife and wiped it and his hands on the dead man's tunic, then looked across at her.

"Are you hurt?"

Severa shook her head and stared uncomprehendingly at the body sprawled across her. There was blood all over its chest. So she hadn't missed after all.

"The knife," she said vaguely. "What did I do wrong –?"

She was not expecting an answer, but Steeleye leaned forward and inspected the body with a professional air.

"Looks like you held the knife high and stabbed down. Amateurs usually do. Next time, hold the knife under the ribs and stab *upwards*."

The dairy was suddenly full of people. Someone hauled the body off her, and then her arms were full of Luned and Gwen and Blodwen and the dog, all hysterical but apparently unhurt. They stumbled outside together, clinging to each other.

***

Outside, the hafod looked as if a storm had struck. The gate was smashed to pieces and the woods and field were full of panicked livestock. Bodies seemed to be strewn all over the yard. Severa stared vacantly, numb with shock. One had a shattered skull, and one lay on its back with a spear sticking in its belly. A detached hand lay in the mud with its fingers curled up like a dead spider. The only men standing seemed to be the four tramps, all splashed with blood and looking hardly less savage than the robbers.

"You're not going to hurt us –?" she stammered.

"Of course not," Steeleye said wearily, "what the hell do you take us for?"

72

She still could not grasp what had happened. "You – you – killed all of them?"

"What, did you want to keep one as a pet?" he said acidly. "Of course we killed them. Let them escape and they're buggers to hunt down."

"But – there were so many –"

"Six," he said dismissively, "and not very bright, either. Lilla was on watch and heard them coming a mile off. Unfortunately we were waiting to jump them until they were all in the yard and you screamed first." He glanced at Luned, who was sobbing and clinging to Blodwen, and Gwen, who was on her knees being sick, and his voice softened. "Send them indoors, Mistress. This –" a gesture encompassed the shambles in the yard "– is not a sight for women. But would you come with me, if you are well enough? I have bad news for you."

She followed him to one of the bodies, which was covered by a blood-soaked cloak.

"Your shepherd, Mistress," he said quietly. "I am sorry. I shouted at him to stay back, to leave it to us, but he did not hear me."

"He would not have understood." She touched her temple. "Poor Gruffuyd was only a baby, up here. How –?"

Steeleye caught her hand before she could touch the cloak. "Don't look. I am afraid he is not a pretty sight. It was quick, if that is any comfort. He would not have known anything about it, and you may trust me on that." He paused. "I gather – the older lady –?"

"Blodwen."

"– is his mother? She should not see him, I think. Can you break it to her?"

Severa nodded, still dazed. It all seemed so unreal.

He glanced at the cross round her neck. "You are followers of the White Christ? Should we bury him?"

"I am, not the others. But yes, bury him. Please."

***

Blodwen screamed and wept all day and the other women tried, without success, to comfort her. The four men beat a hasty retreat from the hysterical huddle in the house and proceeded to get on with clearing up. This at least was familiar territory.

They wrapped Gruffuyd's body respectfully in two of the thieves' cloaks to act as a shroud, found some spades in a shed, and buried him solemnly under a rowan tree in the woods. They did not know the dead man's god, so they buried one of the thieves' spears with him – reckoning that he had died like a warrior and therefore deserved it – and honoured him with bits and pieces of the rites sacred to Thunor, Woden, Lord Frey, the Great Mother and even some half-remembered Christian prayers Eadwine had heard at Father Ysgafnell's monastery. No doubt this would cause some confusion in the afterlife, but at least it should ensure a considerable welcoming committee for his soul and the gods would just have to work it out between themselves.

The rest of the bodies were hauled deeper into the woods, where Ashhere and Drust dug a big hole and Lilla, with a little help from Eadwine, stripped the bodies of valuables and weapons. Between them, they yielded one good-quality cloak brooch, some eating knives, three more spears, a moth-eaten shield and a sword. Drust took the shield, the others shared out the spears, and they insisted that Eadwine take the sword.

73

"It's a good sword," Lilla said in some surprise, giving it a final polish. He turned it so that the light caught the writhing patterns indicating a high-quality pattern-welded blade. "There are runes up here by the hilt, look. Can you tell what they say?"

Eadwine traced the marks with his finger. After some study he realised they were not Anglian runes after all, but Latin letters. He spelled them slowly out to himself, trying to remember which shape stood for which sound. Father Ysgafnell had explained the numerous inscribed stones in Eboracum to him with commendable patience, but it was a long time ago, and he was starting to feel faint with pain and weariness. He tried various combinations until he found a Brittonic word that made sense.

"Bright - blade," he said, at length. "Brightblade. Seems appropriate."

Ashhere rested on his spade and leaned down for a closer look. "I wonder who he stole it from?"

"It could easily have been his own."

"A bandit?" scoffed Ashhere. "Never!"

"Come down in the world, lost his lord and his lands. Like us. Hasn't it occurred to you that this is how we'll end up, if we can't find a king to give us refuge? Thieving from peasants who've nothing worth stealing, until we clash with a stronger band, or some lord who takes his duties seriously, and that's us down there." He gestured at the bodies in the ditch. "If anyone even bothers to bury us."

He could not repress a shudder, and Drust took his arm. "It hasna happened yet, and ye'll work out where we are sooner or later. Yon lord in his stone fort might help us."

"He owes us a favour," Eadwine agreed, "since we've just done part of his job for him. I'll ask – "

He stood up, rather too quickly, and swayed.

"Not today," Drust said firmly. "Ye're going to get cleaned up, and then sleep while we finish the work. Ye're no use half alive."

***

Eadwine really had little choice but to follow the advice, partly because they threatened to sit on him if he did not and partly because his injured body was beginning to complain vigorously. He ached all over, and he had been very lucky not to reopen the wound in his side. He lay down in the hut and went out like a snuffed candle.

***

He slept all through the racket they made rounding up the straying livestock, cleaning the dairy and blocking the wrecked gate with thorn bushes, and even through the mournful complaints of the cows that were still in milch, who lowed piteously and continuously until Severa pulled herself together enough to relieve their discomfort.

It was long after sunset when he woke, to find the others sitting cross-legged around the fire drying their damp clothes and philosophically sharing a basket of nuts, mushrooms and berries.

"Didn't know where they keep the food and we didn't want to disturb them," Lilla said, seeing that Eadwine was awake and offering him a handful of kernels. "The witch – I mean, Severa – looked like a sleepwalker when she was milking the cows."

74

"Makes a change from porridge, anyway," Ashhere said, grinning. "You feeling better now?"

"Much. Is there any water?"

Drust dipped a cup in the bucket and handed it to him. He drank, gratefully.

Someone knocked at the open door, and a woman's voice said hesitantly, "May I come in?"

Severa stood there, looking very pale and shaken, holding a platter and a jug.

"Of course, Mistress," Eadwine answered, astonished. She had never knocked before. "It is your house. You will forgive me if I do not rise."

She came in and handed the platter and the jug to Drust, who happened to be nearest.

"Bread and milk," she apologised. "I'm sorry, there is nothing else, we have not cooked pottage today."

"I think we can bear the disappointment," Eadwine said gravely, and was surprised to hear a muffled snort from behind him. Ashhere's Brittonic must be coming on.

Severa did not seem to have heard. "I am sorry –" she said. "I – I misjudged you. I have not thanked you –"

"There is no need, Mistress," Eadwine answered gently. "I am sorry for your loss." He gestured to the open door, where Blodwen's abandoned sobbing still echoed through the hafod. "Poor lady. How is she?"

"She will recover. For Blodwen grief is violent but it is short. When she lost her fourth husband she wept for a night and a day, and then began looking out for a fifth. It is a good way to be, I think. Life goes on."

She took another step into the hut, and to his surprise she kneeled down so that they no longer had to look up at her.

"Steeleye –" she began, and broke off, twisting her hands together.

He was going to have to get used to that name. "Yes?"

"I – I – came to apologise," she said quietly. "For calling you Judas. Not that I suppose you have any idea what it means, but it – it is an insult. I was wrong. I am sorry."

"I know who Judas was," he answered dryly. "I am not a follower of the White Christ myself, but I have heard the tale."

"Then I am even more sorry." She bit her lip. "How ungrateful you must have thought me –"

He smiled. "To be honest, I was not paying you much attention. If anything, it was probably useful. You distracted him, and you convinced him I was no friend of yours. If it worked you would find out your mistake soon enough, and if it didn't your good opinion was likely to be the least of my worries."

"I – I still do not understand why. You could have joined them and taken what you pleased, or you could have disappeared safely into the woods. Why fight them?"

"I keep telling you we are not thieves. We have eaten your food and slept under your roof. We pay our debts, Mistress. For our own honour, not for your gratitude."

She looked up, and her green eyes were full of tears. "Will you – will you accept the gratitude, nonetheless?"

Chapter 9

"I d-d-don't want to go on my own!" Luned wailed, again. "I'm s-s-scared! W-what if more bad men come? What shall I d-d-do?"

"Scream and run, same as you would if there were two of you," Severa said, keeping the sharpness out of her tone with an effort. "Luned, you have to take the pigs on your own. There's no-one to come with you. Gwen's taking the sheep, and poor Blodwen isn't fit for anything."

Blodwen had cried all night, and between that and jumping in terror at every noise none of them had got any sleep.

"C-c-can't you come with m-m-me?" Luned pleaded.

"No, lass, I'm needed in the dairy. There's all yesterday's milk and the day before's as well as today's."

She closed her eyes, trying not to think of the amount of work she would have to get through. A narrow escape from death, rape or slavery didn't mean you could all take the day off. And there was grain to grind and bread to make, or the herders would go hungry tomorrow, and –

"Luned," she said firmly, "there aren't enough of us to go round. You've got to go on your own."

Luned's startled expression made her turn, to see the youngest tramp, the good-looking boy, threading his way through the milling animals. His limp was almost gone.

He came up to them, took a deep breath, and declaimed, "My-name-is-Lil-la-I-was-a-swine-herd-once-I-will-help-you-with-the-pigs."

Severa blinked. He was regarding her hopefully. "Oh," she said, surprised. "That's very kind of you. Have you herded this kind of pig before?"

His expression became panic-stricken, and he looked round desperately for Steeleye, who was nowhere to be seen. Presumably he was still sleeping, after yesterday. Finding no help, Lilla began repeating his speech, rather louder than before, "My-name-is-"

Evidently he had got Steeleye to translate what he wanted to say into Brittonic and had learned the strange sounds by heart. It was rather touching.

"Luned?" she asked.

Luned gulped, and nodded. Lilla beamed. Luned gave him a shy smile and they trotted off together with the pigs.

Severa wondered how they would manage, since Lilla obviously did not know a word of Brittonic and Luned did not know a word of Saxon. She shrugged. The pigs didn't know a word of either. One problem solved, but it looked as if she still had another to deal with before she could start her own day's work. Gwen was beckoning at her excitedly from the gate, where the sheepdog was chivvying the sheep up the track in a woolly river.

"I don't want to go on my own, either!" Gwen announced, with her eyes fixed on Ashhere and Drust who were hauling the thorn bushes further out of the way. "I'm ever so frightened!" She fluttered her eyelashes hopefully in Drust's direction, but he was intent on the wreckage of the gate and the effect was lost.

Ashhere stepped forward. "I will come," he offered, and Gwen cast a last look at Drust and gracefully accepted consolation prize.

***

Severa watched them stroll after the sheep, Gwen's hand already beginning to wander. Just as well the sheepdog knew the job. She rubbed a hand over her tired eyes, wished vainly that she could lie down and sleep for at least a week, and turned to the dairy, running through tasks in her mind. The day-old milk would have separated by now and she would need to skim the cream, churn it into butter, and turn the skimmed milk into cheese. The same for the two-day-old milk, which would still be usable provided she processed it today. Lucky that it had all been on the other table at the far end of the dairy and had escaped her struggle with the thief. She smiled sourly. Lucky? If it had all been spilt at least she wouldn't have had to deal with it. There was also a bag of curds that had been draining since the day before last, which should have been milled and pressed yesterday and would now have to be done today. And all of today's milk, which she would have to turn into whole-milk cheese because there was no space to let it separate. Mother of God, she thought, we'd be hard pushed to do all that with two or three of us. So clot today's milk first and put the curds to drain, then mill the already-drained curds and mould them, and then skim two lots of cream, make the butter, and clot the skimmed milk if she could get round to it. She could give the skimmed milk to the pigs if she had to, but it would be a criminal waste to give them the cream and lose all that butter –

She passed the door to the grain store, and froze in shock. Surely she must have imagined it. Her nerves were on the jump at every sound – no, there it was again. The grating sound of the rotary quern. Something was grinding grain. Not a person, she was sure. It was a task they all hated, dusty, monotonous and repetitive. In better-off households it was done by slaves, here they reluctantly took turns at it. It had been Gwen's turn this time, but Gwen had gone up to the moors with the sheep. Blodwen was still snuffling in the house. Had Luned been leaving bowls of cream out for the brownies again? More alarmingly, had one of them taken notice? Severa hesitated. It was very, very bad luck to disturb a brownie at work. They could turn the cows dry, or the cheese rotten, or bring you out in a plague of boils. Then she took a deep breath and squared her shoulders. This was *her* household, whatever-it-was was grinding *her* grain, and good Christians feared nothing on God's earth, including brownies. She crossed herself, took the wooden cross firmly in her hand, and kicked open the door.

It wasn't a brownie. It was Steeleye. He jumped. She jumped.

"Oh! What do you think you're doing?"

"Milking a cow, what does it look like?" he snapped back. "Why are you waving that cross at me?"

Severa let it drop. Her hands were shaking annoyingly. "Why are you grinding grain?"

"Because it hurts too much to chop wood and all I know about sheep is that they're woolly things with four legs. Gwen – it is Gwen, isn't it, the pretty one? – was worried that she wouldn't have the time to do this, being away with the sheep all day. I asked her to show me, it didn't seem difficult, it only needs one hand, so I volunteered. Am I doing it wrong?"

He had a lot to learn about Gwen, Severa thought, hiding a smile.

"No, no. But you shouldn't – it's a slave's task!"

"So? Somebody has to do it."

"It's not fitting. You're a great lord in your own country."

He started in shock, then his face set into a mulish expression.

"We are poor men –"

77

"Oh yes, and I'm the Empress of Rome! I don't like being lied to, Steeleye. You carry weapons."

"All free men carry weapons where we come from."

"That belt was expensive."

Eadwine looked down at the broad leather belt with its decorative bronze plates and its heavy bronze buckle. He was so used to it that he had forgotten about it.

"Stolen," he said defensively.

"Really? When you were so keen to insist that you weren't thieves?"

"Not from you," he retorted.

"Your tunic is a complicated weave. Some very skilled woman spent a lot of time weaving that, *and* making the decorative braid, *and* sewing it all together. Only noblewomen have that much time for needlework."

"A hand-me-down from a lord."

"Funny he was just the same size as you. And your friends treat you as their leader."

"So I happen to be the captain —"

"At your age? At least two of them are older than you."

"Talent. Luck."

"More likely noble blood. And you know about fighting, but you're woefully ignorant about anything practical."

"Oh, thank you kindly. So I happen to be stupid."

"Hardly stupid, but you've obviously never had to earn a living. You speak well."

"I talk too much. But that doesn't mean —"

"And," she interrupted, playing her trump card, "there's this!" She held out the splinter of metal she had removed from his wound.

"Ah," he said.

It was a fragment of mail.

Severa pressed home her advantage. "Only lords own mail shirts. The Lord of Navio has one. He wears it on high days and holy days."

He rallied. "Stolen. From a corpse on the road."

"There were two bits of cloth caught on it. One was a scrap of your smart tunic. The other was a piece of linen undershirt. Linen! Ordinary people wear wool. *Maybe* you stole some lord's armour. *Maybe* you even stole his tunic and it just happened to fit you. But do you seriously expect me to believe you stole someone's luxury underwear?"

That made him laugh, ruefully.

"Ashhere warned me you were a witch. I should have listened to him."

"You don't deny you're of noble blood?"

Eadwine shrugged, and winced. "I shall have to stop doing that, it hurts…. How can I deny it?" He paused, rubbing his painful shoulder as an excuse to give himself time to think. Damn, *damn!* He had been much too careless, and this girl was much too sharp. How to repair the damage? He was reluctant to tell her a direct lie — it was too much trouble to maintain a deception — but equally the truth was out of the question.

He said, cautiously, "I am from a noble family, yes. My fathers served with Peredur King of Caer Ebrawg." Well, that was quite true, as far as it went. "Men who have wealth have enemies. There is always someone who thinks he has a better claim to a larger share, and is prepared to back it up with violence. There was a fight. I lost."

He paused, wondering if that would be enough. It was not exactly untrue, but to someone familiar with the Brittonic system of dividing an inheritance between sons and the inevitable fratricide it produced, it should lead her to an entirely plausible, if wrong, conclusion.

It did. "So a brother or cousin or uncle attacked you to get your share of the family inheritance? And would have you dead so you cannot reclaim it?"

He breathed a sigh of relief. "You understand, Mistress? I was not lying when I said 'poor'. Penniless might be more accurate. My family lands and wealth are gone, probably for ever. All I have left is my life, which I would quite like to keep, at least as long as my friends need me."

"Hence you do not want your name known. I can understand that! Telling Blodwen a secret is like carrying water in a sieve. Very well. Your secret is safe with me." She gave him a warm and friendly smile. "Hadn't you better get on with earning an honest living? You'll have to get used to it now, you know."

***

Later in the day he came to help her in the dairy, where she was not even halfway through the work. It quickly became apparent that he was in too much pain to lift or carry anything significant, and Severa was at a loss as to how to make use of him until she had the bright idea of showing him how to skim cream. He was slow at it, of course, even compared to Luned, but anything done was better than nothing, and she was never going to get round to skimming the milk herself.

"You're not bad at that, Steeleye," she said, looking up after a couple of hours to find that he had almost finished. "We'll make a dairymaid of you yet. Are you left-handed?"

He seemed very gratified at the praise. "No. It's because the shield is carried on the left arm."

Severa thought about this for a minute, and gave up. "Sorry?"

He smiled. "Your own shield protects your left side. See?" He demonstrated with a dish-cover. "In a shield-wall, your right side is protected by the shield of the man next to you. But if you're not in a shield-wall, there's nothing to guard your right side. So injuries to the sword-arm are fairly common. The first time it happens, you spend a couple of days relying on your friends to do everything for you, then you realise how very tedious that is and learn to use your other hand."

"This is not the first time you've been wounded then?"

"Not the first, no. Although, possibly, the most painful –"

She came over and took the skimming spoon from him. "Sit down. If you pass out you'll knock all the bowls over and I haven't got time to clean up the mess."

He sank gratefully onto the bench, leaned his head back against the wall, and closed his eyes. He had gone very pale again, and she remembered that it was less than half a month since he had been at death's door.

"Go and lie down," she said, her voice unusually tender.

"Unless I'm in your way, I'd rather stay here," he said. He opened his eyes and tried to find another smile, but this time it didn't work. "It's a very nice hut, but having counted all the onions several times there's nothing to hold my attention, so I think – and remember –"

"Well, stay here and watch me, if that's so much more fascinating. I'll explain the process of cheesemaking to you if you like."

"That's probably over my head, at least until I feel a bit more alive. It looks very complicated. If you can talk while you work, tell me about yourself instead. I had not thought to find someone so exotic on a remote upland farm."

Severa laughed, but there was a forced sound to it. "Exotic? I've been called a lot of things, but never that."

"No? Your looks and colouring are very striking. You're a follower of the White Christ, very unusual outside a city. You speak well. You're an unusually skilled doctor. Your name is Latin. Exotic seems a fair description. It's like finding a rose growing in the middle of the ocean."

She laughed again, more happily this time. "My husband said something similar once, though he wasn't quite so complimentary about it. I do sometimes feel like a blackbird in the snow. It's all due to my grandfather. He had a great reverence for the old Empire. His forefathers were surgeons to Macsen Wledig – Magnus Maximus, my grandfather called him – or so he claimed. *This scalpel,* he used to say, *operated on an Emperor once!* Then he'd wink, and say, *Mind you, it's had four new blades and two new handles since then!*"

Eadwine smiled at the obvious affection in her tone.

"What was his name?"

"Germanianus Severus Aurelianus," she said, rolling the syllables. "Everybody here called him Garbanion, which annoyed him intensely. He wasn't from round here, you see. He came from somewhere far away north and west, near the mountains and the sea, not far from the – the Great Wall, near a great city whose name I can't remember –"

"Caer Luel?"

She looked up from pressing curds into the cheese mould, surprised. "Yes, that was it. How did you know?"

"It's the only city I've heard of near the western end of the Wall. Why did he leave?"

"He quarrelled with his king." She looked sad. "I don't know the details. It made him unhappy to talk about it. He was a fervent Christian – which is why I honour his god for his sake, although without a priest I'm sure I must be doing all sorts of things wrong – and that was one of the causes of the quarrel, but there was more to it than that. So he and his wife and their children and their servant packed up and left. He said – please don't laugh at me – he said there was still an Emperor, a long, long way away in the East, and he was going there. Somewhere where the world was still run properly, he said, with no petty tyrants and no jumped-up kings. Is there such a place? You come from the east."

"Not far enough east, I think. Certainly there's no Emperor where we come from. I talked to a sailor on a wine ship once though, and he told me about a sea with no tides and endless sunshine, far away in the south, and a great city at the end of the world, all built of white stone and gold, where a mighty Emperor ruled in a palace of painted marble. He was probably spinning tall tales – sailors are like fishermen – but I suppose it could have been your grandfather's Emperor."

"I hope so. I'd like to think he was going to a real place – even though, as you can see, he never got there. When they reached Combe village one of the children fell sick and his wife – my grandmother – refused to go a step further until the child was better. The village headman gave them shelter, and by the time the child had recovered it was winter, and then his wife fell pregnant, and then it was winter again. And by then the village had grown to like having a doctor living with them, and built him a house, and his wife had made friends in the village and was enjoying being the wife of an important man. So they stayed another year, and then another, and then his son married a local girl and settled down, and so with one thing and another they never got any further."

"Was he happy here?"

"Not really. He felt stifled, I think, and he always regretted not having gone on. His son – my father – called him a silly old fool whenever he talked about the Empire. So he talked to me about it instead, probably from the cradle and certainly for as long as I can remember. He said the Emperors would come back one day to reclaim Britannia, and that when they did they would value people who remembered the old ways."

"Do you think he was right? That the Emperors will come back one day?"

She shook her head. "No, if the Emperor was coming he would have come by now, surely. It was just something to learn. Anything would have done. You understand that, I think?"

He nodded, recognising the thirst of a questing intelligence for knowledge, on any subject. It was the same imperative that had driven his own eclectic if haphazard education – Ysgafnell's monastery, Heledd and her bards, the sailors on the quays, anyone, really, who could open a window onto another world. But he had had a whole city to explore, full of interesting things and people, and she had had only one old man.

"You must miss him greatly."

She smiled sadly. "Yes. It's silly really – he died over five years ago, before I was married, and yet still I find myself thinking *Oh, Grandfather would be interested in that, I must ask him about it.* He seems almost more real than the living." She paused, turning another cheese out of the mould. "I think – I think it may be because there's no-one else I am close to. Blodwen and Gwen and Luned are nice enough, and I like them, but if I say anything out of the ordinary they look at me as if I was mad – or magical, which is worse. Do you know what I mean?"

Eadwine smiled, thinking of the usual reaction from spearmen when they first found out his liking for Brittonic poetry. "Oh, yes."

"I thought you might."

"But in the winter when you're back in the village, with your husband –"

"My husband is gone."

"Oh, I'm sorry. How did he die?"

"I didn't say he died. I said he was gone." She leaned on the edge of the table, gazing into the middle distance. "He went away on a journey, four years ago this coming winter. It was a week before my sixteenth birthday. I remember waving him off from Derwent Bridge. It was a cold, frosty morning, and the hills were all dusted white with the first snow of the winter. I wanted to walk a little way with him, maybe to Derwent Stone, but he wouldn't have it. I was four months pregnant at the time. He kissed me, and his breath froze in my hair. We laughed about it, and he said he would be back by the spring and mind I had a baby son for him to play with. I watched him stride away up the army-path and into the woods above Combe village. That was the last I saw of him." She looked directly at him. "But he will come back to me. I know he will."

"Yes," he said. What else could he say? "Of course he will."

"So in the meantime his brother is acting as village headman, and as I am still the headman's wife, I run the hafod in the summer. And I wait."

"What of your child?"

"Miscarriage. Twins." She glanced up with a brittle smile. "It's all right, I can talk about it now. I was lucky there was a good midwife in the village. Blodwen's mother-in-law. She moved in with me to make the nursing easier, and never had cause to move out. I learned a lot from her, and I more or less took over from her when she died." She patted the last lump of cheese into shape. "Excuse me, I must get some dock leaves to wrap these in."

Eadwine suspected she actually wanted some privacy to cry, so he did not follow. What a lonely position she was in, neither wife nor widow, bereft but yet not free, bound to the ruins of an old life and unable to start again. There was, he thought grimly, something to be said for losing everything. Then he thought of Eadric, and his grief for his beloved brother came swirling back in a great wave. He too was bound to the ruins of an old life, for he owed it to his father and brother to avenge them – and to Aethelind. What was happening to her? Was she already dead? Or was she still alive, waiting for him to return as Severa was waiting for her husband? The images from his delirium came back sharp and clear, Aethelind beaten, Aethelind enslaved to some brute, Aethelind screaming in pain and terror, and the last words she had spoken to him, now transmuted into a wailing cry, *Don't fail me!* Rumour said the Bernicians did unimaginable things to captured women. Unfortunately, Eadwine had a very good imagination.

A pain in his shoulder recalled him to reality, and he realised that both fists were tightly clenched and he was shaking. No, thinking and remembering was definitely not a good idea. It was all right if he could keep his mind occupied, or if he was exhausted enough to sleep, but otherwise he felt he was drowning in grief and shame.

Severa still had not come back, so he got up gingerly, supported himself against the wall until the floor stopped pitching, and went outside.

***

Severa was leaning against the fence, the dock leaves apparently forgotten in her hands. In the doorway of the house, Blodwen was standing with eyes and mouth agape. Both women looked transfixed, and the reason was not hard to fathom.

Drust was splitting a log. He was driving wedges into the trunk, and pounding them home with a heavy mallet. He had taken his tunic off, and with each mighty blow the great muscles of his shoulders and back flexed and rippled under the gleaming skin. Blodwen's head nodded up and down in time with the rhythm, as if on a string. The log split with a tearing sound, and Drust bent over to retrieve the wedges. Blodwen put her hand to her breast and emitted a faint breathless squeak.

Eadwine grinned, a little wistfully, and made a discreet withdrawal. Drust tended to have that effect on women. Eadric and Cynewulf, his two half-brothers, had the same magnetism, and Ashhere too, to some extent. It was something to do with being possessed of a fifty-inch hairy chest, magnificent musculature and a firm belief that tongues were not intended for talking.

He was not surprised when Ashhere came back down from the moors with a faintly dazed expression and a long curly dark hair caught in his beard, nor that they were invited to eat in the house that evening, where it seemed impossible to find anywhere to look without accidentally intercepting a smouldering glance. Nor was he surprised that neither Ashhere nor Drust came back to the hut that night, although that was distinctly less amusing.

***

Two yawning and bleary-eyed figures crept back to the hut in the half-light before dawn, shushing each other noisily, and tripping over the pig-trough on the way. This was going to be more fun than they had thought –

"I don't want to know what you've been doing," remarked an icy voice as they fell in through the door. "Nor do I greatly mind doing double-duty on watch, although in future I should prefer to have warning. But would you care to explain why you saw fit to desert your posts?"

They shuffled miserably. Eadwine could wound with words more effectively than many men could with fists.

"And kindly don't try to dig your way out through the floor. Well?"

"Er," began Ashhere, feeling about half an inch high. "Er – sorry, lord –"

Even Drust sounded shamefaced. "Er – it willna happen again –"

"I asked you for an explanation, not an apology."

"Er – well – the girls –"

"It wasna rape, if that's what ye think –"

"I am not interested in your personal lives, as you should know very well by now. You can tumble every woman in Britannia for all I care, provided you don't expect me to get you out of trouble for it. But you do *not* shirk your duty and you do *not* leave your comrades unguarded. This is not a holiday. Do I make myself quite clear?"

"Yes, lord," they said, squirming.

***

He was half-expecting Severa to be furious and possibly even to demand compensation, to which as head of the household she would have been entitled under Anglian law, but instead she seemed to consider it a great joke.

"I owe Luned a new hair-ribbon," she informed him, righting the pig-trough and pouring whey into it. "We wagered on which one would get Drust, and it was Blodwen. By a short head." She jumped back out of the torrent of rushing pigs, laughing up at him. "Dear me, Steeleye, have I shocked you? You think they'd sit and virtuously spin with four new men – well, three and a half – to engage their attentions? You might as well expect water to flow uphill. If Blodwen can find some comfort with a passing stranger – or two – who am I to begrudge it? And Gwen – well, is Gwen. Where is the harm? They both know the precautions, and if they forget themselves, it's only a month until Samhain and I can always claim it's premature – there are some advantages to being the midwife." She shrugged. "You saved all our lives, remember. Why should we not show our – gratitude? And you must admit, your friends are easy on the eye. You will not be here long. After Samhain you will leave and we will never see or hear of you again. Why not make those few weeks sweet? There is little enough joy in this world, and such pleasures as come our way should not be spurned. To be faithful in the heart is what truly counts, I think. The other – well, it is natural, like eating and breathing."

Eadwine felt a sudden, inexplicable pang of jealousy, wondering if she applied the same philosophy to herself, and if so whether she and Ashhere – or Drust –

Severa quirked an eyebrow. "Do you know, Steeleye, you have a very expressive face? If it makes you feel better – well, shall we say that neither of them was a very severe test of my virtue?"

***

The hafod soon settled into a very pleasant pattern of life, now with eight people – well, seven and a half – to share the work, not forgetting the dog. Two people, almost invariably Lilla and Luned, drove the swine into the woods, and two more plus the dog took the sheep up to the moors each day, generally Gwen or Blodwen with either Ashhere or Drust. The other three and a half, which always included Severa, stayed on the hafod. With so much more labour available than usual the hafod improved noticeably. The gate was replaced, the drystone wall repaired, the roofs mended, the dairy cat-proofed – as far as possible – and the vegetable patch dug and weeded as never before. Severa found she had time to do tasks that she never normally got around to, like dyeing wool, and even set up her loom in the wool shed and began weaving a large brightly coloured chequered cloth. Around sunset, they all gathered in the house for the meal and then sat on into the lengthening evenings, enjoying one another's company. Lilla was painstakingly fashioning a fishing hook out of some scraps of bent metal he had found, and Ashhere was helping Drust repair the shield. None of the women spoke any Anglian, but Lilla was quickly picking up Brittonic, Drust found that the dialect had many words in common with Pictish, and Ashhere was getting used to the local accent, so they mostly spoke Brittonic when the women were present and Eadwine had less and less need to translate, unless someone wanted to say something complex. The women all spent the evenings spinning wool, and the endless twirling of the drop spindles as they fell was hypnotic –

Eadwine jolted out of a doze and found Lilla poking him in the ribs.

"Wake up and do something useful for once," Lilla said, grinning. "The lasses want us to tell them a tale, and you're the one who knows all the poetry."

Eadwine had no objection. Anything that would delay the moment when he had to return to the hut and try to sleep was welcome, and he had learned a large repertoire of Brittonic poetry from Heledd, her court bard, and the many itinerant bards she patronised.

He began in the traditional way. It was usually a safe bet. "Attend! The High King Arthur held court at Camulodunum –"

"Oh," Blodwen protested, in a disappointed tone, "must it be about Arthur? *All* the tales are about Arthur. Can't you tell us something we haven't heard before?"

"And it was all so far away and long ago," Luned said shyly. "Nothing to do with the likes of us."

"Unless Queen Gwenhwyfar's in it," Gwen suggested. "*She* sounds interesting."

Eadwine hesitated. He knew there was a rich seam of vernacular legend about Arthur's fiery Queen, but he was not very familiar with it. Heledd, his main source for Brittonic legend and history, had disapproved of Gwenhwyfar ('*Not* the conduct of a good Christian queen!', although the one thing nobody had ever accused Gwenhwyfar of was being a good Christian), and the itinerant bards earned their livings at royal courts, where tales of a queen who rebelled against a king were undiplomatic to say the least and therefore not worth knowing. In the battle-poetry Eadwine knew best, Gwenhwyfar's role was confined to waving the warriors off to war in the first verse and welcoming them home again in the last, which was unlikely to satisfy Gwen. Did one of the others know something that would do?

A few minutes conferring with his friends, reverting to Anglian as they always did between themselves, confirmed that between them they knew quite a lot of battle-poetry, mostly odd verses relating to the deeds of supposed ancestors, a few nursery rhymes, some sailing songs that seemed absurdly out of place in these landlocked moors, and a startling number of disreputable drinking songs.

"No," Eadwine warned, seeing Drust clear his throat. "Not *Attacotti Nell*. We're all sober."

"Och, I willna do all fifteen verses."

"Half of them are impossible anyway," Ashhere muttered.

"How much will ye bet?"

"Drust, if you give offence you'll get us all thrown out –"

"Ye dinna have tae translate."

"If you put in your usual performance, what worries me is that I won't need to." He turned back to the women, who were regarding him expectantly. "Er – I'm sorry I don't know any tales about Gwenhwyfar, and you may not like this, but it's not about Arthur and I can guarantee you haven't heard it before." He took a swallow of water, and began again.

"Attend! In the fair land of the Summer Country, where the great oaks grow about a sparkling river, and purple-hued moors rise to the sky –"

Luned nudged Gwen and whispered, "Where's that? It sounds a bit like here."

"Ssssh!"

"– dwelt a kind and simple man and four fair maidens. They were not rich, but they were fair of face, and skilled in all manner of crafts, and their merry voices would silence the skylarks for shame. But in the wilds, grim and greedy, cruel men stalked the fells –"

Eadwine saw they were listening and went on, warming to his theme. He was a born storyteller, and the idea had been running in his head on and off for days. He told of the attack on the hafod, and how the bandits had paid with their lives. Borrowing the triad motif so common in Brittonic poetry, he lauded the exploits in battle of the Three Fighting Tramps of the Island of Britannia, with a whole verse each devoted to Ashhere Steel-Arm, Lilla Swift-Handed and Drust Mighty-Grasp. His friends seemed mightily pleased, for although they had listened to a lot of praise-poetry for long-dead kings and heroes, they had never before featured in any. Then he went on to pay tribute to the dauntless Lady Severa, Daughter of the Romans, and the Three Valiant Dairymaids of the Island of Britannia, these being Luned the Gentle, Gwen the Fair and Blodwen the – here he floundered for a moment – the Magnificent. Even the dog got an honourable mention.

Then his tone changed and became slower and sorrowful.

"– But alas, though they triumphed, great was their loss also. For on that day fell Gruffuyd, son of Blodwen, bravely defending his home against the foe –"

The twirling of the drop spindles had long since been stilled, and the fire was burning low. There was no sound but his voice, now low and sonorous as he spoke a eulogy for Gruffuyd, making of a rather pitiful and pointless death something fine and heroic.

"– evergreen shall his memory be, the best and bravest of shepherds, the kindest of men."

He ended. There was utter silence, broken only by the soft hiss and crackle of the flames.

Blodwen sniffed, gulped, and began to cry quietly. "Thank you," she whispered, "thank you for Gruffuyd –"

"Bravo!" Severa smiled, her eyes green and glowing in the firelight. "Forget being a dairymaid, you could earn an honest crust as a bard. But you forgot to mention Steeleye."

Eadwine laughed, pleased and more than a little relieved that his performance had gone down so well. "Oh, the bard never features in his own poetry. It isn't done."

"Blodwen the Magnificent!" scoffed Gwen, tossing her hair and shooting him an inviting over-the-shoulder look across the dying fire, before glancing at his sling and catching first Drust's eye, then Ashhere's and then Lilla's.

"Just make sure you turn up for your watch," Eadwine warned them, trying not to laugh and wondering if they got any sleep at all. He hoped fervently that Treowin had struck just as lucky in Lundencaster.

***

Aethelferth prodded Treowin's unconscious body with the butt-end of a spear. "Is he dead?"

"Not yet, Lord King."

"He's a stubborn bastard," the Brittonic captain said, not without admiration. Not many men refused to answer Aethelferth the Twister's questions, certainly not for this long.

Aethelferth fixed him with a baleful glare. "Did you catch any others with him?"

"One survived, Lord King."

"Fetch him."

***

Treowin's retainer fell on hands and knees, beside what he took to be the dead body of his lord. A foot took him under the chin and flicked him over onto his back. A large, powerful man with a scar running from his right eye down into his bristling beard was glaring down at him, leaning on a spear.

"Do you know who I am?"

The retainer had only seen him on the battlefield, in full armour, but it was not hard to guess that he was looking at Aethelferth the Twister.

"Y-y-yes," he managed to say, quivering with terror. He tried not to look at Treowin's limp form, crusted with blood and bruises.

"I am a merciful man," Aethelferth said, in what was no doubt meant to be a pleasant voice.

The retainer licked his dry lips nervously. He had heard a great many things about Aethelferth, but that was not among them.

"If you answer a few questions, I will let you go. I promise it. Do you understand?"

The man nodded, as best he could while lying flat on the floor.

"Where were you going?"

The retainer found a spark of defiance in his abject terror. This man had hurt his lord.

"I d-don't know."

Aethelferth twirled the spear and looked down at him with a contemptuous expression. The retainer felt as if someone was hooking his soul out through his eye sockets.

"This," said Aethelferth in a conversational tone, "is a spear. If you do not answer my questions I personally will ram it up your arse and out through your lying mouth. Try again. Where were you going?"

The retainer's mouth moved, seemingly without his own volition. "L-Lun – something – Lun – den – caster."

"Why?"

"M-m-my lord t-told us to –"

"This is your lord?"

"Y-y-yes –!" sobbed the man.

"Is this –" holding up Eadwine's helmet, "your lord's helmet?"

"N-n-no –"

"Whose is it?"

"Eadwine – the atheling – the King – "

The flash of anger in Aethelferth's eyes would have put Woden to shame. "*I* am the King!"

The retainer could do nothing but freeze, like a mouse under a kestrel's stare.

"And why was your lord wearing the atheling's helmet?"

"H-he was d-dying –"

Aethelferth frowned. Treowin had seemed in reasonable health, until quite recently. "Your lord was dying?"

"N-no – lord – the atheling –"

Here was good news. They had all seen Eadwine struck down on the field. So the injury had been serious enough to kill. If Aethelferth could retrieve the body, he could fulfil his pledge.

"You saw him die?"

"N-n-no – lord – I-I mean y-yes – he c-c-couldn't have l-l-lived –"

Aethelferth glared. But he could send someone to check. A recently-dug grave would be obvious, and the corpse should still be recognisable.

"Where did you leave him?"

"I d-d-don't know, lord –!"

It was soon clear that this was true. All the information they could extract was that it had been in a forest near a river, which applied to most of Britannia.

Aethelferth glowered and the retainer cringed.

"A – a forest – near a r-river, lord," he wept, "m-m-my lord didn't t-t-tell me w-what they were called – I – I n-never w-went that far from h-home before – I d-d-don't know any more. P-please let me go. You p-p-promised –!"

"So I did," said Aethelferth meditatively. "Release him."

The unhappy prisoner fell at Aethelferth's feet, covered them with kisses, and fled. Aethelferth gave him a moment's start, then strolled to the door and sent the spear speeding after him.

Outside, there was a cry, followed by a muffled thud.

"Disloyal creep," Aethelferth said. He gave Treowin's limp body a kick. "Bring him round. I want Eadwine of Deira, dead or alive."

***

"Not in the mouth, you bloody fool," Aethelferth growled. "How can he answer if you kick all his teeth down his throat?"

He planted another kick in Treowin's stomach and Treowin doubled up on the floor, retching helplessly.

"Where is Eadwine?" Aethelferth repeated.

No answer.

"Tell us where he is and I will let you go."

No answer.

Aethelferth grabbed Treowin's hair and jerked his head up, staring into his eyes.

"*Where is he?*"

And Treowin spat a mouthful of blood and vomit and broken teeth full into Aethelferth's face.

***

One of the guards, a fat red-faced man, looked on disapprovingly as the beating began again. Such a good-looking youth – handsome face, broad shoulders, narrow hips, long tapering legs – and such a mess they were making of him. Such a waste. The guard shifted from foot to foot and surreptitiously scratched at his groin. Such a waste. But he did not dare to intervene.

***

"Try another question," said Aethelferth's impatient voice. "Is Eadwine dead?"

Through a red mist of pain, Treowin recognised that this could be a way out for both himself and his friend. If he swore that Eadwine had died of his wounds and they had burned the body or thrown it in the Trent, Aethelferth would give up searching for Eadwine and would probably also give up questioning him. Eadwine would be safe from pursuit. But if Aethelferth stopped searching, then Deira too would accept that Eadwine was dead, and that would finish Eadwine's chances of regaining the kingdom. There had to be rumours of secret survival, rumours of a prince – a King – who would return one day. Otherwise the remaining nobles and thanes would accept Bernician rule as sanctioned by the gods, and if Eadwine ever did return he would find himself fighting his own people as well as Aethelferth. He would fail, and Deira would never be restored.

"Is Eadwine dead?" repeated the harsh voice.

Through a bruised and broken mouth, Treowin hissed, "Eadwine – lives."

And that was the first time that Treowin betrayed his oldest friend.

Chapter 10

"I can safely say this isn't going to kill you after all, Steeleye," Severa commented, removing the last of the stitches. She smeared honey over the wound, shaped a clump of sphagnum moss into a fresh dressing, and bandaged it firmly in place. It was early morning, a week after the bandit raid, and Steeleye was sitting with his tunic off on the bench outside the hut, patiently ignoring the chill so she could examine his wounds in daylight. He looked much more tired than she thought he should, and she had been concerned that the wound might be festering again, but in fact it was healing remarkably well. Was something wrong with the shoulder? She ran light, practised fingers along the collarbone. The swelling and bruising was much reduced and she could feel the bone clearly. "And this is doing well too. It's not quite straight, but it's not worth re-breaking the bone to set it properly. Unless you want me to –?"

"No, no," came the hasty reply, "I think I'd prefer if you didn't bother." He winced as her fingers probed the break. "Will I get full use of the arm back?"

"Oh, yes. It's not that far out." She sat back on the bench, wiping her hands on a cloth. "I ought to display you in the village, you know. Proof of my skill."

He laughed, pulling his tunic back on with a shiver. "Not until we leave. No-one should know we are here, if at all possible."

Severa studied him intently, wondering what enemy he feared and if that was the reason for his strained and weary look. She was quite sure it was not her imagination. He seemed cheerful enough, but there were shadows under his eyes and a hollowness about his face that she did not like and could not explain, especially since the pain from his wounds should not now be sufficient to interfere with his sleep. Which meant something else was interfering instead. Fear of pursuit? But it must be a formidable enemy, to alarm a man who could deal so efficiently with six robbers, and in that case the others should surely also be worried, yet they clearly were not. They had all stayed on the hafod this morning, Gwen and Luned having taken the pigs and the dog having taken Blodwen along with the sheep, but apart from keeping a careful eye on her and Steeleye they seemed not to have a care in the world. Drust was picking the last of the crab apples from the top of the tree, Lilla was grubbing around in the vegetable patch and Ashhere was chopping firewood and whistling out of tune. Severa had tried to wheedle information out of them, but although they were not as reticent as Steeleye – particularly when they got carried away topping each other's battle exploits – they clammed up promptly if she tried to turn the conversation towards their captain. He was a puzzle.

"Whatever you fear," she said, with what she hoped was a reassuring smile, "you need not worry that it will find you here. We see nobody from Beltane to Samhain unless it's a panicked father summoning me to his wife in labour and there aren't any of those due for a few months. Here, let me help you with the sling."

"No need, see?" He shrugged off her assistance and tied the knot dextrously with his left hand and his teeth. Seeing that they were finished, Drust came over with the crab apples and Severa borrowed his eating knife and started halving the fruit and flicking the grubs out of the cores. This attracted a flock of excited chickens, along with Ashhere.

"Crab apples go well with roast pork," he observed hopefully.

Severa gave him a rueful smile. "Not here they don't. They go with turnips and barley like everything else."

Ashhere's face fell, and Steeleye grinned. "Cheer up, Ash. Try hunting hares on the moors, if you're still intending to join Blodwen and the sheep."

"Hares?" Drust scoffed. "No chance. Anything faster than a slug can outrun him."

"Sorry about the food," Severa apologised, as she had every day for a week. "I wish I could do better for you. But there isn't anything else."

"That," said Lilla's voice with a gleeful air, "is where you're wrong."

He was holding out a pail in one hand with a triumphant expression. Severa peered into its depths, wondering what feast he had conjured up – and saw a wriggling mass of worms, grubs and a few slugs making determined bids for freedom up the sides.

Her voice was a horrified whisper. "You're not serious –!"

A peal of masculine laughter drowned the words and Lilla held up his finished fishing hook, twirling on a length of thread.

"Who fancies trout for supper?"

"Ow," Steeleye groaned, pressing his hand to his side, "don't make me laugh, it hurts. Oh, Severa, if you could have seen your face!"

She was half-amused and half-annoyed. "How was I to know? For all I know Saxons think slugs are a delicacy."

"Then your education has just been expanded," Steeleye said severely. "But if it isn't a stupid question, what *do* you do with the animals if you don't eat them?"

"Everybody knows what Brittonic men do with sheep," Ashhere grinned.

"Same as Saxons do with pigs?" Severa retorted.

"Och, that's a myth," Drust put in, in the manner of a dispassionate expert. "'Tis just what the women look like from a distance."

Steeleye gave an exaggerated sigh and closed his eyes. "I knew it was a stupid question."

"I expect you salt them for the winter," Lilla said, poking slugs back into the pail.

Now it was Severa's turn to sigh. "If only! No, I'm afraid his lordship and his warband take the animals. To eat, I believe, but I wouldn't put anything past him."

Steeleye looked surprised. "What, he takes all of them?"

She shrugged. "Nine out of ten. More in a bad year."

"Sounds a bit steep for a food-rent. How come he's entitled to so much?"

"Entitled? What his lordship wants, he takes. Food, drink, possessions, women, whatever."

Lilla stared at her with an expression compounded from horror, pity and a fair degree of contempt. "Why do you put up with it?"

"He has a warband. What choice do we have?"

Lilla looked from her to his companions and back again. "We were a warband! But can you imagine what Deornoth would have done to us if we'd tried to take more than the lawful food-rent?"

Steeleye raised an eyebrow. "I should imagine we'd still be looking in the harbour for our heads."

"Oh, and I'm the Empress of Rome," Severa said, annoyed. Did they think she was a fool? "You fought off those robbers. You don't seriously expect me to believe a few farmers with scythes and shovels could have resisted you?"

"You mean a score of large angry men with spears," Steeleye corrected.

"Farmers with spears? Ridiculous."

"Not where we come from. Every man over fourteen has a spear and a shield and follows his lord to war when called, except slaves, cripples and half-wits. They're not as good as the full-time fighters like us, and it's as well not to rely on them if you're expecting heavy fighting, but you'd better not annoy them on their own patch unless you're very sure of your strength."

Lilla was staring at Severa in disbelief. "You mean Brittonic men don't fight? No wonder you get walked all over."

"Being able to fight back didn't do you any good!" she snapped, and saw immediately that she had hit the wrong target. Steeleye flinched as at the handling of an open wound.

"I failed," he said shortly. "That doesn't mean –"

Not 'we', Severa noticed, but 'I'. The others made frequent mistakes with the unfamiliar grammar, but not Steeleye, not in his native language. She interrupted hastily.

"Lilla, your bait's escaping!"

Three slugs teetered uncertainly on the rim of the pail, groping at empty air. Lilla flicked two of them back in, but the third recoiled from his finger, tumbled over the edge and disappeared under a squawking rush of hens.

"There's a lesson in there somewhere," Steeleye remarked. "One minute he's safe and sound in the undergrowth, chewing on a nice dead leaf, not a care in the world. Then he gets snatched up and dumped in this nasty cold pail full of worms and other riff-raff, no shelter, no food, far from home. Is he downhearted? No! he manfully sets himself to escape his prison. Inch by painful inch he struggles up the side. At last he reaches the top. Freedom! he cries. And then – " he snapped his fingers. "Out of the pail and into the chicken. Who says the Three Ladies don't have a sense of humour?"

The others laughed, and Severa gave him a baffled look. "Have you been at the mead or something?"

"No, he always talks like that," Lilla reassured her, grinning. "The trick is to nod politely until he starts making sense again." He picked up his bait pail. "How many trout does everyone want? Two each? Three?"

Drust looked at him scornfully. "Ye'll not catch enough to feed the cat with yon feeble hook." He ducked into the hut and returned with his spear. "Ye want tae watch it done properly, laddie?"

"I can catch more with a hook than you can with a spear!"

"How much will ye bet?"

They climbed the wall and jogged down to the river, still bickering cheerfully.

"Will they catch anything?" Severa asked. "I wouldn't mind a change from pottage myself."

Steeleye stretched gingerly. "Given there's a bet involved, if there's a single fish in the river it'd be well advised to hide under a stone and pray for all it's worth. I wonder if fish have gods?"

"I'll see what I can find on the moors," Ashhere offered. He picked up his own spear and raced off up the track.

"Not slugs," Steeleye called after him. "Even if it is going to disappoint a lady."

"Clown," Severa teased, smiling. As a defence mechanism it was undoubtedly effective. That flash of remembered pain had vanished as if it had never been. She slid off the bench. "Just you and me today, Steeleye. Will you lend me a hand in the dairy?"

***

There was now only one cow in milch, so the dairy work was winding down. Severa poured the new milk into settling pans, scrubbed the cheese mould and set about milling and pressing the curds that had been draining overnight. After a while, she said, "Steeleye – how does Drust catch fish with a spear? Is it possible?"

Eadwine looked up from skimming cream, a task at which he was becoming quite expert.

"He wades out into the river, stands very still until the fish think he must be a tree or a rock, and then – strike!" He made a stabbing motion with the spoon. "Like a heron."

"Doesn't he get wet through?"

Eadwine had perfected a one-shouldered shrug. "He takes his trousers off. And if it's very deep water, his tunic as well."

He waited jealously for her to invent some task that needed doing by the river, but instead Severa merely smiled and murmured, "It's a good job Gwen didn't hear you say that."

She finished churning the butter, washed it, packed it away into a barrel and scalded out the churn. Then she disappeared into her weaving shed, while Eadwine scrubbed the tables and checked the cheeses ranged on the shelves to see if any were fermenting or turning mouldy. Cheese in this state was available to be eaten on the hafod rather than taken back to the village for the winter. There was a certain amount of rivalry between Severa and Blodwen over who made the best cheese, so a neutral observer avoided a lot of unpleasantness. All the cheeses appeared to be fine, so it was devoutly to be hoped that Lilla and Drust were successful. Eadwine chased the cat out of the dairy, shut the door, and went looking for mushrooms in case they were not. There were two or three varieties that were easy even for a non-expert to recognise, and he came back to the hafod in the middle of the afternoon with a laden basket. He chased the cat out of the dairy again, blocked up a hole under one wall that he would have sworn was too small to allow access for a mouse, let alone a cat, and heard Severa swearing vigorously from the weaving shed.

"What's wrong?" he asked, putting his head round the door and then coming in so that he was not blocking the light.

The large cloth was more than half-done, a handsome chequered pattern of dark green, dark blue and dark red. Severa pointed with the weaving sword and swore again, adding another few words to Eadwine's Brittonic vocabulary. The second row of green squares had a thin red line running through the middle of it.

"I must have miscounted," she said crossly. "I'll have to unpick it all and do it again." She kicked one of the uprights, and all the weights holding the warp threads taut rattled. "Damn! Why didn't I check earlier? I wanted to finish it before Samhain!"

"Why not leave it?"

"Because it isn't right!"

"I think it looks rather attractive. More individual."

She looked startled. "You like it? With the mistake?"

"Yes. Anyway, you could put a matching line in when you get to the equivalent row at the other end." His steel-blue eyes twinkled. "Then you can claim it was deliberate. Like a border."

"Brilliant!" She clapped her hands. "I'm so glad you came here, Steeleye!"

He laughed. "So am I, Severa."

Severa felt her heart skip. She liked the way he said her name. His foreign accent suited it, making the name sound – what was the word? – exotic, rather than alien. She looked up at him. He was taller and slimmer than her husband – mind you, most men were – and his face was sharper, more strongly-cut. He looked nice when he laughed, showing very even white teeth and crinkling his eyes up at the corners. In fact, he was quite good-looking, in a way. If only he did not look so pale and tired. Something ought to be done about that.

"Steeleye – " she began, but was interrupted by the crash of the gate and a mighty shout from Drust.

"Here we are, lassies! Fish supper!"

***

Lilla and Drust came across the yard, hauling a heavy-looking basket between them. Drust had his spear over his shoulder and was whistling a jaunty tune. He dumped his end of the basket when they reached the house, looked around for a bench in the sunshine, lay down comfortably on it, folded his arms behind his head, and let out a long-drawn sigh of contentment.

"Wake me up when ye've finished, laddie," he drawled. "Loser cleans all the catch, that was the bet."

Lilla glowered at him. Drust grinned, shut his eyes, and emitted an ostentatious snore.

Eadwine gave Lilla a sympathetic look. "*Never* take a bet with Drust," he said, with feeling.

"Now you tell me," Lilla grumbled. He reached into the basket, took out a trout, and removed the head and the guts with two expert flicks of his knife.

Severa blinked, fascinated. "However did you do that? It looked like magic."

Lilla grinned. "Practice. My home was by the sea, and we near enough lived on herring."

"Herring?"

"A sort of fish that lives in the sea," Eadwine explained, "although not for very long if Lilla's around."

A second trout joined its fellow, and then a third and a fourth. The cat lost interest in the dairy, and Severa chased it away.

"Put the scraps in a bucket for the pigs," she said. "Are there many more?"

She peered into the basket, and her mouth dropped open.

"Mother of God! Are there any fish left in the river? But we'll never eat all these before they rot! What are you going to do with them?"

"Smoke them," Lilla answered, and Eadwine groaned in mock horror.

"You mean we've travelled for weeks through marsh and forest and moor and *still* not escaped your smoked fish?"

Severa laughed, kneading bread. "You don't like it, Steeleye?"

"I'm told it's an acquired taste," Eadwine said, with a straight face. "Can I watch? I've always wondered how you can take a perfectly respectable fish and turn it into something resembling an old shoe filled with bones."

"Ah, you Southrons don't understand good food. Smoked herring keeps for years."

"Since it's invariably the last thing left in the store it's just as well. Picture the scene, Severa. A time of dearth and famine. The barns empty, the fields blasted. The last rat eaten. The last cockroach hunted down. The starving people gather around their chief, an agonising choice before them. On the one hand, a miserable death. On the other, eating the smoked herring." He shuddered theatrically. "I hope it's a decision I never have to face."

Lilla grinned, and flicked the guts of the next trout in his direction. "We shan't save you any then."

"Is that a promise?"

Severa laughed again, and reflected that the hafod was going to seem very empty next year. Come to that, the village was going to seem very empty this winter. She wondered if they might be persuaded to stay beyond Samhain. Nobody travelled in winter if they could help it, and they certainly seemed happy here – except for whatever was troubling Steeleye.

***

Evening meal was much better than usual, both in quality and quantity, all the hot fresh trout and mushrooms that anyone could possibly eat. Lilla and Drust were the heroes of the hour and cheerfully recounted much-embellished fishing tales to a rapt audience. Severa laughed along with the rest, but kept a sharp eye on Steeleye across the fire. He was doing a good job of hiding it, but something was definitely wrong, and she felt she could hazard a guess at what it was.

***

"Coward! You're no son of mine –!"

Eadwine sat bolt upright with a jerk, staring into the night with unseeing eyes as the dream faded. His father's voice had sounded so real. But then, it always did. He sat gasping for air and trembling, waiting for his racing heart to slow, for his muscles to relax – or at least to become less tense – and the appalling images to die away. The fire had died down to embers and it was very dark in the hut, but the sound of even breathing and the occasional snore reassured him that he had not woken anyone else. He must not have cried out. He very rarely did. The early lessons in concealment had been well learned. He had a suspicion that he might not have been quite so controlled during his delirium, judging from the occasional odd glance he received from his friends, but to suffer dreams in a fever was understandable, was not a source of shame. He was shivering with cold now, the sweat trickling over his skin in icy rivulets. Very quietly, he groped for a handful of bracken bedding and rubbed himself down as one might a horse. Then, knowing that he did not want to endure the stuffy darkness of the hut and the peaceful snoring of a man with a clear conscience, he felt around for his clothes, pulled them on and slipped outside.

It was almost as dark outside under the overcast sky, but there was a slight stirring of breeze and although it smelled strongly of farmyard that was at least a change from onions. Eadwine sat down on the bench outside the hut, folded up his long legs and wrapped his good arm around his knees. It was warmer that way, for it must be well into October by now and the air was distinctly chill. He had no cloak and had forgotten to bring the borrowed blanket with him.

A rumbling whisper at his elbow reproved him.

"Ye took first watch."

Drust was on watch. So he had managed to sleep all through Ashhere's watch, three hours or more. That was better than usual.

"I don't need much sleep," he whispered back.

A disbelieving snort. "Ye need more than ye get."

"Drust, I didn't come out here for a chat. Go away."

A grunt of disapproval, and then he was enveloped in folds of warm woollen cloth.

"Drust, you don't need to –"

"Dinna ye freeze as well," Drust grumbled, moving away into the distance to resume his patrol. "Hasna the sense of a babe –"

Eadwine half-smiled. At least Drust was unlikely to gossip with the others. And the cloak was very welcome. He huddled gratefully into the heavy cloth. He would need a cloak before they left. Perhaps he could beg the borrowed blanket from Severa. There was no practical difference between a blanket and a cloak, both were merely large squares of woollen cloth, and the blanket was so threadbare she was probably intending to throw it out soon anyway.

A woman's giggle floated faintly across the hafod, followed by a man's sleepy murmur and another giggle. Well, somebody was awake for a good reason. Good luck to them. His friends must think they had unexpectedly landed in – what did the White Christ followers call it? – heaven. They had food, shelter, unlimited female company, and nothing to be ashamed of. They too had fled a battlefield on which their King had died, but they could excuse the disgraceful action

94

because they had been following their lord. Eadwine had no such defence. His place was beside his father, where Eadric would have been, and his duty was to defend his father to his last breath. Or, failing that, to avenge him on the field. Instead of which he had run away, and the fact that Treowin and Beortred had carried him off the field half-conscious and he had known nothing about it until it was too late did not count as an excuse.

There must have been something he could have done. Perhaps if he had spoken better at the Council he could have convinced them to stand a siege – they had not listened to a word he said, but that only meant he should have been more persuasive. Perhaps he should have tried to hold Derwentcaster. Perhaps he should not have fought the retreat at all, which would have brought him back to the city two or three days earlier. Then perhaps he could have convinced Eadric to defend the city, or at the very least it would have been his task to pursue the raiders and then he would have died in Eadric's place. Perhaps he should have known the invasion was planned, sent spies into Bernicia or something, and then he might have been able to forewarn his father. Perhaps if he had not been stunned he might have given the shattered army something to rally around, and they might have been able to fight a way back to the city and bar the gates. Perhaps he should have sent a messenger to Ceretic of Elmet earlier, before the invasion had begun, and then Ceretic might have had time to march to their aid. Perhaps he should have left the March, given up the independent command that had become so precious to him, and spent more time at court learning the political undercurrents that might have given him a clue to his brother's murder – that might even have enabled him to prevent it. Perhaps he should have tried to organise a night attack on the Bernician camp, instead of helping Heledd and Hereric to flee. Perhaps he should have found Aethelind that night and convinced her to run as far as she could, as fast as she could, instead of staying in the city to be caught in its sack.

So many ifs. It was impossible to know what would have happened with any of them, but given the scale of the disaster at least one of them would surely have been better. The trouble was, even with hindsight he did not know what he should have done instead – only that he should obviously have done something different. What would his father's first words to him be, when they met again in Woden's hall? The same words he heard in the dream? And Eadric? *"Late again, little brother,"* in a half-reproving, half-resigned tone, as if he had expected no better?

He owed it to both of them to avenge their deaths, for he was the closest adult male relative left. It was his unshakeable duty to kill their killers or die himself in the attempt. His mouth twisted bitterly at the thought. He would have died to save them and he had failed. Now he had to kill for them and he was likely to fail at that too. Avenging his father required him to overthrow Aethelferth the Twister, who was now overlord of almost all North Britannia. And avenging his brother required him to identify and track down a secret assassin. Had Beortred been the murderer? He was never likely to know now, as Beortred was dead. Beortred had died to protect him. And what had happened to Treowin? Had he reached Lundencaster safely? Or was Treowin also suffering on his account? And Aethelind – Aethelind –

He clenched his fists until the bone in his shoulder ached. On no account should he start thinking about Aethelind. Concentrate on the matter in hand instead. Find a place of refuge for his remaining friends, before Aethelferth the Twister hunted him down and they insisted on dying for him too. Unlike them, he could not simply enjoy this unexpectedly pleasant interlude without thought for the future. Friends they might be, but the relationship at bedrock was still governed by the oaths of lord and retainer. They were responsible *to* him, and he was responsible *for* them. So it was his duty to find a powerful king to offer them protection.

Which was easier said than done, for he had no powerful connections left. Through his mother he was related to the royal families of Rheged, the North Pennines and Eboracum, which sounded very impressive except that Aethelferth had already overrun all three kingdoms and their royal dynasties were either dead or refugees themselves. One half-sister was married to Aethelferth and the other to Caedbaed of Lindsey, who had already changed sides. All that remained was his tenuous link to Ceretic of Elmet, via Heledd, but even there safety was not guaranteed. Elmet was not a large kingdom, and it was almost encircled by Aethelferth's subject territories. Ceretic would be hard-pressed to withstand Aethelferth in force, and it was not fair dealing to bring trouble knowingly on a host. Quite apart from the fact that a prudent host was likely to switch sides at the first sign of trouble. But there was little choice. Lundencaster was too far to travel on foot with winter setting in, and in any case his welcome there was no more certain.

Eadwine bit down hard onto his knuckles. What use was his royal blood now? It reduced him to a piece on a gaming board, to be guarded, played or sacrificed as political expediency dictated. What use was he to his friends, with his life dependent on some foreign king's charity or political whim? They would be better off without him. He had failed Aethelind, failed the people of the March, failed his father and brother, and he was alive while those he loved were dead – or worse. Not fit to live – not fit to live.

***

Severa hesitated by the house door, watching the motionless shadow huddled on the bench, as if trying to make himself as small as possible. She knew how that felt. Should she leave him alone? If she was right, he certainly would not welcome interference. But she had taken a liking to Steeleye, as well as an interest in him, and she did not like to see him unhappy without at least trying to offer comfort if she could. He could bite her head off if he liked.

Very quietly, she slipped across the yard and sat beside him on the bench. He tensed at her approach, hunched up even more, if that were possible, and turned his shoulder to her. He could hardly tell her to go away, since it was her household, but he could make it quite clear she was not welcome. She was reminded of a hedgehog curling up behind a protective barrier of spines.

"If you slept more," she said, into the frosty silence, "you would recover quicker."

"I don't normally sleep much."

His voice was even more unfriendly than the silence. Beneath every syllable was the unspoken message, loud and clear: *Go away!*

Severa chose to ignore it. She recognised this as well.

"You aren't normally hurt almost unto death," she said crisply. "Something troubles you."

He did not answer.

"Can you tell me what it is?"

"No."

"I think you should."

The invisible spines were raised a little further. "I beg to differ."

"I know you cannot speak to your friends. You are the leader and you must never show any doubts. But you will never have to see me again after Samhain. I am in no position to judge you."

Silence.

"Why do you never talk of the battle? Your friends told me all about it in great detail."

"That must have been fascinating for you."

"I took their tales with a large pinch of salt," she said dryly. "I know nothing of war, but even I know they can't all have won the battle singlehanded."

"Especially as we lost."

Ah, she thought, hearing the bitterness in his tone, now we may be getting somewhere.

"It was not your fault."

Silence.

"It was not your fault your friends dragged you away hurt after the king was killed."

Silence.

"It was not your fault your brother and father were killed."

Severa felt the bench jolt. A hedgehog probably got a similar shock when it felt the first of the badger's talons prise beneath its spines.

"And," she went on relentlessly, "it was not your fault that you could not save Aethelind."

He recoiled, staring at her in horror.

"You can read minds," he whispered, and for the first time she saw him reach to touch the iron handle of his knife.

"If I could, I would know what is troubling you without going to all this effort. You spoke of your father and your brother and of Aethelind – whom I guess to be your wife – in your fever, the first night you were here –"

His face contorted, and she thought for a moment he was going to be sick.

"Frija," he said, very quietly. "You. That was underhand, lady."

"It seemed to give you comfort. I thought you might as well die happy."

"I should have smelt a rat when Frija wanted me to speak in Brittonic," he said bitterly. "I made an utter fool of myself, I suppose."

"I would not say that."

"You don't know!"

"I rather think I do," she said quietly. "You think you failed them somehow. That if you had acted differently, things would have gone otherwise and your father and brother would still be alive. You would have died so that they might live, and now you hate yourself for living when they are dead. And you think they hate you too, from beyond the grave. Is it not so?"

She had guessed right. His voice was unsteady, and he turned his face away. "Truly you read minds –"

"No," she said gently. "I have been there myself. Men do battle on the field, women in the birthing chamber. When I lost my children, I was very ill, as you have been. I was sure that the miscarriage was my fault, that I had done something, or failed to do something, that had killed my children. I relived the time over and over again, trying to see how I should have known, what else I should have done. I dreaded telling my husband, for he had so much wanted a son, and I had failed him. You see – a late miscarriage – of twins especially –

does much – damage – and the midwife said – there will never be another chance. I – I – I – even wished for a time that he would not come back, so I would not have to face his anger – and he – he never did – !"

She broke down. Acting on instinct, Eadwine put his arm around her and drew her to him. At first she resisted, and then suddenly she threw her arms about him and sobbed against his shoulder as if her heart was breaking.

"I am so sorry –" she gasped, after a while. "I – I – thought to give comfort, not to take it –"

"You have, in a way." His own face was wet with tears. "At least I no longer feel I am losing my mind, if someone else has felt the same."

"If I have helped, even a little, I am glad. Blodwen's mother-in-law helped me, a little. But there is not much that really helps – only time – " She sniffed, and sat up. "It does get better. A bit. Eventually. You may trust me on that." She rubbed her eyes. "Do you – did you – have children?"

"No."

"And you were not angry with your wife?"

"We were not married, only betrothed. That was my fault, too. But it is not, surely, something that any man would hold against his wife."

"Do you think so? Do you think he will still want me, when he comes back?"

"If I was him, *I* would."

"Will you go back for your wife – your lady?"

Eadwine had not thought of that, in all the nights his mind had been trudging its weary treadmill. Was it possible that he could rescue Aethelind from whatever had happened to her? Salvage something from the wreck? Was that too much to hope for?

"I don't even know if she is still alive – or if she would have me now – I failed her –"

Severa brushed at her eyes again. "I would have my husband back on any terms."

The certainty in her tone took Eadwine's breath away. Hope flickered up like a dying fire stirred into life. Vengeance was an absolute duty but a cold one, even if it was achievable. It might satisfy honour, but it could bring him no joy. Protecting Aethelind, as he had sworn to do, was also an absolute duty, but one that might have love and life and hope at the end of it. Severa could have given him no greater gift.

***

Hereward strode back to Eoforwic in a black temper. He had seen plenty of the aftermath of war, but the sack of Eboracum was different.

"Animals!" he muttered to himself. "Scum! These aren't foreigners and slaves, these are Anglian girls! Like their own wives and daughters!"

He stomped up to the looted hall, scowling. No doubt they would have to go and fight somebody for a stolen pig, and then butcher it and roast bits of it over the fire, burning their fingers and then choking on half-raw meat coated with charcoal. And then he'd have to sleep on the floor among his spearmen, who could snore for Bernicia, and if he got any sleep at all he would wake up with a crick in his neck and a stiff back. He was getting too old for this, and too bad-tempered. He banged open the door.

The hall had been tidied up, the furniture righted and the fire lit. His spearmen were ranged demurely along one of the tables, politely handing plates and cups down the line. They looked a trifle sheepish, and a lot cleaner than usual.

"Er – lord – the lady said we was to wash before dinner," one of them ventured. He pointed to the end of the table nearest the door, which held an empty basin, a large pitcher of clean water and a towel.

"Dinner?" said Hereward vaguely, and then registered the appetising smell, the cauldron bubbling gently over the fire, the beer barrel and the large pile of freshly-baked loaves. "Oh. Right." He washed obediently – where there was a lady of the house her word was law in domestic matters – and took the place of honour in the middle of the top table. He sniffed appreciatively. This was more like it.

***

Aethelind listened by the door in the family chamber until she was sure the contented chomping from the hall was well under way. Then she turned to the bed. Not her own small bed, which was neatly tucked away against the wall, but the big bed her father had shared with her mother, and then with the numerous concubines of his cheerfully squalid widowerhood. She smoothed down the clean sheets, plumped up the feather pillows, and gave the coverlet a final twitch. She hated disorder and had been itching to manage the house properly for years.

The looters had overturned her coffers and scattered the contents, but there had been more disarray than actual destruction and Aethelind had spent the afternoon setting things to rights. She lifted out her best gown, the rich deep blue one with the embroidery a foot deep around the hem, and laid it on the bed. It would have been her wedding dress, and she shed a few tears for Eadwine before pulling herself together and dabbing her eyes dry. A woman needed a man, and Hereward was strong, had his own hearth-troop, and most importantly he was here. Besides, it was a pity to waste all the embroidery. Her best under-dress had also survived, and she changed into it and smoothed it down. The very best white silk, and she could not guess how much her father had had to give the foreign merchant for it. It looked very modest and virginal, until you realised it was so fine it was almost transparent. Aethelind's father had reckoned, with good reason, that his daughter's face was not her only fortune. Her best jewellery was all gone, but at the bottom of the coffer she found a pair of intricate silver filigree brooches, given to her by Eadwine as a betrothal gift. She had never liked them much – her taste ran more to half a pound of gold and gemstones – but they were graceful and delicate and anyway they were all she had left. She fastened the gown at her shoulders, draping the front rather lower than usual, and tied the girdle into place so that it would accentuate her hourglass figure. The little brooches looked very pretty against the deep blue of the dress. More rummaging located the festoon of beads that went with them, beautifully-wrought beads of gleaming blue glass. The exact colour of her eyes, Eadwine had said when he gave them to her, like a midsummer sky. He was always saying things like that, and again Aethelind mourned briefly for her lost prince before fastening the festoon neatly into place. She hung the household keys from her girdle, slipped her feet into her best house shoes, and then had the happy thought of retying the girdle so that just a glimpse of well-turned ankle showed beneath the hem of her gown. She combed out her long golden hair and considered for some time whether she should adorn it with some ornament, before deciding that the pure maiden look was best and leaving it to flow free. She gave the great friendship cup a final polish – the gold one had been stolen, but she had unearthed the old carved wooden cup from a dusty coffer – and filled it with mead.

She took a deep breath, whispered a brief prayer to Frija, and turned to the door. She was ready.

***

Hereward gaped as the chamber door opened and a vision of loveliness stepped over the threshold. Surely he wasn't that drunk? Anyway, he never saw visions like that when he was drunk.

The vision glided gracefully across the room, carrying a great carved wooden cup in both hands, and offered it to him.

"Good health, my lord," she murmured.

"Er – I thank you, my lady," Hereward mumbled, automatically.

Her fingers lingered on his as he took the cup, but she kept her eyes demurely downcast. Such a beautiful girl, so delicate, so fragile, so in need of a man. For protection, of course.

He could not take his eyes off her as she moved about the hall, carrying the cup to each of his spearmen in turn. The men seemed equally smitten, their heads turning like sunflowers to the sun, but the girl gave none of them a second glance. Very proper. Maidenly modesty. Hereward liked to see that in a girl.

She came to stand before him, and drank from the cup herself. Her eyes met his over the rim, cornflower blue, and there was a flash of invitation in them before she dropped her gaze. Hereward shifted in his chair and wondered how he could get her to look at him again.

She set the cup on the table, and kneeled gracefully at his feet. She raised her head and gave him the full force of her cornflower blue gaze. Her hair rippled over her shoulders like threads of spun gold, framing a face that a man might die for and a long column of slender white throat.

Aethelind saw Hereward's gaze leave her eyes and slide down the front of her gown as if on a magnet. So he had one thing in common with Eadwine. She shifted her position slightly to give him a better view.

"My lord," she murmured, in a low voice that managed to be submissive and inviting all at once.

Hereward gulped, and his eyes came back to her face. "What's your name, lass? Lady?"

"Aethelind, my lord," she said softly.

"Aethelind," repeated Hereward thickly, "that's a lovely name –"

And Aethelind gave him the full benefit of her very best smile.

Chapter 11

"He likes that girl," Lilla commented one evening. Eadwine was helping Severa refill her weaving shuttles, holding the hank taut for her while she wound the thread onto the shuttles. It was a monotonous task that required little concentration and did not interfere with a lively conversation.

"Good," said Ashhere. "Seems unfair that we should have all the fun." He caught Blodwen's eye across the fire and winked at her. "What do they find to talk about so much though, that's what puzzles me?"

Lilla concentrated. His Brittonic was already better than Ashhere's. "Well, right now he's trying to explain about the sea and what a ship is. Earlier it was what plants you use for which colours, and before that it was how do mountain hares know to turn white in winter."

100

"Do they?"

"Apparently."

Ashhere shrugged, thinking that he had managed all his life so far without that piece of information and saw no immediate need for it in the future. "Well, it keeps him happy."

"I hope so," Lilla said thoughtfully.

Ashhere grinned, and nudged him. "He's cheered up a lot since you started going fishing, and he doesn't like trout *that* much."

Lilla laughed. They had all noticed that Eadwine's spirits and health seemed to be picking up in some indefinable manner, and there had been much speculation over the reason. The leading theory, inevitably, was that he might have begun an affair with Severa, although there was so little evidence in support that even Drust was not prepared to take a bet on it.

***

Eadwine was aware of the speculation and chose to ignore it. What he had found in Severa was a rarer commodity, another mind. As long as he took care to keep away from anything that might betray his identity or his origins, he could raise any subject that came into his head and be sure of an intelligent response. He and Severa were from utterly different worlds, his the luxury and violence of a royal court, hers the workaday foundation on which all such luxury depended. And yet they had in common the experience of being different, of not quite fitting correctly into the spaces they were supposed to occupy, of not always thinking and feeling as they were expected to think and feel, and often that produced an echo of recognition so startling it was like a physical shock. She had given him not only pity – which he always distrusted as akin to contempt – but understanding without judgment. Although the dreams still came they were not now so overwhelming, and he was more able to think of the future. He still could not see how his obligations could be achieved, but he had begun to treat them as problems to be solved rather than disasters to be feared. Whatever the truth about Eadric's death, he was sure that Beortred was the key to it, and even if Beortred could no longer speak there might be some clue on his dead body. It would be unfair to Beortred's memory to share his suspicions, but there was another excuse he could use to search for the remains.

***

Severa wound the last shuttle and picked up her spinning, and Eadwine came to sit with his friends.

"I've been thinking," he announced, and laughed as they exchanged resigned glances. "Poor Beortred. Don't you think we owe him a decent funeral?"

"Who is this?" Severa enquired, winding the new thread around her drop spindle before setting it spinning down again.

"We had a companion, on the moors, before Ashhere found you," he explained. "He was killed by a troll and –"

"A what?"

Eadwine realised he had used the Anglian word for troll and searched his memory for the Brittonic equivalent. There didn't seem to be one. He tried to explain about giant human-shaped creatures made of stone, who lived in wild and rocky places and preyed on travellers.

Severa shook her glossy dark head. "None of those round here," she said.

Drust grinned. An ally at last.

"We all heard it!" Ashhere protested, and put his hand to his new wooden hammer amulet. "And I saw it!"

Severa raised an eloquent eyebrow and spun another length of thread. The other women giggled. Ashhere sulked.

"Well," Eadwine said hastily, "whatever it was, something killed poor Beortred while he was trying to protect us from it. The least we can do is go and search for his body and build him a funeral pyre."

"Where did he die, Steeleye?"

"We last saw Beortred among the – the – rock outcrops –?"

"Tors. Which ones?"

"It must have been quite near where you found us, because we can't have got far."

"Nae distance at all," Drust said. "Ye look like ye weigh nothing, until we have tae carry ye."

Eadwine looked across at Severa. "Could you direct us, Severa?"

"I'll do better than that, I'll come with you. We can take the sheep that way tomorrow. There's hardly anything left to do in the dairy and I've hardly been off this hafod all summer. A change will do me good."

**

It was the first time Eadwine had been up on the moors, conscious at least, and the weather obliged with a bright clear day. It was cold first thing, so he borrowed the threadbare blanket to use as a cloak, fastening it with the brooch they had taken from the dead thieves. There had been no opportunity to replace his lost shoe, but he was accustomed now to going barefoot around the hafod so it was no great hardship. He was very pleased to find that he could manage the climb all the way up through the woods without having to stop, although he was grateful that the sheep didn't move especially fast.

They paused a little way above the treeline, ostensibly so that he could admire the view, although he suspected that it was really a tactful excuse to allow him to rest. The view was worth admiring, though. The Derwent valley snaked away north-south, filled by woodland that was now beginning to flame with autumn colours. The trees lapped high onto the surrounding moors, fading gradually into lower vegetation to leave just the flat tops of the high ground bare of tree cover, like overturned boats half-submerged in the sea. Close at hand, the moorland vegetation was an intricate mixture of stringy grass, faded heather, low shrubs and the occasional rowan. The slanting sun lit up the rowan berries like jewels, and picked out subtle hues of gold, russet and brown. The moor formed a wide tilted shelf, and the sheep spread out over it and began quietly grazing. Only the tearing sound of masticated grass, a few bleats, the occasional bird call and the wind sighing through the grass broke the deep and tranquil quiet. It was like standing on top of the world. Eadwine took a deep breath of the fresh, peat-scented air. He had always liked high places.

All along the eastern horizon, an irregular row of boulders and tors marked the edge of a slightly higher plateau. The rock was dark grey in colour and curiously rounded, like stacked cushions or piled cakes of bread. At close quarters it was coarse-grained and abrasive, full of large rounded pebbles and occasional tiny flecks that caught the light and sparkled in the sun.

"What a strange rock," Eadwine said, turning a pebble in his fingers.

Severa glanced at him. It took some doing to be interested in rocks. "Is it? All the rock is like that on these moors. It makes good querns and grinding stones. We call it gritstone."

102

"Seems appropriate," Eadwine said, dropping the pebble. "So you brought me all the way down from here? I'm impressed."

"That's where you were camped," Severa said, pointing out a jumble of outcrop and boulders to their left. "And you had come from that direction."

Eadwine followed her gesture across the brindled moorland. A short distance away to the south, a gritstone tor reared its stepped profile against the bright sky.

"Let's start there."

***

They had steeled themselves for a scene of grisly feast and slaughter. Even Severa, adamant that there were no trolls on her moors, was prepared for the gruesome results of a fall from the tor and several weeks' attention by wolves and buzzards. But there was nothing at all. They searched below the rocks, above them, among them, and found not so much as a bloodstain.

"This is ridiculous," Eadwine said, after they had scoured the area for the third time. "We know this is the right place." They had found his missing shoe and Ashhere's dropped amulet. "We all heard the fight. So why can't we find anything?"

"Trolls eat their victims –" Ashhere began.

"I know that, but nothing left at all? Not even a shoe, or a belt-buckle?"

"They carried him away to their lair?" Lilla suggested hesitantly.

"Where are the footprints? Look at the trampling we managed to make, all along the top of the rocks here. Everyone says trolls are big. Heavy. They ought to leave more of a trail than five men."

"They flew away?" Drust suggested with a wicked smile, flapping his arms up and down by way of demonstration.

"Trolls can't fly," Ashhere said scornfully. "Everyone knows that."

Drust shrugged, and went back to contemplating the view. In his opinion, beasts that didn't exist might just as well fly as not, but it wasn't worth arguing over.

"But what happened?" Eadwine persisted. "It's as if the earth opened up and swallowed him!"

Ashhere, who had been standing near a crevice in the gritstone pavement, jumped back hastily and eyed it with some alarm. Drust grinned and Severa, who was sitting on top of the tor spinning wool and watching their growing mystification with some amusement, laughed.

"Your friend is frightened of something?" she called down. Eadwine translated briefly from Anglian, and she looked thoughtful. "In the village, people say there are cracks in the earth that lead to Annwn, to the Otherworld. At Samhain Eve Arawn the Lord of Annwn leads the dead out to ride over the earth, and if they find you alone out of doors they may drag you back with them." She crossed herself hurriedly. "But those portals are near Navio fort. Not here."

"How does she know?" Ashhere demanded. He eyed the tor askance as if he expected it to gape open and swallow them all on the spot.

"How do you know trolls can't fly?" Drust retorted.

"All right," Eadwine interrupted, before the argument could get going. "So he didn't fly away and the earth didn't swallow him. But he certainly isn't here. So where did he go?"

Drust looked round with more interest. "Ye think he wasna deid?"

"I'm beginning to wonder."

103

"But we all heard him scream," Lilla said, shuddering at the memory.

"Maybe he wasn't killed," Ashhere began, "and crawled away later…." His voice trailed away, as they all shared a mental image of Beortred dying in pain and cold and hunger in this wild place.

Eadwine shook his head vigorously. "That makes no sense either. He would have left some sort of trail, and Lilla would have seen it today. Oh, damn! What are we missing?"

***

"A rare species of flying troll?" Severa suggested, handing round the bread.

Eadwine put his hand over his eyes. "Oh, don't you start."

She laughed. "Myself, I think it most likely he fell from the rocks, confused by mist and fear. Many have done so. But it's strange there is no trace. Could your friend have missed his tracks?"

Eadwine shook his head, swallowing a mouthful of bread and cheese. "Lilla could track the west wind."

"And anything heavier than a bird leaves marks in this soft ground. Why, even I could track Ashhere back to your camp in the boulders, that first day. And the trail you made is plain to see, even after three weeks." She gestured along the edge, where the scar of churned peat was an untidy black stripe. "It's a mystery, to be sure."

"That's it!" Eadwine jumped to his feet, dropping the remainder of his bread. A lamb and its mother, ever alert for such an opportunity, scuffled for it and the mother won. "Severa, you're a marvel!"

She was laughing at his sudden enthusiasm and the baffled looks of his friends. "I am? How so?"

"How could you get away from here without leaving a trail? *By following the one that's already there!*"

***

"By the Hammer, you're right!" Lilla beckoned them forward and pointed to a single footprint among the jumble of churned peat, the first clear print they had seen. It was blurred and smudged by rain, but the outline of heel and toe were clearly visible. It was pointing south.

Lilla put his foot alongside it. "It's about the right size, too."

"Beard of Woden!" Ashhere breathed. "It's as if he was leaving us on purpose and covering his tracks. But why?"

"'Tis tae do with yon strange knife, no?" Drust said shrewdly. "I saw ye looking hard at it, and I saw he didna like it. But I dinna ken why."

"I'll explain later," Eadwine said. "Lilla, could you tell if these prints leave the main trail?"

"Yes, now I know what to look for. You stay here until I tell you to come on."

Eadwine turned to Severa, who had insisted on accompanying them. "Do others go this way, Severa? Shepherds? Hunters?"

She shook her head. "No. We come from the valley up to the hills and back down again by the straightest way. Besides, if a shepherd had been along here there would be sheep tracks, no?"

"Good point. Where do you get to, if you keep on in this direction?"

"If you go far enough, the Great Stone Edge and Heatherford village. Blodwen comes from there, and Gwen is to marry one of the farmers after Samhain. By the valley it is an afternoon's walk from our village."

"And beyond that?" He scrambled up to the tor beside them. "Can we see from up here?"

They crowded onto the topmost platform. The wide shelf of moorland that swelled above the hafod had gone, and from this tor they could see over a subsidiary ridge and down into the Derwent valley. Opposite, a low hill crowned by twin rocky outcrops just poked out of the trees, and beyond it more flat, dark moors swelled above the forest and rolled away into the west.

"That is Kyndyr," Severa said, pointing due west to a cliff-sided plateau. "To its north you have the Bleak Hills, and between them runs the army-path in its valley —"

"An army-path, did you say?" Eadwine interrupted. "You didn't mention that before."

"You didn't ask. Is it important?"

"It might be. Where does it go?"

"Through the hills to another fort, that my grandfather called Ardotalia. And then on north and west to the mountains and the sea, to his own country."

"And in the other direction?"

She swept her hand southwards in a wide gesture. "Around this end of Kyndyr, then along the far flank of the Withy Hill — you can only see the summit from here, but it is a long ridge in that direction — and so between the Withy Hill and the Swine Hill — "

"The conical one?"

"Yes — and so down to Navio fort and the mines below the Shivering Mountain — you see it there, through the gap, it is connected to the Swine Hill by a long ridge. Arawn sleeps beneath it, and when the miners go too deep and disturb him, he turns in his sleep and the mountain shakes and the rocks slide down. Or so it is said."

"Mines? What do they mine there?"

"Lead, and silver, and the Tears of Annwn."

"Which are —?"

"Blue and white and yellow stones. Like these." She reached for the second string around her neck, not the one that held the cross, and lifted out a pendant of dull pewter set with a large blue stone veined with white. "They are valuable, so I keep this hidden. My grandfather was given these by a grateful patient, a matched pair. He gave them to me when I was betrothed, and had them set each into a pendant, one for me and one for my husband." She slipped the pendant back down the top of her dress, and pointed again into the distance.

"Opposite the Shivering Mountain is the Portal of Annwn, the gate into the Otherworld, where the icy-cold Water of Annwn rushes out and flows past Navio. At Navio the army-path branches. One way goes south and west to Calchvynydd, the Limestone Hills. The Lord of Navio is at feud with the Lord of Calchvynydd, and his men patrol a great dyke that cuts the road, and no-one goes that way except the two lords and their soldiers."

So if Beortred had found this army-path, he could not have taken the south-west route.

"And the other branch?"

"East, along the Water of Annwn, until it joins the Derwent." She pointed due south, along the snaking valley of the Derwent. "After it has passed the Withy Hill the Derwent turns more east than south and runs below the Great Stone Edge. It is like this edge we are standing on – flat moorland that stops suddenly in cliffs and then slopes that fall steeply to the river. The army-path crosses the Derwent at our village, Derwent Bridge, then it goes along the north bank to Heatherford, and then it climbs above the village and crosses the Great Stone Edge by a flight of steps cut in the rock, and then it goes east over the moor. The moor is not wide there, and Blodwen says that you can see where the moors stop and the road goes down into the endless forest. Where it goes after that you would know better than me. You are the only people in my lifetime to have come from that direction."

"Wait a minute," Eadwine said, sorting the names and what he could see of the topography into some semblance of order. "You say that if you keep following the moor in this direction, above the valley, you would get to this Heatherford? Where the army-path crosses the moors?"

"Yes."

"From here, how long would it take to walk there?"

"Two, three hours." She glanced up at the sun. "You have time, but when you cross Chilbage Brook – you can just see the fold in the land – you are on Heatherford ground. Their shepherds will see you and they will not welcome four strangers, armed. They will think you are thieves – perish the thought – and I will *not* have you picking a fight with them – Blodwen's family and Gwen's future husband."

"I had rather we were not seen, in any case. The fewer people know we are here, the better."

"Better get off the tor, then. We aren't exactly inconspicuous up here. Your friend is waving for you, anyway. "

Lilla had found the place where they had floundered up out of the morass and on to the firmer ground of the edge, a sorry trail of bog holes and splattered peat. And more than this, he had found a few prints, just one or two and none of them very clear, but undoubtedly continuing south along the edge. They followed the direction, past more outcrops of weirdly shaped rocks, until the land began to fall away south over a wide heather slope into a shallow valley.

"You had better stop here, Steeleye," Severa said softly. "Heatherford's sheep are grazing Chilbage Brook today, and I see Rhun and Rhonabwy with them."

Eadwine spoke a few quiet words, and all four men went immediately to ground, vanishing into the heather or behind boulders with hardly a sound.

"That's a pain," Ashhere grumbled, when the reason for the halt had been pointed out. "Will they have gone if we come back tomorrow?"

"I think I've lost the trail," Lilla hissed. "I last saw a print two or three hundred paces back, and he could have gone anywhere down this slope. It'd take days to search it properly, and the other side looks much the same. Is there a ford over that brook, where we might pick it up again?"

"You can ford the stream anywhere," Severa answered, when this query was relayed. "Plenty of places you can boulder-hop across without even getting your feet wet. You think your friend came this way? To find the army-path?"

"Possibly," Eadwine said cautiously. "It's almost certainly the quickest way out of the district, and it looks as if he – or at least somebody with his size of feet and one shoe missing – was going somewhere."

"Then I'll go and ask Rhun and Rhonabwy. Unless he was very careful, somebody would have seen him, whether he went west through Heatherford village or east over the Edge. Strangers in these parts are news."

"Can you trust them?"

"I won't tell them about you, what do you take me for? I'll say I'm looking for a lost ewe – their sheep and ours are always getting mixed up – and ask for any news. Rhun will tell me all the happenings in Heatherford down to an escaped chicken. He loves to gossip. You stay here."

She put two fingers in her mouth and whistled, the piercing shepherd's whistle that carries over hill and dale, and the two distant figures on the sheep-dotted hillside jumped up, peered across the valley, and waved back.

Eadwine watched her bound lithely down the slope through the heather and hop nimbly across the brook. Graceful as a running deer, he thought, like the spirit of this wild but strangely beautiful landscape –

Drust nudged him for a second time.

"I said, can ye trust her?"

"If she meant us harm she could have sent word to the fort and got us arrested, or murdered us that first night in the hafod when we didn't set a watch, or just left us on the moors to starve. Anyway, you have a better idea? We must find out whether Beortred did come this way."

"Why would he?" Lilla wanted to know. "Was he looking for us, after he escaped from the troll?"

"Not for us, I think," Eadwine muttered darkly.

"What –?"

"Shh, she's coming back. I'll explain later."

***

"He was this tall, Rhun says," Severa reported, holding her hand above her head to indicate someone roughly the same height as Ashhere. "Heavy-built, strong, hard-looking. Scarred face. Not the kind you'd want to get into a fight with. Definitely not wounded or injured. Fair hair and beard, that's how Rhun knew straight off he was a foreigner. Filthy, wet, ragged. Left shoe missing. Cloak might have been green. Carried a spear. Sneezed a lot."

"That's him!" Ashhere said excitedly. "That's him exactly!"

"Rhun saw him in the middle of the day, about three weeks ago. He was carrying a hare on his spear, coming from the north across the moors. When he struck the army-path he turned east onto it, walking fast and looking over his shoulder and all around, like a man in fear of pursuit. The last Rhun saw of him was a black dot, still following the road across the moor as fast as he could go." She looked around at the nodding heads and the puzzled faces. "So your dead friend is alive and well and hurrying back where you came from? Why would he do that?"

***

Eadwine had considered long and hard before deciding to tell his companions his suspicions about Beortred and Eadric's death. He had no proof, and to spread slander about another man was a shameful thing. But if he was going to expect them to risk their lives hunting down an assassin, they had a right to know why.

Lilla was the first to find his voice. "It doesn't seem possible," he said, into the shocked silence. "He seemed so – so honest. I can't imagine him as a murderer."

"Neither can I," Eadwine said heavily. "But how else explain the knife? I've only ever seen one knife that shape in my life."

"But his own lord!"

"I know."

"Ye'll have tae kill him," said Drust.

"I have to have proof first," Eadwine answered evenly. "There is no honour in killing the wrong man while the guilty one goes free. But if it is true that he murdered my brother, yes, I shall kill him. Eadric would expect no less."

The words, so quietly and calmly spoken, were somehow far more menacing than a furious oath sworn by all the gods in turn. Ashhere shivered. There were occasions when he sensed something out of the ordinary in Eadwine, something that made him superstitiously wonder if the family really did descend from the gods, and it frightened him a little.

Drust was scowling. "'Twas a sneaky thing, faking yon fight and fooling us all."

"We fooled ourselves," Eadwine answered, with an edge in his tone. He was annoyed with himself for having shared the careless assumption. If he had not been hurt and forced to linger here, he would have missed the one clue that might lead him to his brother's killer. "But I don't think he faked the fight. The one thing I remember clearly about that night is Beortred's face. I'd take a bet that he was as terrified as we were, that he really believed he was going to his death. And –" he hesitated "– and that he welcomed it. Honourable death in battle is an easy way out of all sorts of tangles, if you can get it. But then in the morning he found he wasn't dead and there was no troll and no sign of us, so he decided to run."

Ashhere's puzzled expression deepened. "Run from what?"

"Us," said Drust, as if it was the most obvious thing in the world.

Eadwine ran his hands through his hair and started absently twisting it into knots. "Maybe – I don't know."

"Ye'd guessed his secret. He knew ye'd have tae kill him. So he'd have tae kill ye first or flee."

"If he was the murderer," Eadwine said slowly. "Don't jump to conclusions. We've done too much of that already. Stick to what we know." He began checking off points on his fingers. "I know Eadric was murdered. I'm sure it was with Beortred's knife. When Beortred thought I had guessed that, he tried to get himself killed and then he ran away. I agree that makes it look likely that Beortred was the murderer. But it doesn't prove it."

"If he wasn't," argued Lilla, "why run?"

"Good question. But if he murdered Eadric, why was he so keen to stay with me in the first place, knowing that if I ever found out I'd be obliged to kill him for it? And the last thing he said was *I couldn't save your brother but I'll save you*. If that was a lie it was a very good one, and Beortred never struck me as a good liar."

"Did you know him, then?"

"Well, I thought I did. I met him at Eadric's hall, before I came to the March. He seemed a decent sort. Uncomplicated. A good hunter, a good fighter, not overly given to thinking, absolutely trustworthy."

"And now we think he stabbed his own lord in the back. It doesn't make any sense," Ashhere complained. "Not to me, anyway."

"Nor me either," Eadwine agreed. "But one thing I am sure of, Beortred knows something very important about the murder. So I have to find him."

"How?" Lilla wanted to know. "I can't track him any further."

"Princess Heledd feared that whoever assassinated Eadric would try to kill Hereric too. If she is right, and if Beortred was the murderer – or if he knows who is – then eventually he will make for Loidis."

Ashhere's brow furrowed. "Is that where you were sending them? Well, if *I* didn't know, how would he know?"

"He wouldn't. Rhonwen is the only person in Eboracum who knew their destination, except Heledd and me. But it wouldn't be hard for someone of average intelligence to guess."

Drust sniggered. Eadwine ignored him. "Heledd is a Princess of Elmet. Where else could she go? Besides, Ceretic will hardly keep Hereric's presence at his court a secret, assuming they reached Loidis safely, of course. The last atheling of Deira could be a useful gaming piece to have on your half of the board. I think we can be fairly confident that Beortred will soon know where they are. Whether he will follow them is another matter. But there's only one way to find out. Are you willing to come with me?"

"We'll follow you to the death," said Ashhere stoutly.

"Of course," Lilla said. "We were going to Elmet with you anyway."

"That was before I expected to find a murderer there."

"Doesna matter," growled Drust. "When do we leave?"

Eadwine flexed his damaged shoulder, grimaced, tested the muscles in his side and grimaced again. "As soon as I'm mended. There's nothing more to wait for. I know the way there now without having to bother with the Lord of Navio. Which I must say is a relief, because he sounds a nasty piece of work."

Drust gave him a look that might have been called admiring. "I said ye'd work out where we are."

"Not exactly, but I know how to get to Elmet. The army-path, remember. Severa said it went to this place called Ardotalia and then to her grandfather's country, and she told me earlier that he came from Caer Luel."

They looked at him expectantly, puzzled but trusting.

"The main road to Caer Luel branches off from Dere Street at Catraeth and goes over the Pennines," he expanded. "But one of Heledd's wandering skalds told me you can get from Loidis to Caer Luel without going via Catraeth. He didn't see why he should have to pay tolls to Deira if he wanted to travel from Elmet to Rheged. So there must be another army-path over the Pennines from Loidis, and that must join on to this army-path to Caer Luel that goes through here, probably somewhere near this Ardotalia place, or a bit beyond. If we follow this one north and then take the first branch east that ought to land us in Loidis eventually. We'll need food for three or four days, I should think. I'll talk to Severa in the morning."

***

"Leaving?" Severa said, with something that might have been disappointment. "Yes, I know, I know. You were always going to leave at Samhain. I just hadn't thought – Yes, yes, of course I'll give you provisions. You can have the smoked fish, for a start. I'll make you twice-baked bread for travelling, but do make Gwen do her fair share of the grinding and *don't* accept her excuses. But why suddenly talk about leaving now? It's something to do with your dead friend, who isn't dead after all, isn't it? But you'll stay 'til Samhain? I was relying on you to help us drive the livestock back to the village. You wouldn't let us down?"

***

"Dead?" repeated Aethelferth, surprised. "Are you sure?"

"Soft Southrons, Lord King," said the fat guard, sweating. "No grit."

Aethelferth swore, and kicked a chair across the room.

"Throw the corpse in the ditch," he said briefly. At least he could deny the bastard a decent burial.

"Already done that, Lord King."

"Get out."

Once safely out of the hall, the fat guard relaxed a little and mopped his sweating face on his sleeve. He had got away with it. The handsome prisoner was not dead but securely tied up in a peasant hovel not a quarter of a mile from this hall. The fat guard scratched, pleased with himself. He could hardly wait for the night to come again.

***

In the sacred grove, Aethelferth stared at the mail shirt, helmet and sword hanging from the oak tree and swore again. Fear griped in his belly. It was three weeks since the battle, and still there was no atheling's body to go with the armour. Still he had not fulfilled his pledge. Everything he had worked for, everything he was, everything he lived by was dependent on continued success in battle. Dependent on the continued favour of the Terrible One. Was he to lose that because of one wretched youth? Never! If it cost all his life, all his kingdoms, he must keep his promise to the war god. And now the miserable impostor, who knew where Eadwine was, had gone and died and Aethelferth was back to the beginning.

So start at the beginning. He knew Eadwine had been wounded on the field. They had all seen it. Where, and how badly? He reached out to the mail shirt and turned it over in his hands, noting the broken links and the score marks – and the rent. He poked his hand through it. A gash, three fingers broad, over the left side of the waist. And it was not from some old skirmish, for the broken rings were thickly coated with recent blood. Royal blood?

"That stubborn bastard didn't have a hole in him there," commented the Brittonic captain, drawing the same conclusion.

"Where did you catch him?"

"On the Great South Road, past Lindum, four days after the battle."

Aethelferth studied his fingers poking through the bloody hole in the mail shirt.

"A gut wound," he said. "A man with a gut wound cannot ride far or fast. So Eadwine left the road, to hide and lick his wounds. South of the Aire, for if one crossed they probably all did, but north of where you caught up and probably north of Lindum. But on which side?"

"East," said the Brittonic captain promptly. "Trying to get to the coast, get a ship –"

"It's a long way through Lindsey, and with the Trent to cross, and Caedbaed has all the roads and fords watched. He would have been caught." Aethelferth frowned. "West. Into the forests, into the hills, where no king rules. Probably making for Elmet, to join the other brat at Ceretic's court. Yes. Go and find him."

***

Ceretic listened, a sly smile on his face. This was the second envoy in three weeks on the same subject. Whatever the reason for Aethelferth's concern with Eadwine, it seemed to be bordering on obsession. An obsession that could turn out to be highly profitable for Ceretic. How much could he extract from Aethelferth for Eadwine's death? The legendary treasure of Eboracum? Another province from Aethelferth's vast conquered territories? Perhaps the rest of the Pennines, perhaps Craven or part of South Rheged. Oh, yes, Eadwine could be an extremely useful bargaining counter. It was time to join the hunt.

Chapter 12

Severa sighed as she dismantled her loom and put it away. The large chequered cloth was finished – complete with matching impromptu border – and there were still three days to go until Samhain. She should have been pleased. But instead it merely reminded her that in three days the four men would leave and she would be alone again in her empty house for the winter. She would miss them. If she was honest with herself, she would miss Steeleye. She would miss his quick mind, that skipped from one idea to another like a squirrel through the treetops, and his courtesy, and his instant comprehension, and – admit it – his long legs and his swift smile and his expressive face and his piercing hawk's eyes.

She bit her lip, angry with herself for such a thought. No good could come of it. She had liked Steeleye from the first – despite her sensible suspicion of armed strangers – and compassion had quickly turned into an easy friendship that had filled the dying summer with light and colour and laughter. To allow it to turn into anything else would be folly. A crippled hawk might take temporary refuge in a chicken hut to save its life, but as soon as it could fly again it would be gone, back to its own world of the free sky and the hunt. Steeleye no longer needed a sling, and although it would be some time before his disused muscles recovered their full strength and suppleness, to all intents and purposes he was cured. He rarely stayed on the hafod now, usually joining his friends on the hunting expeditions that had become a regular part of life, and although he never spoke of where he would go or what he would do, she knew he was busy with plans. Plans that did not – could not – include her. All she could be to him was a notch on his belt-buckle, and in a few weeks time he would even have forgotten which one she was. Far better to stay true to her absent husband. Iddon had given her a respected position in a village away from her family, he had valued her for her dowry, her household skills and her breeding potential, and if the tender memories she treasured were largely a product of her imagination, he had at least treated her with due respect. His absence beyond a year gave her the right to declare the marriage ended, but that would reduce her status from headman's wife to childless widow, and she had no desire to return to her family's grudging charity. So she steadfastly insisted that Iddon was still alive, and that he would come back some day, and clung to her position as his wife, not his widow. And she was content. Or she had been.

***

She folded up the finished cloth and went outside. It was near dusk already, the yard was full of fallen leaves, and the ground under her feet was chill and sullen. Samhain was fast approaching, and all the world was getting ready to die. Lilla and Luned, who were now almost inseparable, were driving the pigs in through the gate, followed by Ashhere and Steeleye carrying hunting spears and a couple of limp ducks. So there would be duck tonight as well as the haunch of venison from the hind Drust had caught a few days previously. It was going to be quite a feast, especially as she had also yielded to the chorus of entreaties and agreed to take a few jugs of mead out of the stored casks. A feast without mead was apt to be as much of a flop as a bird without wings, and the foreigners deserved better than that. Besides, they had done more to earn it than his lordship of Navio, God rot his heathen soul.

Blodwen shouted from the house doorway for more logs, and after a short exchange Lilla and Luned took the ducks and disappeared into the dairy hand-in-hand – possibly, Severa reflected, the birds would not be very thoroughly plucked – Ashhere took both spears into the hut, and Steeleye started chopping firewood, chanting to himself in the foreign language.

Severa crossed the yard, feeling oddly nervous.

"Did you lose a bet?" she enquired, dodging a flying bark chip.

He laughed, but did not pause in his task. "No, it's good exercise." He switched the hatchet to his left hand for a few blows, then back to his right with a grimace. "Damn, I need it. I'd be hard pushed to win an arm-wrestling contest with Luned."

"You aren't doing too badly," she observed, watching the logs split and fall away from the chopping block. He was clearly stronger than his slim build would suggest, and the thought brought a fleeting image to her mind that she shied away from. She changed the subject. "What were you singing?"

"A sea-song, a boat-song. It gives the rhythm for the oars, so all the rowers pull together." He gave her a swift glance and a smile, and Severa felt her heart turn over. "It works for chopping wood too."

The sea. Another reminder that he came from a world she could hardly begin to imagine. "You miss the sea, don't you? You talk of it a lot."

"Do I?"

"Yes, you do. Will you go back there?"

He split the last log and stooped to heap the wood into the basket, his face hidden. "I don't see how," he answered, on a sigh. "Too many enemies. But there's another sea in the west, isn't there? Your grandfather's sea. Perhaps I'll go there. Afterwards."

After searching for his lady, Severa thought, and felt a breathtaking stab of jealousy for the woman she knew nothing of beyond a name, the woman who held his heart.

"You still intend to leave at Samhain?" Silly question. They were all itching to be off, would probably have left a week ago at least if he had not promised her to stay until Samhain. "I – I have a gift for you."

She held out the chequered cloth.

He seemed as astonished as he was pleased. "For me? Really? Are you sure? A whole month's work – it's too much –"

"You need a cloak," she stammered. "I – I – er I'm afraid it's not much – nothing special – and I know you must be used to much better weaving – " Like the woman who made his tunic, she thought, and again she feared the unreasonable jealousy would show on her face. "It's – it's the best I can do – I hope you don't mind –"

"Mind? It's perfect. I am forever in your debt. And –" he sank his voice to a conspiratorial whisper "– only I know the secret about the border, which makes it doubly precious."

Severa laughed shakily, overcome with a foolish feeling of relief. "It was intended for you all along," she confessed, blushing for the first time in years. "That's why I was so annoyed at the mistake. I don't want you to remember me as an sloppy weaver –"

She broke off, cringing inwardly. Such a silly thing to say! What had possessed her?

Steeleye did not laugh at her. When he spoke, his voice had lost its bantering tone and was soft, almost tender. "That is hardly likely."

"That you would remember me?"

"Ah, Severa –" He took her hand in both of his. "I think you can be sure I will remember you."

His fingers were stroking the soft skin on the inside of her wrist, over and over. So slight a contact, and yet her pulse leaped and her breath caught in her throat. Was it the same for him too? She could not tell. It was too dark to see his face clearly. But whatever he felt, or did not feel, in three days he would be gone, back to his own world, back to his lady.

She took her hand back, trying to judge the movement to give neither offence nor encouragement. She had no practice at this – Iddon's 'courtship' had been confined to strictly practical matters.

"I must get on," she said, doing her best to sound calm and unruffled, though it was difficult as she seemed to have lost the knack of breathing smoothly. "I'll be needed to help with dinner."

It was a transparent lie, for Blodwen was perfectly capable of roasting a haunch of venison and two ducks, but it gave her an excuse to make an unhurried, unflustered escape – until she spoilt the effect by blundering into the log basket.

***

Eadwine knew better than to rush to her assistance, and let her pick herself up and make her way into the house on her own. He had had something of a shock himself. For a few weeks he had been aware that he was attracted to Severa, but he had not acted on the feeling and nor had he had any idea that it was so strong. He had shrugged off the flicker of desire as a natural consequence of returning health, and had even been wryly amused that he should find himself drawn to Severa, when it would have been so much more convenient to have taken a fancy to Gwen or Blodwen. Both of them had started to take an interest in him as he recovered and had made it clear that they would be more than happy to tumble him, if only to complete the set. Neither invitation had been a surprise, or a serious temptation, and both had been adroitly declined with no offence on either side. He had some practice at that, since unless one was physically repulsive being propositioned was an occupational hazard of being rich. Seducing an unmarried woman, whether maid or widow, was an offence against the head of the household, but like most offences it could be settled by paying compensation to the injured party – and as the compensation was expected to reflect the offender's means, careful choice of paramour meant a pretty daughter or sister or even a slave girl could earn more than the price of a good cow for an hour or so on her back. Eadwine never took advantage of such offers, not if he spotted them in advance. He disliked being fished for. Even if there were no strings attached, on the whole he felt little desire for an agreeable tumble with a pretty woman who would forget him as soon as she pulled her

113

skirt down. It never seemed very – satisfying. Another shameful aspect of his temperament that he had learned to keep hidden while growing up in his brother's libidinous shadow and later in the boastful environment of a warband.

So why did he feel differently about Severa, when he knew he would never see her again? More importantly, what was he going to do about it? He now knew the attraction was mutual. But he was betrothed. He did not owe Aethelind fidelity in any official sense, for under Anglian custom the woman vowed fidelity and the man vowed protection, whether married or betrothed. But he had already betrayed her once by failing to protect her from the Bernicians. Was he to betray her again by falling for the first attractive bit of skirt that came his way? Surely he should keep faith with his betrothed in *something*, even if it was not the right thing.

Worse, Severa was married, and on this both customs were in firm agreement, at least in theory. A married woman owed fidelity to her husband. She had the right to end an unhappy marriage, but not to cheat on it. Practice had an unfortunate tendency to diverge from theory, as Eadric's long list of adulterous conquests confirmed, but it was still profoundly dishonourable to seduce another man's wife. And yet, Severa's husband had been gone for nearly four years. No-one, except possibly Severa, thought he was ever coming back. Did she still count as married? Had she kept faith with her husband all that time? Or did she consider herself a free woman, looking for someone to love?

***

Severa refilled her cup with extreme care, and passed the mead jug on its unsteady way. The duck and the venison were all finished, the dog had invited itself to the party by stealing the leftovers, and the atmosphere had evolved from relaxed through convivial to hilarious. For Severa and her kind, mead was for special occasions only and the jug had only gone round once before all four women were giggling. Drust had been prevailed upon, without much reluctance, to perform *Attacotti Nell* – to describe it as a recital really did not do him justice – and although he had offered to translate it into Brittonic it had soon become clear that this was utterly unnecessary. The women shrieked with laughter, the men cheered and clapped, and Blodwen contributed a sixteenth verse that would have been eye-watering if it had made any sense.

Not to be outdone, Gwen launched into a tipsy rendition of the *Maiden's Lament*, a traditional song whose title was a mystery since it was not a lament and its protagonist was not a maiden, at least not for very long. Everyone had had a little too much to drink by now, and the circle round the fire was starting to separate into couples – or rather, three couples and two left over.

Severa gazed at Steeleye over the rim of her cup, watching the play of the firelight on his sharp hawk's face, the soft fall of his dark hair across his forehead, the way his eyes crinkled at the corners just before he laughed. He reached to hand the mead jug on, and she thought how gracefully he moved, and how beautiful his hands were, and how much she would like to snuggle up beside him and to kiss the little hollow at the base of his throat. Sitting opposite him had started out as a sensible precaution, but now it seemed more like a lost opportunity. She remembered his fingers on her wrist and the tender thrill in his voice. She wanted to feel the touch of his hands, and the warmth of his skin against hers in the quiet dark. The mead coursed through her veins like liquid fire. Never mind that his heart was given to some other woman. Never mind that he would soon be gone and she would never see him again. He could spare one night for her. One night that would last a lifetime.

114

Without warning, his glance flicked to meet hers across the fire. She looked away hastily, afraid that she had made a fool of herself, afraid that he did not want her, afraid that he would think her ridiculous or, worse, pitiful. But when she ventured to steal another glance at him, he was still looking at her, caressing her with his eyes, and nothing else in the world mattered.

***

Gwen lost her place in the song and collapsed into Ashhere's lap in a heap of incoherent giggles, and someone had the bright idea of sharing the celebration with the local water-goddess, to thank her for a successful summer and ask her to keep the hafod under her protection over the winter. As they were all feeling very well-disposed to the world in general, it did seem a shame not to include the goddess, so they all reeled giddily out to the glade where the stream emerged from the woods and gathered round while Blodwen poured a libation and mumbled a heartfelt, if somewhat slurred, petition. It was a beautiful night, clear but not too cold, with a bright gibbous moon sailing high amid a sky full of stars. Under its light the rapids and little waterfalls on the stream became a skein of silk and pearls framed by black velvet shadows, a fitting abode for a water-goddess. Eadwine lingered by the stream after the others had turned away, adding his own silent prayer. Whatever power the goddess possessed probably extended no further than the hafod, but all deities were worthy of respect and a homeless exile with a murder to avenge was likely to need any friends he could find.

"Steeleye –" murmured a woman's voice close behind him.

The tone was low, husky, inviting. He turned.

The three couples had disappeared, and he and Severa were alone in the glade.

Her face was silvered in the moonlight. He reached out, traced the line of her cheek with a gentle finger. She tensed at his touch, and for a moment he feared he had misread the signal, feared she would take flight like a startled deer. Then, very deliberately, she reached for her braid and shook her hair loose about her shoulders.

He had never seen her hair unbraided before. It swirled to her waist like a cloud of shadow netted with moonlight, dark as charcoal, soft as velvet. He lifted it in his hands, astonished at its weight, ran a strand through his fingers. Her eyes were wide, her lips warm and inviting. She might have been the water-goddess herself risen from the stream. His heart leaped, and more than his heart. He took her hands and drew her closer. She tilted back her head and smiled up into his eyes. The invitation was as clear as it was irresistible, and there was no possible response but to kiss her.

Her mouth was warm, tasting faintly of mead, and her arms went up around his neck, her hands twining in his hair. He pulled her close, saw her eyes widen as she felt the rising proof of his desire, and then her hands moved to his hips and pulled him closer still, before sliding up his back under his cloak. Every nerve in his body tingled with flame. He slipped the clasp of her cloak, trailed kisses down her throat and along her shoulder above the neckline of her dress, and was rewarded by a little gasp and shudder of startled ecstasy. Her hands were trying to find their way under his tunic, balked by the belt around his waist, and with a pleasurable jolt he felt her fingers struggling to unfasten the buckle. She lifted her face to be kissed again, murmuring some words he could not catch, and a name.

"Iddon –"

Her husband's name.

The shock was like being doused with icy water. If it was vaguely hurtful to be forgotten afterwards, to be used as a substitute for another man was utterly humiliating. He had not known she was so drunk. He released her as if he had been slapped.

"He will come back to you," he said unsteadily. "He will come back –"

Not trusting himself to say more, he turned from her and left the glade, not caring in what direction.

Severa dropped to her knees, sobbing.

"Blessed Lady," she whispered to the stream, "oh, Blessed Lady, forgive my sin, forgive me. How could I help it –? Oh, Blessed Lady – forgive me –" An anguished wail. "It was never like that with Iddon –!"

***

Any bad temper or unhappiness the next morning was easily attributed to the hafod's collective hangover. Even the dog was snappish and out of sorts. A multitude of tasks had to be done, making the hafod weathertight for winter, mending casks and barrels and baskets, and packing up the fleeces, the spun wool, and the food stores to be taken back to the village for the winter. There was more packing than usual, for there was a lot of dried and smoked meat as well as the usual sacks of cheese and barrels of butter and honey and mead, and Severa also had to put aside travelling provisions – biscuit, dried meat and smoked fish – for her departing guests. The chickens fluttered into everything, the cat made a nuisance of itself, and it was very easy to avoid anyone you did not feel ready to talk to.

Some time after noon, Severa finally found the courage to approach Steeleye. She had failed to sort out her confused thoughts, but she felt she owed him an apology, although exactly what for she was not sure. For trying to seduce him? For failing? For not being to his liking?

She found him in the wool shed, patiently unknotting a tangle of rope and looking very pale, very tense and very tired.

"About last night –" she began uncertainly.

His smile was kind, assured, and entirely natural. "You were drunk, lass. Nothing happened. Forget it."

Severa was not sure whether to be relieved or disappointed, and decided it was much more sensible to be relieved. Whatever foolishness she had felt was all the fault of the mead – sweet ensnaring mead, as the poets called it, with good reason – and was therefore not real. She had stayed true to her husband. She could keep her old life.

***

Eadwine saw the look of relief cross her face, and knew he had said the right thing. Poor lass, how desperately she must love her husband to be so devoted to him after so long, and how hideously ashamed she would have been in the morning. He shuddered inwardly at the thought. Last night had been a lucky escape, although it hadn't felt like it at the time.

***

"Samhain Eve," Severa said didactically, "is outside time. It belongs to neither the old year nor the new. The boundaries between the worlds break down, the dead walk the earth, and the gods may take on human form. The gates to the Otherworld open, and Arawn Lord of the Dead rides out at the head of a great host of ghosts and spirits. Like a wild storm they sweep over the earth, scouring the worlds for the Great Mother. Eventually they capture her, and in her absence all things on the mortal earth begin to fade and die. But also at

116

Samhain Arawn couples with the Great Mother, and in the spring, at Beltane, a child of fire is born, who releases the Great Mother from Arawn's clutches and with her return all things on the earth are reborn. So Samhain Eve is the greatest festival of the year, because without it there would be no rebirth."

"So it's a big party, then?" pressed Ashhere, getting to the point of interest. His enquiry had been prompted by the invitation from the village headman to celebrate Samhain Eve with the villagers that night, and he wanted to know if 'celebrate' meant what it said. Eadwine had been unhappy about accepting the invitation, having originally intended to make half a day's travel before dark, but it was becoming clear that getting from the hafod to the village was going to take all day. The drove was headed by the village headman and two other men, who had arrived late the previous day with a string of dispirited pack ponies that were now plodding along laden with sacks, barrels, bundles, baskets of protesting chickens and the hafod's cat. Behind them came the cows, some of them garlanded with wreaths of leaves and berries 'to give the brownies somewhere to ride', as Luned shyly explained, and behind them came the pigs, then the sheep and finally the dog. The cows paced with ponderous dignity, having made the journey numerous times before, but the sheep were always stopping to graze particularly succulent-looking weeds, and the pigs were always trying to dash into the woods to root for nuts and fungi. Keeping the whole ungainly cavalcade together and moving, even with eight people to share the herding, required much breathless running up and down and wielding of sticks and butt-ends of spears. The day was bright, dry and cold, with a stiff breeze sending down showers of russet oak leaves, the exercise kept everyone warm, and the prospect of another feast at journey's end could only add to the holiday atmosphere.

Severa prodded an errant pig back into line with the dexterity of long practice. "It is the greatest feast of the year," she called back. "All six villages gather together on Shivering Mountain – some people also call it the Mother Mountain – and cattle and pigs and lambs are killed in honour of the wedding of Arawn and the Great Mother. It is a lucky night to conceive a child, even if the father is unknown, because the child might have been fathered by Arawn himself in disguise. So many men wear masks, and a man who chose his wife for her dowry may seek out the woman he would rather have had. There is feasting and drinking and music and dancing all night until the dawn comes and the Host of Annwn returns to the Underworld, taking with them the Great Mother and sometimes even living people who have been overtaken by the Host. It is a dangerous night to travel abroad. Or so it is said." She crossed herself. "I am glad you are staying."

"So am I," grinned Ashhere.

"We leave at dawn," Eadwine warned, shouting from across the river of livestock. "And I mean dawn, no matter how bad your hangovers are."

***

Derwent Bridge was an untidy cluster of houses and barns on the east bank of the Derwent, a respectful distance upstream from the solid-looking timber bridge that carried the army-path over the river and gave the village its name. The settlement had probably once been grouped around the crossing itself, but had prudently migrated further and further away as armies became less and less disciplined. It was surrounded by a scruffy thorn hedge, which served to keep the animals inside rather than as any form of defence, and ploughed fields and hay meadows spread out across the valley floor. The great forests of the upper valley had been largely cleared here, leaving only small woods managed for timber and firewood, and steep pastures swept up to a gritstone edge high above the village. A smithy and pungent-smelling tanning pits occupied the extreme eastern edge of the village – since the prevailing wind was from the west, most of the village was upwind of the sparks from one and the smell from the other – and the rest of the space was dotted with wattle or timber houses thatched with moor grass, each with its attached barn and a little colony of sheds and outbuildings. Cattle lowed from some of the barns, greeting their returning relatives, and the inevitable flock of squawking chickens scratched about underfoot. Villagers claimed their livestock and began catching up on six months' worth of gossip, the pack ponies were unloaded into the headman's house, and Severa was immediately accosted by half a dozen people wanting advice on ailments ranging from skin rashes to suspected pregnancies. The four strangers were initially regarded with suspicion and some alarm, until the sack of smoked venison had been produced and the tale of the bandit raid recounted – with far more poetic license than Eadwine had ever dared apply in verse – after which they were urged to stay not just for Samhain but for the whole winter if they liked. There was only one problem.

"You must leave your weapons here if you are going to the feast," Severa explained, amid giggles from the village women and a chorus of jokes that a man needed only one kind of weapon at Samhain. Drust had made some more conquests. "Otherwise the gods will be offended and you will bring us all a year of bad luck. Or so it is said. And it is certainly a sensible custom, for drinking tends to mean fighting, and less damage is done with fists than with blades. Leave them in my house if you like. No-one will go in there."

There was no option, so Eadwine reluctantly agreed. A guest had to follow the customs of the country, like it or not. Severa's house was much like the others, a simple structure of wattle and thatch. As they approached, a man came lounging out and leaned against the door jamb, blocking the entrance. He was a comely fellow of about thirty, with a discontented expression as though life had treated him badly, though when he saw Severa he mustered an unconvincing smile and held out a hand.

"Sweet sister," he greeted her. "I've come to take you home."

Severa folded her arms, ignoring the proffered hand. "As I have told you many times, my home is here. I do not need a place as a household drudge, especially not from you, brother dear. Kindly move out of the doorway."

The man let his hand drop, scowling, but did not move out of the way. "A childless widow has no claim on her husband's family. Your place is with us now."

"But I am not a widow," Severa told him coolly. "Unless you have news of Iddon? No? I thought not. He will come back to me one day, and when he does he will expect to find me here. In his house, waiting for him. As a wife should."

"You loyalty does you credit, dear," put in a blonde woman, patting Severa's arm as she might pat a dog. "But it is four years since he went away. Four years! Face it, dear, he must have met with some accident. You are young, you should start a new life –"

Severa looked contemptuously at the hand on her arm until the older woman, embarrassed, removed it. "If by that you mean you want your husband made headman instead of acting headman, and you want to take my place as headman's wife, say so."

"I'm thinking only of what's best for you, dear –" the woman began.

"How kind," Severa said, in a tone so dry that it could have preserved meat for a season. "Thank you for your concern, dear good-sister, but what is best for me is to stay here."

"Don't think you're going to hook another man!" snapped the brother. "You'll find nobody to take used goods with no dowry. Our father had to pay handsomely to buy you a husband. If you couldn't keep him and he ran off with the money for some other woman, that's not my problem. I'll not buy you another!"

Severa went very pale at the jibe, but answered steadily, "I am not in need of another man, brother dear. I have a husband, as I keep telling you. If you need a household slave because you married a pretty scatterbrain who can't run a dairy, then pay for one." She swept a challenging glance round the crowd and raised her voice a little. "Have you proof that Iddon is dead, or that I have been unfaithful to him?"

No-one spoke. Eadwine saw the village headman exchange a glance with his blonde wife and shrug his shoulders, evidently reluctant to get involved in women's quarrels. Severa's brother swore. The other villagers looked on with indifference - no, not quite indifference, more a latent hostility. Although no-one spoke against Severa, none spoke in her support either. Even the three other women from the hafod were silent. As the herbwife and doctor she had the villagers' respect, but as an outsider they recognised her as different and mistrusted her for it. Eadwine thought it would take very little to tip the silence into hate, and realised for the first time that Severa's position was as precarious as his own.

Severa turned back to her brother and her sister-in-law. "Until you have proof, I remain Iddon's wife, not his widow, and my place is here. Now kindly move out of the doorway of my home."

"You should be grateful," the brother blustered, moving out of the way as Severa stared him down. "You'll beg me to take you in one day! You'll beg –!"

Severa ignored him, turning her shoulder to him in careless dismissal, and led the way into the house. Apart from a summer's worth of dust and cobwebs it seemed tidy and well-kept, but its most striking features were the constant reminders of a man's presence. A bowl, a jug and a shaving knife on a shelf under the single window. A man's tunic, lovingly mended, hanging on a peg. A pair of well-worn house shoes set by the hearth to warm. You would think the man of the house had just stepped out to see to a chore and would be back at any moment. Eadwine swallowed hard as he propped his spear in a dusty corner. What must it be like, living with the constant presence of a ghost? Did Severa wake every morning, surrounded by her husband's possessions, and hope that today would be the day he returned to her? He felt like a guilty trespasser, even though he had almost convinced himself that all he felt for Severa was a temporary lust brought on by too much mead. Just as well that he was leaving in the morning, and only had to avoid her for the Samhain feast.

***

The village elders selected a heifer and two pigs as the village's contribution to Samhain Eve, men shouldered barrels and women hefted baskets and babies, and as the sun slid down to perch on the western hills a noisy cavalcade set out for Shivering Mountain. The army-path was not as broad or as thoroughly engineered as the major roads Eadwine knew around Eboracum, being not much more than a rutted track barely wide enough to take a cart. In places a sizeable tree had taken root in the middle of the road, or a particularly deep water-filled pothole had formed, and here a new track skirted to one or other side around the obstruction so that the road had lost its straight character and was beginning to weave and wind like an ordinary path. In a few more decades it would disappear as if it had never been. It followed the north bank of a little river, with the rock-crowned summit of the Withy Hill rearing up to the right and a flat-topped steep-sided moor to the south. After a mile or so the valley began to swing north, curving around the flanks of the Withy Hill, and a second valley appeared to the south. The villagers, who until then had been merrily singing something about a fairy cow, a witch and a thief, abruptly fell silent in the middle of a verse and began to hurry, as a man does when he sees rainclouds ahead and hopes to reach shelter before the downpour.

It was not long before Eadwine understood the reason. The track passed through a copse of scrubby hawthorn rustling with roosting sparrows, and emerged onto a much larger army-path at a right-angled bend. Even though scrub had reclaimed the verges and weeds had colonised the ditches, this was a real highway, a military road engineered with uncompromising straightness through the landscape, broad enough for two carts to pass with ease, surfaced with pounded gravel and flanked by deep drainage ditches. One arm struck south-westwards through the new valley while the other marched north-westwards, visible in the distance as a broad pale scar making a purposeful rising traverse up the flank of the Withy Hill. In the crook of the right angle, on the south side of the river, sat the fort, as hard and square and dominating as the road. It was far smaller than Eboracum and not in such good repair, as if it had been abandoned or neglected for a long time in its past and only desultorily repaired. Its stone walls were missing a few blocks, and the headquarters building inside had lost one end of its roof in an avalanche of red tiles, but somehow the air of dilapidation made it more, not less, threatening, like a scarred thug with some teeth missing. Eadwine saw Severa cross herself, and many of the others reached to touch amulets or sprigs of rowan as they hurried forward up the north-western branch of the army-path, casting fearful glances at the fort on the other side of the river as if they were passing a dragon's lair. Eadwine felt his lip curl. A lord should inspire this sort of terror in his enemies, not in his own people.

Some distance ahead, a blackbird whirred from its roost and swooped low across the road, shrilling its alarm call. Eadwine tensed, all his nerves on edge. Most likely the bird had been disturbed by a rat, or even by another bird after the same roost, but his hand automatically felt for the sword-hilt that wasn't there. Damn the Samhain custom!

He felt it at first rather than heard it, and before his conscious mind could put a name to the sound a vivid memory of defeat and disaster came swirling back, a memory of blood and a broken shield-wall and pursuing cavalry. Horses, many horses, approaching at a fast trot.

"Off the road!" Severa shrieked. "It's his lordship! Off the road, quick!"

Eadwine was astonished at the order, and still more by the reaction. Like any young man who could afford a good horse, he had often come hurtling round a bend intent on an impromptu race only to find the way blocked by a herd of ambling cows or a farmer with an overloaded hay wagon. Such encounters generally resulted in mutual cursing and either a screeching halt or a nimble piece of avoiding action, with or without an accident. It had never occurred to him to expect the cows or the farmer to clear the road – just as well, because it never occurred to the farmer either. But here everyone immediately began scrabbling to get off the highway and drive the animals with them. Easier said than done for many people, for the whole village turned out for Samhain Eve regardless of age or state of health. Eadwine scrambled down into the ditch to help an old man bent double by the joint-evil, and saw Drust doing the same for the pregnant women and Lilla and Ashhere chasing down errant toddlers further along the road.

He could see the approaching riders clearly now. Four or five men in bright cloaks, all with spears and swords, and several spare horses carrying what looked like a stag and a couple of hinds. The Lord of Navio and some of his warband, returning from a successful hunt.

Most of the villagers were off the road now, except for Luned trying to chase the pigs over the ditch and a knot of men gathered around the heifer, who had balked with her forefeet in the ditch and her hind feet on the road and would go neither back nor forward. Luned managed to shove one of the pigs into the ditch, where it got stuck in a patch of brambles and squealed piteously, convincing the other to bolt for freedom across the road. Luned ran after it, hoping to drive it across the other ditch, and that was a mistake. She passed much too close to the struggling heifer, which suddenly found a target for its frustration and indignity. A hind foot flailed out, and Luned went flying into the middle of the road like a child's rag doll, straight into the path of the oncoming horsemen.

They would have had time – just – to slow or swerve to avoid her. But instead, the leading horseman whooped with the savage joy of a hunter sighting prey, and with horrified disbelief Eadwine saw him deliberately kick his horse into a gallop and alter course to charge directly at the stricken girl.

Luned was struggling to her knees, clutching her stomach and coughing. Voices yelled at her from all sides, proffering much advice but no actual help. Nobody with any sense was going to run into the path of a galloping horse, especially not one ridden by the Lord of Navio. Eadwine was just about level with Luned, could see that she was too dazed or too petrified with fear to run. He sprang from cover. One long stride took him across the ditch, two more took him to Luned, and his momentum was enough to carry them both tumbling across the road almost under the hooves of the leading horse.

Eadwine heard the horse snort, felt a heavy hoof strike his thigh a glancing blow, heard another hoof thud down inches from his head, and then he came to a crunching halt amid a tangle of bracken and brambles. A split second later, Luned came to an equally crunching halt on top of him. He struggled to sit up.

The horse, guided by its instinct, had tried to dodge round them, as Eadwine had guessed it would. But the rider had hauled its head round too sharply, throwing the horse off its stride, and then it had tripped over Eadwine's leg. Now it snorted and stumbled, trying to recover its balance and failing. Its rider lurched forward. The horse staggered under the shifting weight, lurched another step, and went heels over head into a heap of flailing limbs. With a yell of outrage the rider pitched over its head, skimmed across the metalling like a well-bowled ball, and vanished into the ditch in a trail of broken twigs and flying nettles.

Some of the villagers cheered, most of the rest laughed, and as the remaining horsemen pulled up in a welter of sliding hooves some of them were sniggering too. Either their fallen colleague was not popular, or they thought he deserved what he got.

The sniggering stopped abruptly as a bedraggled figure hauled itself swearing out of the nettles. He was a big man, several inches shorter than Eadwine but twice his bulk, and even in the fading light it could be seen that he was in a towering fury.

"I'll kill you for that!" he spluttered.

Eadwine had managed to struggle out from underneath Luned, who was surprisingly heavy, and help her to her feet. She was sobbing and shaking, but apparently unhurt. No thanks to this oaf.

121

"Serves you right," he retorted. "If you can't control your horse, don't try to ride people down."

The man scowled. He had little piggy eyes, a florid face, a nose like a battering ram, and an unpleasantly slack mouth that now hardened into an avaricious line. "Who are you? You don't belong on my land."

"A passing traveller," Eadwine answered, with belated caution. Luned was rigid with terror, clinging to his arm and trying to bury her face in his shoulder, and some distance away he could see Gwen cowering flat behind a bush – Gwen, who would flirt with anything in trousers and should surely have been expected to give five burly spearmen the eye. What was it about this mountain brigand that could inspire such fear? He seemed no more than an ordinary thug.

The piggy eyes narrowed. "Passing traveller, eh? Who gave you leave to enter my lands?"

"I did," Severa interposed, coming up and putting her arm around Luned in a fashion that could only be described as motherly.

"You!" The Lord of Navio recoiled as if from a snake, then recovered himself enough to sneer, "Found yourself a new man at long last, have you? Some tramp who'll take a barren outlander with no dowry?"

"I am Iddon's faithful wife, as everyone in this valley knows," Severa answered. "This man helped us with the drove and is staying to mark Samhain Eve with us."

She lifted her chin and met the lord's gaze fearlessly. For a moment there seemed to be some unspoken contest of wills between them, and then the piggy eyes wavered and looked away. The fallen horse had by now thrashed and struggled to its feet, panting and shaken but otherwise unhurt, and its owner now retreated to it and mounted in some haste. He forced a laugh. "Well, well! Passing travellers are always welcome in my lands. Stay for Samhain by all means. Stay all winter if you like. Come to the fort tomorrow and feast with me."

He wheeled his horse, signalled to his men, and was gone.

***

"Hush, Luned, hush," Severa murmured softly, trying to comfort the sobbing girl. "He's gone, lass. He won't touch you again, you're too old for him now."

"Too old?" repeated Ashhere, puzzled. "But she's only fourteen –"

He broke off as the shocked realisation dawned, and Severa shrugged in weary affirmation. "His lordship likes them young."

Lilla's fist clenched, and if he had had a spear the Lord of Navio would probably have been a dead man that night. "I'll kill him!"

"No, you won't!" Eadwine said sharply, although he would gladly have done the deed himself. "We have our own business to mind, and it's past time we got on with it."

***

The holiday atmosphere was gone, and they hurried on in gloomy silence, now needing torches to light the way. Eadwine dropped back down the line until he found Severa walking alone at the rear.

"He's afraid of you," he said quietly. "Why?"

She gave him a sidelong glance. "Your Ashhere's not the only one who thinks I'm a witch."

"What did you do to him?"

"No more than he deserved," she said vengefully. "It was the autumn before I was married. He'd left me alone until then, probably from fear of my

122

grandfather. A lot of people thought my grandfather was a wizard. But when he died, his lordship thought it was about time he exercised his 'rights'. I was nearly fifteen, so in his view he'd waited quite long enough. It was pig-slaughtering time, shortly after Samhain, and I happened to be making black pudding when he came into the house, said he had a present for me and started taking his clothes off. He was alone. People don't resist him. But I was furious, and so lost after Grandfather's death that I didn't care if he did kill me. I raised my hand as if I was throwing something at him, upbraided him in what Latin I could remember, and swore that if he laid a finger on me I would curse him so that his finger – or whatever else – would rot and turn black and drop off, that I would fill his belly with writhing snakes of fire, that I would make his skin flake and crack and flay off in sheets – and rather a lot of similar things that I can't remember. Then I threw the cauldron at him." Her eyes glinted. "It was a criminal waste, but it was very satisfying. He fled out into the village, in front of everybody. Naked as a plucked chicken, slimed from head to foot in black pudding, and with great gobbets sliding down his chest and dribbling off his – his – well, you know. It wasn't boiling so he wasn't scalded, but I suppose it was hot on his skin. He looked down at himself and he must have thought he was being turned into a toad or brought out in a plague of boils on the spot, because he screamed and threw himself down in the dirt and started thrashing and writhing about, trying to scrape the stuff off. I laughed and laughed, and he shot me a look of pure horror and bolted, stark naked and covered in black pudding and mud and rubbish, right through the village and back to his fort as if the whole Host of Annwn was after him. He never tried to touch me again."

Eadwine burst out laughing. "Good for you!"

"You think I did right?"

"Of course you did right. Except maybe you let him off too lightly."

"Iddon didn't agree with you," she said, rather sadly. "He had second thoughts about marrying me when he heard, but I was well dowered, so he overcame his – misgivings." She brushed her hair back from her face. "He was right, I am sure. No good can come of annoying his lordship. It is just as well you are leaving tomorrow. He will not forget being humiliated like that, nor forgive it."

"If the Lord of Navio is the worst enemy I have to face, I will be well content," Eadwine said dryly.

***

It was not long before they left the army-path for a narrow drove track that crossed the river at a shallow stony ford and passed another village, already deserted for the festival. A straggling wood climbed the hillside behind the village, and on its fringe stood a small hut, half-hidden in scrub. Here Severa halted.

"I do not celebrate Samhain," she explained, sounding a little apologetic. "My grandfather abhorred the festival, and I try to honour his memory. I keep vigil here."

Eadwine surveyed the hut, which seemed to be an ordinary thatch and timber cabin such as a shepherd might build for temporary shelter. "Why here?"

Severa opened the door and held her torch to illuminate the interior. It was as unprepossessing as the exterior, empty except for a raised wooden platform about three feet in height and depth and about six feet long across the rear wall of the hut, like a sleeping bench. Above it a cross had been drawn on the wall in charcoal. There was a strong smell of mice and thousands of their little black droppings littered the floor and the bench.

"It is a holy place," she said. "Or at least, a holy man lived here once. He was very devout and very mad, but my grandfather revered him greatly and used to send me with food, which the holy man gave to the mice." An ironic smile. "They at least are still here. The holy man died years ago, the winter after I was married, and the villagers think his ghost haunts this place. They say there was a terrible smell here for months that winter." She shrugged. "I do not know anything about that, of course, but I think if my grandfather was going to come back to earth at Samhain, he would come here. I would dearly like to see him again." She jammed the torch upright into a holder cut into the centre of the wooden platform, and the cross on the wall seemed to dance and waver in the smoky light. "You had better hurry, if you are going to the feast?"

"No," Eadwine said slowly. "No, if the dead are going to walk tonight there are some among them I wish to see."

"It is dangerous, they say –"

"I am not afraid."

***

That was not completely accurate, he reflected, groping his way uphill by the deceiving light of the full moon. It would be fairer to say that he was prepared to run any risk for the chance to speak to his brother again. Severa's description of the Host of Annwn reminded him of the Wild Hunt led by Woden on stormy nights, when the dead racketed through the air like drunken warriors on a spree and sensible people stayed indoors. Sometimes it seemed to him that all the gods were the same, merely called by different names in different places, just as Eboracum was called Eoforcaster by some people and Caer Ebrawg by others. The Wild Hunt could travel the sky from edge to edge in an hour, so who was to say that Eadric was any less likely to be here than in Eboracum? And since the dead rode through the air, the best place to be found by them would, logically, be high on the summit of a hill.

The slope eased, rolling out into a heather-covered plateau, and ahead of him reared the crenellated summit tor of the Withy Hill. He did not know the way, and the moonlight was deceptive, but the rock was reassuringly rough and solid under his hands. A few minutes of scrambling brought him to the summit, where the rising wind keened in the rocks and tugged at his cloak. A huge yellow moon sailed majestically overhead, escorted by a flotilla of stars. Across the valley he could see the curving line of the ridge leading to Shivering Mountain, and below the summit the dark hole gouged by repeated landslips gaped like an open maw. Great beacons ringed the hilltop, their flames leaping up into the sky to ward off the spirit host, and the rhythmic roll of drumbeats echoed from the rocks, part summons, part warning.

Standing alone on the highest rock, leaning into the wind to keep his balance, Eadwine cupped his hands to his mouth and called aloud the names of his dead. There were too many, far too many, his mother, his father and brothers, the men slain on the March and in their desperate retreat and in the battle that should never have been fought. Perhaps also Treowin, perhaps even Aethelind. The wind whipped away the names into the east, and on Shivering Mountain the flames and the drums rose and fell like the breathing of some gigantic animal.

After a while, he retreated from the tor and found a place among the rocks out of the wind, watching the moon and stars wheel their timeless dance through the night. Nothing came in answer to his summons, and yet his mood lifted. Eadric had never been one to come when called; that was a disappointment but no surprise. But Aethelind had not answered, Aethelind whose heart was one with his had not come. And that must surely mean that she had survived, that she was alive somewhere and perhaps waiting for him, as Severa was waiting for Iddon. He turned his face to the north-east, in the direction Eboracum must lie, and sent forth a silent message: *I am coming, my love! I am coming to you!*

Eventually, feeling strangely at peace, he slept.

***

In the hall at Eoforwic, Hereward rolled sleepily out of bed and padded across the chamber to the window without bothering to put his clothes on. He pushed back the shutters. It was a fine day. A few birds were singing and it was getting light. Hereward yawned and stretched like a contented dog. He felt good this morning. A good dinner and a soft bed with a warm woman in it. What more could a man want from life?

He turned back to the bed and stood looking down at Aethelind. She was so pretty, lying in her cloud of tumbled golden hair, and with the covers not quite drawn up to her neck –

The girl opened her eyes and smiled at him without moving. Her gaze travelled slowly over him from head to toe, then slowly back up again before stopping about halfway.

"My Lord," she murmured, throatily.

Lord was one of the god Frey's titles. Frey was a fertility god, and all his images had one very prominent feature in common. Hereward looked down, and blushed rather proudly. He climbed back into bed.

***

Would it have been like this with Eadwine, Aethelind wondered to herself. She suspected he would grunt less and kiss more. She had liked his kisses – and there were one or two liberties that were permitted between betrothed couples – She quivered a little at the memory, and Hereward's big simple face beamed happily.

"You like that?"

Aethelind tactfully guided his pawing hands, and discovered that, yes, she did like that. Hereward was clumsy but he had not been brutal. It was supposed to hurt the first time, anyway. She ran her hands hesitantly over his tangled fair hair. It was thick and springy and would probably look quite attractive if it was clean and properly cut. In fact, Hereward was quite good-looking, in his broad, blond, uncomplicated way, like a large friendly hound. Perhaps he could be trained.

Hereward rolled off and lay gasping like a stranded fish. Aethelind watched his broad chest heaving and the light catching his golden chest hair. Yes, he was definitely a good-looking man. It had hurt hardly at all this time. In fact, she thought she would quite like to try again. Preferably after she had given him a bath.

This time, he didn't fall asleep as soon as he recovered his breath. Instead, he heaved himself up on one elbow and looked down at her.

"Aethelind –?"

"Yes, my lord?"

"The King has granted me this hall and the lands."

"Yes, my lord." She had guessed that would happen.

"I want you to stay here."

"Yes, my lord." Success. He would guard her along with the rest of his property. She was safe until he tired of her, and it was her business to make sure that did not happen soon.

125

Unexpectedly, he reached out and stroked a coil of her hair where it lay loose on the pillow.

"I'm sorry about your father, lass."

"Yes, my lord." A strategic tear slipped from one eye and trickled down the side of her cheek.

Hereward's gaze rested on her face. His eyes were a warm blue, not at all like Eadwine's cool grey-blue. Much nicer, Aethelind thought, guiltily. And she was feeling an irresistible impulse to run her fingers through his chest hair. Eadwine's chest had been almost hairless. She could still remember the disappointment.

"You were a maid." Hereward said.

"Yes, my lord."

He reached out and blotted away the tear with a corner of the coverlet.

"I'll marry you," he said gruffly, and got out of bed.

Marriage! She would have a home of her own and a household to run and servants to order around and, if Frija was kind to her, babies. Aethelind had no need to think about her smile this time.

"Yes, my lord!"

***

Eadwine woke as the first pink fingers of dawn strayed over the dark hills in the east. Samhain Eve was past, and as far as he knew he had been visited by nothing more supernatural than a dog fox passing by on its own business and something small and furry that had taken cover under his legs from a hunting owl. But for some reason he felt refreshed, as if after a night of peaceful sleep. On Shivering Mountain the fires were dying down, though the noise was if anything louder than ever, the drumbeats replaced by shouting and yelling. Well, at least that should wake even a man with a two-barrel hangover. He grinned as he ran down the eastern slopes of the hill into the Derwent Valley, leaping through rocks and heather with reckless abandon. He did not bother to divert downstream to the bridge, but instead stripped, threw his clothes in a bundle to the far bank and plunged into the river, revelling in its cold freshness. Down here in the valley the sun had not yet risen over the hills, and his breath hung in clouds in the air as he dressed. They had left their provisions for the journey hidden in the woods above the track yesterday, so that they could not get muddled up with the village's food, and he retrieved them before hurrying down into Derwent Bridge.

The village was still deserted, which was annoying. It was properly light by now, and he wanted to be on his way. Where had his friends got to? Was he going to have to go up to Shivering Mountain and roust them out of hedges and ditches? He buckled on his sword-belt and was considering whether he could carry all their weapons, Drust's shield and four packs – and deciding that the answer was probably no – when he heard someone approaching. One person, not three, and much too light of foot to be any of his friends.

A sobbing voice called his name, "Steeleye –!" and faded away into a despairing wail.

He ran to the gate, and a small dishevelled figure threw itself weeping into his arms. Luned, white, exhausted, struggling for breath and trembling as if the Host of Annwn itself was on her heels.

"They've got him!" she howled. "They took him to the fort! Oh, Steeleye – they've got Lilla!"

Chapter 13

Eadwine hauled himself up onto the river bank for the last time, wrung out his cloak and the skirt of his tunic, tipped the water out of his shoes and squeezed as much as he could out of his hair.

"I – th-thought you'd drownded –" Luned quavered.

"And then you'd have been stuck on the wrong side of the river with nobody to carry you back across," he teased, before remembering that to Luned even crossing the tributary river was liable to be a terrifying venture into unknown territory. "It was only a loose rock, lass, and I didn't even drop anything – Shh!"

He threw himself flat on the bank among the piled packs and gear, and pulled Luned down too, as a troop of horses clattered past along the road. Raising his head cautiously to peer through the bushes, he saw that there were about half a dozen riders, all bearing spears and heading in the direction of Derwent Bridge. Leaving the road and crossing the river had been a good decision, if an uncomfortable one.

Luned's eyes were saucer-shaped in her pale face. "Were they looking for us?"

"As they didn't see us, it doesn't matter." He loaded swords, packs and Drust's shield over his shoulders, and picked up a spear in either hand. "Come on, let's get up into the woods before any others come. Are you sure nobody uses these woods?"

"No," Luned panted, trotting beside him with Lilla's sword buckled proudly over one shoulder, the two lightest packs on her back and also with a spear in each hand. Between them, they were just able to carry all the gear. "No, on account of the river's being hard to cross, and the only bridge being right up under his lordship's nose at the fort –" she shivered. "– so you can't drive pigs across and you can't get a cart in for firewood, so nobody comes here at all."

The woods clothing the steep slope on the south side of the tributary river certainly looked as if no-one had entered them since the dawn of time. Gnarled oaks, venerable ashes, tall sculpted pines, hazel bushes, hawthorn, brambles, bracken and ivy all grappled for light and air. There was no trace of a path made by anything bigger than a woodlouse, and the floor was an ankle-twisting tangle of mossy hollows, suddenly-collapsing hidden burrows, rotting tree stumps, projecting roots and snaring brambles. Low overhanging branches that snagged packs and caught at clothes and hair added another hazard. At least it looked as if his instinct had been right – this would be a good place to hide. No horseman could follow them in here.

Burdened as they were, it took half a morning of slipping, stumbling struggle to traverse the north slope and work a way round onto the western flank of the hill. Here Eadwine stopped, much to Luned's relief, and left her with the packs and most of the weapons while he went on alone.

***

He had guessed that, if his understanding of the geography was correct and his sense of direction had not utterly vanished, somewhere on this western flank he would find a vantage point over the fort. He had been right. A few minutes' cautious prospecting found a slight knoll, clothed in oak and hazel, which seemed to look straight across to the fort. If he could climb one of the trees –

A sound in the distance made him tense, every nerve jangling a warning. The staccato crack of a snapping branch and the rattle of thorny twigs suddenly caught and as suddenly released. The shrill note of a bird's alarm call. The sliding tumble of falling earth as something – someone – slipped on the loose slope.

Luned was sound asleep where he had left her, curled up among the packs like a mouse in its nest. He picked up two spears, shrugged off his cloak and shoes, and went hunting.

This was his element. This silent stalking of prey through the shadowed woods. He knew how to avoid the dry patches under trees where drifted leaves might rustle, how to roll his weight smoothly with each step so that his bare feet felt every irregularity in the ground and not even a twig would turn or crack, how to sense a thorn snagged in his clothing and stop to release it before it made a sound.

Something pale flashed briefly through the trees, just where he had expected the intruder to be. He balanced one of the spears in his hand. Even left-handed, he could split a sapling at this distance. Someone was creeping through these woods, where no-one ever came. Someone in a pale garment, someone who was trying to move quietly but who was no expert in woodcraft.

Someone who was singing a snatch of *Attacotti Nell* in a low voice, a voice that, although breathless, was much more musical than Drust's and had a strong Brittonic accent.

Eadwine relaxed. He could think of three people who might sing *Attacotti Nell* with a Brittonic accent, but only one of them was likely to have ventured into unknown woodland.

***

Severa shook out her wet skirt – she too must have forded the river – and sat down on a log beside Luned. "No, I didn't know you were here until you jumped out at me," she admitted. "How did you appear out of thin air like that?"

"Magic," said Eadwine, pleased that his woodcraft had not deserted him.

Luned looked awestruck, and Severa quirked an eyebrow. "Yes, and I'm the Empress of Rome. But it wasn't hard to guess where to start looking when you weren't in the village. Where else would you be, except in the woods where nobody goes? And I thought you'd be trying to get a look at the fort." She peered through the hazel bushes screening the knoll. "You mean to get them out?"

"Lilla said you shouldn't!" Luned interrupted. "He said I was to warn you to hide so they wouldn't find you, and tell you to go right away and not bother about them. 'Tell him to save himself', that's what he said."

"And you've told me, and we've done the first part of it," Eadwine retorted. "So it's up to me if I ignore the rest of his advice."

Severa put a comforting arm round the girl's shoulders, and looked across at Eadwine.

"How?"

He ran a hand through his hair. "Good question. Were they hurt?"

Severa shook her head. "Not when they were taken past the chapel. They were all walking, as far as I could see between the guards."

"His lordship said they wasn't to be hurt or – or – or – anything –" Luned faltered. "Alive and unharmed, he was yelling when I ran away."

Severa nodded. "That sounds like he wants them for slaves. His lordship does well out of the slave trade. He raids all summer, all the lands within a few days' ride, and about now – after Samhain but before the snow closes the passes – a trader generally comes over the hills on the army-path and brings iron and

128

copper and salt and gold in and takes lead and wool and slaves out. His lordship keeps the little girls for himself, his warband gets the pick of the women, the trader takes the boys, the women the warband have finished with and the men he can get a good price for, and the ugly men work in the mines until they drop –"

Luned shook her head vigorously. "No, no, no. It's not that, it's not. They were looking for Saxons."

Fear ran icy fingers up Eadwine's spine. "Why?"

"There's a big reward for one. Some Saxon prince, they said. They were shouting a name. A funny name it was – "

Eadwine knew what the name would be even before Luned had stumbled through the unfamiliar syllables. They had stayed here too long, cocooned in illusory isolation, and now the outside world had caught up with them. Did Aethelferth the Twister have allies even this far south? Surely not. But how else had the Lord of Navio found out about Eadwine of Deira?

"Never heard of him," he said steadily.

Severa was frowning. "Why search here, of all places?" she wondered. "A Saxon prince would stand out like a white hare in a snowless winter. Big and blond and beefy and dim and talking his foreign language –"

"With horns," Luned added.

Severa laughed, and then her face changed and for a heart-stopping moment Eadwine thought she had guessed. She shot him an odd glance. "Are you sure your Ashhere isn't a Saxon prince in disguise?"

"Oh, I'm quite certain of that," Eadwine answered, with the conviction that comes of telling the absolute truth, and the relief of being asked the wrong question. He peered through the branches, trying to get a good view of the fort. "Where are they held?"

"In the fort," Luned said, accurately but not very helpfully.

"In – in a room underground," Severa amplified. "I followed them to the fort and heard his lordship give the order."

"A cellar? Where is it?"

Neither woman knew for sure. All they knew was that the fort had a cellar somewhere and that his lordship used it for especially valuable or especially difficult prisoners. But it was said to be made of stone and to have stone steps leading into it, and that was almost certainly enough to locate it. Nobody had built in stone in Britannia for two centuries, so a stone cellar could only be part of the original fort. Eadwine knew three forts intimately, at Eboracum, Catraeth and Derwentcaster, and had a passing acquaintance with half a dozen more. They varied dramatically in size, but they were all built to the same basic design, rather as if the ancient emperors had got a job lot from the giants. The cellar must be the vault under the shrine at the back of the great hall. He knew precisely where the one in Eboracum was – it was still the royal treasury – and he would take a bet with Drust that the one here was in the same position. Assuming that the central building was not built to some strange pattern.

He looked up at the veteran oak rearing above him, flexed his weak shoulder, cursed it mentally and scrambled up onto the lowest branch. By working back and forth around the tree he was able to climb to a considerable height before he ran out of branches.

Now he could see the fort clearly, spread out below him in an eagle's-eye view. It was about a quarter of a mile away, directly across the south-western branch of the army-path, and about a hundred feet below his vantage point. He breathed a sigh of relief. It was of the familiar rectangular design, oriented north-east – south-west with the long sides parallel to the army-path and a gate in each wall. The north-east wall, one of the short sides, was neatly placed across a meander in the river to enclose a flat meadow about half the size of the fort itself. A heap of rubble marked the site of a partly-collapsed building, and the rest of the meadow was dotted with grazing horses – most useful for a mounted warband, to have at least some secure grazing where the horses could neither escape nor be attacked. He was looking directly onto what was clearly now the main gate, positioned not quite half-way along the south-east wall and served by a short track leading off the army-path. Opposite this gate stood a lord's hall, built of wood and roofed in thatch, with the gable ends carved into wolf's heads. Smoke trickled up from the roof, a constant flux of people hurried in and out, and two doorwardens leaned on their spears on either side of the main door. The Lord of Navio's hall, where he feasted and his warband slept. Behind the hall, a rear gate led out to another track heading in the direction of Combe village. In the exact centre of the fort sat the central building complex, arranged around a square paved courtyard. The side of the courtyard furthest from the old main entrance was formed by a long aisled hall, with central clerestory and red-tiled roof. The rest of the courtyard was surrounded by high walls, with an entrance facing the south-west gate. Eadwine knew that if you walked in through that entrance you would be looking straight across the courtyard and through the hall's main doorway to the shrine in the centre of the rear aisle. And directly underneath that shrine would be the vault.

So there was where he had to get to. How? The central building was obviously little used now, its place usurped by the timber hall, but it seemed in fairly good repair. Only the north-west corner of the aisled hall looked damaged, where the roof had lost its tiles and sagged alarmingly. That might be a way in, if he could get that far.

He transferred his attention to the defences. Unfortunately, they were also very standard. A high stone wall, twice the height of a tall man, surrounded by a pair of ditches each a good twelve feet wide and probably around four to six feet deep judging from the size of the saplings growing out of them. On the three sides that did not face the river, there were also signs of a third, smaller ditch well outside the main pair. The main gate looked depressingly sturdy and only a small postern was open. There was no reason to think the other gates would be any different. A sentry stood by the postern, and more sentries patrolled the rampart walk along the top of the walls. Eadwine watched for a while and observed that there were four, one to each wall. Assume one guard at each gate, and the two doorwardens, that made ten on duty that he could see. He frowned. Ten made a reasonable-sized warband. How many men did the Lord of Navio have? Half a dozen had passed them this morning, and now another dozen came riding along the army-path.

"His lordship has visitors," commented Severa's voice, near at hand. She climbed up one more branch, lithe as a cat, and perched a little below him. Luned, it seemed, had sensibly stayed on the ground.

"Visitors?"

"The banner. His lordship's symbol is a wolf's head –"

"Very appropriate." In Anglian custom a wolf's head signified an outlaw.

"– and whatever it is on that banner, it isn't a wolf's head – Are you all right?"

The world seemed to grow dark around Eadwine, and he heard blood rushing in his ears. The banner snapped in the wind as the horsemen turned off

130

the road and took their horses to drink at the river under the corner of the fort. A leaping salmon, glistening silver in the sun. The badge of Ceretic of Elmet. And that explained the sudden pursuit. The Lord of Navio might never have heard of Eadwine of Deira, but Ceretic of Elmet certainly had, and was offering a reward for his capture. Was Ceretic in alliance with Aethelferth – voluntarily or by force? Had he unwittingly sent Hereric to his death?

His vision cleared, to show Severa looking at him with a concerned expression.

Eadwine ignored it. "How many men in your lord's warband?"

Severa frowned, and he was half-expecting an answer as unhelpful as Luned's reply of 'lots' to the same question. "Forty," she said, after a pause. "Give or take one or two."

Forty was not a warband, it was a small army. And there were another dozen of Ceretic's men at least.

"Do you know how many are on guard during the night?"

"One on each gate and one on each wall, same as during the day," came the immediate response. "I don't know about inside. We don't go inside if we can help it."

"Not even to deliver the food-rent?"

"His soldiers and slaves come and take what he wants." She glanced up. "Next time they want a cartload of something – hay, perhaps – if you are in the village I might be able to distract the guards long enough for you to hide under the load. That would get you into the fort. But I don't know when that might be. And I can't see how you get out again. Damn – that isn't much use to you –"

"It would also be very dangerous for you," he said quietly. "I do not ask your help, Severa."

"I offer it anyway," she returned. "Why else do you think I came?"

"No. I can't accept. All we have to do is escape –"

"All!"

"– but you have to carry on living here, and his lordship will be a very angry man if we succeed. I would not wish his wrath to fall on you."

"He's afraid of me. You said so yourself."

"Angry men often forget their fear. Severa, I am grateful but I do not ask or need your help."

"No? How are you going to get into that fort? You can't disguise yourself as a peasant or a slave because, frankly, you don't look like either and his lordship's men know everyone in the valley by sight. Also, some of them saw you on the road yesterday and if they recognise you you'll be dead. His lordship didn't dare hurt you then because violence on Samhain Eve offends the gods, but he won't have forgotten you. You can't climb the walls. You can't break down the gates. You can't hide in a sack or a beer barrel because the ones we use are too small. You can't get in."

Eadwine had run through most of those options himself and reached much the same conclusion. "There has to be a way!"

Severa threw him a flashing glance like a shaft of sunlight piercing clouds. "I said you can't get in. But I can. And then, after dark, I can open a gate."

"No! It's too dangerous!"

She gave him a cool, level stare. "You think a life of ever-dwindling hope is worth clinging to at any cost? You of all people? You were my guests. You think I'm going to let that bastard betray my hospitality, break my trust? I mean to get

131

your friends out of there, on my own if need be. For my honour, not for your gratitude."

Eadwine understood. This was the ethic that drove warriors into battle or vengeance against all reason, when the fear of death shrivelled beside the need for self-respect. But he could not bear to imagine what the Lord of Navio might do to Severa, if she was discovered.

"They won't let you in," he protested, knowing it was hopeless. "You're known here –"

"To his lordship's men, yes. Not to them." She nodded to the riders by the river, who were lazing on the grass while their horses grazed. "They're soldiers in a strange land, and there's one thing they always need a woman for."

Eadwine's concern was replaced by a stab of jealous shock. "You wouldn't!"

"As a matter of fact," she returned tartly, "I was thinking of washerwoman. But now you come to mention it, the one with the banner isn't half bad."

"Severa –"

"You mind your business and leave me to mind mine," she retorted. "I'll get you into that fort, and together we'll get your friends out. Are you coming?"

Her face was alight with excitement and her eyes were sparkling as she disappeared back down the tree with the insouciant ease of a squirrel. This was a side of her he had not seen before. He was reminded of a young deerhound, ears pricked and tail high, eager for the hunt. Or of a young warrior, lissom and lithe and full of life, light-heartedly setting out to the battle that might end in death. He shivered, as if at a sudden cold wind, realising for the first time how thin the threads were that bound her to life. Day after monotonous day, facing the resentment of her sister-in-law and the relentless pressure from her brother, with only the slender hope of her husband's return standing between her and a lifetime of drudgery in her brother's household. And she had lived like that for four years.

Severa was combing out her hair when he reached the ground, and he glared at her.

"You said washerwoman," he accused.

She ignored him, sweeping her hair into a provocative curtain over one shoulder. "Which gate would you prefer, if I have a choice?"

"The river-gate. That end of the fort looks quieter, unless he keeps his hounds in the stables?"

"N-no," Luned faltered, blanching at a terrifying memory "– the hounds live in the big hall."

Severa fastened her cloak. "What else do you need to know?"

"How many guards are in the big central stone building, and where they are. How are you going to tell me?"

She paused. "Good question. Perhaps I can slip out and back in again."

Luned swallowed hard. "I'll come with you. I can come out with a message."

Severa put an arm round her. "Ah, lass, no. I wouldn't ask you to go in there again –"

Luned's chin tilted, giving her a mulish expression. "I'm not frightened." A sniff that proved she was lying. "I want to help Lilla!"

***

Eadwine watched as the two women, hand-in-hand, crossed the road and sauntered over to the men lounging under Ceretic's banner. It was soon clear that their company was very welcome. Before long two of the men were showing

132

off to Luned with an admittedly very impressive display of swordplay, and most of the rest had clustered around Severa. He could even swear he heard shrill giggles carried on the wind, although that was probably his jealous imagination. The standard-bearer seemed especially taken with Severa, offering her a drink from his flask and then lifting her up onto his horse – taking maximum possible advantage of where to put his hands, Eadwine observed sourly – and taking her for a cheerful canter up the road and across the meadow to a conveniently placed clump of trees where he dismounted and drew her into a very long, very active embrace.

Eadwine glowered across the valley like a thunderstorm, and scowled even more when Ceretic's men went into the fort and took the two girls with them. All afternoon he watched the garrison going about its duties, taking careful note of the number of men and their comings and goings. He worked out the guard roster and the watch pattern, and noted that the guards patrolling the wall had a tendency to turn well before they reached the corner towers, and sometimes would stay sheltering from the wind in a convenient angle of the gate tower for minutes at a time. All the time he tried not to imagine what Severa might be doing with the burly standard-bearer. It was absurd to be jealous over a woman he had no interest in whatsoever.

***

Luned came back to the knoll in the late afternoon, with a message from Severa that there were two guards in the aisled hall and two more at the entrance to the courtyard, and that he should be waiting outside the river-gate after it was full dark.

"And she told me to go home," Luned finished, "and to say she was called off sudden to a birthing if anyone asked where she was." She sniffed. "You will be able to save Lilla, won't you?"

"I believe so," Eadwine answered. "I can promise you I'll do my best."

"Will you tell him –" she hesitated, and began again. "Last night – he said – he said he couldn't marry me. Because he had to follow you, see. And I – we – quarrelled." She scrubbed tears from her eyes. "Tell him – tell him I understand. And look after him!"

***

Lilla had a splitting headache and a roiling pain in his stomach. This was not unexpected for the morning after a feast, although usually they did not result from a club and the butt-end of a spear, respectively, not unless you had really offended someone with a very short temper. It was also unusual to be lying face down on a stone floor with your feet tied together at the ankles and your hands tied behind your back. He opened the one eye that wasn't swollen shut. It made no difference whatever. Either he had gone blind or he was in some very dark, very deep dungeon shut away from the sun.

The second possibility was preferable, so he concentrated on that. Besides, he had a vague recollection of bouncing down a flight of stone steps, and someone falling on top of him.

"Ash? Drust?"

A groan answered him, and then Drust's voice, his Pictish accent thicker than usual. "Ach, Holy Mother, ma heid! Whit in heill dae they put in the mead here?"

"If you hadn't tried to fight them they wouldn't have hit you so hard," Lilla responded unsympathetically. "Ash? Are you there?"

A muffled snort, and he became aware that something was wriggling under his feet. He moved them.

133

"About time," came Ashhere's voice. "Where are we?"

"Somewhere in the fort."

A pause, and then Ashhere asked the question no-one wanted to. "Eadwine – ?"

No answer.

They all held their breath, observed that no-one else was breathing in the cell, and exhaled a collective sigh of relief.

"I told Luned to warn him," Lilla said.

"Guid laddie," said Drust, approvingly. "He'll get us out."

Lilla sensibly did not say what the second half of his warning had been.

They wriggled around in the cell and discovered that it was tiny, about eight feet long by six or seven feet wide, and not high enough to stand up in. The walls were made of square-cut stone blocks and the floor was apparently a single slab of stone – none of them had come across cement before. A short flight of steps led up to a trapdoor, which was either very heavy or very firmly bolted down because they were unable to move it. Much to their puzzlement, the cell also contained some big heavy stone slabs lying on the floor or propped up against the walls, covered in carvings and the strange markings that looked like runes but weren't. They could not guess the strange stones' purpose, although Drust was happy to invent one.

"Wouldna mind a chance tae belt yon guard wi' one of these," he muttered.

"If you sit up straight, and let me get behind you," Lilla said, squirming across the floor until he was back-to-back with Drust, "I think I might be able to untie you –"

His bonds did not seem to be tied as tightly as his friends', perhaps because he was the least beefy or perhaps he had just been lucky? At any rate, his fingers had not gone numb. He worked patiently at the knots binding Drust's wrists. One of them seemed to be coming loose –

"Sh!" Ashhere hissed, and they hastily threw themselves flat, Drust rolling onto his back to hide the evidence.

A crack of light glanced in, followed by the grating sound of wood on stone and a square of brilliant light as the trapdoor at the top of the steps was heaved up. Lilla could make out the silhouettes of two men, one broad and squat like an enormous toad, the other giving an impression of medium height and muscular build. He shut his eye hastily. If they thought he was unconscious there was less chance of being beaten or questioned. They were talking, and the Brittonic words swarmed round his aching head like the buzzing of bees, vaguely threatening but completely meaningless.

Until a name caught his attention.

"– Eadwine of Deira –"

Lilla felt his blood congeal in his veins and his heart skipped at least one beat. He listened for all he was worth.

Another voice was speaking now, in a high nasal whine. Lilla recognised it as the Lord of Navio who had nearly ridden them down yesterday. It sounded aggrieved.

"– price of five slave girls in gold, you said –"

"For the right man," returned the first voice. It was clipped and hard and confident, and it did not much care for the Lord of Navio. "Not for any random tramp."

"– and they're all alive, like you said –"

"None of them is *him!* No, you'll have to make what profit you can from these on your own account. I'm not paying you for them."

"There was another one – the bastard who tripped my horse on the road –"

"I'm only interested in Saxons."

"These are Saxons –"

"Not the right one."

"How do you know?"

"Because I was King Ceretic's envoy to Aelle's court, and I met Eadwine of Deira last winter. I'd recognise him anywhere."

Lilla's heart bunked off for another short break, and then started hammering against his chest as if trying to escape. Despite his warning, he knew Eadwine would try to rescue them. And he would walk unknowingly into a trap.

Chapter 14

Eadwine crouched in the inner ditch beside the river-gate. As soon as the sun had set and the dusk had begun to descend he had shifted their packs and weapons up to the tiny chapel above Combe village, reckoning that if the locals all thought it was haunted it was likely to be a safe hiding place. Finally he had crossed the river where it meandered past the fort and had crawled from shadow to shadow across the meadow. He was sure he had not been seen. Now he had nothing to do but wait, watching the moon rise and torturing himself with thoughts of Severa and the handsome standard-bearer. Let her call *him* Iddon too, and see how *he* liked it – !

Eadwine rubbed his eyes as if trying to dispel the image. He had no idea why he should be thinking such things, nor why they should hurt when he was *deeply* in love with someone else. How had the wretched woman got under his skin like this? Perhaps Ashhere had a point after all.

Above his head, the gate creaked. He drew his dagger, which was handier than a sword at close quarters. A line of deeper black appeared as the gate opened a crack, very cautiously, and someone inside whistled a few lines of *Attacotti Nell.*

He slid in through the crack like a corporeal shadow and Severa swiftly closed the gate and dropped the bar back into place with hardly a sound. On the wall above, the sentry's footsteps plodded unconcernedly on. There seemed to be no-one else near.

Eadwine waited until the steps on the wall passed above the gate, then caught her hand and ran with her to the concealing shadow of the nearest building.

"Where's the gate guard?"

Severa's voice was a matching whisper. "Waiting for me behind the stables."

He scowled in the darkness. "While you find somewhere quiet and private, I suppose."

"While I fetch more ointment," she corrected, dryly. "Being known as the witch has its uses. He has terrible piles, poor man."

Eadwine stifled a laugh. Drink or food or even a woman could all have been consumed without the guard leaving his post, but an embarrassing ailment demanded privacy. "You have a talent for this."

He edged along the wall and peered round the corner towards the interior of the fort. The back of the stone headquarters building reared against the sky, and beyond it firelight streamed from the open doors of the hall. It was still early in the evening, the feast was in full swing, and the interior of the fort was busy with people. Servants bringing food, drink, firewood and torches, stable hands seeing to the horses, women fetching water, knots of people standing around gossiping, latecomers strolling to the hall, well-oiled revellers wandering in search of the latrines. There was no chance of passing unseen. The trick was to pass unnoticed.

He put his arm round Severa, drew her close so that her head leaned against his shoulder, and strolled out from the shadows.

"We'll be seen!" she protested.

"Doesn't matter." He paused by the next building, a cattle byre judging from the noises inside, and looked casually around. No-one was paying them any attention. He meandered on to the next shed. A hurrying groom sidestepped them with an apology and a muffled snigger. They were near the damaged end of the headquarters building now, where he had hoped to find a way in, but the guard on the north-west gate looked irritatingly alert. He stopped just within the guard's field of view, backed Severa against the end wall, stooped and kissed her.

"Sorry," he murmured, coming up for air.

"I'm not," she hissed back, and wrapped her arms around his neck.

Out of the corner of his eye Eadwine could see the guard grinning.

"Giggle," he whispered. "Or shriek, or something, but not too loud –"

He stepped backward, pulling her off-balance so that she staggered against him as if drunk, giggling helplessly, and led her behind the headquarters building. A man skulking round the fort on his own would almost certainly have been challenged. But a man and a woman creeping into the ruins together? Everyone knew what they were up to.

It was dark and quiet under the stone wall. Broken tiles and fallen stones littered the ground, and a couple of sizeable bushes and a rowan tree had taken root. The moon sailed high in the sky to the south, casting deep shadows on this side of the building. Eadwine peered up at the wall. The end wall still stood to full height, but a section of the clerestory had fallen in and taken part of the roof with it, leaving a gap where the back wall stood only about eight feet high. He paced the distance from the corner. The collapsed section was nowhere near the shrine room, which was always in the middle. It would lead into one of the old offices, which in turn would lead into the hall, and from the hall he could get to the shrine and the vault. But there were two guards in the hall to get rid of first, and it would have to be done with no noise at all that might raise an alarm.

"Severa? I may need your help again. You were useful just now."

"Useful," she repeated, in an odd tone. "Oh. Good. Delighted to help."

Eadwine was studying the stonework intently, running his hands over it. No obliging creeper to climb up, but the masonry was chipped and cracked from centuries of neglect.

"Good," he said absently. He flexed his stiff shoulder, stood back slightly and jumped lightly for the top of the wall. A couple of footholds, a strong pull with his left arm, and he was up, lying flat along the top of the wall. No-one shouted a challenge. He peered over the other side. Moonlight slanted in patches through the broken roof, and all there seemed to be on the inner side was a floor littered with more roof tiles. A rat skittered across the floor and disappeared into a hole, rattling the tiles as it went. Eadwine held his breath. No-one came. So small disturbances were considered normal. Very slowly, he lowered himself over the inner side until he was hanging at full stretch from both hands, and let himself drop the last few inches to the floor. He made no more noise than the rat, and attracted no more attention.

He climbed back to help Severa scramble over the wall and together they crept to the inner doorway and peered cautiously out into the shadowed expanse of the great hall. It was lit only by a torch stuck in a wall bracket by the arch that led out into the courtyard, and by the moonlight that filtered in through the clerestory windows high above. Straw was piled high at the near end, and there was a strong smell of bat droppings and mice. Along the rear wall the old doorways were black shadows like missing teeth. All the doors had been looted for firewood long ago. The two guards were lounging in the archway, showing no inclination to leave the comforting circle of torchlight. One was short and stout and picking his nose with great attention to detail. The other was tall and talkative.

"– I told you that 'orse wasn't no good," he was lecturing. "Bent fetlocks, see?"

His short colleague grunted, and began excavating his other nostril.

"– now what you should've done, right," continued the tall guard, "you should've took a good look at 'is fetlocks. Always tell a good 'orse by 'is fetlocks, you can –"

"Right," said the short guard, with the glazed despondency of one who sees an evening that promised to be merely dull turning into one of screaming tedium.

"– see, if the fetlocks is good an' straight, right, that 'orse'll win races wi' a sack on 'is back –"

The short guard slouched against the wall and stifled a yawn. Beside him, the voice droned on.

"– Good fetlocks, that's what you need, right, never let you down –"

In his other ear, from the dark interior of the hall, a woman's voice murmured, "Hello, big boy."

The short guard turned, astonished, and was further astonished to find a woman's softly curved arm go round his neck and a woman's hand sliding down over the front of his trousers. He left his spear leaning against the wall and groped into the darkness, a foolish leer on his face. Behind him, the flood of horse expertise came to an abrupt end in a muffled thump and a brief scuffle, but the guard paid it no attention. His evening was suddenly full of unknown promise.

Which ended unhappily when the arm round his neck clamped its hand over his mouth and the other hand clenched tightly and painfully in a very sensitive place. The guard froze, his eyes watering.

"Now then, big boy," murmured the voice, in the same silky tones, "don't make a noise or you'll be a very small boy indeed, you understand? Good lad. Now just you step this way, round the corner –" a sharp tug dispelled any thoughts of disobedience "– where my friend can hit you with half a brick. Good lad."

Severa stooped over the prone body, scrubbing her hand on her cloak.

"Have you killed them?"

"Shouldn't think so," Eadwine grunted, struggling with the guard's tunic. "If you're not going to help me get their clothes off, go and fetch a couple of armfuls of straw."

"Straw?"

"Just do it!"

***

Ten minutes later, the captain of the night watch glanced in from the entrance gate and noted with satisfaction the two dark figures leaning on their spears under the arch. All was quiet, all was well. He exchanged a joke with the guards on the entrance gate and strolled back to his dinner.

***

In the dark shrine room, Eadwine and Severa were struggling to haul a very heavy stone grave slab clear of the trapdoor.

"Should have made the guards shift it before you tied them up –" Severa panted.

"Quiet!"

They heaved again, heels braced against the floor, and the slab slid a few more inches.

Severa felt along the edge of the trapdoor. "It's free!" She grasped the handle.

"Don't lift it!" Eadwine hissed. "Are you mad?"

Severa recoiled from the trapdoor as if it would bite. "What –?"

Eadwine picked up the guard's spear and levered the trapdoor open a crack with the butt-end, standing well back.

"*Attacotti Nell?*" he whispered into the gap.

There was a brief disappointed silence, and then the sound of a very large and heavy stone being set down with some care.

"What kept ye?" said Drust's voice.

***

Eadwine peered very cautiously over the top of the wall. The cluster of sheds and stables seemed deserted now, and nothing moved in the bushes or the shadows at the foot of the wall.

"All clear," he whispered into the dark interior. "Cross one at a time and wait in the bushes. Severa, you come first and keep watch from the corner."

Some shuffling from below indicated a certain amount of competition to give the girl a leg up. Eadwine lowered her to drop gently on the far side, and swung his leg over the wall to follow.

At that moment a man came round the corner.

Severa shrank back into the shadows. Eadwine tensed to spring, but the newcomer was a little too far away and in any case seemed to have noticed nothing amiss. He was weaving a little as he walked, apparently having had a skinful and looking for a convenient place to get rid of some of it

The man belched, reeled against the wall, got his balance back, and then hitched up his tunic, unfastened his waist-cord and pulled the front of his trousers down. A small sigh of anticipated relief, and a pool started spreading around his feet.

Severa, crouching in the shadows, froze. Eadwine, balanced astride the wall, froze. If only the man did not look up! If only he was the type who liked to jet some inoffensive insect off its stalk, or draw a picture on the stonework.

Unfortunately, he was the type who liked to survey the world around him. He rocked back on his heels, and tipped his head back to contemplate the sky and the stars.

Eadwine leapt as soon as he saw the man's mouth open, but it was too far to prevent the man yelling his alarm before they tumbled together into the mud.

The other man was much superior to Eadwine in weight and strength, but he was slowed by drink and hampered by his loosened trousers. He succeeded in smashing the dagger out of Eadwine's hand to send it flying against the wall, and then Eadwine planted his knee hard in the man's belly, rolled on top of him as he tried to double up, and forced the man's face into the mud to choke off his second shout for help. An elbow driven hard into the kidneys, a chopping blow to the back of the neck and the man lay still.

Eadwine picked himself up, breathing hard. Severa had retrieved his dagger and looked ready to use it, and Ashhere was halfway through climbing over the wall. But it was too late.

"This way, men!" a voice called. It was a young, well-bred voice, with the precise intonations of Elmet. "Follow me!"

Half a dozen men at least, judging from the noise, under a keen young captain who believed that mysterious yells for help in the night were part of his concern. Too many to fight, and no time to run. Eadwine snapped at Ashhere, "Back!" and swore savagely under his breath. He was caught, and he would never have been here but for the woman's crazy idea.

The company of soldiers ran round the corner, and Eadwine turned on Severa and struck her to the ground.

***

The young officer found himself confronting a squalid scene. One man sprawled on his face with his trousers round his ankles. A woman cowering against the wall. A second man – no, only a youth, not much more than a boy – standing over her, shouting threats in the hideously rustic local accent.

"– you bitch! Slut! Just like your mother you are, not wed two months and you're whoring a fancy man behind my back –"

"I never!" wailed the woman, clutching at his upraised arm. "I never did! I'm a good girl, I am!"

The officer grimaced in disgust, and not just at the stink of urine. His lord was right, these mountain brigands lived like swine and rutted like stray dogs.

"What's going on here?" he demanded, although really it could hardly have been more obvious.

"That bastard was shagging my wife!"

"He made me do it –!" bawled the woman, bursting into noisy tears. "I'm a good girl, I am!"

The man on the floor groaned, and Eadwine took the opportunity to deliver a swift kick to the head. He lay still again.

"Hey, hey, easy, lad –!" began the officer, and broke off as the outraged husband turned on him like a tiger, clearly more than half-drunk and in the throes of a jealous fury.

"She invite you as well? Eh? Eh? You want a fight as well? Eh? Eh?"

The officer stepped neatly out of the way. It was not honourable to turn weapons on a drunk, even a belligerent one.

"Now then, you come along quietly –" he began, and was interrupted by a shriek from the woman.

"You take your hands off of him! He's my husband, ain't he? You mind your own business!"

The officer gave up. There was no honour in a sordid brawl between two drunks over a woman, especially a woman who wasn't going to be grateful for being rescued. He and his men had better things to do with their time, like watching grass grow. They beat a dignified retreat.

***

Eadwine watched them out of sight, whispered over the wall, "Ash! All clear!", and helped Severa to her feet. He was grinning with the fierce delight of success, and something more.

"You were superb!" There had been no time for instructions or explanations. She had understood in an instant what he was trying to do, and had played up to him brilliantly. "You're a marvel, Severa, a marvel!"

"Truly?"

Her hand was warm in his and she moved closer, but Drust came puffing last over the wall and it was time to go.

***

Ashhere pulled the door of the chapel closed behind him and stepped reluctantly out into the freezing wind, shouldering his pack and wishing in vain for dry clothes. It had been easy enough to get out of the fort. Heavy clouds frequently obscured the moon, allowing them to thread a way unseen through the dark and slumbering stable blocks, and the two guards who should have been patrolling the north-east and north-west walls had been sheltering from the wind and playing a peaceful game of dice with their colleague at the river-gate. Eadwine had had the foresight to bring a rope, so all they had needed to do was creep up the stairway to the deserted ramparts and climb down the rope to freedom. Ashhere had hoped for a rest and a meal at the chapel, since there seemed to be no sign of any pursuit, but they had only paused to grab dried meat and bread out of the packs before setting off along a steep path through the scrubby cattle pastures above Combe village. He bit off another chunk of dried venison, realised the others were already well ahead, and had to run to catch up. Severa was leading, setting a great pace for so small a woman, but then she wasn't carrying a week's worth of supplies and she wasn't soaked and freezing from wading the river. She had stayed in the fort to retrieve the rope, and then simply walked out of the back gate and up the track to Combe. Nobody ever challenged a woman carrying a couple of buckets. At least, that was her explanation. Ashhere was entertaining certain private thoughts about cats, or possibly bats. He touched both his amulets in turn. He had decided to keep the replacement as well. Thunor would be twice as helpful now.

***

Two miles away and five hundred feet below, a couple of sleepy guards were reluctantly shuffling through the stone courtyard to begin their watch.

"Right, Mabon, Hywel," – huge yawn – "off you go, you lucky beggars –"

No response from the two figures propped either side of the archway.

"'Ere, wake up, you lazy sods –" He reached out and shook the nearest figure by the shoulder. "Mabon?" A harder shake. "Mabon!"

The head lolled slowly forward, forward, forward, rolled off and fell to the floor –

"Aaargh!"

– where it was revealed to be a roughly spherical bundle of straw stuffed into Mabon's woollen cap.

"*Captain!*"

***

"I think they've found your straw men and the trussed chickens in the cellar," Severa commented, as the horns blared in the valley.

"Sooner than I hoped," Eadwine answered, quickening his pace. "Lucky there was a big feast for the visitors. We'll have another hour before anyone's sober enough to ride."

"Yon eager pup wasna drunk," Drust observed, " and I'll bet his boss wasna."

"So we get a move on."

"They'll ride ahead and block the road," Lilla panted, a few paces behind, "and if they recognise you –"

"I wasn't planning to go by the road."

They had reached one of the cols on the ridge joining the Swine Hill to Shivering Mountain. On the far side another blind valley bit into the hills, and beyond it the fitful moon gleamed on a line of dark cliffs crowned by rocky teeth.

"That's Kyndyr!" Lilla exclaimed. "Luned says there's no way over it!"

Severa laughed, as clear and buoyant a sound as the skylark's song. "There is if you're with me! That valley is Combe's hafod, and I spent seven summers retrieving stray sheep from Kyndyr. No-one else would go there."

"Don't blame them," Ashhere muttered, fumbling for his amulets.

She laughed again. "Don't fear, I won't let the trolls eat you! Come on!"

She leapt away down the path, her hair flying in the wind, and Ashhere wondered why she seemed so happy on a freezing moor in the middle of the night. Women were contrary creatures, right enough. He did not see that Eadwine was close by her side, nor did he notice when each reached for the other's hand.

***

First light found them in a bleak wilderness of peat. More precisely, at the bottom of a twisting channel where an icy stream had carved its way through the peat to the underlying gritstone. The whole plateau top was riven with these channels, like the cracks in a giant cowpat, and they were deep enough that even a tall man could not see over the sides. Ashhere had no idea where they were. All he knew was that they had walked all night with hardly any rest, first taking narrow paths through thick woodland and across a marshy valley floor, then crossing a river at a deep ford, then a lung-bursting climb up an ever-steepening rocky valley that pierced the hillside like a sword slash, and finally this maze of peat, sometimes following the channels and sometimes having to thrash and slither over the ridges from one channel to another. In daylight it would have been arduous. At night, having to grope for each step and continually stumbling on rocks and disintegrating peat, it had been unimaginably slow and exhausting. They were all wet, cold, weary and peat-stained, and Ashhere half thought he would have preferred to take his chances with the Lord of Navio's soldiers on the road.

The channel they were following now was wider and deeper than most, and the trickle of water in the bottom was almost wide enough to be called a stream. In the distance ahead, the half-light showed two giant grey shapes standing guard on either side of the channel. Ashhere supposed they were trolls, or ancient standing stones of malevolent power, but he was too tired to care. He plodded on, and with diminishing distance and growing light the two shapes resolved into a pair of gritstone tors. Beyond these sentinels the channel made a wide bend to the left and the stream gathered volume to become an infant river running in a sandy bed. A little further on, and it threaded through a jumble of gritstone boulders and plunged over a rocky fall to vanish in a dark hollow scooped out of the plateau side.

Ashhere stared at it, uncomprehending. His first thought was that they had wandered around in a circle and come to the ravine they had climbed up in the night, but he did not remember a waterfall. And slowly he realised that the sun was rising behind him, and the blue-shadowed plains rolling away to a distant horizon were in the *west*.

"You have crossed Kyndyr," said Severa's voice, behind him. "Not many men can say that! The safe way down is another mile further on. I will show you, but first stop and drink. This is the best drinking water for miles."

She was right. The water was clear, cold and refreshing, and they drank, refilled water bottles and skins, and washed off the worst of the peat. Eadwine produced a leather flask of mead and handed it round, and that, together with the watery sunlight filtering through the clouds, completed the cure. A gritstone edge led north and west from the falls, giving easy walking on flat slabs and sandy peat, and as they followed it the plateau edge became less and less precipitous and the boulders less and less frequent.

Severa stopped beside the last of the boulders, where the edge faded away altogether and the way ahead dropped gently down into a shallow saddle.

"The army-path runs in a deep valley beyond those moors to the north," she said, pointing to their right. "But you should cross the low ridge directly ahead, north-west, and then any of the streams on its far side will lead you down to the river and so to Ardotalia fort. What you will find there I do not know, but it is not in his lordship's lands. This is as far as my knowledge goes." She included them all in a brilliant, brittle smile. "I wish you well. May the Father and the Son and the Blessed Lady Mary look on you with favour." She held out her hand to Eadwine. "Fare you well, Steeleye. May you come safely to your home and your lady."

Eadwine took the proffered hand. It did not seem real that they should part, not now, not yet. He had intended to thank her, to say some brief and decorous farewell and then set off on his way. But as she stood looking up at him, her long hair swirling about her face, he no longer cared about hunting a murderer, avenging his father and his beloved brother, even about seeking Aethelind. Nothing seemed to matter, except that he would never see Severa again.

"Come with us."

It was an utterly stupid thing to ask. He had no home, no land, no money, no means of supporting a woman, and he was committed to a task that was almost certain to end in failure and death. He was not even free. Yet all he could think of was that he could not bear to be without her.

She buried her face in his shoulder. "Oh, Steeleye!" Her voice was not much above a whisper. "I *can't*."

He stroked her hair. She was not free either. But what kind of life would be waiting for her now?

"Navio will find out that you helped us. He hates you, Severa."

She drew a shuddering breath and raised her head. "I'm not afraid of him."

"I am. I fear for you."

Her eyes met his. "Is that the reason you want me to come?"

He knew he should have said yes. He should have lied to her to make this parting easier. But even as he was trying to think of the words, he slowly shook his head.

A spark flickered up in the expressive eyes. "Then what is?"

"This."

Her lips were soft, her body warm and pliant against his, her arms around his neck, her hands tangled in his hair. He was no longer aware of cold or fatigue, no longer saw the moorland or felt the searching wind. All that mattered, in this world or the next, was the woman in his arms.

It was Severa who drew back, laying her cheek against his chest so that he could no longer see her face.

"I don't want you to go," she whispered.

"I must."

"I know." She let him slip his fingers under her chin and tilt her face up to his. "You belong to someone else." She kissed him again, with a despairing fierceness. "Oh, I am a fool, a fool!" She pulled away, dashing the back of her hand across her eyes. "Go! Go now, before it is too late. And forget me!"

***

Eadwine looked back once. She had climbed up onto one of the boulders, as though to keep them in sight as long as possible. Her hair tossed wildly against the pale sky, and one hand was half-outstretched as though in entreaty or farewell. He checked his stride, hesitated a heartbeat, and turned back – but she was gone. The rocks and the sweeping moorland were empty, bereft of human voice or figure. She was gone, and he set his face once more to his onward journey, knowing that he could not do the only thing she had asked of him. He would never forget her.

Chapter 15

Severa stumbled down the rain-slicked path through Combe village, not caring who saw her. The sun was already setting, and it would be dark before she got home. She did not care about that either. All her future seemed dark. During those few hours of shared danger she had tasted the exhilaration of risk and fear and success, and something more. It was as if she had come truly alive for the first time. Now the routine of village and hafod seemed no more than a joyless living death, a drudgery without hope and without reward. For nearly four years she had waited for Iddon's return, and now she knew she did not want him back. Life with Iddon had given her status, comfort and security, insofar as those things could be had in the Lord of Navio's orbit. It had never given her joy or colour or laughter or desire, and because she had never experienced these things she had not mourned their lack. Until now.

She sobbed aloud in sudden agony. Steeleye had asked her to go with him. What had possessed her to refuse? But what choice had she had? He was going back to his betrothed, and if he found her he would marry her, and then what could she be to him – a mistress at best, more likely a discarded slut to be abandoned on the roadside. She scrubbed an angry hand across her eyes. It was all her own fault, it served her right, she had always known no good could come of it. Like a chicken trying to flutter after a hawk, she had made a fool of herself. But oh God, to watch him go, and to a woman he did not even love! Another sob shook her. He couldn't have kissed her like that if he was in love with someone else, he could *not*. Unless he was a duplicitous deceiving two-faced rat, and he wasn't that, surely he wasn't that. Although she remembered the ease with which he had deceived the guards, and before that the bandits. When he was playing a part everything changed, his face and his posture and even the tone of his voice, as easily as putting on a mask. He could have deceived her just as easily, and she was going to spend the rest of her miserable life longing for someone who had already forgotten all about her.

"Oh, God!" The cry was torn from her. "I wish I was dead!"

A door opened, spilling a wash of light over the track. People crowded out of houses and barns, surrounding Severa in a wide circle. The voice of her sister-in-law shrilled, high and clear, "See, I told you! I told you there was no birthing! Slut! Liar! She's been with a fancy man! She's not fit to be a headman's wife!"

The cry was taken up. Severa had endured mockery before, but this had a note of fear in it, as though they believed that attacking her would pacify some other malevolent force. What it was she did not know – until the Lord of Navio pushed his horse through the crowd. With him were a dozen men with spears and a wolf-net, and Severa's brother scampered at his side.

"I'll take her, my lord!" He plucked at the Lord of Navio's saddle in his eagerness. "Give her to me. It's my duty to take her in. I'll see that she's punished, I swear it."

Severa gazed at him, too numb to care. What did it matter whether she wore away her life in domestic drudgery in Iddon's house or in her brother's?

The Lord of Navio did not answer. His gaze was fixed on Severa, his lips drawn back in a feral grin, and she realised that she had a third choice.

She found her voice, bitter despair lending it a mocking note. "Punished for what, brother dear? Adultery?" She laughed, never taking her eyes from the lord's face. "Oh, I have better things to do than that!" She raised her hand, and saw Navio flinch a little. Yes, he remembered.

Her brother was still flapping and pleading. The Lord of Navio pushed him away as he might spurn a tiresome hound. "No. *I* will take her."

***

Severa stared straight ahead in the smoky hall. The wolf-net was tight over her head and upper body, pinning her arms to her sides, but she had not even tried to struggle.

The Lord of Navio glared at her from his high-seat. She was drenched from the day's rain, weary and bedraggled, but the green eyes met his with a defiant contempt that brought back humiliating memories of black pudding and a village's mockery. Bitch! The stuff had been disgustingly greasy, and a vile stink had clung about him for weeks afterwards. He had even had to take a bath. But he would get rid of her this time, and with a bit of luck he could get that prettified dandy from Elmet to do it, and then any curse would fall on him.

"What were you doing in the fort?"

Her voice was calm, almost bored. "Conjuring demons to fill your belly with writhing snakes of fire."

"Ha! It didn't work!"

"I didn't say it would be immediate."

"Who was the man you were with?"

"The Lord of the Underworld."

Some of the watching spearmen shifted uneasily. The Lord of Navio scowled. He would dearly like to throw the bitch to his spearmen and then to the dogs, but most likely neither would dare touch her. His stomach grumbled, and he waited anxiously for any sign of a writhing snake of fire, but it seemed to be only indigestion.

"How did the prisoners escape?"

"I turned them into toads and they crawled away through the stones."

He turned triumphantly to the lord from Elmet. "See? She admits it!"

A frosty stare. "The prisoners were yours, not ours. Is this charade to go on much longer?"

The woman laughed. "If you want to murder me, your lordship, it seems you'll have to do it yourself. Tell me, do you still eat black pudding?"

There was a snigger from the back of the hall. Someone else remembered the incident. The Lord of Navio glowered. And he had another score to settle with her.

"Where's the bastard who tripped my horse?"

"He went south."

"Ha! My men on the dyke never saw him!"

"I turned him into a starling and he flew over their heads."

"Where were you today?"

"On Shivering Mountain, sacrificing a black goat to the Lord of the Underworld. Before Beltane comes you will be struck down, your breath will choke in your throat, your skin will turn grey and peel off in sheets —"

"Enough!" The Lord of Navio had blanched.

The envoy from Elmet exchanged a superior glance with his standard-bearer. How these peasant brigands clung to their rustic superstitions! But he put a hand to his crucifix, just in case.

The Lord of Navio was on his feet. "You will die, bitch!"

"It comes to us all in the end."

The standard-bearer failed to stifle a laugh and turned it hurriedly into a cough. By the Blessed Lady, but the girl had spirit! He had once seen a woman like her in the entourage of a very rich wine merchant, all high cheekbones and golden skin, redolent of strange countries under a hot sun far away, and had determined to own one himself some day. Now he looked at the tangled mane of black hair and imagined it combed smooth, imagined her clothed in silks and serving wine in his hall to his envious friends, and then later there would be more wine, but no silk —

"My lord!" He stepped forward. "Will you sell her as a slave girl? I will give you gold for her."

The green eyes widened momentarily, flicked over him as though he were the one on sale, and then were veiled by thick lashes. God —! He would be the envy of all his friends.

The Lord of Navio turned slowly, his piggy eyes narrow.

"So she can put a curse on me from afar? You think I'm a fool?"

The standard-bearer did, but it was not the moment to say so. Over his head, the frosty voice of his lord said, "We would not dream of interfering, my lord. Please excuse the interruption."

The Lord of Navio's voice filled the hall. "She must die!"

Nobody moved. The woman laughed again. "Remember," she taunted, "any man who touches me with blade or hand will die. His hands will drop off, his teeth will fall out, he will drown in his own blood." A mocking glance swept the hall. "Who wants to be first?"

"Stone her!" A heavy wooden platter struck her face with enough force to draw blood. The Lord of Navio grinned wolfishly. "Ha! She can die without being touched. Stone her!"

"My body will rise from the grave to haunt you," mocked the woman. The thread of blood down her cheek gave her a demonic look, and the standard-bearer was half-relieved that his bid had failed.

No more missiles came. The Lord of Navio was practically dancing in fury.

"No body! No grave! Push her into the fire!"

The girl's voice was scornful. "And my ashes will curse the place of my death until the end of time."

"Cowards!" screamed the Lord of Navio at his shuffling spearmen. "What do I feed you for? Get a horse! An old one," he added hastily, in case horses could be cursed too.

Severa made no resistance as they tied the trailing line of the wolf-net to the horse's harness, and that seemed to encourage the spearmen. A few even found the nerve to throw stones at her as she was marched up to Combe village and forced into the chapel.

"This place is already cursed!" bawled the Lord of Navio, as his men hauled a heavy rock against the door and stacked the walls high with the village's firewood supply. "Let her die here with her heathen demons!"

He thrust a torch into the pile. The wood sputtered and caught. More torches were thrown in, and the fire grew. Much of the firewood was wet from the day's rain, and clouds of choking smoke billowed across the hillside. The wet thatch flared in ragged patches and spat showers of sparks into the air to whirl away on the wind and die as they fell to the sodden earth. A few mice fled squeaking from the flames, their fur smoking, and the Lord of Navio and his spearmen ran to stamp on them in case one was the witch's spirit escaping.

One of the heavy roof timbers fell in with a crash, sending up a sheet of sparks and a thick swirl of smoke that blotted chapel and hillside temporarily from sight. Soon the others were outlined in fire, eerily beautiful against the dark sky, like a skeleton clothed in flame. As the first beam fell in there was a long-drawn bubbling scream from the blaze, a scream that could have come from the tortured depths of the Underworld. And then nothing but the roar of the fire.

***

"This fort's deserted like the other two," Lilla reported back, in the murky half-light of a wet morning. "Doesn't anybody live in this country at all?"

"Not any more, by the look of it" Eadwine answered, hoisting his pack. "Heledd's bard said some people call it Makerfield, the Field of Ruins. I thought he was exaggerating."

"Bloody awful place," Ashhere grumbled. "No food, not a building with a roof, *and* it rains all the bloody time."

This was not quite true. It had in fact stopped raining at least twice during the two days and two nights since they had left Severa, but the transition from cold depressing drizzle to cold depressing gloom and back again was of purely academic interest. And the country was as desolate as its weather. Expecting to find local warlords ensconced in the surviving fortifications, they had approached Ardotalia fort and the two small walled towns with extreme care, and found all of them to be roofless ruins apparently inhabited only by mice. Villages and farmsteads were reduced to weed-grown hummocks, patches of nettles on the old middens, and the occasional charred or broken timber. Wells were stagnant or blocked with debris. Fruit lay rotting on the ground in dilapidated orchards. On both sides of the road, fields and pastures were turning back to scrub. If there were any inhabitants, they kept themselves well hidden. The only sign of human life they had seen in thirty miles were a few bleached

146

bones scattered among the weeds. It was a salutary reminder to all of them – except Eadwine, who had known from the beginning – that exile was not going to be all friendly farms and pretty women. Drust had hardly said a word for two days, Lilla appeared to be sunk in a fit of the sulks, and Ashhere occasionally found himself thinking wistfully of the Lord of Navio's dungeon.

"At least that was dry," he muttered to himself, trying unsuccessfully to adjust his pack so that the straps did not cut into his shoulders through his wet tunic. "Not surprising nobody lives here, what a dump, no good to man nor beast –"

"Shows what you know about it," Lilla snapped, behind him. "It's good country, this, flat and fertile. Look at the size of the nettles. It's poisoned. Or it's cursed."

"It's a country without a lord," Eadwine cut in, before Ashhere had even managed to reach for his amulets. "The king was killed in our grandfathers' day and since then it's been raided and fought over and raided again. It's been claimed by half a dozen kingdoms and defended by none of them, and Irish pirates raid from the coast into the bargain. No farmer can make a living with rival armies passing through every year. Plant crops and they'll be trampled, build a house and it'll be torched, breed livestock and they'll be stolen, raise a family and they'll be enslaved or murdered. So one by one the farmers give up. No farmers means no warlords. Now it looks like even bandits can't make a living here." He shot a sharp glance over his shoulder. "And you can think on that, Lilla, while you're cursing me for not taking revenge on the Lord of Navio. Quite apart from the fact that four against fifty is lousy odds, how long do you think they'd have survived without a lord? Bastard he may be, but he has to keep his sheep alive so he can fleece them."

Lilla flushed. "I never said –" he began defensively.

"No," came the dry response, "you didn't have to." He lengthened his stride. "We'd better get moving. I want to cross the moors before dark. It'll be cold up there."

The army-path, which had been following an ever-narrowing valley, now decided that the valley was no longer going in the right direction and abandoned it to zig-zag steeply up the side, emerging onto a plateau of soggy moorland blanketed in equally soggy fog. Visibility was no more than a few hundred yards, but the army-path carved a straight course into the grey distance, giving the comforting impression that it thought it was going somewhere. Ashhere, who had been hopelessly lost since they left home, hoped it was right.

He hurried to keep up with Eadwine. "Cross the moor? What's on the other side?"

Something that might have been a sigh. "Elmet, of course."

"You can't go to Elmet now!" Lilla burst out. "Were you listening to me? They're looking for you there as well!"

"It's nice to be popular, isn't it?"

"That thane of Ceretic's said he knew you!"

"So? He's in Navio, not in Elmet."

"There'll be others! If you're recognised –!"

"I know." Eadwine ran a hand over his chin. "I've got an idea about that."

Everyone they had encountered since leaving Deira, from Severa to the Lord of Navio, had assumed he was Brittonic. Partly because he was dark and slim when popular prejudice declared all Saxons to be blond and beefy, but mainly because he spoke the language as if it were his mother tongue – which, of course, it was. Language was the great identifier in Britannia. The Brittonic dialects and the Anglian dialects were utterly different in structure, sounds, grammar and stress patterns and the only words they had in common were the handful that both had borrowed from Latin. Communities spoke one or the other, never both. Many people spoke some of the other language if it was useful to them – in parts of Deira the headmen of neighbouring villages usually knew enough to settle boundary disputes, negotiate marriages and borrow one another's stud livestock – but it was invariably obvious which was the native tongue and which was learned. In mixed marriages, women expected to learn the language of their husband's village and their children would be raised speaking the husband's language, whichever way round it was. Fluent Brittonic instantly labelled him as Brittonic. The bandit raid had provided him with a Brittonic sword, a Brittonic spear and a Brittonic brooch, and now, courtesy of Severa, he also had a genuine Brittonic cloak. His hair had been sorely in need of cutting since the summer and was now nearly down to his shoulders, not far off the length favoured by Brittonic men. About the only part of his appearance that might suggest his Anglian origin was his scruffy beard. Sadly, it would have to go. A reason for travelling would complete a plausible disguise. Severa had joked that he could earn a living as a bard, and while he hoped he would never have to rely on it for his bread, it was a useful idea. Many bards did wander the land from one court to another, particularly young men who had yet to find a rich patron. They were usually from the weapon-bearing upper classes, invariably educated, and often had servants or other hangers-on. He fitted the pattern fairly well. And no-one searching for a Saxon prince was likely to look very hard at a Brittonic bard.

Accordingly, as soon as they descended from the moors and reached the first valleys and farms of Elmet, he haggled for some hours with a village headman and obtained a harp and a razor in exchange for his carved ivory comb and the decorative bronze plates from his belt. And three days later a tall, willowy, languid young man, with a harp under his arm and a nick in his chin, was to be seen lounging nonchalantly against a wall at a lord's hall on the Wharfe, waiting with a crowd of other suppliants for Princess Heledd to come out of church.

***

"I didn't recognise you!" Heledd exclaimed. "You look so different! It was only when you asked for alms in Latin that I knew it must be you!" She hugged him again. "Oh, I'm so glad to see you! But what possessed you to come here? Don't you know there's a price on your head?"

"Rather a good one, so I hear," Eadwine answered, sinking gratefully into a chair and stretching his tense muscles. After that fleeting instant of stunned recognition, Heledd had casually hired him to entertain the hall in exchange for a meal and a bed for the night, and being the focus of all attention for most of the evening had wound his nerves up tighter than his harp-strings. It was not easy to play, and sing, and get the words in the right order, while expecting at every moment to feel a heavy hand on his shoulder or a knife in his back. He had got through two tales of Arthur and the Dream of Prince Macsen – long-dead heroes were the safest subject in a foreign hall where he did not know the local politics – before Heledd had announced that she would retire to her private chamber as she had a headache, and perhaps the bard would be good enough to come with her and play some soothing music to ease the pain. Lamps were lit, mead brought, her servants and ladies shooed out, and now, finally, they were alone.

"I'll say it's a good price!" Heledd returned. "He doesn't like being beaten. All Britannia knows you escaped, and all Britannia is sniggering behind its hand watching Aethelferth the Twister hunting shadows. When it isn't plotting how to obtain the reward, that is."

"Tempted?"

"Don't tease. I owe you my life and Hereric's. But others might be."

"Ceretic, for instance? Yes, I know. At least he stipulated all of me, alive, not just my head. One must be grateful for small mercies. What of you? Is he treating you well?"

"Of course he is. His father was my brother. He'd be universally despised if he did anything against me and mine. Besides, I'm not dependent entirely on Ceretic's goodwill. On my mother's side I'm kin to the Lords of Wharfedale, and cousin Constantine welcomed me with open arms, gave me the use of this hall and the estate that goes with it. We were always close. You need not fear for me."

"Is Hereric safe?"

She nodded vigorously. "He is at court with Constantine's youngest brother. Ceretic is taking an interest in him, and he is with the other youngsters training for a place in the warband. Almost like a foster-son."

"Can you trust Ceretic?"

"With Hereric, yes. In the first place, he would not sink so low as to betray a blood-tie. In the second place, Wulfgar and Wulfraed are with Hereric as his bodyguards, and it's a brave man would incur their wrath. What they lack in brains they make up for in brawn. And in the third place, Ceretic does not dare annoy the Lords of Wharfedale. Constantine controls his northern border and he knows it. Besides, the Twister does not seem much interested in Hereric. It's you he wants. I don't know why."

"Oh, thank you."

Heledd wrinkled her nose. "Don't be obtuse. What I mean is, you're not the only atheling left. Both your cousins survived."

"Osric and Aethelric? Good for them. How?"

"Osric got lost on the way to Eboracum, met some survivors, ran home in a panic, and his wife bundled him and everything else she could carry onto a ship bound for Kent. It must have been the most overloaded vessel since the Ark. The last I heard, they were settled in at Aethelbert's court for the duration."

Eadwine laughed softly. For anyone else, getting lost on the way to a battle would have been at best a polite fiction. For the hapless Osric it was quite likely to be true. Osric blundered through life with an air of hopeful puzzlement, apparently unable to do anything right but always willing to try again.

"And Aethelric?"

"Aethelric is King of Deira."

Eadwine jolted upright so sharply that he spilled his mead. "You're joking!"

"No. He was captured a few days after the battle, and Aethelferth put him in prison for a while. Then when he went back north he probably thought his new province might be quieter if he let them pretend they've got their own king. So he got Aethelric out of prison, dusted him off, and installed him as King of Deira. I'm told Ceretic wet himself laughing when he heard."

"I'm not surprised. Aethelric King! I've seen jellyfish with more backbone."

"I think that's his chief attraction. No chance of him starting another revolt."

Eadwine tensed. "Revolt? What revolt?"

"Oh, it didn't amount to much. The Twister parcelled out the land among his thanes, as you'd expect, and it seems a handful of peasants somewhere in the north took exception to their new lord and threw him out." She shook her head. "Brave, but stupid. You can guess Aethelferth's reaction. He sent a warband north, with instructions to take no prisoners."

"They didn't deserve that," Eadwine whispered. Somewhere in the north. In his country? Some of the farmers on the March were probably boneheaded enough to revolt against Aethelferth the Twister.

"Nobody deserves that," Heledd said sombrely. "He sent Black Dudda."

Eadwine drew a sharp breath. "Again?"

"What do you mean, again? Do you know him?"

"He led the invading army, before Eboracum. I crossed swords with him then, and he came off worst. If he's taking it out on the March, on my patch –!"

"If he is, there's nothing you can do about it," Heledd cut in sharply. "You shouldn't even be here. You should be a long, long way away, out of the Twister's reach. Is that why you came to me? You need money? A ship? I can find Constantine's wine merchant, and I think we have a distant cousin somewhere in Gaul –"

"No."

"Then what do you think you're doing here?"

"Hunting my brother's murderer."

He explained his suspicions about Beortred – the unique knife that matched the murder weapon, Beortred's suspicious secret flight. Heledd listened, frowning.

"Captain Beortred? I can hardly believe it."

"I didn't want to believe it either."

"And you would risk your life to take revenge?"

"I owe it to Eadric. He would expect no less."

"The good opinion of a ghost," she remarked dryly, "is not something I would set great store by. You are as big a fool as he was."

"That is my concern," Eadwine retorted, annoyed. "But if you care little for your husband's honour, do you care more for the life of your son?"

Heledd paled. "*Hereric?*"

"It was you that said it. He who killed the father may also try to kill the son."

"And you think he will come here?"

"Not if I find him first."

She swallowed. "But it is such a risk. For you. Could not someone else –?"

"Hereric is Eadric's son. All that is left of Eadric on this earth. I'd protect him with my life. Now will you help me?"

"What do you need?"

"Nothing too taxing. First, refuge. For me and my three companions."

"Then you're hired for the winter as court bard. Your friends will have to make themselves useful, though. They can sleep with the servants."

"I assumed we all would. Second, news. I want to know if anyone remotely answering Beortred's description is seen. You were always well-informed, and that doesn't seem to have changed."

"Constantine has a lot of spies," she said, with a crooked half-smile. "He hears things, shall we say. So do I. There are a few refugees from Deira in Elmet already. Mostly people with family ties here, but anyone who has nowhere to go comes cap in hand to me, widow of the Aetheling. Astonishing the number of people who claim to have been in Eadric's service. I had no idea we had such a big household."

He sat forward eagerly. "Who? Can you give me names? And where they are living?"

She shrugged, with a yawn. "If you don't mind it taking all night. Let me see –"

A tap at the door made them both stiffen and Eadwine reach a hand to his dagger, but it was only an elderly woman who entered, looking around her with eager curiosity.

"Begging your pardon, my lady, but I was just wondering if you and the – gentleman – would be wanting anything?"

"No," Heledd said firmly. "Go to bed, Eurdyl. *Now*. Irritating woman," she confided, as the door closed behind the disappointed gossip. "Still, I suppose we have been in here for quite some time now."

"Shouldn't I play the harp or something?" Eadwine suggested, feeling the colour rise in his face. "They might wonder – I mean, they might think –"

"Oh, they'll think you're my toy-boy. *Everybody* knows about rich widows and their bards." She gave him a sunny smile. "Don't look so shocked! Did you think epithets like 'Silvertongue' referred to singing? You can be such an innocent."

Eadwine glared at her, feeling foolish, hurt and a little disgusted by her levity. How could she not mourn the death of the finest man in the world?

"You seem to have taken your husband's death very well."

"Listen," Heledd said, in a changed tone. "You cannot expect everyone to mourn him as you do. I know you thought him a god come to earth, but it was not so. You hardly saw him for these last three years, or you might not be so blind. Waiting to be king had soured him. He wanted it so much, and here he was turned forty and Aelle was still blundering along refusing to die, interfering in everything and heaping honours on his bastard son. Honours that should have gone to you – Eadric's faithful shadow and therefore no threat – but instead were going to his rival. He feared that by the time Aelle finally had the decency to die he would be too old and the Council would pass him over. Eadric was never a patient man, and the anger was eating him up. Sometimes he flew into such a rage that I feared for my life."

"Eadric would never harm a woman," Eadwine insisted.

She sighed. "I knew you'd say that. But you don't know what you're saying. You never crossed his will."

***

Eadwine left Heledd shortly after and picked his way carefully among the snoring bodies in the hall to the main door. Ashhere was sitting on watch beside the weapon rack, with Lilla and Drust stretched out on either side. He moved over when he saw Eadwine, leaving a vacant sleeping place, but Eadwine declined the offer with a smile and a shake of the head. He knew he ought to sleep, but he also knew he would not be able to. He pulled his cloak tighter round his shoulders, groped for the door latch, and slipped silently out into the night.

It was cold, damp and overcast outside, but at least it wasn't raining. He paced up and down along the length of the hall, the steady rhythm helping to shake his thoughts into some sort of order. Heledd's attitude was a disappointment – she seemed happier as a widow than she ever had as a wife – but that was none of his business, no matter how angry he was at the insult to Eadric's memory. What mattered now was finding Beortred and avenging

Eadric's death. And then he would be free to find Aethelind. He hugged the thought to him. Heledd's news that Aethelferth was still searching with unabated ferocity had sent his spirits soaring. All Britannia knew he had survived. Therefore Aethelind, wherever she was, would know he had survived. She would know he would come for her. All she had to do was wait. He imagined finding her, unhappy and dishevelled perhaps, but still with that voluptuous beauty undimmed – and she would throw herself into his arms – and he would carry her away –

At which point his imagination failed him. Try as he might, he could not see Aethelind, the girl who had balked at the minor discomforts of living on the March, enduring the hardship and danger of life as a hunted exile. Whenever he thought of Aethelind, he saw her sitting placidly in the sun with her embroidery, or (more often) in his bed. Not even his fertile imagination could conjure a picture of Aethelind opening the gate of a hostile fort, or deceiving enemy guards, or facing down the Lord of Navio. Aethelind would not be his active ally. She would have to be looked after, escorted, guarded, taken care of. In short, she would be an unmitigated nuisance –

He stopped short as if he had walked into a wall. Had he really just thought that? About his beloved Aethelind? For shame! A woman's place was in the home. It was the man's place – his place – to provide that home. So he would find a way. Somehow. Aethelind was pledged to him by a solemn promise, and he would keep faith with her.

***

Heledd's information sources yielded no word of Aethelind. But they did provide the names of people who had fled Deira and were now living in Elmet, and those people turned out to have relatives and friends and friends of friends, scattered all over the kingdom. Searching among them all for news of Beortred was a long task. The choice of travelling bard as a disguise proved to have two huge unforeseen advantages. In the first place, it stilled – or rather, channelled – all the inevitable gossip that surrounded the presence of a stranger at Heledd's court. Anyone enquiring who he might be was sure to receive the answer "Ooo-ooh, he's the lady's new *bard* [nudge, wink]", and by the time someone had smirked, "I hear he's very good, you know," and got the reply, "And he plays the harp quite well too," and they had all fallen about digging each other in the ribs and sniggering, the gossips' interest appeared to be satisfied. And in the second place, it gave him complete freedom of movement. Whereas the arrival of armed strangers caused respectable people to bolt inside their houses and bar the doors, the harp under his arm guaranteed an instant welcome from shepherd's hut to lord's hall. He could travel in dead of winter, alone or with one or more of his companions, and they could be sure of a meal of some sort, even if it was turnip soup and stale bread, and shelter for the night, even if it was in a barn or a shed. In this fashion, Eadwine crossed and re-crossed Elmet many times that winter, from the villages perched on islands in the eastern fens to the sheep farms in the foothills of the moors, and from the Wharfe in the north to the Don and the Sheaf in the south. He met men who had fought in Eadric's hearth-troop, men who had fled the burning in Eboracum Vale, and a great many more who turned out to have nothing whatever to do with Deira. None of them was Beortred, and none of them had seen or heard anything of Beortred, either. By the time Yule – or Christ Mass, as Heledd's household called it – had come and gone, and the days were getting longer and colder, he was beginning to question whether Beortred had ever intended to pursue Hereric to Elmet at all, and, by extension, whether Beortred had had anything to do with Eadric's murder. He had failed to pick up the trail, and must cast about for a new lead. And then Heledd relayed the gossip that yet another envoy from Aethelferth was on his way to Ceretic's court. It had to be important, for no-one travelled in winter if they could help it. An exchange of galloping messengers, and Heledd's younger cousin whisked Hereric away on a hunting trip deep in family territory. If the envoy was coming to demand Hereric, no-one was prepared to trust entirely to Ceretic's word for his safety. And Eadwine, knowing that the most likely place he would be recognised was Ceretic's court and that recognition would mean instant death (if he was lucky), set out as unobtrusively as possible for Loidis. He went alone, much to the alarm of his friends, who tried to insist on accompanying him until he pointed out sharply that they were far more likely to attract attention than he was.

***

Accommodation was cramped at Loidis with most of the court and a foreign ambassador in residence, and a travelling bard of no reputation was a long way down the pecking order. Eadwine was consigned to an outbuilding, which suited him very well as being out of the way, and gave him an opportunity to get himself knocked down in a dispute over bed space. One black eye, a swollen jaw and a few more bruises later, even Hereric might have had some difficulty recognising him.

***

Ceretic's hall was crowded. Ceretic himself was lounging comfortably in his high-seat, with most of his advisors ranged on carefully placed flanking benches. The envoy from Aethelferth had been given a chair on the dais, a mark of respect, but not *too* much respect, for it had been carefully chosen to seat him just a little lower than Ceretic. His bodyguards were consigned to the ordinary mead-benches at the foot of the dais, where they sat looking frankly bored. Some of Ceretic's warband had just come back from hunting and were monopolising the fire, and anyone else who could find an excuse to be there had come along to watch. The formal reception of a foreign envoy often turned into a verbal battle that was as much a display of the king's prowess as a duel or a wrestling match. No-one paid any attention to a young bard, plainly down on his luck, mending a broken harp-string in a dark corner.

At first Eadwine thought he had walked twenty miles and picked a fight for nothing. The envoy was arguing with Ceretic about the tariffs charged to the Frisian and Frankish slave traders. Aethelferth had apparently demanded higher tariffs from the traders at Eboracum, whereupon they had negotiated better terms from Ceretic for access to the Aire for the coming season. Aethelferth was not pleased. Ceretic was. The subsequent wrangle was a tour de force of courteous obstructionism on Ceretic's part that left the envoy red-faced and furious and Eadwine stifling admiring laughter. He had last met Ceretic about eight years previously and remembered him as a pimply youth with a permanently sulky expression. Clearly there was more to Ceretic than met the eye. He wished the Bernician bodyguards would be quiet so he could hear properly. They had been served with wine – a great honour, for wine was brought great distances from Gaul – and they didn't appreciate it.

"Poncy stuff," complained a stentorian whisper in the Bernician dialect.

"Yeah."

"Tastes like sheep's piss."

"Yeah, right."

"Dunno what these poncy toss-pots see in it."

"Too right."

153

Eadwine leaned closer to the leader.

"Excuse me," he whispered, speaking Anglian but with a strong Brittonic accent, "like you not?" He pointed to their cups, which despite their complaints were all empty. "Want you mead?"

He beckoned to a passing servant, and a few words in Brittonic procured a mead flagon and beaming grins from the bodyguards.

"Cheers, mate!"

It worked. They shut up.

Aethelferth's envoy, comprehensively outmanoeuvred on his first subject, turned to another. Aethelferth wanted tribute from Elmet, and hostages as a token of good faith. Ceretic objected, not surprisingly, for paying tribute and yielding hostages was an admission of weakness that no king would contemplate except by force or the threat of force.

"Of course," he was saying smoothly, "naturally your lord can count on my full support as his ally, especially as he is having so much trouble in Deira –"

"There's no trouble in Deira!" protested the envoy, rather too fast.

"Really? Then Black Dudda is burning villages on the North March because the occupants are in full agreement with their new king?"

Muffled laughter from the audience. Aethelferth's envoy went brick-red. "He's burning villages because the scum won't pay their tribute! That's what happens to people who withhold tribute from Aethelferth!"

This time the reaction from the hall was a hiss, compounded of roughly equal measures of anger and alarm at the implied threat. Aethelferth had never been beaten in the field, and not many people thought Ceretic of Elmet was likely to succeed where mightier kings had failed.

"However –" Ceretic glanced around the hall, and his next words dropped into hushed silence like pebbles into a pond – "it may be that I have something to offer your king that he would value more highly than cattle and silver. My men are on the trail of Eadwine of Deira."

He's bluffing, Eadwine thought, over the pounding of his heart, *he has to be. If he really knew anything, he could have picked me up any time in the last two months, handed me over on a plate*. It took all his iron self-control to stay still and silent, not ten feet from two men who wanted him dead and fifty more who could enforce their will, like a hounded stag lying in cover and waiting for the hunters to pass by.

No-one moved. No-one even looked in his direction. By the time the rushing in his ears had subsided enough to let him hear again, Ceretic had cut off the envoy's eager response and was speaking as smoothly as ever,

"– but you must give me time. He is far away. Well guarded. Not impossible to capture, but difficult – and of course if I have to divert men to collecting tribute –"

Why me? Eadwine wondered, listening as Ceretic expertly tied the excited envoy up in diplomatic knots, at the end of which Aethelferth's envoy had conceded all claims to tribute for at least a year and Ceretic had conceded a few vague promises. *What makes me worth so much to the Twister? He can tolerate Hereric living here and Osric living in Kent, and Aethelric under his thumb in Eboracum, but he wants me dead at any price. True, Hereric is a child and nobody would follow Osric or Aethelric anywhere except out of curiosity, but am I really so much more of a threat? What makes me different?*

***

154

He was still puzzling this question when the feast got under way. Unsurprisingly, though to his considerable relief, he was not required to perform. Ceretic maintained his own establishment of court bards, who praised their glorious/valiant/generous – hint, hint – king to the rafters in relays for hours on end. Eadwine was just wondering whether he trusted his disguise enough to make his way up to the dais and try to engage the Bernician envoy in conversation, when a loud voice interrupted his thoughts.

"Hey, you! Singer-boy!"

It was four of the Bernician bodyguards, weaving their way across the hall in the cheerful early stages of inebriation. A swift glance round confirmed to Eadwine that there was no obvious route of escape. He managed a feeble smile as they came close.

"You talk Saxon?" demanded the leader, brandishing a mead flagon.

Eadwine remembered just in time to apply a Brittonic accent. "Yes, want you I do something for you?"

The mead flagon encompassed the current bard and the rest of the hall in a dismissive gesture. "We're bored wi' this poncy heathen rubbish. You know any real poetry?"

"Er –"

"Proper battles," expanded one of the others. "This is all King La-di-da Arthur. Bo*ring* –!"

"Poncy!"

"'Is wife sounds a bit of all right, though –" put in a short man with a cauliflower ear.

"Yeah, but you never 'ear nuffink about 'er," interrupted the first speaker, saving Eadwine from having to explain that he didn't do *that* kind of poetry. "It's all poncing about on 'orses. We want t'ear about real fighting, see?"

"Have a drink," offered the biggest of the four, flopping down onto the bench and rocking the table alarmingly. The others followed suit, gathering into an expectant huddle.

"Um – what about the Grendel fight from Beowulf?"

"Yeah!"

They were an appreciative if unsophisticated audience. He quickly learned that they got restive in speeches that lasted more than two lines, so Hrothgar and Beowulf became models of unaccustomed brevity and the fight itself expanded to epic dimensions. They cheered every time Beowulf landed a punch, hissed whenever Grendel got the upper hand, and roared "Yes!" in unison when Beowulf finally nailed the monster's bloodstained hand up above the door.

"'Ere, that was good, that was," belched the leader, in a cloud of alcoholic fumes. "That bit where 'e rips the arm out, right, with the spout of blood hitting the roof, that weren't in it last time I 'eard it. I'd of remembered that bit. You making this up?"

"Some of it, yes," Eadwine admitted cautiously, and got another thump on the back.

"Good on yer, mate! 'Ere, can you make up anythin'? Can you make up summat about us?"

"We'll tell you what 'appened, an' you turn it into poetry, right. Summat short –"

"–but wi' plenty of blood an' guts –"

"– what we can learn an' tell our mates back 'ome –"

"We'll pay yer!"

"We'll find the bloke what done that to yer face an' kick the shit out of 'im."

The big one captured a passing serving girl and banged a flagon of mead down on the table. "Have a drink!" Then, struck by a generous thought, "Have the girl an' all!"

"After you," Eadwine said politely.

"Ta, mate, yer a gent –!"

"Come on, you make summat up for us! It were like this, see –"

To his horror, Eadwine found himself listening to a confused account of the battle at Eboracum from the winning side, though fortunately they interrupted each other so much that it made no sense at all and it was certainly impossible to relate any of the numerous fatalities they claimed to real people. Come to that, since between them they claimed more casualties than the total size of the Deiran shield-wall, most of them probably weren't real people, merely the generic 'enemy' whose sole claim to fame was the inventive method of their despatch by the hero. The major difficulty was describing all their claimed exploits without repeating himself. Luckily, every bard and skald in history had had the same problem, and the corpus of heroic poetry in both languages was replete with metaphors, similes and kennings. His customers ran out of material before he did.

"Beorn Bear-Grip," mumbled the biggest one, "I like that. Yeah. Have a drink."

"Good battle, that was," said Cauliflower Ear, now at the stage of mellow reminiscence.

"Beorn Bear-Grip. Good name. Have another drink."

"Yeah," agreed the captain, rescuing the mead flagon as Beorn subsided gently off the bench like a mountain landslide, "a lot better than what was s'posed to 'appen –"

Eadwine pricked up his ears. This might not be such a waste of time as he thought. "Oh? What was supposed to happen? A siege?"

The captain slapped his thigh. "Siege! 'Ere, you 'ear that lads? A siege! Ha! ha! ha! After we'd burned all the fields an' all? That's a good 'un, that is!"

"So what was supposed to happen?" Eadwine prodded, when the roar of raucous laughter had died down. "You were going to storm the city?"

"Storm that! Beard of Woden, when I first saw that city I nearly pissed meself. Never seen nuffink like it. Even old Ox-brains could of defended that 'til 'e died of old age. Nah, the King weren't never goin' to storm that. 'E ain't stupid."

"Beorn Bear-Grip, tha's me, y'know," slurred a happy voice from under the table.

"'E ain't called the Twister for nuffink, you know," the captain went on, ignoring the interruption. He leaned forward, making Eadwine wonder if you could suffocate from halitosis, and announced, in what was supposed to be a confidential whisper, 'E'd got somebody what was goin' t'open the gate." He leaned back and tapped the side of his nose triumphantly. "Not many people know that."

Eadwine had no difficulty looking suitably stunned at this revelation. The Bernician camp on the morning of the battle! The warriors lined up for attack even though they had no scaling ladders! Here was the explanation. A traitor in the city. *Who?*

The captain mistook shock for awe and beamed, highly gratified. "That were my job, see? Just before first light, me an' a few other lads crawled up the ditch to the posh gate on the river. Creepy it was, I swear I 'eard a rat rustlin' about —"

No, Eadwine thought, trying to keep his face set in an expression of mild interest, *that was me, and I knew you weren't rats.*

"— An' I were to give a password, and the gate were goin' to be opened, an' as soon as it did I were goin' to blow a horn to signal the rest o' the lads to charge, see? They was all lined up just round the corner, an' we'd of gone through that city like rhubarb through a sick dog."

"Who —?" Eadwine began, but his mouth was too dry to speak. He swallowed. "Who was going to open the gate?"

"Dunno. 'E never showed up. I give the password, all correct, an' all I got were the sentry shoutin' from the top of the wall. There was some row goin' on up the river, all the ducks squawkin' an' quackin' like there was a fox in the roost, an' I reckon the city was all woke up an' 'e got cold feet."

"I reckon the King planned it like that," observed Cauliflower Ear, nodding sagely.

"Not the way 'e was swearing, 'e didn't."

"Ah!" said Cauliflower Ear, in the manner of one imparting great wisdom. "We won, dint we? 'Ere, that bit where I chop the fella's 'ead off an' gut 'im on the backswing, do that again. I like that bit."

"— Bear-Grip — hic! — 's me, y'know — hic!"

Eadwine got away some time later, leaving them snoring contentedly in a pool of spilled mead, and escaped into the blissful silence of an icy-cold winter night. How *could* he have been so stupid? Of course Aethelferth the Twister was never going to besiege Eboracum. Burning the surrounding fields had *proved* that, if only he had had the wit to see it. And of course Aethelferth was never going to storm the city either. He remembered his own words to Hereric, *Could you climb the walls? No. Could you break down the gates? No.* And he had thought that made the city impregnable. He had never thought to say, *Could you bribe some traitorous scum to open the gate?*

He clenched his fists. What kind of man could stoop to that? What kind of man would deliberately condemn his comrades, and his lord, and his king, and everyone else in the city, to Aethelferth's tender mercy?

One who could stab his own lord in the back.

It had been Eadric's hearth-troop on duty at the river-gate that night. It had been Beortred who, in Eadric's absence, was captain of the guard. Beortred who would have had the perfect opportunity to be at the gate at the appointed time for treachery.

Beortred who now had a great deal to answer for.

Chapter 16

Eadwine left Loidis the next day. If Beortred had been in Aethelferth's pay to betray Eboracum, no doubt Aethelferth had paid him to murder Eadric as well. That would explain why Beortred had apparently gone back east over the moors, and also why there was no sign of him in Elmet; he had probably been feasting in his master's hall all winter. Though some things were still not explained. If Beortred was Aethelferth's agent, why had he helped to rescue Eadwine from the battlefield? Why insist on staying with him as long as possible? Why had he apparently been willing to give his life to save the others? If he had been planning to deliver Aethelferth another atheling of Deira, why had no warband descended on Severa's hafod? There had been ample time, yet when the searchers did come they had been from Ceretic, not Aethelferth. And from the readiness of Aethelferth's envoy to make concessions, Aethelferth clearly had no idea of Eadwine's whereabouts

Eadwine sighed, hunching his shoulders in a futile attempt to keep the stinging sleet out of his face. It still did not quite make sense. Something was still missing, and he could not see what. If only he could have talked it over with someone! Someone intelligent, someone who would challenge his reasoning, help him see it in a new light. Someone like Severa.

He shook his head impatiently, as if to shake the thought out of his mind. Nearly three months since they had parted, and *still* he found himself thinking of her far too often. Why should he miss her so much? He had never missed Aethelind like this during their lengthy separations. It had better pass. In the meantime, finding Beortred had become both more important and much more difficult. Eadwine was reluctant to go searching for him in Bernicia. A few months ago, shattered by grief at Eadric's loss, dying honourably in a futile attempt at vengeance would have been a welcome prospect – indeed, dying in any way at all had been a welcome prospect. Now, though he was still prepared to die in the attempt, he was determined above all that it should be a successful attempt. Which was unlikely if he went blundering into Bernicia, where any stranger remotely fitting his description would be immediately taken to Aethelferth. It would be possible to travel across enemy territory quickly and secretly, moving by night, but only if he knew exactly where Beortred was. Heledd's spies seemed to be confined to Deira, possibly even to Eboracum, and would be no help at all. But the man who lived at the other end of this cold and wet tramp down the river might be.

Unfortunately the slave trader, a cheerful Frisian who had married a local girl and built himself a commodious hall and a wharf where the great north-south army-path forded the Aire, had never been near Eboracum or Bernicia in his life. But he had cannily offloaded all his stock before the winter storms closed the ocean, and was happy to recommend his brother, who was back in Frisia for the winter but who had a partner in Elmet who would be delighted to sell the bard a slave girl to do his cooking and keep him warm at night. The partner lived twenty weary miles in the other direction, had one girl that he wasn't selling until he had finished with her himself, but was readily drawn into talking shop with a sympathetic listener. Yes, there had been some slaves taken after Eboracum, but only those fugitives found long after the battle when the fighting frenzy had died down. There followed a lengthy diatribe on Aethelferth's lack of business sense – such a waste, corpses were no good to anyone, didn't he know that strong healthy men fetched good prices these days, and good-looking youths even more, Rome and Byzantium couldn't get enough, and how was a poor honest man to make an honest living if kings went round killing their enemies – Eadwine listened patiently, and when he could get a word in edgeways mentioned casually that he had heard that Lady Heledd of Wharfedale was interested in ransoming men of her late husband's warband.

At which the slaver brightened up considerably. Ransoms were a good deal, because friends and family could be expected to pay far more than the going rate, plus the extra benefit that there was no need to fund transport to Rome. He scratched his head. Well, now you come to mention it, he had another partner – a purely informal arrangement, you understand, a cousin of his wife's best friend

– who dabbled in the trade and who had moved down from Eboracum just this winter, and still had some stock he was stuck with until the spring came, and who would be *most* interested to help the Lady Heledd if he could. What was the late husband's name again? Prince Eadric of Deira? Oh, a very rich widow, then? He brightened a bit more, mentally calculating his commission for introducing a more than usually profitable sale. Funnily enough, he had one or two other acquaintances who might be able to help the lady –

Poor Heledd, Eadwine thought, as he tramped the roads for a week assiduously spreading this rumour through the trading communities on both sides of the river, she would be swamped with slavers chasing after the prospect of a fat ransom, but she would just have to cope. She – or at least Cousin Constantine – could afford to pay a few ransoms, and nobody searched more efficiently than a merchant anticipating a profit. Between them the traders knew everyone and went everywhere, and now they and their news would filter back to Heledd. If any of Eadric's warband had survived and been captured, a few good men might be freed into the bargain. And some of them might be able to tell him more about Eadric's death and Beortred's involvement, for either no-one had told him the details at the time or he had been too grief-stricken to hear.

He was well pleased with himself when he forded the Aire for the last time, on a bitterly cold and clear day that was, annoyingly, cold enough to scatter the river with ice floes but not cold enough to freeze it solid, and ran up the steep slope of the army-path to get warm again. There was a longer, easier way round on tracks and droveways that was much less exposed to bad weather than this high windswept road over the watershed dividing the Aire from the Wharfe, but the direct route would take less than half a day back to Heledd's hall. It was over a month after Yule, the days were noticeably longer already, and there would be three-quarters of a waxing moon to light his way in the early part of the night if he ran out of daylight. Besides, he was young and fit and carrying only the harp, and he could run for the sheer pleasure of it. As he climbed higher the road became puddled with ice, not water, and the moor on both sides was freckled with snow. A hare, also patched with white, shot from cover almost under his feet and tore across the moor into the distance. Drust would have grabbed for his spear. Eadwine was content to watch, marvelling at the animal's speed and at the way it blended instantly into its background as soon as it stopped. Overhead in the peculiar limpid blue that only comes in a winter sky, a kestrel hovered, balanced on the breeze with brindled tail spread and bright eyes scouring the wintry ground. The hare was too big to tackle, and the voles were lying low. With a shrug of one shoulder – so slight a movement – the hawk slid away on the breeze to try its luck elsewhere. Eadwine pulled a fold of his cloak up around his ears, grateful for the warmth, and left the ice-glazed road to walk on the peat alongside. It was frozen not quite solid and crunched just a little at each footfall, neither jarring nor sinking under his feet. Extraordinarily pleasant to walk on. Severa had said that the moors were at their best in winter. She was right. He hugged the cloak closer round his shoulders, thinking of her weaving it and wondering what she was doing now and if she was thinking of him – and then remembering, impatiently, that he was betrothed to Aethelind and had no business daydreaming of anyone else. Somehow he found it impossible to daydream about Aethelind, so he ran the rest of the way across the moor and bounded down into Heledd's valley just before the sun set behind the hills.

***

"You've got a rival," one of the kitchen girls greeted him, smiling her thanks as he held the woodshed door open for her and helped her carry a log basket across the yard.

"Rival?"

The girl jerked her head in the direction of Heledd's chamber. "She's got a new bard. Arrived today." A dreamy sigh. "Such a dear young man."

***

Before Eadwine reached the hall, he had gleaned the further information that the dear young man had hair like spun sunlight – a poetic image that he stored away for future use – and wonderful bright sparkling blue eyes, that he was tall as a tree and strong as a bull, that he could probably have laid every woman in the household end to end if he had had the mind (or the stamina), and that he couldn't sing a note. *That* sort of bard.

***

Eadwine recognised the newcomer immediately he entered the hall. Evidently the slavers worked even quicker than he had expected. The dear young man was Imma son of Imma son of Imma, an undistinguished junior member of Eadric's warband, very fair, very well-muscled even after months in captivity, and gazing at Heledd with a look of utter devotion that was undeniably appealing. The raw red welts encircling his wrists and neck, where the slave shackles had bitten into the flesh, gave ample explanation for his gratitude, though Eadwine suspected it was probably more to do with having been taken notice of for the first time in an unremarkable life. He retreated behind a pillar, though he had no great fear that Imma would recognise him – connecting a Brittonic bard with an exiled prince of Deira required some originality, which was not a strong trait in the family of Imma son of Imma son of Imma – and in any case, Imma was far too concerned with recounting his story to his saviour to notice anything else.

It seemed Imma had been wounded in the battle – here he rolled up his sleeve to a chorus of feminine oohs and aahs and displayed a jagged red line from wrist to elbow –

("Huh," scoffed Ashhere, somewhere in the background, "call that a scar?")

– and he admitted that he had fled the stricken field and saved his life by hiding in a bramble thicket all day and most of the following night, in terror of the enemy horsemen. When it seemed quiet he had emerged and set off to try and make his way back to his mother on the east coast. But he was weak from his injury and from hunger, having nothing to eat and not being very good at stealing, and after a few days he had been captured by a group of Bernician warriors. They took him to their lord, who kept him chained up but fed him and sent someone to treat his wounds, and when he began to recover he was sold to a Frisian merchant, who later sold him on to a Frank. By this time it was after Yule and the Frank was not willing to risk a ship in the winter gales, so Imma had found himself locked up again to wait for spring or a buyer, whichever came first.

"And then the merchant came down and asked if anyone had served Eadric of Deira," he concluded. "At first I was afraid, because I thought my lord's enemies might be trying to find and kill all those who had served him, like they're trying to find and kill his brother, and I hid myself and said nothing. But then I thought it was better to die than live as a slave, so I spoke up. And here I am. Forgive me, lady. I did not think anyone would try to rescue me. Truly you are a great and generous lady, and I ask nothing more than to be allowed to serve you faithfully for the rest of my days."

Heledd, who had not in fact been trying to rescue anyone and had been as astonished as Imma to hear that she had offered to ransom him, accepted this undeserved compliment with queenly grace. A lady could not have a warband, of course, but perhaps she should have a personal bodyguard, and perhaps Imma would be its captain?

("Huh," came a disgruntled mutter from the back of the hall, "talk about falling on your feet!")

At the word captain, Imma's delighted face became aghast.

"Captain, my lady? *Me?* But what about Captain Beortred?"

Heledd frowned, puzzled. "What about him?"

"Aren't you going to ransom him too? My lady, you must! I beg you!" Imma flung himself on his knees at Heledd's feet. "I know he says it was his fault Lord Eadric died, but it's not true! Lady, you must believe me! I know it's shameful to survive if your lord is killed, but Beortred wasn't with them! He ran after them, and when we found them he was cradling Lord Eadric's dead body in his arms and crying that he came too late! Lady, you must believe me, you must!"

"Imma, Imma, please," Heledd said helplessly, "you aren't making any sense. Sit down quietly and tell me what you mean, slowly and carefully. Remember your language is not my native tongue." An inspiration struck her. "Bard!"

"My lady?"

She beckoned Eadwine forward. "You speak Saxon. Translate if we need it."

A puzzled look crossed Imma's face as Eadwine took a seat nearby. "Who are you? Haven't I seen you somewhere before?"

"I had the honour to sing in your lord's hall a few years ago," Eadwine answered, silently cursing Heledd. "Perhaps we met then, though I do not remember you."

"Nobody ever does," said Imma, with a disarming smile. "You speak Anglian very well."

Eadwine wound his Brittonic accent up a couple of notches. "A poor traveller who sings for his supper has to know a lot of languages, lord. Will you tell the lady everything you know about Lord Eadric's death?"

It was the first time in his life – and quite probably it was also going to be the last – that anyone had called Imma 'lord', and that convinced him of Eadwine's lowly position.

"It was after the raiders burned the ships and the wharf," he began. "Lord Eadric was so angry he would not wait for Captain Beortred or anyone else. There were four men with him when he heard and he marched out with them at the double –"

"Eadric set off *on foot* after a mounted warband?" Eadwine interrupted, incredulous. "Are you sure? I mean – er – the lady wants to know exactly what happened."

Imma had begun to bridle, but calmed down when Heledd was invoked. "Yes. Certain. I was helping to fight the fires, and saw them go. Captain Beortred was with us, and when he saw that Lord Eadric had so few men with him, he shouted across the river to him to wait, to let him collect more men. Lord Eadric shouted back that he was to mind his own business. But Captain Beortred said he wasn't going to let his lord go into danger without him at his side, and he threw down his bucket and ran after them. Without even going to fetch his spear or his shield or sword or anything. He had to go down to the bridge, see, so he was a long way behind, and if he'd gone for his weapons he wouldn't have caught them up. That's how brave he was, to run into danger with only his knife, trying to protect his lord. Will you tell the lady that?"

161

Eadwine translated for appearances' sake, and added in Latin *I want to question him. Back me up.* Heledd smiled sweetly and responded, also in Latin, *Why do you think I called you over? You might as well get my money's worth.*

"We got the fires out after a while," Imma continued, "and Lord Eadric hadn't come back. So some of us went out after him. And we found them." His lip started to tremble and he bit down on it, hard. "All dead. Cut down from behind. The Bernicians must have turned back and attacked them. And in the middle Captain Beortred, weeping like a woman with Lord Eadric's body in his lap, crying out over and over again Too late! Too late! Forgive me lord, forgive me!"

"Forgive him for what?" Heledd asked.

"I don't know, lady. For coming too late, I suppose. Though he must have got there before the fight was over, because his knife was all blood right up to the handle. I remember that, because none of the others had even drawn their swords or bloodied their spears."

"I do not think I have understood this," Heledd said slowly. "They did not fight at all? How is that possible?"

"They didn't run away, lady! The horsemen must have been waiting in ambush, taken them by surprise."

Eadwine frowned. Eboracum Vale was flat, open country, not well suited to ambush. He had thought Eadric and his men had been overwhelmed by a vastly superior force and gone down fighting.

"Where was it?" he asked.

"At the ivy-covered oak on the border of Lord Eadric's lands, not two miles from the city. Those horsemen are devils, lady! They appear from nowhere, murder, and vanish again!"

No they don't, Eadwine thought, his frown deepening. They appear out of woods, from behind hedges and out of dips in the ground you haven't looked in. Men do *not*, in my experience, appear out of nowhere, and especially not men with horses. And ambush is something I have a lot of experience in. That oak stands all by itself at a crossing of tracks surrounded by flat farmland. It's a meeting point, a landmark, visible for miles. A cat would be hard pushed to ambush a mouse there. No way could enough men hide there to kill five men before any of them can strike even one blow in return. Especially not men led by a commander of Eadric's experience. Unless by archery? Archers could kill from a distance, though it was not something that mounted warriors generally went in for.

"Did they die by arrows?"

Imma shook his head unhappily. "No. They had all been cut down by sword or spear." He shivered. "Some had been wounded first, and then killed later as they lay on the ground. My younger brother was among them." He swallowed hard, and Heledd leaned forward and patted his hand kindly. "We – we thought the horsemen must have swept down on them so fast they had no time to do anything. Except Lord Eadric, of course. His sword and spear were both covered in blood."

Eadwine sat up sharply. So Eadric had fought but his warband had not. Fought who?

"Were there any Bernician dead or wounded?"

"No, nothing. Just hoofprints."

Well, the Bernicians could have carried their dead and wounded away, but this was starting to look like a peculiarly one-sided fight. It reeked of treachery –

162

luring Eadric to a pre-arranged meeting point with only a handful of men, there to be betrayed and slaughtered. But treachery by who? Eadric had made all the decisions, it seemed. Beortred had literally been tagging along behind.

"Was Beortred wounded?"

Imma shook his head. "No. Well –"

"Go on," Heledd prompted.

Imma tapped his temple. "He was – strange, lady. We thought his mind was unhinged by grief. He wouldn't let go of the body, and he sobbed and wept like a child. *Too late, too late, I would have died for you,* he cried, over and over again, all the way back to Eboracum with Lord Eadric's body on the bier. And he spoke true, lady, I am sure of it. He would have died for Lord Eadric. We all would. It wasn't his fault he came too late!"

"Truly Imma, I knew nothing of all this," Heledd said thoughtfully. "Captain Beortred seemed well enough at the funeral."

"He was more himself by then, my lady. Better for a man to avenge his lord than mourn overmuch, as the poets say. He called us all together by the pyre and said that it was up to us to make sure that Lord Eadric's name was held in honour for ever. As long as men respected his name, he would never really die. So he said we would fight for Lord Eadric's brother until his son came of age, and wherever people heard of our deeds Lord Eadric's name would be remembered and honoured –"

Imma sniffed, and Eadwine felt his own throat constrict. To live for ever in song was every warrior's ambition, to uphold their lord's reputation every warband's highest duty. Reputation mattered more than life itself, for while all men died eventually, reputation lived for ever. But it would not bring Eadric back, would not change the fact that he would never see his brother again –

"– We all knew there was a battle coming," Imma was explaining to Heledd, who was holding his hand again, "and Beortred was determined we would fight well in it. He even made us do double-duty on watch at the gate all night. Two of us on every post, in case one fell asleep. And in the battle he told us to protect Lord Eadric's brother as if he was our own lord. You must ransom him, lady, you must! He doesn't deserve to be a slave!"

"A *slave?*" Heledd questioned, startled. "Beortred is a slave?"

Imma nodded so vigorously it seemed his head would fly off. "Did you not know, lady? I was sure you must have found him, since you found me. He was captured somewhere to the south and when I was sold to the Frisian he was already there."

"Is he still there? I can send to the Frisian –"

"No, no, lady, he was sold. Only a few days after I came there. A buyer came looking for strong men for his lord, who was going away north. I was still weak so I was not good enough. Beortred was. You know how strong he was, lady."

"Who was the buyer?"

"I don't know, lady."

Eadwine heard this as if in a dream or from a great distance. *Beortred* a slave? If he had been in Aethelferth's pay, why wasn't he living it up on his reward? Captured on his way to Aethelferth, and Aethelferth had refused to ransom him? Possible. Aethelferth might well discard a man he had no further use for. But if Beortred had doubled the guard on the river-gate, Beortred could not possibly be the traitor. Unless he had a fit of remorse after murdering Eadric? But then why had he not warned anyone of the plot? No, Beortred could not be the traitor. Beortred was covering up for the traitor. Preferring to risk an attack on his gate – which might well result in his own death and many others' – rather than reveal the traitor's secret. *Who was it?* Whose reputation could Beortred value more highly than his own life? He should owe that sort of loyalty only to his lord –

Eadwine felt icy sweat prickle down his spine. No, that was impossible. Impossible!

He found his voice. "When was this? Who was the merchant?"

Imma's face screwed up in concentration, and he counted on the fingers of his free hand. "About the middle of October. I don't know the man's name. Greasy fair hair, beard a family of eagles could nest in, two teeth missing, limped on his right leg."

"Where was he based?"

"Eboracum."

***

"I don't like it," Lilla objected. "It's too dangerous. What if you get caught?"

Eadwine laughed softly, settling his pack more securely on his shoulders. "In my own city? Don't be absurd. Anyway, Aethelferth's in Bebbanburgh and Aethelric couldn't catch a cold."

"I don't see why you have to go into Eboracum anyway."

"Because," Eadwine said patiently, "I have to find out who Beortred was sold to and where he was taken. Otherwise we might be wandering round Deira for weeks and that really *would* be dangerous. Meet me here two nights from now. Don't eat all the food and keep out of trouble."

Lilla sat down on a fallen log with a sigh, watching as Eadwine's slender shadow was swallowed up in the deeper shadows of the wood. He was tired, but more than that he was anxious. They had left Heledd's hall the same night as the ransomed housecarl had arrived, and covered the distance to Eboracum in two relentless night marches. Eadwine would only let them rest during the day, when they lay hidden in woods or wasteland, and he clearly grudged even that. Lilla thought he would have run all the way to Eboracum without a break, if it had not been for the need to avoid being seen. Whatever he had inferred from Imma's story had obviously disturbed him greatly – more, Lilla thought, than was justified by the mere prospect of running Beortred to earth. But his tentative enquiry had been rebuffed with uncharacteristic sharpness. Whatever was wrong, it was something very close to Eadwine's heart.

"Cheer up," Ashhere said, sitting down beside him. "He'll be fine, and in the meantime we can put our feet up. Mine are killing me."

"I hope you're right." Lilla looked round, but all he could see was the moonlit clearing in what seemed to be a fairly sizeable wood. "Where are we? Anyone know?"

"West of the Ouse, about an hour's walk from the city," Ashhere informed him, for once not the directionally challenged one. "There's an old charcoal burner's hut by a stream, over that way. It's not used any more, on account of half the logs being rotten, but it's not likely to have fallen down yet. How about we wait there? It'll be out of the weather at least."

Rather to Lilla's surprise, the abandoned hut was exactly where Ashhere had said it was, and more or less intact.

"How did you know this was here?"

"This is home. Pa's hall is a couple of miles away, and we own all the land round here." It was Ashhere's turn to sigh. "Used to. I suppose some bastard from Bernicia's got it now."

Lilla looked at him in some surprise. "How can you bear it? To have your land occupied by someone else?"

"Well, if Eadwine can bear it, I'm sure I can," Ashhere said comfortably. "What is it with you and land, Lilla? Pa got given this estate by the king twenty-odd years ago, Eadwine will give me another when he comes into his own. Easy come, easy go. I can't see what's so special about a muddy field or a herd of smelly pigs. Though I've a mind to go and see if I can find out what happened to Mam and my sisters. One of Pa's old spearmen farms just the other side of these woods."

Drust's voice was doubtful. "Ye sure that's wise, laddie?"

"Why not? Eadwine didn't tell us to stay in the same place for two days. Anyway, what's sauce for the goose is sauce for the gander."

"What do you mean by that?"

"Oh, come on, Lilla, you're supposed to be the bright one. Two days to find one trader? When he's in such a tearing hurry? I'll bet you he's going to look for his girl."

***

In the hall at Eoforwic, Aethelind turned over in bed and prodded Hereward until he rolled onto his side and stopped snoring. He was turning out to be a very satisfactory husband, obedient even in his sleep. Especially since the child she was carrying had started to kick and confirmed beyond any doubt that she was pregnant. Hereward had been as thrilled as a child with a new toy, torn between wanting to show her off all round the estate – look, what a clever boy I am! What a clever girl I married! – and wanting to keep her wrapped in thistledown as if she was suddenly made of glass. He had compromised by inviting every last soul on the estate and everyone else he knew to a feast so huge they had to press the barn into service and the estate stumbled around in a blissful alcoholic haze for days afterward. Even Aethelferth, far away in Bebbanburgh, had sent his best wishes and a gift for the lady by special messenger, a rare honour that had practically reduced Hereward to tears, as he worshipped his king second only to the gods. Indeed, Aethelferth seemed to be taking a particular interest in Hereward. He had attended their wedding, seemed most impressed that Hereward's bride had once been betrothed to a prince, and made sure to call in whenever he was in Eboracum. Hereward could hardly believe his luck. A beautiful wife! A rich estate, which lay south of Eboracum and had largely escaped the war! His king's favour! And a baby on the way, the ultimate seal of the gods' approval! All the local temples were doing very well out of Hereward this winter.

The temple of Frija was also doing rather well, if more discreetly, out of Aethelind. Truly Lady Frija had heard her prayers! The estate had accepted Hereward as its new master happily enough. Their old lord had been a fair master, and they were sorry he was gone, but he had died in battle, which was the right and proper way of things, and the new lord was young Lady Aethelind's husband, which was also the right and proper way of things. Hereward was cheerful and approachable, took his duties seriously in settling disputes at the moot, and had a warband powerful enough to protect his new lands from raiders, thieves and the increasingly desperate beggars displaced from burned Eboracum Vale. He settled some of his more senior spearmen as sub-thanes on outlying pockets of land, where they could use the food-rents to maintain their own small warbands and would in due course marry, start their own families, and take up farming – insofar as that meant handing out well-meant if impractical advice, or leaning over the wall of the sty scratching the back of a favourite pig. Eoforwic was well content with its lot. And Aethelind, snuggled under the covers with Hereward's warm bulk beside her, was well content with hers. She was sorry that Eadwine was dead – she always thought of him as dead, even though she knew he was not, it was more comfortable that way – and she missed the prospect of being a Princess of Deira some day. But she had found that she did not miss being compared to midsummer skies or shining stars at evening or the sparkling of clear water, nor did she miss his stubborn refusal to let her have her own way and live near Eboracum. Hereward's mute adoration or reliable 'Yes, my love' were far more to her taste. Now, though she still shed occasional tears for her lost prince, she could hardly remember what he looked like.

Chapter 17

Father Ysgafnell concluded the pre-dawn Mass and watched as the rest of the monks filed out of the tiny church. He must be getting old. How else to explain this grey, sad feeling? He would be sixty-three in a few months. The same age as Peredur, his flawed, beloved king, would have been if he had lived. If he had not gone down beneath the Bernician blades on the blood-soaked field of Caer Greu. Twenty-five years ago, yet it seemed as if it was only yesterday. And now the descendant of Peredur's murderers – yes, murderers, for it had been no fair fight – ruled in Peredur's city. *Vengeance is mine, saith the Lord,* Ysgafnell quoted to himself. All very well, but I wish You would get on with it. I want to live to see it. He shuffled the chalice and the lamp onto a tray, balanced it on his single hand with the ease of long practice, and pushed open the door to the sacristy, feeling the weight of years on his shoulders.

A shadow moved on the far side of the door. A shadow that resolved itself into a tall, lean young man with dark hair tied back from a bony hawk-like face. A face Ysgafnell had last seen twenty-five years ago, on the eve of battle –

"Here," said a familiar voice, when his hearing cleared, "drink this."

Ysgafnell realised he was sitting on the floor – how had he got down there? – and someone was supporting him with a strong arm round his shoulders and holding a cup to his lips.

"No," he croaked out, "no – it's the communion wine – sacred to God –"

"I think your need is greater than his just now," said the voice, with its familiar warmly ironic undertone. "Are you not always telling me yours is a forgiving god? Here. Drink."

Ysgafnell swallowed obediently, choked a little, and swallowed again. He clutched at the arm holding the cup, a thin, sinewy arm in patched woollen cloth, the bones reassuringly solid under his grasp.

"My boy!" He let his head sag back against Eadwine's shoulder. "Oh, my dear boy. I thought you were a ghost!"

"Mine?"

"No." Ysgafnell turned his head, scanning his companion's face. It was not his imagination at all, the resemblance was there. "No, your grandfather's. You're the image of Peredur when he was your age. In looks, that is. I hope you've got your mother's mind."

"I rather hope I have my own," Eadwine said dryly. "Let me help you up, Father. I came to ask you a favour, not to make you faint, but I can't linger."

"Ask away, lad."

"I'm looking for a slave trader. Finn Lousebeard, from the description. He trades wine for slaves, so given your god's taste in drink, you're probably one of his better customers these days. Can you tell me where he is?"

"He's here for the winter, in Eboracum. But you'd best not go near his place. He's very thick with the Twister's men."

"So I would expect. He's got a profit to make. But he sold a man I'm anxious to trace, and I need to know who to. All I know at the moment is that it was to someone going north in the middle of October and looking for strong men."

"Ah! I can help you there! Finn was trumpeting that sale all over the city. A dozen strong fellows to carry the food and gear for a warband, no expense spared. Why these heathen Saxon imbeciles won't use horses is beyond me, in my day —"

But Eadwine had no time for Ysgafnell's military wisdom, not today. "Who was the buyer, Father?"

"Black Dudda."

Eadwine drew a sharp breath, and the blue-grey eyes became very cold. "For his harrying of the March, of course. I should have worked that out for myself." He ran a hand through his hair. "Father — what exactly has he done to the March? I noticed there are more beggars on the roads than usual. Alive and dead."

"As to the March, I don't know," Ysgafnell said doggedly. He had no intention of provoking Eadwine into tangling with probably the most effective and certainly the most ruthless of Aethelferth's lieutenants. "The beggars aren't from there. They're all from Eboracum Vale and Derwent Vale, folk who were burned out and hadn't got kin to take them in."

"*Still?* Hasn't Aethelferth done anything about it?"

Ysgafnell shrugged. "Not his people, not his business."

"He conquered them," Eadwine said through clenched teeth, "so they're his business now."

Ysgafnell shrugged again. "They're Brittonic, mostly. Why should it bother a Saxon king?"

"It bothers me."

"You're different. You're Coeling."

To Ysgafnell, whose family had served the descendants of Coel for generations, that was the highest compliment he could pay. He was taken aback when Eadwine turned on him fiercely.

"That has nothing to do with it. In what way do my father's people belong here less than you? We were given land on the coast by the Emperors when no-one else would live there for fear of raiders. It was we who fought the raiders, we who kept Eboracum and the Vale safe behind us, and we who had our children taken as slaves. When the last Emperor refused help and left Coel the Old as Protector, we kept faith with Coel and his descendants. We guarded the coast while they guarded the Wall, we fought beside them in their wars. There was as much Deiran blood as Brittonic blood spilt at Catraeth and Arthuret and Caer Greu. And when there were no more Coeling kings we *still* kept faith and we are *still* here, *still* guarding the coast and the March. In what way is this less our country than yours?"

Ysgafnell tried to take another step back and found he had backed against the wall. Eadwine had never raised his voice, yet the words lashed like a steel whip. Ysgafnell threw up his hand as if to ward off a blow.

The cold anger died in Eadwine's eyes and he stepped back. "I am sorry, Father. You need not fear I would raise a hand to you." He sighed, looking suddenly grim and much older than his years. "I am aware we have not done a good job lately. Both Deira and Eboracum overrun with enemies, and there is nothing I can do about it. For now. But it will be mended one day, Father. It will be mended."

***

Ysgafnell walked his visitor to the gate, as if shepherding a penitent on his way, and saw him off with a more than usually heartfelt blessing. Then he went back to the church with elastic step and lit a candle in thanksgiving. Peredur's killers were going to pay at last, and Ysgafnell was determined to live to see it.

***

Eadwine paused when he reached the main street. He had no more reason to stay in the city, but it was now broad daylight and would be awkward to leave. The gate was out of the question, as a bored guard was clearly visible in the arch. A stranger would be stopped and questioned, and half the people in the city probably knew him by sight and would not be averse to earning more money than a rich man would normally see in a lifetime. He had a fold of his cloak drawn over his head as if to keep out the wind, and tugged it further forward to keep his face in shadow. Could he climb back over the wall? It had been a simple enough climb in the dark, much easier than scaling the sea cliffs with Lilla in search of guillemots' eggs, for the wall around this half of the city was reduced to its rubble infill in some places, a legacy of the days when civil authority had broken down but people still built in stone and considered the civilian city wall a convenient quarry. But there were too many people around, he would be seen. He could leave by the river, since unlike the military fortress the civilian city had never had a wall along the river and apart from the wharves either side of the bridge the bank was thick with vegetation. But swimming the river in the depths of winter was not an appealing prospect. More sensible to lie low for the day and climb the wall after dark. He would still rejoin his friends a day earlier than he had expected, since he had not after all had to tramp around every one of Finn Lousebeard's numerous halls up and down the river. That had been a stroke of luck. The Three Ladies must be feeling helpful for once. He turned back into the interior of the city.

***

It looked the same as it always did, with its incongruous mix of towering stone buildings surrounded by little thatched wattle houses, patches of ground cultivated for vegetables or crops, tethered goats, scratching chickens, a few lonely pigs in their pens, grubby children fetching water or minding their younger siblings, stray dogs and a few beggars scavenging for scraps. Occasionally some wealthy man would ride down the thoroughfare that connected the gate with the river-bridge, a trader or one of the remaining Brittonic lords who, unlike their Anglian counterparts, built their halls within the security of the massive walls. The change of king appeared to have made little difference to the Brittonic half of Eboracum. Not, perhaps, surprising, for half a century of dynastic warfare until the Coeling dynasty ran out of kings had accustomed Eboracum to frequent and often violent changes of ruler. The powerful men who were left were those who trimmed their sails to the prevailing wind, and the powerless had little more interest in the occupant of the fortress across the river than they had in the Man in the Moon, provided the fighting happened somewhere else.

Eadwine threaded his way into the heart of the most heavily built-up part of the old city, now a maze of collapsed walls, blocked streets, fallen columns and shattered tiles. No-one herded animals here, and no-one had bothered to try to clear the rubble to grow crops or make a vegetable garden. It was a crumbling desert, inhabited – so popular folklore said – by malevolent ghosts who crushed unwelcome intruders to death and ate their flesh. Such tales had been attraction rather than deterrent to a curious child, and Eadwine had found the ruins fascinating, despite the disappointing absence of ghosts. Who built them, and what for, and why did everyone he asked give a different answer? Then, later, the ruins had been his refuge, a safe haven where he could be sure of being completely alone. He had never shared this particular secret even with Treowin. No-one would ever guess that if you climbed through a hole in a wall *here* and scrambled over a fallen arch *here* and skirted a collapsed roof *here* and went through another hole in another wall *here* – you emerged in a colonnaded courtyard with a fountain trickling into a pool in the centre and a gigantic wild rose bush covering the whole of one side.

Eadwine stopped sharp, nostrils flaring. The smell was faint but it was there, the unmistakable metallic whiff of human waste. And, yes, a shallow latrine pit had been inexpertly dug, very recently. His hand went to the hilt of his sword. The intruder was not in the courtyard, for the central part of the courtyard was carpeted with thick moss, the weeds around the edges were too low to conceal a man, and there was clearly nobody hiding in the thorny space behind the leafless rose bush. That left the surrounding ranges. The one under and behind the rose was no more than a heap of rubble, and the two side ranges were dangerous with rotten floors and sagging walls, but part of the range opposite the rose bush was intact. A wide doorway, its doors long gone, opened from the colonnade into a large room with a colourful floor made of thousands of tiny tiles. Eadwine held his breath. Something was moving inside, something much bigger than the usual mice or roosting owls. He drew his sword very quietly. Was he not safe even here, in this courtyard that was known to only one other person in the world?

He sprang through the doorway.

"*Rhonwen –?*"

She had shrunk back into the furthest corner when he burst in, and now crouched there whimpering, wide-eyed with terror. Eadwine sheathed his sword and let his pack drop to the floor, conscious that his knees were weak with relief. Not a thief, not an enemy, just Rhonwen. He was guiltily aware that he had not given her a thought since he left. How changed she was! Could four months do that to someone? Ragged dress, ragged cloak, dirty bare feet, hair in lank rats' tails, and that rictus of terror.

"Rhona?" He held out his hands. "Do you know me? I won't hurt you –"

She did not get up. Instead, she half-scrambled, half-crawled across the floor and grovelled at his feet, sobbing incoherently.

Eadwine was beginning to fear she was mad. He kneeled down and put his arms round her, and she seemed to understand that, clinging to him as a drowning man might cling to a floating scrap of wreckage. She was shaking with cold and painfully thin, every bone sharply defined under the shabby clothes. He unpinned his cloak and draped it around her shoulders, then disentangled one arm from her clutching hands and groped for his pack.

"Are you hungry, Rhona? Eat? Food?"

169

She snatched at the first thing he fished out, a chunk of garlic sausage, and devoured it in two bites. The stale end of a loaf went the same way, though with a little more trouble, giving Eadwine time to rummage for the rest of his provisions – dried meat, cheese and biscuit – and spread them on a cloth on the floor.

"Eat," he said, though she was already grabbing for the cheese. "Take what you want. There's plenty."

He propped his sword against the wall and retreated into the courtyard to drink from the trickling fountain. The water was cold and pure as ever, and he wondered again where it came from and where it went after it left the overflow channel and disappeared somewhere under the side range. He had tried to find out once, but that particular exploration had ended ignominiously in a rotten floorboard, a fall into a dark cellar, a sprained ankle, a couple of rat bites and some nasty splinters in his hands by the time he had climbed out. This time he was much more careful, and successfully garnered some not-too-rotten floorboards and some of the smaller struts from the collapsed colonnade roof behind the rose bush.

Rhonwen was still eating when he returned with his armful of wood, though not quite so desperately, so he averted his gaze and busied himself with making a fire. Mosaic floors were hopeless for building fires on – proving that whoever built this place either did not live here in the winter or knew nothing about heating – but previous experience had shown him that a hearth of carefully stacked bricks and tiles allowed enough air to circulate underneath to keep a small fire going. The smoke would find its way up through the gaps between the ceiling boards into the room above, and from there it would eventually filter out through the windows of the upper storey and the missing tiles in the roof, far too slowly to be seen from outside. There was a heap of dry bracken in one corner, presumably serving as a bed, which furnished him with a handful of kindling, and patient work with flint and steel eventually persuaded a tiny tongue of flame to lick along the driest piece of wood. He sat back on his heels, and risked another glance across at Rhonwen.

She had consumed more than Drust would get through in two sittings and was licking the crumbs from her fingers and regarding him with an embarrassed expression. To his relief, for if she was embarrassed she could not be mad.

"I'm so sorry," she managed to say, speaking with exaggerated care as if she had only just learned to talk. She wiped her hands and face on the edge of her cloak, and looked at the grimy cloth with distaste. "You must think me disgusting."

"I am sorry to see you like this," he said, truthfully. "What are you doing here? I know I said it would be a good place to hide, but not for four months."

"Is that how long it's been?" Rhonwen seemed genuinely surprised. "All the days are alike here. Fear and hunger, hunger and fear. Never a kind word. You can't imagine how glad I am to see a friendly face! Something to remind me that I'm human." She shuddered. "The Twister's men caught me, after the battle. He knows I was your – that we used to be – he made me look for you among the bodies –"

"Oh, Rhona –"

"I ran away that night. They were all looking for you. I came here because it always felt safe here, when you used to bring me here. I knew they wouldn't find me."

"But how have you been living?"

She shrugged, and looked at the floor. "I beg. I steal. I scavenge scraps out of pig troughs. Once or twice I – I – I – sold myself –" She bit her lip, and looked up with a desperate plea in her eyes. "But only once or twice! When I was so hungry I thought I would die of it! Please – please don't hate me for it!"

"Hush," Eadwine soothed. "You have more reason to hate me. But truly I never thought you would come to this. I thought you would have gone back to your uncle's."

"He'll sell me back to the Twister. I'd rather starve."

"You are starving," Eadwine said gently, glancing at the meagre remains of three days' rations, "and you can't go on living like this, Rhona."

Another shrug. "I've nowhere else to go."

"Heledd would take you in. She was truly fond of you, Rhona."

"I know," Rhonwen said dully. "She gave me some of her jewellery. But what use is gold? You can't eat it. You can't buy a loaf of bread with it – all it does is make you worth robbing –"

"She wouldn't have known that. Look, you could go to her now. It's only a day's walk to Calcacaster, even if you're not used to it, and then two more to her new home in Wharfedale."

Hope flared and then died. "How am I to get there? I don't know the way. I never went outside Eboracum in my life. And the roads are full of beggars and thieves and the Twister's spearmen. You know what would happen to a woman on her own." She shuddered again. "At least here they pay me for it –"

"Oh, *Rhona*." He sprang to his feet, pacing up and down the room. "Look – I'll take you to safety, if I can. But I have things to do first. I must know how my brother died. I must avenge him. I can't delay, though it breaks my heart to see you like this –" Another turn of the room. "I should have done better for you!"

Rhonwen stared at him, startled. "What could you have done? You were exhausted. You'd fought a battle, you'd been browbeaten by the Council, you'd just heard about your brother. It's a miracle that you managed to send Princess Heledd and the boy to safety. There was nothing more you could do. Why, you couldn't get your betrothed out of the city, let alone me –"

"Aethelind!" Eadwine stopped pacing as if struck, a great dread rising in him. "What happened to her?"

Rhonwen bit her lip and looked down at the floor. So it was bad news. All his nightmares came flooding back. "*What happened to her?* Is she – is she dead?"

"No, no! She's at Eoforwic – but –"

The dread turned to joy with a speed that left him dizzy. All his stern resolutions were swept away. Aethelind alive! And so close! He could find her, save her, keep one promise at least.

***

Common sense reasserted itself somewhere on the bridge, and Eadwine slowed from a run to a walk. Less likely to attract attention, though he was already the target of some idly curious stares. Fortunately he had left cloak, sword and pack in the courtyard, and his stained and mended clothes were not so far out of the ordinary. He kept his head bowed and shoulders hunched to shield his face.

No-one challenged him. There were no guards on the bridge, and the fortress was closed and barred. Neither king must be in residence. No great surprise there, for Aethelric shared the normal Anglian distrust of stone buildings and detested the city as much as Aelle had. He would be wintering at his hall on the family estate on the Humber, and Aethelferth would have left only a skeleton garrison to guard his new possession. Little point even in collecting tolls, for there was not much traffic in winter at the best of times, and even less than usual now. The wharves on the west bank had been rebuilt, probably by Finn Lousebeard, who could recognise a monopoly when he saw one and had stayed when his compatriots moved down to the Aire, but no-one had bothered to repair the damage on the east bank. The strip between the river and the fortress walls was still scarred and blackened by fire, and the high tide did not quite cover the charred skeletons of ships littering the foreshore.

Eadwine turned downstream from the end of the bridge. The last time he had trodden this path had been with Hereric, on the way back from his brother's funeral pyre a lifetime ago. He passed the south corner of the fortress, passed the burial ground, and looked ahead to Aethelind's hall, dreading what he might see.

But Aethelind's hall looked untouched. More, it looked prosperous. The barn was undamaged. The yard was tidy. The fences were in good repair and the ditches clear. The pigs snuffled and grunted in their pen. The chickens were plump, glossy and well-feathered. A large hound dozed placidly in the hall doorway. A woman, one of Aethelind's old servants, stooped over a laundry tub near the well. Two men, strangers to Eadwine, were skinning a sheep's carcass, and two more were chopping wood. Smoke curled gently from the opening in the hall roof, and a faint smell of roasting pork and fresh bread wafted over the scene.

Eadwine stepped smartly behind the hedge as one of the wood-choppers glanced in his direction. One of the Twister's thanes must have taken the hall, kept Aethelind as a servant or a slave – or worse. How to find her? But if it was washing day, and someone else was working the tub –

He made his way cautiously along the outside of the hedge, on the narrow strip between hedge and river bank. The property occupied all the land between the burial ground and the point where the Foss flowed in from the north-east to meet the Ouse, but before it reached the confluence the hedge faded out into clumps of hawthorn and hazel and scattered weeping willows, giving Aethelind's family their own private river frontage. A few sheep were allowed to graze it in summer, keeping the grass short and sweet. Aethelind's father used to fish from the bank. And Aethelind always hung laundry here to dry, where it was open to the sun in the south and there was no risk of anything being stolen.

Eadwine peered cautiously out from between two hazel bushes. She was there. Aethelind as he had first seen her and fallen in love with her, hanging a tunic to dry on a thorn bush. Dimpled arms and curvaceous figure and that wonderful cascade of golden hair glittering in the sunlight. He expected his heart to leap at the sight of her. Strangely, there was not the least response. Instead, he had a vivid, disturbing memory of a cloud of shadowy hair and sparkling green eyes and a small lithe body and a clever cat's face. The vision sparked first a sharp pang of loss, and then another of annoyance. He had no business thinking of Severa. Aethelind was his true love, his betrothed, the woman he was bound to by a solemn promise. He stepped out from hiding.

"Aethelind!"

She swung round, biting back a startled gasp, and recognised him in the space of a heartbeat. For a long moment there was silence. Aethelind was thinking: *I remembered him as handsome!* And Eadwine was thinking: *Did I ever really find her attractive? So fair and plump and placid, like a dairy cow.*

But promises were made to be kept. He held out his hands to her.

"Aethelind – my love –"

172

She did not rush into his arms. Instead she made a fluttering gesture, as if she were swatting away a wasp.

"Go away! The King wants you dead!"

Her voice grated on his ears, high-pitched and strangely lacking in expression, like a little girl's. But she was still his Aethelind.

"As you can see, he hasn't succeeded," he said, smiling, but she did not seem at all delighted. She looked around anxiously, even guiltily, and made another flapping gesture.

"What are you doing here? Go away, quickly!"

"I came to rescue you."

She did not seem delighted at that either.

"But I'm in the middle of the washing!"

His smile was long gone. This was not funny. Every moment he remained here his life was in peril, and she was worried about her laundry?

"Leave it," he ordered. "Come with me now, quickly."

"I – I can't! You don't understand -"

She laid her hands on her girdle and smoothed her gown over her swelling stomach. Eadwine stared, horrified. She was pregnant, four or five months gone by the look of it, and that could only mean one thing.

"Oh, Aethelind – what you must have endured! But it's over now, it's over. They'll never touch you again – and I swear to you, I'll care for the child as if it were mine –"

"No," she said, backing away. "No. You don't understand. Hereward – "

"He did this to you? He's the rapist?"

Aethelind had reached the bushes and could back away no further. "He's my husband."

Eadwine could hardly have been more shocked if she had thrown a knife at his head. It was some moments before he could speak, and when he did his voice was shaking.

"A – a forced marriage – it doesn't count. You can leave him – come away with me –"

She folded her arms. "I don't want to. I want to stay here."

"With *him*?"

"I like him," she said obstinately. "He does what I tell him and he never says things I can't understand. I have a home and a household and I'm going to have his baby."

"Is that all you want?"

"What did you think I wanted?"

"I see," he said, and his voice was a dead calm. "Then I wish you every happiness, lady."

Aethelind felt a hot blush stain her cheeks. How dare he speak to her as if he despised her, as if *she* had done something wrong!

"Eadwine –!" she hissed.

He turned back.

"You do understand?"

But she never knew what he would have said, for at that moment four of Hereward's spearmen came from the direction of the hall.

"Him?" one of them sneered. "Nah, he's only some beggar, nuffink to worry about –"

"Lord Hereward said the King wanted anybody what come near the lady," protested one of the others.

"Nah, not some foreign tramp, just kick him out –"

Eadwine judged he could talk his way out of it. They were doubtful, only one showing any enthusiasm. Used to be a servant of the lady's, down on his luck, hard times, hoping for a day's work – all Aethelind had to do was agree with whatever he said.

But Aethelind did what she always did in a crisis. She screamed.

"It's not my fault, Eadwine! I never told them!"

At the name all doubt vanished instantly. All four men sprinted forward, bellowing to unseen comrades. Eadwine spared Aethelind a single contemptuous glance, and fled.

The hawthorns on the bank slowed him down. Someone grabbed at his arm, wrenching the crown of the sleeve out of the armhole, but the grip slackened with a cry of pain as the hawthorn branches whipped back into his assailant's face. Someone else grabbed at him from the other side. Eadwine lurched towards the man, throwing him off balance, and kicked him hard in the groin. It would only gain a split second, but a split second was all he needed. He broke through the last branches onto the bank. As he dived, two men thudded onto the spot where he had been.

Aethelind ran to the bank when the shouting had stopped. No corpse. No prisoner. Just a knot of men standing on the bank, arrows nocked and spears poised, intent on the river.

"There!"

Halfway across and some considerable distance downstream, a dark head broke the surface. Three spears and two arrows splashed into the water around it.

The swimmer threw up his arms with a strangled cry, and the river swallowed him. All that remained, drifting slowly downstream on the ebbing tide, was a small oily slick of blood.

Chapter 18

Ashhere peered out from behind an oak tree. A solitary ploughman was plodding up and down the field behind a ponderous pair of oxen.

"Psst!"

The ploughman glanced up, saw nothing, shrugged, and carried on. Ashhere felt his mouth go dry and his palms begin to sweat. The ploughman was the image of his elder brother Fordhere, last seen in a ring of bloodied blades as the remnants of Aelle's hearth-troop closed around their defeated king to defend him to the death. Could it be –?

"Psst!" he hissed again, more urgently.

This time the ploughman stopped and looked round with more care, his gaze scanning the field edge, the ditch and the tangle of brambles before coming to rest on the figure capering and waving beside the oak. His mouth dropped open, then split into a grin of delight and disbelief.

"*Ash?*" He bounded the few steps to the end of the furrow, hurdled the ditch and enfolded Ashhere in a crushing bear-hug.

"Ford!" cried Ashhere, pounding his brother's mighty shoulders. "Ford! It *is* you!"

"Ash!" cried Fordhere. "Little brother!"

"By the Hammer! I thought you were dead!"

"Beard of Woden! I thought you were!"

"You first, little brother," Fordhere spluttered, when the flood of incoherent swearing and mutual back-slapping had died away. "How come you're not dead?"

"No, no, you first. What are you doing here?"

"Working the land," grinned Fordhere, gesturing at the oxen which had shambled to the end of the furrow and were nosing for something to graze on in the ditch. "Like Grandpa. Ploughman to ploughman in three generations."

"But the battle! How come you weren't killed?"

"I didn't run away!"

"I never thought you would have."

Fordhere relaxed, looking a little sheepish. "Sorry, Ash. Didn't mean to bite your head off. I'm a bit touchy about it, is all. Because I *didn't* run away and I won't have anyone saying I did."

"I wouldn't dare," said Ashhere, with feeling. "But what happened? Did Pa get away too?"

Fordhere shook his leonine head and dashed the back of his hand across his eyes. "Pa took a spear in the throat. Just as we'd given up any hope and formed a ring round the banners. I got the bastard that did it, though. Split him open from shoulder to breastbone while he was trying to get his spear back." He mimed a slashing sword-stroke to the right shoulder, and grinned in fierce satisfaction. "Bastard. Not that it did me much good, 'cause two of his mates come after me then, both together. Don't rightly know what happened next. I hit one of 'em, and then the next thing I knew it was morning and some mangy cur was snarling and snapping with its head in the guts of a corpse next to me. That made me sit up, I can tell you! I'd been pretty badly knocked about, and I was covered in blood, and all my gear was gone, so I suppose I'd been looted and left for dead. There was nobody about apart from the dogs and some seagulls, and I was dying for a drink, so after I'd stopped being sick I tried to crawl to the river. I didn't get very far." He grimaced. "I wasn't in very good shape. Anyway, some enemy warriors found me first. I thought they'd skewer me on the spot, but instead they got very excited. They gave me water and one of them ran off and fetched their lord. By the time the lord arrived I was feeling a bit better and thinking that Thunor must be holding his hand over me, so when the lord wanted to know who I was I said I was a poor married serf from the coast and I hadn't got any money and hadn't done any fighting and I'd only come to carry food for my thane's warriors."

"And they fell for it?" Ashhere questioned, incredulous. He touched his hammer amulet. "Thunor must have been watching over you!"

"He was that," Fordhere agreed, grinning broadly. "Good job Pa never managed to get any polish on us, eh? It'd never work for a real nob. And when I say I'd been looted, I mean looted. Every stitch. So I suppose there wasn't anything to show I was lying. The funny thing was, though, they seemed most interested in my hair. One of them poured water on it and scrubbed it with a cloth, and they seemed very put out when they saw it was fair. Dunno what that was all about. Anyway, they lost interest in me and let me go, and after a couple of days I managed to crawl here and old Leofric took me in. Remember him?

Pa's best spearman, has the fattest pigs and the fattest wife in Deira. And here I am. Mam and the girls are here too. Leofric fetched them from the hall as soon as he heard. He may have been retired for years, but he's still Pa's man to the death. Besides, Leofric hasn't got a son and his wife's sick, so he's glad of the help." He gestured at the weed-strewn field, becoming animated. "D'you know, this is the first time in three years this field's been ploughed? Crying shame, it is. And there's another field beyond the stream that's just as bad. I reckon I can plough and crop both of 'em this year, if Red-beard sends us kind weather. We'll need more beasts to manure them, so next year I'll get the neighbours to help me dig a drainage ditch so cows can graze the wet fields below the house in summer. The new thane says his mother expects to get twice as much milk out of their cows as Leofric gets out of his, so he's promised to swap me one of his father's breeding bulls for some breeding stock from Leofric's pigs, 'cause he says he's never seen pigs as fat as them in his life, and his dad likes fat bacon –"

"The new thane?" Ashhere interrupted, breaking into his brother's happy plans.

"He's called Eofor, comes from somewhere in the Tyne valley. Decent sort. Funny to think we were probably trying to kill each other a few months ago. Seems a bit silly now. He helped Mam look for Pa's body and build the funeral pyre and raise a burial mound. He's confirmed Pa's grant of Leofric's land, and as Leofric hasn't got a son he confirmed me as Leofric's heir. Good of him, because he could just as easily have given it to one of his own men and reduced Leofric and me to staying here as serfs or going back to the family folk-land and scrabbling for elbow-room at ten men to half a hide. Mind you –" he winked "– I reckon his sister fancies me. She's here keeping house for him until he finds himself a wife. Pretty lass, smiles all the time, plenty to get hold of. Knows a lot about dairying, too. I reckon she'll do me very nicely. It's about time I settled down."

"But," Ashhere began, lost for words. "But he's the enemy! What about vengeance?"

"I avenged Pa on the field. And you're not dead, so I don't have to avenge you."

"For your lord! For the king!"

"Aelle?" Fordhere shrugged. "He wasn't much good, you know."

"Yes, but he was *ours*!"

"He was useless," Fordhere said curtly. "It might have been all right for you, up in your backwater where there's never any fighting –"

"Huh! We fought all the time!"

"– but I can tell you we got sick of losing. He'd lost his luck, and ours with it. The gods were fed up with him. They're on Aethelferth's side. Aethelferth won the battle, right? He killed Aelle. So that proves the gods think he should be King. I'm not about to argue."

Ashhere swallowed. "What if Eofor asked you to fight for the Twister – I mean, Aethelferth?"

For the first time, Fordhere looked uncomfortable. "Oh, my fighting days are done, little brother. I'm not a thane any more."

"You're a free man, so you're obliged to fight for your lord if he asks you to."

"I'll defend my land and my family against all comers, like any free man. And as long as Eofor's a decent lord and Aethelferth's a decent king, I'll fight where they ask me to. That's fair dealing." He clapped Ashhere on the shoulder. "Don't look so sad, little brother! Fortune of war. Come and have a drink and meet Eofor. You'll like him. Don't worry, he doesn't hold grudges —"

Ashhere shook his head, backing away.

"Oh, come on, little brother. I'm dying to hear how you got away and where you've been all this time —"

"I," said Ashhere through his teeth, "have been keeping faith with my lord."

Fordhere's cheerful grin faded. He gulped. "The atheling?" he managed, in a whisper. "Is it true he survived? Beard of Woden! Last I saw of him he was laying into their line like a man in a hurry to get to Woden's hall." He looked round wildly. "Is he here? Ash, tell him to go away! He's a fool if he thinks he can raise an army here. He'll get no support."

"That won't surprise him," Ashhere said bitterly. "He found that out before the battle, when he was the only one who *hadn't* lost to the Twister's men and you lot shouted him down. If you'd done what he said, maybe you'd still be a thane and not a ploughman!"

Fordhere looked at his feet. "The gods were against us," he mumbled. Then, with more spirit, "Anyway, why should we listen to a lad with a head full of moonshine? What's he ever done? Outside of his own family and followers, who's ever heard of him?"

Ashhere thought vaguely that at least one Pictish tribe, several Bernician chieftains and a large number of raiders and pirates all had cause to remember Eadwine's name with fear. But there was no point saying that, since none of them were people Fordhere knew and therefore they didn't count.

"Ash, listen to me," Fordhere persisted. "I won't tell anyone, for your sake. Even though the reward would make me richer than a king! But tell him to go away! We don't want more trouble."

"He has a brother and a father to avenge," Ashhere said stubbornly. "And he won't turn aside from that."

"Against Aethelferth?" A grudging respect crept into Fordhere's face. "He's got guts, I'll say that for him. But — little brother — it doesn't have to involve you. Stay here, settle down. Mam would love to have you back, and Leofric's daughter always liked you —"

Home, family, security. A roof over his head. Food on the table. Perhaps in time his own hearth to come home to, his own wife and children. Ashhere was sorely tempted. Eadwine had already released him from his oath, in that bitter exchange on the banks of the Ouse. But he had insisted on staying bound then, when he had nowhere to go and no-one but Eadwine to look after him. It was not fair dealing to leave now that he was offered a cosy corner to hide in. Besides, he was not yet ready to abandon the spear for the plough, or to exchange a lord's commands for a wife's.

"No, Ford." He clasped his brother's hand. "I wish you well. But I follow my lord until death."

***

Eadwine clung to the root of an alder tree overhanging the west bank of the Ouse, gasping for breath and struggling to do it quietly. Both halves of the city had erupted like an overturned anthill, swarming with men, women and children all intent on fishing a king's ransom out of the river. Most were rushing downstream, as he had hoped, looking for a floundering swimmer or a floating corpse. Already a surfacing grebe, a log and a dead sheep had been the targets of a flurry of missiles, and some way downstream a man was leaning out over the water enthusiastically trying to hook what he would soon find out to be a waterlogged tree. Others, with more sense and more likelihood of success, were launching boats from the wharves, and on the opposite bank a baying pack of hounds came tumbling out of a yard. Hounds! Could they follow his trail back to the courtyard, back to Rhonwen? No, his old habit of secrecy about the Brittonic half of his life had provoked him to divert through a tanner's yard on the edge of the ruins, and no hound yet whelped could follow a trail through a tannery. Rhona was safe. It was only his own head he had thrust into the noose. He had badly underestimated Aethelferth the Twister. Of course Aethelferth would have found out his connection with Aethelind. Eadwine's half-sister Acha was Aethelferth's wife and through her Aethelferth probably knew all manner of personal details about Eadwine. Certainly about his betrothal – Acha had made her opinion of the match very clear at the time and at regular intervals since. And if Aethelferth was prepared to forego a whole year's tribute, he would certainly not have neglected to set a watch on Aethelind, and probably on everyone else he thought Eadwine might try to contact. Just as Eadwine would have done himself if their positions were reversed. It was fortunate that Acha had always maintained a haughty disinterest in his Brittonic connections, or he would most likely have been arrested at the monastery. What had he been thinking of, blundering along like a dozy partridge into a snare? He had not been thinking at all, that was the trouble. Consider it a valuable lesson. If he lived long enough to learn from it.

His breath was coming more easily now. Soon he would be able to move again. He put his hand to his upper left arm, where a spear or an arrow had torn a bloody gash in his flesh. Very lucky that the blade had not stuck. It hurt abominably, but the limb still worked.

Someone was coming down the bank, parting the bushes and prodding into the thicker vegetation with a spear. Eadwine took a deep breath and dived without a ripple. Just as well the river was always thick with silt. As long as he was under water he was invisible. The only flaw in this strategy was that he needed to breathe.

He surfaced again further upstream, this time in the shelter of a weeping willow not far below the downstream end of the civilian city wall. No missiles greeted him, and no yell of recognition. The bush-beater was downstream, disturbing a protesting moorhen. A boat glided past on the current and he pressed back into the bank, hidden behind a trailing branch. But it was only halfway through the day, if that, and he had no hope of prolonging this aquatic hide-and-seek until nightfall. For one thing, the cold would kill him in that time. Already his muscles were stiff, and the wound on his arm had almost stopped bleeding. For another, the tide was ebbing. Eboracum was a long way from the sea and the tidal fall was not great, but it was quite enough to shrink the water away from the concealing fringe of vegetation and leave him exposed on the foreshore like a stranded fish. But if he left the river anywhere near the city, the bank was so thick with searchers that he was certain to be seen long before he could find anywhere to hide. There was one chance. Just one.

He dived again, soundless as a water vole, and laboured upstream in the shallows. Good swimmer though he was, it was hard work against both tide and current, dodging submerged debris and trailing branches, surfacing for a snatched breath only when his lungs seemed on fire. He was past the monastery now, surely somewhere near the place. He blinked water out of his eyes, squinting to see clearly. Two alders with their trunks entwined – yes. The hollow in the bank where the kingfisher lived – yes. And there it was, leaning over the water like a protective sentinel, its roots so entwined that they formed a little peninsula where the bank had been cut away on either side, the veteran willow tree that had probably been growing on the river bank before the city was ever founded. Local folklore said the giants who built the city had left it standing so they would have somewhere to rest in the shade. Eadwine reached for a jutting root as if for a friendly hand. Now for the difficult part.

A thick branch swung low over the river. Eadwine stretched up. He could reach it, just, but his hands were so numb the fingers would not grip. Frantic with fear, shrinking behind the willow roots, he breathed on each hand in turn, flexing the fingers until some strength came back. He tried again. Both hands gripped the branch. Inch by inch, muscles groaning, he pulled himself up. His clothes streamed icy water, trying to glue him to the surface. The cold struck him to the marrow. He clenched his teeth to prevent them chattering. Beads of sweat stood out on his face, mingling with the water. Pain burned through the torn muscle on his left arm. He had been able to do this as a boy, when nothing more than a bet with himself hung on it. He must be able to do it now, when a slip and a splash would cost his life.

His chest was level with the branch. Another heave and he was lying across it, the weight off his arms at last. Blessed relief! But no time for rest, not yet. At any moment someone might nose a boat under the protective screen of branches, or force a way through the bushes on the bank. He dragged himself fully onto the branch and reached upwards and right for the next one. It shook under his weight. He had been lighter last time, and the tree not so old. But it only had to hold him for an instant and then he would be safe. If it was the right tree. If it had not changed.

It was the right tree, and it had not changed. The hollow heart was still there. What had been roomy for a skinny twelve-year-old was a tight fit for an adult, but it was enough. Feet first, he wriggled into the opening and let himself slither down into the dry, dusty, cobweb-hung, woodlouse-rustling, beetle-chewed interior. There was just space to fold himself up so that his head and shoulders were hidden below the lip of the hole. Now he was invisible. Unless he made a noise, no-one would find him without chopping the tree down.

Time crawled by. He crouched in the gloom, soaked and shivering, his cramped muscles screaming for relief. The wound on his arm throbbed as the feeling came back and the blood began to flow again. He groped for a handful of cobwebs and bound them in place with the thong from his hair, not much caring whether it did any good or not. Humiliation hurt far worse. Look at what he was reduced to, hiding like a worm in his own city. No wonder Aethelind had abandoned him for a better man. She hadn't wasted any time either, had she? He thought of Severa waiting four years for her husband. How long had Aethelind waited for him? Four days? Four hours? Nor had she gone to this other man through force or necessity. She *preferred* him. And that hurt worst of all. What she had shown with brutal clarity was that she had never cared for him in the way he had believed. He had been at best convenient, at worst – oh, horrible thought! – a necessary evil, the price of a home and a household. Everything else had been merely a figment of a besotted youth's imagination. He had made an utter fool of himself, from clumsy beginning to ignominious end. And no woman, obviously, would want a fool.

He closed his eyes on that bleak thought and gave himself up to bitter reflections on folly and betrayal.

***

Night took a long time to come. Huddled with his misery in the hollow tree, Eadwine was aware chiefly that the chill intensified and the dim light filtering down through the opening faded. It was a great temptation to ignore it, to stay here and hide his shame for ever, or to slip back to the river and let it roll his corpse down to the sea. But, shamed or not, failure or not, he had still a duty to avenge his brother's murder. Eadric would scorn him if he failed, and he had never been able to bear Eadric's scorn.

It was some time before he summoned up enough will to move, and some time longer before his cramped limbs had regained enough life to obey him. Crawling out of the hollow and climbing round the trunk to drop quietly to the ground on the landward side of the tree was an intricate and difficult business. He paused for a moment when he was down, placed both hands on the gnarled trunk and said a silent prayer of thanks to the guardian spirit of the tree. Then he dropped to hands and knees and wormed a cautious way through the bushes.

His instinct had been right. Not all the searchers had gone home at dusk, not by any means. It was a cold, clear night with a brilliant full moon. Quite a pleasant night to be out in search of valuable prey. One glance told him he had no chance of crossing the wall tonight, for he would be seen as soon as he gained the rampart and pursuers would close in long before he had climbed down the far side. It might be possible to wait for high tide and then swim round the end of the wall under the bushes. Another soaking would make little difference, as his clothes were still wet from the first one. He could probably swim that distance even encumbered with sword and cloak and pack. Probably. Or he could wait until tomorrow night in the hope of cloudy weather that would obscure the moon. What wind there was had veered westerly, and that usually meant rain. Usually. Either way, the first task was to creep under cover of ditches and fences and shadows back to the courtyard to retrieve his gear. He was not going to crawl back to his friends weaponless, like a beggar – there was enough of his lacerated pride left to rebel against that. And if he was fated to die, better with a sword in his hand.

***

Rhonwen knelt by the fire and fed another fragment of wood into the flames, paying no attention at all to the task in hand. She had heard the commotion in the city and a few nervous searchers had even ventured into the ruins, though none had come into the courtyard. Now she huddled by the fire, watching the doorway and praying as she had never prayed in her life.

"Hail Mary, full of grace," she muttered. "Hail Mary.... Blessed be thy name.... Blessed art thou among women.... Oh, Blessed Lady Mary, do not let him be taken. Do not let him lose his life because of a silly girl. Hail Mary, full of grace..."

One moment the doorway was empty, in the next a tall thin figure was leaning against the frame. Rhonwen jumped to her feet.

"You're alive! Oh, you're alive!"

Eadwine did not move or respond as she ran to him. His face was in shadow, half-hidden by tangled hair, and she felt a sudden surge of hope that perhaps he had never got as far as Eoforwic, perhaps he did not know. His sleeve was cold and clammy under her touch, his hands chill as ice.

"Come to the fire," she pleaded. "How did you escape them?"

"Crawling and hiding. I'm good at that."

The flat misery in his tone was unmistakable. He knew, and it hurt.

"Come to the fire," Rhonwen insisted again. "There's blood on your sleeve. Are you hurt?"

He flinched away, like a dog from a strange hand. "A scratch."

"Let me see."

"It doesn't matter."

"Please. I would be happier if I could see for myself."

That worked, as she had known it would. He pushed the torn sleeve up above his shoulder and sat passively while she cleaned the dirt out of the gash and bandaged it with the cloth the cheese had been wrapped in. Rhonwen surreptitiously studied his face in the firelight. He looked hurt and bewildered and very young. Very like the shy fifteen-year-old she had first indulged, thinking it would be a shame if all that eager innocence was spoiled by some hard-faced tart on the waterfront. Well, that shallow little blonde had spoiled it now all right.

He glanced up with one of his quick movements and caught her looking at him. Her pity for him must have shown in her face – it could hardly fail to – and he had always hated being pitied. He pulled away, shoulders hunched and arms locked around his knees.

"Why didn't you tell me?"

Rhonwen lowered her eyes. "I'm a coward," she admitted. "I didn't want to be the one to hurt you."

"So you let – you let *her* do it instead."

His voice was bitter, accusing. Rhonwen glared at him.

"You wouldn't have believed me!" she shot back.

He turned his face away. When he spoke, all the anger had gone from his tone and his voice was muffled. "No. No, you're right. I wouldn't have believed – I'm sorry, Rhona –"

She drew closer and tried to put her arms round him. How often they had sat together in love and laughter, in that summer long ago. But the roses now were faded and the stones were cold.

"I wish them well," he said, after a while. "At least, I think I do. I always wanted her to be happy. But – I thought – I thought it would be with me –"

Rhonwen drew his head down to her shoulder, stroking his hair. There had always been a strong motherly component in her affection, more so since she had, very gently and firmly, ended their affair – only to see him fall headlong for a girl who was even less suited to him. Perhaps he would realise that now. Perhaps he had realised it already, for he seemed more shocked and humiliated than broken-hearted. She smiled softly, and placed a gentle kiss on the crown of his head. *Blessed Lady Mary*, she said silently, *send him another woman, and get it right this time.* And in the meantime, she thought, a little reassurance would not go amiss.

"Eadwine," she said softly. "My dear."

He raised his head from her shoulder and she looked into his eyes. He was probably blaming himself, trying to figure out what he had done wrong. Any minute now he would make some excuse to go off by himself, and she was certain he should not be allowed to do that, not tonight.

"You're kind, Rhona," he said gently. "Thank you. It is time I was going –"

She took his hand. "Don't go. Not yet. Stay here with me."

He smiled, a little sadly, and her pulse jumped. His face was cleaner-cut and stronger now, his figure still slender but with the suggestion of well-proportioned muscles under his clothes. No longer a bony adolescent but a young man. Reassurance? Her feelings for him were not entirely maternal after all. Nor was he the only one in need of comfort.

"It's so lonely here –" she whispered, and her voice and hands were trembling.

"Yes," he agreed softly, and folded her hand in both of his. "Are you sure, Rhona? You said never again."

She smiled shakily. "Never is a long word. Stay, my dear. For old times' sake."

***

Eadwine woke many hours after dawn. The fire had been tended, he was snugly covered with his cloak, the water bottle and the remains of the food were set out within easy reach, and Rhonwen was kneeling in the doorway using the murky half-light of a wet winter day to sew the sleeve of his tunic back into the armhole.

"I ought to get nearly killed more often," he said drowsily. "Mending done. Breakfast in bed."

Rhonwen looked up, and her smile had regained some of its old sparkle. "I was wondering if you were going to sleep all day. How do you feel?"

He stretched, tentatively. The wound on his arm hurt, but not enough to be alarming, and all his limbs worked. "In one piece, which is more than I deserve. Is the weather as good as it looks?"

"It's vile. Rain then sleet, and it hasn't got properly light all day."

"Excellent!"

"What?"

"That means a dark night. I should be able to get over the wall without being seen."

She bit off the end of the thread and came to sit beside him, her face anxious. "You're going already? But it's not safe!"

He laughed, but there was a hard undertone to it. "It never will be, Rhona. Not for me, not any more. What would you have me do, live in fear of my own shadow? I've got a fair chance. Two days with no luck in the city, they'll mostly be looking downriver for a body by now, and if the Three Ladies are feeling helpful they might even find one. There are generally a few to choose from. And on a dark wet night all sensible people stay indoors." His fingers smoothed the frown from her forehead. "They won't catch me."

"They nearly did yesterday!"

"True," he agreed, ruefully. "But that was my own fault. I'm sure I must have done stupider things in my time, but I can't think of any."

"I think it was very brave."

"Stupid," he repeated, "but lucky. In more ways than one." His hand traced the line of her cheek and came to rest on a bruise on her shoulder. Now it was his turn to frown. "Did I do that? I'm sorry, Rhona —"

She hid a smile, wondering when he would notice the nail marks on his back. "I never felt it," she said truthfully. "I needed a night like that as much as you did."

It was still endearingly easy to make him blush, and she leaned down impulsively to kiss him.

"You're cold," he said, after a while.

"Freezing," she agreed.

He caught the hopeful tone in her voice and offered, "It's warm under here."

She snuggled up without waiting for a second invitation. "Mmm, so it is! The doctor can weave as well as she can sew. Tell me about her."

He yelped as her fingers found the puckered scar at his waist. "Keep still, if you want to talk. Remember you have the advantage over me."

"Advantage?"

"You're dressed."

"And you" – with a long, lingering caress – "are not. That's easily remedied," and her dress joined his clothes on the floor.

Later, as she was drifting off into a sated sleep in the warm circle of his arms, she realised drowsily that it was at least the second time that he had avoided telling her anything about the doctor, and she smiled to herself. Perhaps the Blessed Lady Mary was already working on it after all.

***

"I mean it, Rhona," Eadwine said, buckling his sword-belt in the fading dusk. "You can't stay here. Even if you have learnt how to light a fire."

"How long before you can come back for me?"

"Maybe never," he said soberly. He reached for his cloak and fastened the brooch on his shoulder. "Anything could go wrong."

"But if it doesn't?"

He considered. "Well, no-one is going to kill a good horse racing north to tell Aethelferth they let me slip through their fingers. So it will be a while before he hears. But he will hear, and if he's as keen to get hold of me as he seems, he'll either send someone south or come himself." He drummed his fingers on his thigh, thinking. "I've probably got half a month. If I'm not back here when the new moon is born, I'm probably not coming. Or not all of me, anyway."

Rhonwen shivered. "I wish you wouldn't joke about it."

"Sorry." He ran a hand through his hair. "But that doesn't mean it won't happen. Look, Rhona. You know the monastery in the south of the city?"

She nodded.

"If I don't come back, go there and ask for the abbot. Father Ysgafnell is his name. He knows me. More to the point, he also knows Heledd. I rather think he is her chief spy in Eboracum. And unless Christians really can talk to the birds, which I doubt, that means he sends her messages. So he can send you."

"For love of you?" Rhonwen asked, doubtfully.

Eadwine laughed. "No! But his god has expensive tastes, and you said Heledd gave you jewellery. You can't buy bread with gold, but you may be able to buy a priestly escort to Heledd's hall. What did she leave you? May I see?"

She pattered across to the far corner, where a hole in the floor gave access to the underfloor cavity, and came back with a cloth bag.

"Is it enough?" she asked anxiously.

Eadwine shook the shining tangle into his hand. "Oh, very nice." He turned the pieces over. A woman's silver bangle, a string of polished jet beads, a small gold finger-ring set with a red stone, and a man's large heavy gold brooch. "This should be more than enough –"

He broke off, staring at the brooch as though it had bitten him. A double-headed snake, body writhing in fantastic contortions, mouths open, malevolent fangs bared. The symbol of the Bernician royal house. The badge of Aethelferth. The badge of a traitor. *Rhonwen?* But no, Rhona was living in terror of Aethelferth, she could not be in his pay. Heledd? But Heledd had difficulty walking more than a few hundred yards and hardly left her apartments. She could not have crossed the city in the middle of the night to open a gate, even if the guards would have obeyed her. A terrible dread began to gnaw at him.

"Where did you get this brooch?"

His voice sounded strained even to his own ears. Rhonwen's face was out of focus, and her voice seemed to come from a great distance as she answered.

"It was on Lord Eadric's body, the day he died. We found it as we were laying him out. Neither Lady Heledd nor I had ever seen it before. Ugly thing, isn't it? Sinister....."

The picture glittered into place, like the moment when the water in a pool stills and the reflection looks back whole and unbroken, perfect in every detail. Not Beortred. *Eadric*. Embittered by waiting, afraid of being supplanted by a younger rival, eaten up with anger, desiring above all else to be king. An easy target for Aethelferth the Twister to manipulate. First contact made through Acha no doubt, believing she was fulfilling the traditional queenly role of peaceweaver between two warring kingdoms. Discussion. Negotiation. All very amicable and reasonable. And under it all one of Aethelferth's notorious plots, twisting like the serpent, feeding Eadric's discontent until it flared up into hatred and treachery. What did he promise you, Eadric? Cynewulf's death or banishment? And then to make you King of Deira, in honourable alliance with Bernicia? A partnership of two kings, brothers by marriage and brothers in deed. And for that you agreed to betray Eboracum to him. So you set off not to chase down a mounted warband on foot, but to meet Aethelferth or one of his captains at the ivy-covered oak, probably to agree which gate you would open. To make it look like a skirmish you stood by while the Bernicians slaughtered your men – no, worse than that. Your spear and sword were covered in blood. You killed them yourself. Oh, Eadric, Eadric, how could you sink so low? No deed is more shameful. You cut a few superficial wounds, accepted Aethelferth's token so that his men would recognise you as one of their own when they broke into the city. And then Beortred came blundering in, poor, simple, honest Beortred hurrying to protect his lord. He saw you speaking with the enemy. He saw you slaughter your own men – his comrades – as they lay wounded on the ground, and in his anger he struck you down with the only weapon he had to hand. Honest, loyal Beortred, killer of his own lord. No wonder he was distraught. But he could not say what he had done, because he would have had to say why, and if he could no longer defend your life he could still defend your honour. So he kept quiet, he doubled the guard on the gate, and he attached himself to your nearest adult male relative. Me. Until he thought I knew he had killed you. Poor Beortred, who was never a good liar but who could not tell the truth because it would shame his lord. So he ran away still burdened with his terrible secret, no doubt hoping to start a new life with a new lord far away, and met a slaver instead.

Yes, now I understand. But, Eadric, what were your plans for our father and for me? Did Aethelferth promise you our lives? You surely could not have believed he would keep such a bargain. Did you not care? Or did you sell us too, as part of the price? My brother, my hero, I would have died for you, but that was not the way I had in mind –

Eadwine clenched his hand over the brooch, welcoming the pain as the edges cut into his palm. A murderer. A traitor. A man without honour. Who deserved his shameful death.

"My dear?" Rhonwen's voice was small and terrified. "My dear, what is it? You look as though you've seen a ghost!"

Something snapped in Eadwine and he began to laugh, a manic sound, brittle as shattering glass.

"No," he gasped, "no, no, no! Now I know why I haven't seen a ghost!"

Chapter 19

"What *happened* to him in the city?" Lilla panted, struggling to keep up with Eadwine's punishing pace. "I've never known him so unhappy, or in such a hurry."

"Woman trouble," grunted Drust, shifting his shield on his shoulder.

Lilla frowned. "I don't think it's a woman. He's got that haunted look back, like when he first heard his brother was dead. Only worse."

"When he's miserable there's always a woman at the bottom of it," Drust insisted.

"Shows what you know. He's no womaniser."

"That's why they make him miserable. He lets them mess with his head and heart. If he kept them to the one part that's concerned with women he'd be a lot happier." He shifted the shield to his other shoulder. "I reckon he's told that blonde piece he's finished with her and he feels bad about it."

"Break a promise? Never –" Lilla broke off, struck by a new possibility. "Maybe he was looking for his girl and found she's dead."

Drust snorted. "Her? Girls with tits like that don't get killed."

"Maybe she's a prisoner –"

"And he feels obliged tae rescue her and doesna want tae, because he likes the little witch better? Aye, that's the sort of stupid thing he'd fret over."

"You're wrong!" Lilla snapped, all the more hotly because he thought it might well be true.

"Aye, weel. My shield says when this is over and his brother's avenged, we go back and pick up the little witch."

"And my sword says we come back to Eboracum and rescue his girl!"

"What are you two gossiping about back there?" Eadwine shouted over his shoulder. "Get a move on!"

"Coming, lord!" Lilla called back, and turned to Drust. "Done?"

"Done!"

***

Two nights' journey, marching from dusk to dawn without pause or rest, following little-used paths and tracks winding stickily through the woods and marshes of Eboracum Vale. Much of the farmland was a drear landscape still, ashen under the winter sleet, with here and there a ploughed field or a stack of timber beside the charred hump of a farmstead marking where some hardy souls had begun to return and rebuild. Dawn on the third day brought them to the southern edge of the moors, a country of scattered farms in hard-won valley clearings tucked among high and lonely hills. This land had been their home four months ago, their own country, where they could count every man as a friend. Now they came creeping back to it under cover of darkness, like thieves in the night.

And found it wrecked beyond all recognition.

***

They had been braced for trouble, after Eadwine had passed on Heledd's news of rebellion and punishment. They were familiar with the aftermath of raids, livestock taken and houses burned and survivors living hungry in the ruins or crammed into the homes of kinsmen and friends. But nothing had prepared them for Black Dudda's inventive savagery.

Every farm and smallholding was broken and roofless, either deserted or occupied only by the dead. Here were Aelfweard and his wife Hild, a famously lugubrious couple who farmed a benign, south-facing, well-watered valley and yet were always gloomily predicting crop failure or cattle plague or the wrong sort of weather, now merely charred skeletons lying with their legs broken in the burned-out wreck of the farmhouse. Cuthwulf and his three sons, who lived in cheerful bachelor chaos, brewed the best ale in Deira and were seldom sober, hanging in a disintegrating row from their door lintel. Sigelind, three times widowed, recently married for the fourth time and pregnant with her tenth child, floating face-down in the duck pond with her children drowned around her and her husband's headless body thrown down the well. Locca and Leofa, who farmed adjacent lands on opposite sides of the same stream and who maintained a permanent tight-lipped quarrel with no known origin. Four times a year they had stalked into the folk-moot, bristling with righteous indignation, and accused each other of pissing in the stream, moving the boundary stones, letting their cattle get into each other's hayfields, and insulting each other's daughters. Four times a year Eadwine had listened to them with an admirably straight face, exchanged resigned glances with their long-suffering wives, and awarded each of them exactly equal amounts of compensation. Now Leofa was a scatter of calcined bone in the burned-out ruin of his house, and Locca was a heap of evil-smelling shreds being shovelled into a shallow grave. Nothing and no-one had been spared. Every animal had been slaughtered and left to rot in the fields, even down to the chickens. Every house had been destroyed, even down to a tiny hovel in the bottom of a valley that was too steep for crops and too wet for pasture, where a single couple had scraped a precarious living from charcoal-burning and trapping and now lay with shattered limbs and shattered skulls outside the broken doorway of their home.

It was as they were rolling these bodies with as much decorum as possible into a hastily-dug grave, that they heard the moaning. All four instinctively recoiled, hearts hammering and hands reaching for amulets, but the moan had come not from the corpses but from the hut. A half-grown boy was dragging himself, inch by agonising inch, out into the light. His hands, feet and knees had been smashed to bloody shards and he was trying to crawl on his elbows. Jagged splinters of bone gleamed through torn flesh, and both his legs were blackened, stinking and swollen. Gangrene had set in.

"Water," he groaned, "water–"

The four travellers stood rooted to the spot, paralysed by pity and revulsion in equal measure. There was something obscene about this creeping, crippled horror with its corrupting flesh, something less than human.

"Ida –!" Eadwine choked, and went to him. "Here, lad –"

The boy sucked thirstily at the proffered water bottle, coughed, choked, and sagged back against Eadwine's arm. "Hurts –" He rolled his head from side to side as if trying to escape the pain. "It hurts – "

"Lie still, Ida," Eadwine said softly. "Who did this?"

"Butcher – the Butcher –"

"Black Dudda?"

"Aye – his servant killed – by th' outlaws – he said we done it – we never! We never done nowt – he said we knew who had – said he'd break our bones – one by one – til we told him where they hide – we didn't know nowt – nowt – it *hurts* –" Ida's bleeding hands flopped against Eadwine's chest in desperate appeal. "Hurts – make it stop –"

"I'll make it stop, Ida. I promise. See, help is coming, look."

He gestured to the right. Ida turned his head. Eadwine's dagger flashed, and Ida lay still in his arms, blood gushing from his cut throat.

***

"Outlaws?" queried Drust, as they heaped earth and stones over the enlarged grave.

"Exactly," said Eadwine, through clenched teeth. He rolled the last stone into place and got to his feet, his face set in an expression of cold anger that none of the others had ever seen before. "Come. I want a word with these outlaws, so we have hunting to do."

***

Not even Drust dared to question Eadwine in this mood, even when it turned out that 'hunting' was meant literally. They ran down a young stag in the late afternoon, and Eadwine insisted on hauling it out of the valley and carrying it along a high moorland ridge – much to Ashhere's alarm, since they could hardly fail to be seen on the skyline if hostile eyes were watching – to a deep, steep-sided, woodland-filled hollow in the moors. Wade's Cauldron it was called, after a giant called Wade who carved it out to cook his wedding feast and still, according to harassed mothers, prowled the moors in search of naughty children for dessert. Here Eadwine made them stop, light a large fire in a clearing backed by a rocky outcrop, and set about roasting haunches of venison.

"Er – should we damp the fire down?" Ashhere ventured, feeling a little braver now that he was comfortably full of his first hot meal in days.

"No," Eadwine answered. "I'm expecting company to dinner."

"Er –?"

"Be quiet, Ash!"

Silence fell, broken only by the crackle of the flames. Ashhere could hear his three companions breathing, the distant hoot of an owl, the rustle of a mouse in the leaf-litter – except it was a very *heavy* mouse –

Eadwine sat bolt upright, alert as a kestrel sighting prey.

"Come into the light, friend," he commanded.

The mouse scuffled to a startled stop. Eadwine moved his hand to his sword hilt.

"I said, come into the light."

A man limped out of the shadows. A small, scrawny man, not much bigger than an adolescent boy, but with a snake's speed of movement and a thin face alive with all the mischief of the world.

"By the Hammer!" said Ashhere, astonished. "Weasel!"

***

"Ar!" grinned the newcomer, helping himself to a chunk of venison. "An' 'oo was you expecting then?"

"Not you, at any rate," Eadwine said frankly. "You're losing your touch, Weasel, if we could hear you coming."

The little man grinned more broadly, if that were possible. He was of indeterminate age and mysterious origin, a thief and a pickpocket on Eboracum's busy waterfront until, for some reason no-one else was quite sure of, he had attached himself to Eadwine and by extension to the warband. He was not a warrior, nor was he quite a servant, he was always getting into trouble and out of it again, and he had a useful knack of getting into unexpected places and finding out undisclosed information. He was sharp as a needle, charming as a puppy, tricky as a fox and trustworthy as a cat. He could get up a woman's skirt faster

187

than a rat up a drain, talk his way out of trouble with her husband, and steal the family silver into the bargain. His name, inevitably, was Weasel. It was probably not the name his mother had given him, though opinion was evenly divided over whether he had ever had a mother in the first place. He had been badly injured in the foot trying to loot an enemy corpse at the fords of Esk, in the first skirmish against the Bernician invaders four months ago, and so unable to follow the retreat to Eboracum. Eadwine had sent him off the battlefield to take what refuge he could find with the villagers of Beacon Bay, and that had been the last they heard of him.

"Ar, the foot mended, thank you for asking," Weasel explained. "We 'eard you got away from the battle, so when I could walk I started 'eading south, back to the city, an' in Derwent Vale I 'eard they'd got you at Wicstun, so I 'itched a ride in a cart an' went there instead."

Eadwine laughed. "What, a rescue attempt? Don't tell me you came over all virtuous, Weasel."

"Ar, there was 'undreds of folk goin' to see the show. Big event, big crowd, good pickings," said Weasel, unabashed. "But I were too late, any'ow. They'd finished days before I arrived."

"What do you mean, finished?"

"At the 'Ome of the Gods. Ceremony over, priests gone 'ome. Yer armour's 'anging in the sacred grove. Very pretty it looks too."

Eadwine blanched. "Treowin took my armour! What happened to him?"

"Ar! Well, I dint know that, did I? I thought it was you." He sniffed. "Bit sad, really. Until I 'eard the rumour."

"Weasel, I am not in the mood for riddles. *What happened?*"

"Ar! Wish I'd seen it. Made the Twister look a right fool, everybody seeing 'e'd got the wrong man an' all. Couldn't give the gods the wrong man."

Eadwine sagged with relief. "They spared him? They spared Treowin?"

"Ar. Can't get nothing out of a corpse. Mind you, I 'eard he died before 'e said anything. Can I 'ave some more dinner?"

"Weasel –!"

"Stupid idea, trying to keep a feller prisoner in the middle of 'is own lands," Weasel continued, enjoying the effect he was having. "'Is sister was offerin' gold for 'is rescue. Lucky I were on 'and. Always pleased to oblige a lady, me. Mind you, I earned it. Took me weeks to find 'im, 'idden away in a shack. Even most of the guards dint know 'e was there. 'E sent you a message."

"Weasel, if you stop once more, I swear I'll strangle you –!"

"Ar, an' then you'll never know the end."

"*What message?*"

"Three guesses."

"*Weasel –!*"

"Ar!" said Weasel, grinning. "Well now, I think 'e'd like to tell you 'imself."

He turned, beckoned, a twig cracked under a clumsy footstep, and a tall, dark figure stalked out of the shadows.

***

It was Treowin, but greatly changed. His face, once so handsome, was now marred by a broken nose and a puckered scar on the left side of his jaw. Two of his front teeth were missing and two more were broken. His right arm terminated in a stump where the wrist and hand should be.

"Eadwine?" He blinked uncertainly in the light. "Is it you?"

Eadwine embraced him like a brother. "Can you doubt it? Alas, my friend!" He looked at Treowin long and searchingly. "I fear you have suffered greatly." For Treowin was trembling slightly from head to foot, not the shaking weakness that comes from weariness or wounds, but a kind of heightened tension like a harp-string tuned to breaking-point, or a highly-bred horse quivering under the touch of an unfamiliar hand. And there was a strange expression in his eyes too, excited and yet somehow furtive, like a child bursting with an important secret.

Eadwine stepped back, feeling suddenly uneasy. "Come. Tell us your tale —"

"You must go away!" Treowin blurted out. "Far, far away! Now! At once!"

"I have an errand that will not wait and that no-one else can do," Eadwine said calmly. "You would not have me leave my brother unavenged?"

Treowin did not appear to have heard. "You're mad to come here! The Twister —"

"Has offered gold for my head. I know."

"He has vowed you to Woden!"

The circle of firelight seemed to shrivel and fade, and the others involuntarily shrank away from Eadwine, as if they expected the dread war-god to stride out of the darkness to snatch his prize.

"This explains much," Eadwine murmured thoughtfully, when Treowin had stumbled to the end of his terrible tale. "It means Aethelferth can never give up hunting me."

""It means you're a dead man!" Treowin cried. "Unless you go away, far away, where other gods rule."

"As to that, we shall see." Eadwine drew a deep breath. "There are many gods in the nine worlds, and they are all subject to the Three Ladies, just as we are. If the Ladies weave me in their web, Woden or any other god cannot cut me out. And if they choose to snip my thread, no god's favour will save me." He looked around at his friends. "For my part, I will take my chances with my fate, whatever is woven. But I would not compel anyone to follow me."

Silence for what seemed like a long time.

Then Drust cleared his throat. "The Great Mother hasna heard of this upstart ye call Woden." He held out his hand to Eadwine. "I follow ye, lord."

"And I —" quavered Lilla, "I follow Lord Frey and I have not heard he has any quarrel with you, lord."

"N–n–nor Red-beard," stuttered Ashhere, clutching both his amulets tight in his fists and bracing himself for a thunderbolt.

"For my king, I would defy every god in the nine worlds!" declared Treowin.

"An' me, I follow my belly an' no god ever give me a decent meal," drawled Weasel, and belched. "That for the lot of 'em!"

Ashhere winced, but the sky remained placidly empty of flaming thunderbolts.

"I thank you all," Eadwine said, when he could speak. "And I hope you have no cause —" he glanced at Treowin and corrected himself, "— no further cause to regret it." He stretched stiffly and glanced up at the stars. "I wonder where tonight's intended guests are? That owl was a long way off, but they should have managed to walk here by now."

"Er – owls don't walk —" Ashhere began, and subsided when Lilla elbowed him in the ribs.

"Ar!" said Weasel. "I told 'em not to use that signal. Tawny owls live in the valleys. Up 'ere, what you wants is a wolf, or mebbe a fox."

Eadwine gave him a dangerous look. "Are you involved in this, Weasel?"

Weasel looked hurt. "Me? I could of done better'n a cartload o' firewood an' a couple o' dead slaves! But Fulla won't listen to the likes o' me."

Eadwine frowned. "Fulla? Thirty-ish, built like a barrel on legs and with about as much brain, reckons the answer to any problem is to hit it, keeps sheep with half a dozen cousins on the marshy land above Boggle Bay? That Fulla?"

"That's 'im," Weasel agreed.

"How in the name of all the gods did he start a rebellion? I didn't think he could lead the way out of a burning house."

Weasel grinned. "Depends what you call a rebellion. Seems the new lord what come after the battle told 'em all they 'ad to pay double food-rent an' not do military service no more. Fulla dint like this – 'e enjoys strutting about with a spear – so 'e said 'e weren't going to put up wi' being treated like a slave an' 'e weren't going to pay the extra rent."

Eadwine groaned and put his head in his hands. Weasel cackled with laughter.

"It were quite a show, Fulla bellowing an' Deornoth bellowing back, an' Fulla's wife railing at 'im for a mutton-headed fool an' swearin' she'd not let 'im back in the 'ouse til 'e saw sense. Wish I'd been selling tickets. Any'ow, a few more numbskulls join Fulla an' they stamp off to tell the new lord they'll pay the lawful rent an' no more, an' 'e laughs at 'em an' tells 'is guards to chuck 'em in the river, 'cos the law now is what 'e says it is. Well, this gets everybody riled, not just the muttonheads, an' the upshot is a couple of 'undred folk descend on 'is hall one night an 'is lordship an' 'is guards get trussed up in a cart an' hauled off to the king." Weasel's voice became suddenly sober. "They was expecting the king to 'ear their case an' either tell 'is lordship to behave 'imself or send 'em a new lord more to their liking. But what come back was Black Dudda, wi' the messengers' 'eads on a spear." He shivered. "Folk 'ere dint know what 'it 'em. Me 'an 'im –" he nodded at Treowin, "– 'ad just come up 'ere 'cos 'is sister said 'e were too dangerous for 'er to keep in Wicstun, an' it were like a year's worth of raids all rolled into one. After that most folk – them that was still alive – kept their 'eads down an' 'id away in sheds an' shielings out o' the way. But Fulla an' a few cousins an' some other numbskulls 'ang around up 'ere eating rats, beating up easy targets, stealing from other folk an' calling 'emselves outlaws."

"They are brave men!" Treowin exclaimed. "All they need is a little guidance –"

Eadwine turned sharply. "Have you been egging them on?"

"Lord," Lilla interrupted nervously, "listen –"

Crashing in the undergrowth, heavy breathing and a bitten-off curse heralded the eruption of half a dozen large hairy men, all wielding clubs or spears, into the circle of firelight.

"Stay where you are!" bawled the leader, through his bristling beard. "Don't move or we'll smash your heads in!"

"Fulla, I presume?" Eadwine remarked, quite unmoved. "Do join us. I was expecting you." He gestured expansively to the fire. "I am afraid I cannot compete with Wade's wedding feast, but you will find there is plenty to go round."

Fulla hesitated, thrown by this unexpected reception and uncertain how to react, but his followers were already pushing for places around the fire and eagerly reaching for venison, so he really had little choice but to follow suit. In a society where hunger is never far away, the man handing out the food always has the advantage.

"I hear you have been busy in my absence," Eadwine said, with deceptive calm. "Do tell me about it."

***

It transpired, after much patient questioning, that Fulla and about a dozen other men had taken to the high moors, where they attacked Black Dudda at every opportunity. The one flaw with this was that Black Dudda had a warband of thirty-odd hardened warriors and little reason to venture onto the high moors, so opportunities were not very common. So far they had managed to murder one of Black Dudda's spearmen in bed with a local girl, they had ambushed a hunting party and wounded two of them, not very severely, and they had killed two of Black Dudda's slaves who had been driving home after dark with a cartload of firewood. In revenge, Black Dudda had slaughtered the spearman's girl and her entire family, burned every boat in the Esk harbour, and destroyed four farms and all their inhabitants. Somewhat discouraged by this, Fulla's men had then taken it upon themselves to punish people they considered disloyal, which consisted of abducting and abusing three local girls for sleeping with the enemy, and beating up half a dozen farmers from Beacon Bay and the Esk valley.

"You did what?" Eadwine demanded, a dangerous edge in his voice.

"They were coll – collabo – turncoats!" Fulla blustered.

"Ar, an' one of 'em wouldn't let 'is daughter marry yer cousin," Weasel piped up, ever one to tip the frying pan into the fire.

"They were paying their food-rents to the Butcher," Treowin explained, as though that settled the matter.

Eadwine looked at him, and then at Fulla. "And?"

Fulla squirmed. "Er – that's it really –"

"If no-one paid their food-rents, the Butcher would starve and have to leave," Treowin lectured. "And if no-one in the whole of Deira paid, then Aethelferth the Twister would have to leave. Starve them out."

"Treowin, the man has a small army," Eadwine snapped, thinking back to Severa's valley and the Lord of Navio. "If the rent isn't paid he can *take* what he wants. People have the choice of paying their rent or having it taken and having their homes burned as well."

"And if he burns every farm there'll be nobody to feed his warband!" Treowin said triumphantly. "And he can oppress us no longer!"

"Only because there'll be nobody left to be oppressed!" Eadwine retorted. "You will make a wasteland and call it freedom."

"Oh, well, a few peasants get killed," Treowin agreed airily, oblivious to the black looks he got from some of Fulla's companions. "It is a price worth paying for freedom! Are we cowards, to live like slaves?"

"Aye!" bellowed Fulla. "We've got the balls to stand up for our rights!"

"Nobody denies you've got balls, Fulla," Eadwine said wearily. "Just don't bloody think with them all the time."

"What are we supposed to do?" Fulla flared. "If a wolf attacks your sheepfolds you fight back!"

191

"Woden's breath!" Eadwine exploded. "If a wolf attacks your sheepfolds you collect all the spearmen in the area, you track it to its lair and you kill it! You do not twist its tail until it turns round and bites someone else's head off!"

"We didn't start it!"

"You refused to pay your food-rents and lynched Aethelferth's chosen lord! How the hell did you expect him to react?"

"We only threw him out," Fulla mumbled. "We didn't kill him or anything. Anyway –" defensively "– it worked before."

"When you threw out my predecessor, you mean? Listen, Fulla, my father ruled Deira by right of blood and Eboracum by right of marriage. So he ruled by law and custom. He thought you a bunch of pig-headed loudmouths, but custom in Deira says that if freemen in folk-moot challenge a lord's actions, the king has to hear the case. It was easier for my father to try sending you a new lord, so you got me. But Aethelferth rules by right of conquest. Why do you think he wants Deira? So your food-rents support *his* thanes and their warbands. More warriors for his army so he can use them to conquer other kingdoms, other territories. He doesn't care about defending Deira so your military service is no interest to him. If you won't pay your food-rents to a lord of his choosing, you're of no value to him. You might as well be dead. In fact, if you won't pay he would prefer you dead, so he can settle his own freemen and serfs on your lands. That is what Black Dudda is doing. Can you not see that?"

A frown formed on Fulla's heavy face, giving him something of the look of a perplexed bullock. He and his followers looked at each other, then at Treowin, then back at Eadwine.

"He never told us that."

"'Cos you're peasants an' a price worth paying," Weasel chimed in.

"Now listen here –" Treowin began hotly.

"Shurrup," grunted Fulla, and went into a muttering huddle with his companions.

"Here," said one of them after a while, looking up and addressing Eadwine, "all that about the wolf an'all. Does that mean you reckon you can get rid of the Butcher?"

"Yes," Eadwine answered, very steadily. "I am the Warden of this March and I have a duty to protect its folk from thievery and murder. That includes Black Dudda. But you must do it my way."

The huddle reconvened.

"Right you are, lord," announced Fulla, getting up and walking round to Eadwine's side of the fire. "We'll do what you say."

***

"A hall-burning!" Treowin urged. "Surround his hall and torch it and roast the Butcher and his men alive!"

"Aye, and any local lasses they've taken," scowled Deornoth. He was the headman of the village at Beacon Bay, a worried-looking man with a pinched, hungry face. Behind him his wife huddled in the doorway of the clifftop fish-smoking shed that was now their only shelter, trying to comfort a baby that wailed incessantly.

"No worse'n the Butcher's already done," Fulla growled. He had tried burning the hall down himself, failed miserably, and was keen to have another go.

"Aye," snarled Deornoth, "because of your stupid attacks!"

192

"Now you look here –!"

"Sit down, Fulla," Eadwine ordered wearily. "And you too, Deornoth. There'll be no hall-burning. In the first place, burning Black Dudda's hall also means burning his food stores, and –" glancing at the hungry woman and child "– we have better uses for them. And in the second place, it's possible to escape a hall-burning, if you're agile and if the roof beams fall before they burn through. I want Black Dudda dead for certain." *And I want Beortred alive*, he added silently, though he kept that thought to himself.

"So what are you going to do?" Deornoth demanded.

"We need to destroy all Black Dudda's warband, and in such a way that someone else gets the blame. So far what Aethelferth's men have encountered here is a mob of angry farmers and a rabble of outlaws. Not warriors. So Black Dudda and his men have to die in battle."

"You want to fight them?" Deornoth was incredulous. "Do you know how many men he's got?"

"Thirty-two, Weasel tells me, including one who was sick with the flux last week but should be well again by now."

"We can't fight that many!"

"Says who?" boasted Fulla, banging the butt-end of his spear against the hut wall and making the baby yowl a bit louder.

"You'll do as you're told!" barked Treowin, at the same moment. "How dare you defy your king!"

"I'm not asking you to fight them, Deornoth," Eadwine said, ignoring both interruptions. "I'm asking you to help me fight them. You were willing to do that four months ago, and he had two hundred men then."

"True," agreed Deornoth despondently, "but four months ago we didn't know he could do this to us." He gestured round at the pitiful shelter and the picked bones of his two prize dairy cows. "Everything we've done since then – and especially everything that oaf's done –" pointing at Fulla "– has just made things worse."

"Then all the more reason to fight!" cried Treowin. "Better to die in the shield-wall like heroes than grovel in stinking huts like cowards!"

"Treowin, will you hold your tongue!" Eadwine snapped, reaching the end of his patience. "When I want your advice I'll ask for it! Please excuse my friend," he added, turning to Deornoth. "His enthusiasm runs away with him."

"All right," said Deornoth, somewhat mollified, as Treowin slunk off with a hurt expression, "what do you want us to do?"

"Two things. First, let me ask for volunteers to help in the fighting. Like last time, anyone who can hunt with a spear or shoot for the pot. Not hand-to-hand. You remember how much damage you did at the fords of Esk, before they even got within reach of us."

"Aye," agreed Deornoth, more confidently. "Aye, we did that! Volunteers, mind?"

"Volunteers."

"Agreed. And the second thing?"

"Three of your elders to go to the king –"

"Aethelferth the Twister?" spluttered Deornoth.

"No, no, the other king. My esteemed cousin Aethelric."

"He's not a proper king," snorted Fulla, and spat in contempt. "Your little weaselly friend says he always has two of the Twister's thugs with him, pulling his strings."

"Quite so," agreed Eadwine. "But Aethelferth likes to pretend Deira still has its own king, so let's go along with that. Three men to go to Aethelric, swear loyalty to him, throw yourselves on his mercy and beg his protection because your lands are being wasted by Pictish raiders. Make sure as many people as possible hear, especially the Twister's minders. Aethelric'll be at his hall near the fort on the Humber. Just follow the army-path on the edge of the Wolds south until you run out of land."

"What d'ye expect Aethelric to do?" Fulla sneered.

"Dither," answered Eadwine, with absolute certainty. "But when word comes that Black Dudda and his warband have been killed by Pictish raiders, the Twister will believe it. No more reprisals."

Deornoth looked dubiously out at the empty sea. "I can't see no Pictish raiders."

"No?" Eadwine said, grinning across at Drust. "I can see at least one."

Chapter 20

"Again!" Drust roared.

The twelve volunteers took a deep breath and yodelled a spine-chilling war cry.

Eadwine raised an eyebrow. "Well?"

"Och, they'll do. Yon Sassenachs willna ken the difference, any road."

"Doesn't sound like your war-cry."

"Ye've got a good memory. 'Tis my cousin's. He'll be pleased if he gets the credit. Black Dudda has a reputation. His balls are worth nailing up above your door."

"I hope you don't mean that literally."

"Och, ye needna watch."

Eadwine surveyed the volunteers, who were hopping about in eager anticipation like dogs expecting a walk. "Will they pass for Picts?"

"With the right shields, aye. From a distance."

"What's the decoration for?"

Fulla and one or two of the other men had woven feathers into their hair and beards, giving the impression of a badly-plucked chicken that had collided with a broom.

"They think we do that!" Drust said indignantly. "What do they take us for, some kind of ignorant savages? *And* they wanted to take all their clothes off and paint themselves blue. In this weather!"

Eadwine assumed an expression of innocent enquiry. "Do you only do that in the summer?"

Drust gave him a withering look. "Did ye get the weapons?"

"Yes. Black Dudda's men have destroyed or stolen all the weapons they could find, but they haven't found every hiding place." He held out a small round shield. "Thirteen of these. Only eight of the right spears, but plenty more of our own. By the time anyone gets a close look at a spear point they're not likely to notice the design." He shot Drust a sharp glance. "Would you like to give them out? It's your gear."

Drust's shoulders, which had slumped a little at the bleak memory of defeat, straightened. "'Tis nae disgrace tae lose tae a noble enemy. I didna believe that before."

"Adversary," Eadwine corrected. "Opponent. Foe. *Not* an enemy. Not now, not then."

"Ye wouldna beat me that way again, ye know."

"I should hope not. *If* I ever have to fight you again, Drust, I'll think of a different way to beat you. Tomorrow, I am glad we are on the same side."

***

Eadwine made his round of the camp in the dusk, as he always did when he knew they were expecting a fight. They had thirty men, not counting Weasel. Fulla and his eleven erstwhile outlaws, all irresponsible young men who would pick a fight to liven up a dull evening, had been assigned to Drust. They were all thrilled at the prospect of exchanging their role as outlaws for the far more exotic one of Pictish raiders, and were gathered noisily round one fire like a gaggle of starlings, hanging on Drust's every word as though he were a god come to earth. A few of the more impressionable local girls had been attracted in, and Drust had already had to crack heads together to break up the ensuing fights – which had only added to his prestige. Eadwine was well satisfied with them. Their part in tomorrow's plan was the simplest one, consisting mainly of appearing in the right place and making a lot of noise, then wading in when, as he hoped, the fight collapsed into a general melee. They should be capable of that.

Twelve rather steadier men, two women and five half-grown boys had volunteered from the coastal villages, along with Deornoth himself, and were gathered around a different fire, talking quietly among themselves while they fletched arrows, tested bowstrings and sharpened spears. Lilla and Ashhere were with them, and Ashhere was describing the skirmishes at the bridge on the Trent and the paved ford in glowing terms. Eadwine considered advising him to tone it down a little, and decided against it. Anything that reinforced the need to obey his orders instantly and to the letter would help, and tomorrow everything would depend on timing. This little group would have to respond to his commands as efficiently as his own limbs if they were to stand any chance at all, which was why he had picked out the steadier men for his group. Thirty against thirty-two sounded reasonable odds, but not when the thirty-two were all hardened warriors and the thirty had only five professional fighters among them, one of whom had only one hand.

"Sulking," said Lilla, in response to his enquiry for Treowin. "We asked him to join us but as soon as he'd eaten he sloped off."

***

Eadwine found Treowin in the direction Lilla had indicated, sitting morosely on the ground and staring into the middle distance. He threw himself at Eadwine's feet.

"I never meant to interfere! I only wanted to encourage them! I would die for you!"

"I never doubted your courage or your loyalty, Treowin," Eadwine said gently, feeling a little embarrassed. He stooped and raised Treowin to his feet. Again there was that odd thrilling tension in Treowin's body, and again Eadwine was the first to step back. "But if you take offence at every order, you will find that a far greater handicap then the loss of one hand."

Treowin took this the wrong way, as usual. "I can still fight, you know! I'm left-handed, and I found a shield I can strap to my arm." He drew his sword and mimed a few very effective-looking cutting strokes. "I fought with the outlaws!"

"I know you did. I heard you fought very well."

"Then why are you angry? I thought you would want them to fight back." Treowin sounded bewildered, like a child that has been slapped for no reason.

Eadwine sighed inwardly, and sat down. Treowin sheathed his sword and sat beside him, now with something of the manner of a dog hoping for a pat. "Are you still angry?"

"No. I'm thinking what to say. Look, it is true that you have fought in more shield-walls than I have, and in that respect you have more experience than me. But here we are always fighting an enemy far stronger than we are, and all is different. March fighting is stealth and murder, Treowin, nothing but stealth and murder." He sighed. "Maybe there is glory in the shield-wall, as the poets say, though it did not seem so to me at Eboracum. But here there is never any glory in the means. So you must never, never lose sight of the end. Have you given thought to why lords and warriors exist? Yes, I know that men of our class are born to it, and a sword is more interesting than a plough, and more girls are drawn to a man with a spear than a man with a spade, but apart from that? Why should some men drink and fight while others work? It is because not all men are capable of being warriors. Why do you think I asked for volunteers rather than ordering all Deornoth's folk out on military service, as I have the right to? Because the twelve who have come have made their own choice and will be far more effective than fifty who are compelled unwilling to the fight. But does that mean those who do not want to fight are worthless? Of course it does not. I do not grow corn or build a house or work iron, yet I expect to benefit from the skills of those who do all those things. It is only fair that those men who do not have the temperament to fight benefit from the skills of those who do. They feed us, we protect them. A lord is the helmet of his people, Treowin, not their scourge. His job is to bring the greatest good to the greatest number of his people. This is not the same as bringing the greatest harm to his enemies, and nor is it the same as bringing the greatest glory to himself. By murdering Black Dudda's slaves and beating up those who pay their rents, you did Black Dudda little harm and you brought down much suffering on the heads of other people. My people. That is why I was angry. Do you understand that?"

"Yes, yes!" Treowin agreed, so eagerly that Eadwine suspected he had not taken in a word. "You're right, of course you're right."

"Then come to the fire. My friends are willing to accept you, if you give them a chance. And tomorrow they will see how well you can fight."

Treowin hesitated. A man and a girl ran past hand-in-hand and disappeared, giggling, behind a gorse bush. Treowin stared after them, and swallowed. "Tomorrow –" he began and broke off. He swallowed again and jerked his head in the direction of the 'Pictish' campfire, where Drust was beginning a raucous performance of *Attacotti Nell*. "They might all be dead tomorrow! And they sing and tell tales and gamble and – and – lie with women!"

"Seems a reasonable way to spend your last night on earth," Eadwine said mildly, wondering what this was leading up to.

Treowin appeared not to have heard. "And there isn't any mead!" It was almost a wail.

196

"Ah," said Eadwine, grasping what seemed to be the root of the problem. "I'm afraid that's our way up here. I have very few rules, but one of them is that none of my men gets drunk without my permission. I don't care to go into battle knowing that the man who's supposed to be watching my back is already wishing he was dead to get rid of his hangover. We get drunk after the fight, not before."

"You fight sober?" Treowin made it sound like a superhuman attribute.

"More or less."

"Even the militia?"

"I find they copy the professionals," Eadwine said easily. "Will that be new to you?"

Treowin nodded miserably. Eadwine sought for something reassuring to say. "If you fight well when you're drunk, Treowin, you'll fight even better when you're sober."

Treowin did not look convinced. He was staring moodily at the gorse bushes, where the giggling had given way to a rhythmic sighing.

Eadwine got to his feet, reluctant to eavesdrop further, and held out his hand to Treowin. "Come on, back to the fire and show me how you use your shield. It must be years since we've sparred together and I want you to fight at my side tomorrow."

Treowin's face lit up. "Gladly!"

***

"They aren't coming," Treowin worried, peering out of the heather. He and the rest of Eadwine's group lay flat near the top of a shallow peaty slope, hidden from view in the deep heather. Here and there tall bog-cotton stems marked the position of wet ground and moorland pools. A chill north-east wind blew under an overcast sky, but the ground was not deeply frozen and only a thin skin of ice skimmed the pools. It would be a difficult place for fighting, all treacherous ground underfoot, which was why Eadwine had chosen it. Ahead, the slope plunged abruptly into a deep, steep-sided wooded valley. A sticky track, worn down to the orange-coloured clay that underlay the top six inches or so of peat, climbed out of this valley, crossed the shallow slope at an angle, and then turned south to climb a very slight rise. Slight, but just sufficient to provide a reverse slope to conceal Drust's band of 'Pictish' warriors. Only Drust was visible, and then only if you knew exactly where to look. The big man was still as a stone, and blended into the heather like a red grouse on its nest. He too was watching the track. It was the most direct route from Eadwine's old hall in the Esk valley, now commandeered by Black Dudda's warband, to Guardian Howe, an ancient burial mound at an important crossroads on the high moors and the traditional site of the local folk-moot. They were expecting Black Dudda's warband to come panting up the steep slope from the valley. Any moment now. But the track was still empty.

"What if he doesn't come?" fretted Treowin.

"Keep your head down!" Eadwine hissed. "He'll come."

"Why should he?" grumbled Deornoth, who was getting unsettled by Treowin's fidgeting. "He wouldn't come onto the high moors for Fulla."

"Fulla's head isn't worth its weight in gold."

Deornoth blinked. "He knows you're here?"

"He does now. Weasel went yesterday to tell him I'm hiding at Guardian Howe with only three friends, waiting to be joined by Pictish allies."

"By the Hammer," muttered Deornoth, awed. "You play for high stakes, lord."

"My stake in this is the same as yours."

"What if they don't believe him?" worried Treowin.

"Oh, they will," Eadwine said easily. "Weasel looks like the kind of man who'd sell his own mother for a couple of drinks. People suspect him of all manner of things, usually quite rightly, but nobody ever yet suspected him of loyalty."

"How do you know he won't sell you? Tell them we're waiting here."

"He doesn't know. The only thing he asked me was if we were going to use Roman thorns again, because he doesn't want to cripple his other foot."

Lilla stifled a laugh. Weasel's outrage when he had run into the fords of Esk to loot a body and trodden on a caltrop had been a sight to behold.

"I wish they'd get a move on though," groused Ashhere, looking at the leaden clouds massing like bruises on the north-east horizon. "It's cold enough already, and there's rain in those clouds."

"Snow," corrected Lilla.

Eadwine looked at him sharply. "Snow? Are you sure?"

"That direction, this time of year, no question. Does it matter?"

"How long?"

Lilla studied the clouds thoughtfully. "Afternoon. Maybe not til nightfall."

Eadwine relaxed. Snow could ruin his plans, but it would all be over one way or the other long before nightfall.

"Ah!" breathed Deornoth. "Here they come."

Two bobbing heads had come into view over the break of slope, where the track changed gradient and plunged down the steep valley side. Their owners were soon visible, gasping for breath and sliding unsteadily in the slippery clay. One of them was already covered in it, having evidently slipped and fallen somewhere further down the slope. Not for nothing was the track known locally as Lousy Hill Lane. The watchers lay absolutely still, scarcely breathing, as the rest of the warband came into view. Black Dudda barged his way up to the front, resplendent if rather mud-spattered in mail shirt and helmet. Four other men had mail shirts, three of whom also had helmets, and the rest were clad in wool and leather. Weasel danced along beside Black Dudda, pointing eagerly ahead up the track. Eadwine smiled to himself. So far, so good.

Then he tensed and stiffened, as four more men came labouring up over the breast of the hill. They had no weapons or mail and they were tied together by rope halters around their necks, not unlike a train of pack horses. Black Dudda was evidently anticipating a night on the moors, as Guardian Howe was more than half a day's walk from the Esk valley, and had brought his slaves to carry supplies. Eadwine grasped Deornoth's arm.

"Beortred's there! Look, the big fellow third in the slaves' line, fair hair, scarred face. Pass the word! He is not to be killed, understand? I want him alive! Lilla, get over to Drust as soon as we move and warn him. I want Beortred alive!"

"Right. He's to be kept for you."

Eadwine gave him an odd look. "Yes. Yes, that's a better way of putting it. Tell them that."

***

Black Dudda's men came pounding on, striding more easily now the slope had eased, though still out of breath. They passed Eadwine's hidden group, and reached a certain light-coloured boulder at the side of the track. Eadwine held his breath, waiting –

Drust did not let him down. A terrifying war-cry ululated over the moors. The empty ridge ahead sprouted a line of howling savages, waving Pictish shields, brandishing spears and screaming for blood.

Black Dudda had been half-expecting to encounter a Pictish warband, and he was a professional.

"Shield wall!" he roared.

Weasel skipped smartly into the nearest hollow, having long since perfected the art of lying low until there was looting to be done. The slaves shambled to a bewildered halt.

Black Dudda's thirty-two warriors, professionals to a man, squared up, shoulder to shoulder, ranked three deep, the front row gleaming with mail shirts and helmets and presenting an unbroken line of overlapping shields to the Pictish warband.

While the rear row presented eleven unprotected backs to the group of seventeen men, two women and five boys who rose silently from the heather behind them and unleashed a storm of arrows, light hunting spears and rocks.

**

Eadwine had warned them that the first barrage would decide the fight. Ashhere saw five men fall, spitted with spears and arrows or dazed by crashing rocks, before they even realised their danger. Six more went down even as they turned to face the new enemy. It looked as though it would all be over in a few minutes.

But then the storm of arrows and rocks slackened. There were few missiles left.

"Come on!" Eadwine shouted, and leaped forward.

"Eadwine for Deira!" bellowed Ashhere. "Eadwine for Deira!"

Deornoth was on one side of him, also yelling madly. Ahead, Treowin and Eadwine ploughed into the remains of the Bernician rear rank, Eadwine with a sword in one hand and a spear in the other, Treowin with a shield strapped to the stump of his right arm and a sword dancing in his left hand. They fought as one man, perfectly matched, each parrying blows aimed at the other, and what was left of Black Dudda's rear rank buckled before their fury. The Bernician shield-wall broke up as some of the front rank turned to help their comrades behind. On the other side, Drust and Fulla charged in shrieking rage. The shield-wall, assailed unexpectedly from both sides and stumbling on a slippery track and treacherous ground, crumbled into a muddle of individual fights.

Ashhere and Deornoth ran to catch up with Eadwine, Deornoth stooping briefly to grab one of their hunting spears from the back of a fallen enemy. The man groaned as the blade was wrenched out of his back, evidently still alive, and Ashhere stabbed down hard with his own spear. This was no time or place to take prisoners. Ashhere registered a spearman coming from his left, caught the blow on the shield he had borrowed from Drust, and then punched the heavy iron shield boss into his opponent's face. The man staggered back, and Ashhere ran on.

"Eadwine for Deira!" he yelled, and beside him Deornoth copied the cry and jabbed his hunting spear at an enemy arm. More by luck than judgement, the blade connected, the man twisted away, and Ashhere and Deornoth were up with their two comrades. Eadwine's spear was gone and Treowin had moved to his left side, so that each had a sword-arm free on the outside of the pair and Treowin's shield provided some protection in the middle. Ashhere and Deornoth moved up close behind them, making a tight knot of four men all protected by each other's blades.

But they had no support. The volunteers had run out of missiles, had no weapons, no armour, not even shields, and they hung back from the savage blades and the blood and the screaming. One man had run with Eadwine's charge and now reeled out of the melee with one arm hanging off and half his face cut away. A Bernician warrior slashed at him with a sword, almost contemptuously, and the man crumpled crying into the heather. The ends of the Bernician line began to curl round Eadwine's group. Ashhere saw they would soon be enveloped and surrounded, but there was not a lot he could do about it except hang on and guard his lord's back.

The battle had shifted ground, and they were on the right of the line now, on the side where the track sloped down into the valley. Ashhere saw Beortred dragging the other slaves with him, aiming for a wounded Bernician warrior sitting dazed on the ground trying to staunch blood pouring from a thigh wound. The wounded man jumped up as he saw Beortred, seized a spear and lunged at him. Beortred grabbed the next slave in the line and swung the man bodily to block the blow. The spear stabbed right through the slave's back and lodged with the point projecting from the chest. Beortred held the dying slave upright with one arm, grabbed the wounded Bernician with the other, and smashed his forehead into the Bernician's face. All three fell to the ground in a heap, and Ashhere caught a glimpse of Beortred sawing the neck rope on the projecting blade of the spear, before a swirl of movement blocked his view. The press ahead suddenly slackened, and the little knot of four stumbled forward into clear air. They had carved right through the Bernician warband.

But Black Dudda was far from beaten. Indeed, the fight was swinging his way. More than a dozen of his men were still standing, forming into a new shield-wall around their commander. Black Dudda was bellowing like an enraged ox, swinging his great gory sword left and right, and the supposed Pictish warband was scattering in terror before the onslaught. Drust and Lilla, back-to-back, were engaged in a fierce fight with two men in mail and it was all they could do to defend themselves. Fulla's men were backing away, frightened. For all their martial talk, they were farmers and shepherds, unused to the horrific violence of hand-to-hand fighting. They were not ready to face a shield-wall, and Eadwine had never intended that they should.

He shouldered his way to the front. "Black Dudda!"

The big man turned. "Who wants him?"

Eadwine stooped and snatched up a fallen shield. He faced Black Dudda, shield in one hand, sword in the other, and cried for the third time,

"I am Eadwine son of Aelle, and you are not welcome on my land!"

Black Dudda snarled. "Turd! Bastard! Offspring of a whore and a weasel! I'll get you this time!"

He lunged with his heavy sword, aiming low where the blade would cripple unprotected lower legs. Eadwine leaped up high into the air and the blade passed harmlessly under his feet. He swung at Black Dudda as he landed, but Black Dudda was also fast and deflected the blow with his shield. The two men circled each other, breathing hard. Up and down what was left of the line, private fights were broken off. Men stepped back to watch, knowing that a duel between the commanders would decide the issue. The first flakes of snow came swirling down.

"No Roman thorns now!" mocked Black Dudda. "No fires, no weasel tricks! No walls to hide behind! You can't fight like a man!"

He made a feint to the right, then snapped back like a snake and struck at Eadwine's sword-arm with a blow intended to take off the hand at the wrist. Eadwine saw the move in time and whipped back out of range. His foot caught in a tangle of heather, he staggered, momentarily off balance, and Black Dudda leapt forward with a yell, aiming a savage cutting blow at Eadwine's unprotected head. Eadwine flung up his shield just in time, Black Dudda's heavy blade bit deep into the rim and snagged amid a tangle of splintered wood, and Eadwine jerked the shield towards him so that Black Dudda had to lurch forward a step to avoid having his sword tugged out of his hand. Eadwine jerked the shield in the opposite direction, the sword tore loose, Black Dudda was thrown off balance and with an athletic roll and twist Eadwine regained his feet, ducked under Black Dudda's wild stroke and sliced his own sword into the back of Black Dudda's lower leg.

It was only a flesh wound, not reaching the bone, and Black Dudda stayed standing.

"You little shit," he snarled, and rushed forward again, this time cutting at Eadwine's right shoulder. Eadwine had no mail shirt, and his splintered shield was all but useless. He darted back and only the tip of the sword reached him, raking three inches of blood-welling furrow down his breast.

Black Dudda's face contorted into a feral grin. He swung at Eadwine's legs again, knowing that he need only slow his agile enemy to gain the victory.

Eadwine leaped again to avoid the blow, but this time he stumbled as he landed. Black Dudda roared in triumph and brought his sword slashing down.

Ashhere started forward with a cry, his heart in his mouth, but Treowin, who had trained with Eadwine since boyhood, flung out his shield-arm and held Ashhere back.

The stumble had been a feint. Eadwine pivoted on his toes, and Black Dudda's blow whistled harmlessly past his head. Black Dudda lurched, off-balance now that the stroke had failed to connect with anything except empty air, and Eadwine's sword cut hard into Black Dudda's wrist. Bright blood spangled the snow, and Black Dudda staggered, his sword drooping uselessly from nerveless fingers. Eadwine dropped his shattered shield and swung his sword in a great two-handed blow. The blade struck Black Dudda in the angle of neck and shoulder, between the helmet and the mail shirt, and bit deep into muscle and bone. The big warrior crumpled to his knees. Even then, dying, he drew his dagger and slashed left-handed at Eadwine's legs, trying to bring his enemy down with him. Eadwine stepped back – no need to jump this time – and Black Dudda toppled forward into the snow, his weight wrenching the sword from Eadwine's grasp. He twitched once, and lay still. Snowflakes began to settle gently on his back.

The remaining Bernicians cried out in dismay. Their leader was dead. The gods were not on their side. They stared for a heartbeat in frozen horror, and then they fled.

Now the farmhands came into their own again. The hated occupiers were on the run, frightened men trying only to save their own lives, and a fleeing warrior is no match for two or three farmers – or even women and boys – with scavenged spears and fish-gutting knives.

***

Eadwine heaved the dead slave off the Bernician stunned by Beortred, slashed the warrior's throat to make sure, and picked up the severed end of the neck rope.

"Where's Beortred?"

Weasel looked up from rifling Black Dudda's belt pouch, and pointed. "He went that way."

A trampled line in the fresh snow headed out into the moors, going east and a little north. Straight into the teeth of the approaching storm.

"Drust!" Eadwine shouted. "Take half Fulla's men and clear up here. No prisoners! Do whatever your people do to enemy bodies, collect all the war gear and anything else worth having. Leave a Pictish shield and spear here. Ashhere, Fulla, take the rest of Fulla's men and see to our dead. There mustn't be anything left here to show the locals were involved. Treowin, Lilla, take everyone else and the slaves and carry our wounded into shelter, then get down to the hall. Clear up any of Black Dudda's men left there, find the stored food and distribute as much as you can before nightfall. Deornoth will tell you who's most in need. And take Weasel in case there's a hoard hidden. I'm going after Beortred. I'll meet you at the hall."

Lilla grabbed his arm. "No, lord, no!"

Eadwine shook him off as if he was brushing an unwelcome insect from his coat. The battle-fury was still on him, his face set and his eyes wild.

"I must find Beortred!"

"The snow!" It was snowing steadily now, already difficult to see more than fifty yards, and the heather stalks drooped under a soft white blanket. Lilla grasped Eadwine's arm again. "Eadwine, the moors are lethal in snow and darkness! If you can't reach the Esk before nightfall, don't try to cross the moors. Fulla has cabins and sheepfolds on the stream draining into Boggle Bay, you can't miss it, just follow the stream. Take shelter there. Promise me, lord!"

"All right, Lilla, I promise. Now let me go!"

***

Eadwine ran on over the moors, alone. The snow was falling faster now, a few inches already covering the ground and beginning to form drifts. Beortred's track was fast disappearing. It was gloomy under the leaden sky, and low cloud brushed the highest ground. Wind-driven snow scoured Eadwine's face like icy needles. He came labouring to the top of a rise and realised he had lost the trail.

"Beortred!"

No answer. But – yes – there was a dark figure slipping through the gloom ahead, outlined against the snowy ground.

"Beortred!" Eadwine yelled again, and gave chase.

This was the last rise before the sea, and ahead the land sloped away north-eastwards for a mile of rich clay farmland and pasture before ending abruptly in high sea cliffs. Beortred was just visible in glimpses ahead, ducking in and out of gorse bushes and hedges. He was a heavy man, and finding the combination of slippery clay and fresh snow hard work. Eadwine, lighter and more sure-footed, was gaining fast.

"Beortred!" he shouted. "Wait!"

He plunged through a tangle of gorse and paused for breath. The gradient steepened ahead of him, the last sloping field before the sea. To his left, a stream had cut a little wooded ravine. There was no sign of Beortred.

"Beor –"

Some soldier's instinct, some sixth sense, gave him warning. He twisted aside in the instant that a spear hurtled out of the bushes edging the ravine and flew past inches from his waist. Beortred erupted from the ravine like a wild boar and butted head-first into Eadwine's stomach, sending both men skidding backwards down the slope in a welter of churned mud and flying snow. Beortred had no weapon, but he was getting on for twice Eadwine's weight and strength. One mighty fist crashed into the side of Eadwine's head, the other punched up under his ribs. Eadwine fought back as best he could, half-winded and half-stunned, and managed to jab his elbow hard into Beortred's belly. A sword was no use at close quarters and he could not reach to draw his dagger. Besides, there had been quite enough of knives in the back where Beortred was concerned. It was like hitting an oak plank, but Beortred grunted and his grip slackened a little. Eadwine thrashed sideways to avoid the next blow and the struggle tumbled a little further down the slope.

"Beortred!" Eadwine choked. "Bloody fool – the cliffs –!"

Pinned flat under Beortred's bulk, he had no way of knowing how near they were to the edge, but he could hear the thunder of surf on rocks mingling with the howling of the wind. These cliffs where the moors met the sea were notoriously unstable, built of crumbling shale and soft boulder-studded clay, and it was not unknown for several feet worth of cliff to collapse into the sea in a winter storm. It was not a good place for a brawl.

He tried to gouge his thumbs into Beortred's eyes, but Beortred seized his wrists and slammed them back against the ground.

"You won't kill me!"

"Not – trying – to – " Eadwine gasped, dizzy with the pain. He applied all the leverage he could to his back and shoulders, managed to shift Beortred's crushing weight, and crunched his knee up into the big man's groin. Beortred groaned, his grip broke, and Eadwine succeeded in scrambling out from under.

"Not trying to kill you!" he got out, but Beortred came for him again. He rolled to avoid the punch in the throat that would have broken his neck, but the other hammered into his chest like the kick of an enraged stallion and felled him, helpless, to the ground.

"Now leave me alone!" Beortred roared, raising his foot to stamp on Eadwine's head.

But the foot never connected. Eadwine jerked sideways, Beortred's foot met the earth in a shuddering shock, and Beortred lurched, arms flailing for balance. Eadwine saw the ground tilt and start to slide, understood in a flash and threw himself forward as Beortred dropped in a shower of soil and stones. His fingers encountered and grasped a clutching hand, and he cried out in pain as all Beortred's weight came on his left shoulder. The instinct was to let go and relieve the crushing agony but he overrode it and held on, gritting his teeth and reaching forward and down with his right hand. He found Beortred's wrist and grasped it, spreading the weight onto both his shoulders. A few loose stones skittered away but most of the remaining cliff edge held firm. He was lying flat on his face, only his head and shoulders projecting over the edge, and it did not feel as if Beortred's weight would be sufficient to pull him into the gulf. Not yet, at least.

"Get hold of something!" he yelled.

Beortred's panic-stricken face peered up. Below his dangling feet, gulls soared on the storm and a flat pool-pitted rock platform stretched from the foot of the cliff out into the hungry waves. "Don't let go!"

"Not going to!" Eadwine panted. The effort of holding Beortred's weight was like iron bands crushing his chest. It was hard to breathe. Another chunk of clay broke away under his elbow and plummeted down to smash apart on the scar two hundred feet below. "By the Hammer, man, get a grip! I can't hold you much longer!"

Beortred's feet were scrabbling without success for a hold. "You're sworn to kill me!" His left hand clawed at the cliff face and caught a jagged chunk of sandstone embedded in the clay. The weight on Eadwine's shoulders eased.

"I'm not trying to kill you, you bloody fool! Can you pull yourself up?"

Beortred pulled on the sandstone rock, which shook alarmingly. "But you know I killed your brother!"

"Yes, and I know why." The rock came loose in Beortred's hand, and his full weight crashed onto Eadwine's shoulders again. Eadwine felt the sharp pain in his left shoulder as a muscle tore under the strain. "Get hold of something, Beortred! You're too heavy for me." He gasped, sweating with pain and effort. "I know he was a murderer, I know he'd sold out to the Twister, it wasn't your fault –"

Beortred howled, a terrible cry of desolation and despair. "Nobody knows that and lives!"

Eadwine saw a blur of movement. Beortred's left arm, still clutching the sandstone rock, lashed upwards with savage force. A blinding, splintering pain in his head, and then everything dissolved in a white flash.

Chapter 21

Eadwine lay staring vacantly at the dust motes swirling above a slab of mouldy cheese, wondering idly whether Severa knew the dairy roof had blown off and why there were seagulls crying overhead in a landlocked mountain hafod. Probably Severa had never seen a seagull, so he ought to find her and show her these, just as soon as he felt well enough to move.

"Yaaark – aark-aark-aark!" in his ear, and a herring gull sailed past inches from his face, tilted a wing and side-slipped with masterful grace down towards the slab of cheese.

The world came back into focus with a sickening lurch. The slab of cheese was the flat rock scar at the base of the cliffs two hundred feet below. The dust motes were fat snowflakes. He was lying on his belly at the edge of a sea cliff, his arms and head dangling forward over a sheer drop.

He scrabbled back away from the edge, a little avalanche of soft snow sliding off his back. The movement made his head spin and his stomach turn over, and he vomited weakly into the snow. His bruised abdominal muscles complained vigorously at this further punishment, his chest and back ached, and there was a burning pain in his left shoulder. It felt as if he had come off worst in a more than usually murderous fist fight. Which, of course, he had.

He put his hand up to the throbbing pain centred in the right side of his forehead. A deep jagged cut just above the eyebrow, slimy with clotted blood, a large and very painful swelling, but – he probed tenderly, shrinking from the pain – the bone seemed to be intact. No doubt that the blow had been meant to kill, but not even Beortred had the strength to smash a man's skull when he had to strike upwards and left-handed.

"Beortred!" he shouted into the storm. The cliffs were not absolutely vertical. Bands of soft clay and shale formed steep slopes, sometimes stable enough to support vegetation, between short walls of harder rock. Beortred might be lying on a ledge. He deserved to be. It was not fair that a good man should die because of Eadric's treachery.

No answer. He tried again, cupping his hands to his mouth. "Beortred!"

Still no answer. Kneeling, he peered very cautiously over the edge, but there was no ledge big enough to support anything more than a kittiwake's nest. And there was a suggestion of something dark and indistinct on the scar below, glimpsed through the whirling snow.

Eadwine dragged himself to his feet. He had to know. Wearily, his head pounding, his damaged shoulder screaming its protest, he descended the ravine. The rocky bed of the stream was rough and choked with undergrowth, but it dropped at a safe angle through the cliffs until it terminated in a trickling waterfall about thirty feet above beach level. A slither down mud and slippery disintegrating shale delivered him safely to a narrow beach.

"Beortred!"

No answer. But he knew the site of their struggle had been above the headland to the right. After a few yards the beach gave way to a platform of slabby rock, almost level but treacherous with slippery seaweed and water-filled hollows. Barnacles crunched under his feet. These flat reefs, known locally as scars, were covered by the sea at high tide.

He rounded the point of the headland. Yes, something dark was lying on the scar. A seal, he told himself, until he was close enough to see its shape. Then he thought: A shipwrecked sailor. It couldn't be Beortred. Beortred could not be dead. It would not be fair.

He stooped over the body. "Beortred?"

No answer. There could not be, of course, not with the back of the head smashed like that and the brains spilling out over the rocks, nor with the splintered shards of rib gleaming through the crushed chest.

"Well, Eadric," he said aloud, "I suppose this means you're avenged. I hope you're satisfied."

He dropped to his knees on the rocks and took Beortred's flaccid hand.

"Your loyalty was greater than mine," he whispered. "You were prepared to die, and kill, for him even when you knew what he had done. I was not. You deserved a better lord."

He could not leave Beortred there, to be squabbled over by seagulls and tossed by the waves until all that remained were slimy rags of flesh clinging to bleached bones. A good man deserved an honourable resting place. A funeral pyre or a grave were impossible in this place, and he was not strong enough to haul Beortred's body up the ravine, but there was one thing he could do. He unpinned Beortred's cloak and wrapped the body in it, scooping up as much of the spilled brain as possible and laying a large flat stone on the chest. Beortred's belt and brooch secured the cloak, and Eadwine grasped the shoulders and began laboriously dragging the body over the scar to the thundering surf. He would send Beortred to Njord, the god of the sea, the father of Lord Frey and Lady Frija. Njord's handmaidens were said to search the sea bed for the bodies of drowned sailors and carry them to his hall, which was much like Woden's hall but under water and not quite as boisterous. There would be no shame for Beortred in that company.

The air was full of salt spray driven on the wind, and the larger waves broke over the scar in a surging wash that briefly floated Beortred's body and tugged it to follow as the wave ran back to the sea. Njord was eager to welcome his new guest. The waves grew deeper and greedier as Eadwine neared the edge of the reef, and it was a struggle to keep his footing on the slippery rocks. At the edge he kneeled, breathless and sore, and rolled Beortred's body into position. The next wave broke right over his head, he heaved Beortred's body off the scar into the sucking backwash, and seized hold of a rock to avoid being swept with it. For a fleeting moment he was sure he saw the shrouded body gliding down into the green depths as serenely as a seal, and then wave and body were gone and he was coughing and clutching the rock while the icy wind howled and his body shrank from the cold. It was a great temptation to let go of the rock and let the next big wave take him out to join Beortred in the tranquil depths. But he had made Lilla a promise, and the promise was on land.

The journey back without the burden took far longer than the journey out, and the crumbling shale by the waterfall came near to defeating him. At the top he fell in a heap in the bed of the ravine, wishing that the pounding in his head and the red-hot needles in his shoulder would stop so that he could go to sleep. They did not, and he retained enough awareness to know that if he slept he would be frozen to death by morning. Boggle Bay, Lilla had said, and follow the stream to Fulla's cabin. That sounded straightforward enough. Very slowly, he began to clamber up the ravine.

The daylight was almost gone by the time he emerged onto the clifftops, and snow lay thick on the ground. All signs of his struggle with Beortred were already obliterated. But the snow was a blessing in one respect, for it made the white edge of the land visible in contrast to the dark sea below. Three miles along the clifftop would take him to Boggle Bay. An hour's pleasant stroll on a summer evening. Huddled into his wet cloak, he set off. The buffeting wind was at his back now, pushing and bullying him. The cold ate into his bones. Soft snow took him up to mid-calf at every step, and deeper windblown drifts filled every dip and hollow. Soon he could no longer feel his hands or feet, and he stumbled on every irregularity in the ground. He fell waist-deep into snowdrifts and had to burrow his way out like a mole. After a while, standing up proved to require too much co-ordination and he was reduced to crawling. His left shoulder was unreliable in taking his weight, though mercifully the pain had faded. Indeed, he could hardly feel his limbs at all. When he fell and found his head resting on his arm in the snow, it was as if he was lying on a piece of wood. He lost all track of time and place. It was difficult to see much in the howling dark, except the white line of the cliffs stretching ahead, and even that blurred into two and writhed snakelike through the dancing snowflakes. He had forgotten what he was doing or why, but he still knew vaguely that he had a promise to keep. It was like being drunk, or in a high fever.

A sliding tumble down a long slope terrified him back to a vague grasp on reality. This must be the descent into Boggle Bay. He was supposed to do something here, though he could not remember what. Something about a stream. Streams were generally to be found at the bottom of slopes, so he floundered downhill until he stumbled across a thin ribbon of icy black water, and recalled hazily that he was supposed to follow it for some reason. But he was so tired. All he wanted was to lie down and sleep. He was no longer cold. In fact, he felt quite warm, and would be able to move much more easily if only he could get rid of the heavy cloak that was weighing him down, but his fingers were too numb to work the brooch. The snow no longer stung at his face and eyes but instead seemed soft and caressing, like gently floating feathers or apple blossom whirling in the first gale of spring. He tried to catch some, but unaccountably the ground seemed to tip sideways so that he was climbing up it, and that was not fair for he had climbed the shale and the ravine already and did not see why he should have to do it again. The drifts were warm and welcoming, feather beds inviting him to snuggle up in one. But he had a promise to keep. He could not sleep yet.

Something bumped against his bowed head. Something was in his way. It was too dark to see, but the obstacle was flat and vertical. He blundered along it and came to a corner. A thin line of yellow light outlined a rectangular shape, and the bleating of sheep frightened by the storm mingled with the shrieking wind. Eadwine stared at the yellow line. The small part of his mind that was still functioning screamed that this was important, but he could not remember why. Was he supposed to do something? But he was too exhausted to do anything more. His shoulder gave way again and he fell sideways against the obstacle. A dog barked. Blinding light spilled over him. Hands pulled at him, lifted him. He was faintly conscious of voices, disjointed words that made no sense.

"– more than half frozen, poor lamb – those icy clothes – how he found his way – the storm – let him sleep –"

And that seemed like a very good idea.

***

Warmth. That was the first sensation he became aware of. He could not remember why that was such a blissful feeling, nor why it seemed so important. There was a vague shadow in his mind, like the ghost of a dream, of a descent into the freezing wastes of Hel, a nightmare journey through an underworld of icy cold and shrieking devils. The second sensation was pain, a dull ache in every muscle, a burning itch from the shallow sword cut on his chest, and a throbbing, blinding headache apparently centred in the right side of his forehead. Wriggling his eyebrows confirmed the presence of an uncomfortably thick, heavy bandage. Eadwine opened his eyes, cautiously, and found he was lying on his left side on something that felt like blanket-covered straw, looking across a fire into the mournful eyes of a hound bitch curled around two very small lambs. This was very puzzling. What was more puzzling was the smooth warmth of a body cuddled against his back. Somebody was in bed with him.

He rolled over and found himself looking at a big blowsy woman with kind brown eyes and a face that could best be described as wholesome. He blinked. It was not the first time he had woken up with a pounding headache and a strange woman – followed on that earlier occasion by a large father and brother trying to look indignant instead of jubilant as they demanded their compensation – but it was the first time he had had no idea how he had got there or who his companion was.

He said, uncertainly, "Do I know you?"

The wholesome face broke into an equally wholesome, if gap-toothed, smile. "Tunhild. Fulla's wife." A meaty hand felt for his fingers and a large bare foot slid down his ankle and tickled his toes. "Ah, you're warm at last! I knew it would work." She nodded in the approximate direction of the hound bitch on the other side of the fire. "Old Lass there is busy and you're too long for her, any road. But I reckoned I'd do. I told 'em you weren't dead when we heard the bang on the door and the shepherds brought you in out of the snow. I said to 'em, I said, if he's crawled all this way he ain't daft enough to die on the doorstep, you just give him to me. Though I were scared to begin with. Cold as a stone, you were, and not hardly breathing –"

Snow. Fulla's cabin. Beortred. Black Dudda. Eadwine rolled out from under the blankets, heedless of Tunhild's interested gaze. His clothes were spread out by the fire. They were stiff with dirt and salt and blood, and had the unpleasant smell one would expect after not having been off his back for weeks, but they were dry and warm.

"Awww," protested Tunhild, "are you going? An' I was looking forward to staying in bed with a nice young man all day, and my husband not able to say a word about it neither."

Eadwine laughed, buckling his belt and kicking his feet into his shoes. He stooped and kissed her on both cheeks as a son might kiss his mother, then dropped to one knee and kissed her hand as if she had been a great lady. "Alas, Mistress Tunhild, much though it grieves me, I cannot stay. You are a pearl among women, and I am forever in your debt. Some day I hope to be able to show my gratitude. But now I must go."

He jerked open the cabin door.

"Behold the King!" a voice yelled, and a cacophony of noise broke out. Ragged cheering, the banging of spear-shafts against shields, a hunting horn, somebody yodelling Drust's Pictish war-cry, and over it all Treowin's voice leading a chorus, "Hail the King! Hail the King!"

Eadwine's first thought, after the initial shock, was for Tunhild's modesty, prompting him to slam the door smartly behind him. His second was a profound sense of gratitude that he had got fully dressed before leaving. And the third was a keen sense of the ridiculous at the idea of anyone hailing a scruffy, unwashed, unshaven, uncombed youth as King.

"Calm down," he tried to say, reluctant to shout because of his headache. He made a dampening-down gesture with his hands and mercifully the noise began to abate. "Calm down. What's all this about?"

It looked like a well-attended folk-moot. There were perhaps a hundred people crowded into the sheepfolds and around the cabin door, men, women and even a few children. He recognised them as people from the coastal villages and the Esk valley, who astonishingly must have thought it worthwhile walking several miles through a foot of lying snow to come here. Some were those who had fought in the skirmish with Black Dudda's warband yesterday. Fulla was there, jigging up and down with the bedraggled feathers still sticking in his beard, Weasel was happily chewing on a chicken leg, and Ashhere, Lilla and Drust were gathered in a group at one side, bruised and bandaged but not seriously hurt. The snow had stopped and a watery sun stood well into the south. He must have slept all morning.

Deornoth stepped forward, a bruise on his face and with his left arm in a sling. He crossed his right arm across his chest, right fist to left shoulder, in the formal gesture of fealty, and intoned, "We here, freemen in folk-moot, accept Eadwine son of Aelle as King of Deira. If any man disagree, let him speak now."

Silence.

"Those who agree, speak now."

"Aye!" roared the crowd. Fulla, getting carried away, howled Drust's war-cry again.

Eadwine could only stare, momentarily speechless. From his earliest memory he had always known Eadric was going to be the King. He had expected to be his brother's lieutenant, guarding the March for him, or perhaps being appointed as Warden of the more prestigious West or South Marches.

"I thank you, Deornoth, and all of you," he said gravely. "You do me great honour. But alas, Deira is not in a position to choose its own King."

"You defeated Black Dudda!" Deornoth said eagerly. "You can defeat Aethelferth the Twister! Restore our freedom!"

"Aye!" cried Treowin. "Throw off the tyrant's yoke! Restore the rightful King of Deira!"

Ambition kindled in Eadwine's heart. On his father's side he was King of Deira by blood. On his mother's side his lineage went back even further, back to Coel the Protector whose authority derived from Rome and to Coel's wife whose foremothers had been queens in Britannia since the dawn of the world when the gods still walked the earth. And what was Aethelferth? A barbarian from beyond the Wall, the descendant of a pirate chief.

"The right is mine," Eadwine acknowledged. "But a king is not made by right alone. Aethelferth can field a thousand warriors. That is thirty warbands like Black Dudda's, and yesterday we were hard put to it to beat even one. He is too strong for me to challenge yet."

"No, no!" The enthusiastic voice was Treowin's. "The rest of Deira will join us! They will rise for their rightful King!"

Eadwine regarded him with some astonishment, wondering if Treowin really believed that. "Why should they? Most of Deira knows me as my brother's shadow, if at all. On the Council I was generally in a minority of one. Here on the March I have lived and fought for three years, but away from here I have no military reputation. I have commanded no great armies, fought no major battle." A mutter of protest from the crowd made him smile. "You may well think I could have done better than those who did, or at least that I could hardly have done worse. And you may very well be right. But the fact remains that Aethelferth has led the armies of Bernicia for twelve years as their King, and has campaigned from sea to sea across the North. Do not forget that he won the battle at Eboracum, and many will take that as a sign that he has the favour of the gods. And you think they would fight him for an untried youth?"

Ashhere thought of his brother Fordhere, who had said much the same thing, and knew that Eadwine was right.

"We fought!" Fulla boasted. "We wouldn't bow down to the Twister! Yon soft Southrons should follow our lead."

Eadwine's voice was glacial. "Yes, you fought and what it got you was Black Dudda. And you were not fighting for me, were you?" He swung round to include Deornoth and the rest of the crowd in a sweeping glance. "Any of you? You threw out Aethelferth's lord not because he wasn't me, but because you thought he was treating you badly. And that is my point. Most people care how they are ruled, not who by. Where Aethelferth has put in lords who are less arrogant – or where the folk are less bloody-minded about their rights than you are here – there will be little appetite for more fighting. People may grumble, especially when they find out, as you already have, that Aethelferth has no respect for Deiran law and custom. But it is one thing to grumble and quite another to shed blood. Most will put up with it and get on with their lives as best they can. So must you, for now." He drew a breath. "I am leaving today. Leaving the March, leaving Deira." He held up a hand to still the dismayed ripple in the crowd. "Hear me out! Aethelferth already knows I was seen in Eboracum at the height of the last moon. He will already be on his way south to take me. One of Black Dudda's men got away yesterday, and no doubt is even now fleeing north. He will most likely meet his master somewhere on Dere Street with the news that I have turned up here with Pictish allies. Tomorrow, or the day after, you can expect to see Aethelferth with a warband, if not an army, marching up the road from Dere Street. If I am still here it will go hard with you. I would not wish that."

"You will abandon us?" Deornoth looked and sounded aghast.

209

"Not abandon. Never that. Say rather that I go to build greater strength elsewhere."

"To Lundencaster!" exulted Treowin. "Aethelbert of Kent will give you support!"

"And replace Aethelric with me and Aethelferth the Twister with himself," Eadwine said dryly. "All that will achieve is a change of tyrant. Is that what you want of your King?"

"No, it bloody isn't!" declared Fulla and Deornoth in unison, before Treowin could speak.

"I thought not," Eadwine said, smiling. "I will do better for you than that. I will win back Deira by the sword, and I will rule as King and not as some foreigner's pet or puppet. But it will take time. So I ask you to wait. Be patient. The worst will be over now on the March. Black Dudda is dead and even among Aethelferth's men his savagery is extreme. You are not likely to see his like again. When Aethelferth arrives here, he will be so concerned with hunting me that he will have little thought for anything else. Blame your injuries and Black Dudda's death on Pictish raiders, tell Aethelferth I left with them, and humbly – yes, humbly, Fulla – ask his protection. Aethelferth does not care for you as a king cares for his own people, but you are of value to him if you do as you are told. You will get a new lord, perhaps a good man, perhaps another arrogant fool, perhaps a drunken sot who never stirs from his hall. Put up with him. Pay your food-rents. Keep your heads down. But keep your spears sharp and bring up your sons to fight when I call. For though I do not know how, or when, this I promise you. I will come again."

Chapter 22

"Where will you go?" Rhonwen wanted to know. She was lying with her head comfortably pillowed on Eadwine's chest, in the hayloft above Heledd's barn. This had become their place in the half-month since he and his equally bruised and battered men had brought her here from Eboracum, true to his promise. There was enough of the winter hay left to make a bed, it was warm from the cows in the byre below, and it was far quieter than the main hall.

Eadwine kissed the top of her head gently. "It's best you don't know."

She was not surprised at the response, indeed she had not really expected an answer. Although their physical intimacy was as sweet as ever, in other ways he had grown apart from her. He seemed older somehow, harder and fiercer, and there were parts of his heart that were walled off from her. Which she was finding very interesting.

"Can't you stay here?"

"Alas, no," he said, with mock despair. "Having been ousted from my promising career as a rich widow's toy-boy, I have to make my own way in the world –"

Rhonwen rolled over, laughing. "You don't miss much, do you?"

"What, is it supposed to be a secret? Heledd has started doing her hair differently and looks ten years younger, Imma gazes at her like a particularly dimwitted sheep, and her tapestry hasn't made a thread of progress since I was last here. Good luck to her."

"She was afraid you would be angry with her."

"Heledd is concerned about my good opinion? Whatever for?"

"Your brother –"

"Oh. I see." He sighed. "Have I been such an insufferable prig as that?"

"Well, not exactly. But she knows how much you loved your brother."

"Eadric is dead," he said flatly. "It's over."

This was one of the walled-off places, but Rhonwen could not resist probing again. "Did you find out who killed him? What happened?"

"As I told Heledd. Beortred killed my brother, Beortred is dead, there is no threat to Hereric, and it is over."

"But –"

"There is no more to tell, Rhona."

She conceded defeat. "When must you leave?"

"Daybreak. Hereric is expected within the next few days, and I must be gone before he gets here. Hereric couldn't keep a secret to save his own or anyone else's life. Neither could Wulfgar or Wulfraed." He heaved another sigh. "That is the real cost of exile, not the loss of land or title. My heart burns to see Hereric again, and yet I must run from him as from an enemy. I may never see you or Heledd again either."

"Will we hear of you?"

His eyes glinted in the candlelight. "All Britannia will hear of me by the time I'm done. If I am to depose Aethelferth without putting another foreign tyrant in his place I have to build a reputation that will convince others – many others – to follow me. But it must be under another name. For now." He kissed her again, long and gently. "Enough of me. What about you?"

"I shall buy myself a husband. I'm near thirty, you know. It's about time I settled down, and now I have a respectable dowry to set against my not-so-respectable past."

"Speaking of which –" He reached across her in the hay for his belt pouch, and dropped something golden and glittering onto the blanket. "Here's your brooch back."

Rhonwen caught the object as it rolled. It was a bangle in twisted gold, a beautiful piece of work.

"It's all there," Eadwine said, a little hesitantly, "except a small amount I let the goldsmith keep for his trouble. You did say the brooch was ugly."

"It's lovely." She slipped the bangle onto her wrist and embraced him. "Such a kind thought, too, much nicer to have jewellery I can wear –" She stopped. "That brooch told you something terrible, didn't it? And now it can't tell anyone else. What was it?"

"'Anyone else' includes you, Rhona."

"Don't you trust me?"

"It's not my secret to tell." He placed a warning finger across her lips. "So don't ask." He lay back, with one arm comfortably propped behind his head. "Have you a purchase in mind? What about that fellow trying to convince Heledd that what a rich widow really needs is a noble widower?"

Rhonwen wrinkled her nose. "Not my type. His standard-bearer isn't bad, though."

She expected him to chuckle and wish her luck, but instead something very like jealousy flitted across his face. "You aren't the first woman to say that," he said waspishly, and added, "You're well in there. He likes dark-haired women."

Rhonwen looked at him in some astonishment. "Do you know him?"

He had regained his composure and his lighthearted manner. "Not to introduce you, if that's what you were hoping. I know his lord, though. He was Ceretic's envoy to Eboracum all last winter."

"Is that why you've been keeping your head down since he arrived?"

"Yes," he said wryly. "It gets very tiresome. There are too many people in Elmet who might recognise me, and I can't hide in barns for ever. So we have to go a long way away."

"Ashhere thinks you're going to Pictland."

Eadwine grinned. "Good. So does everyone on the March. We even set off north, before doubling back to Eboracum. Aethelferth can have a happy time trying to work out which of his Pictish allies has given me shelter behind his back. That should keep him busy for a while."

"Is Ashhere right? Your friends have got a bet on it."

"They always have a bet on something," he yawned. "I try not to pay attention."

Rhonwen giggled. "Did you know, there was a bet that you were going back to Eboracum for Aethelind? That's why that shield changed hands and then changed back again when it got light and they saw it was me."

Eadwine groaned sleepily. "I wish they'd find something else to wager on."

"Well, your decisions affect them, so it's not surprising they try to guess what you're going to do." She studied him. He was drowsy and relaxed, off his guard. A good time. "The other half of the bet was that you were going back to the hills for the doctor."

His eyes snapped open and his whole body tensed. "It's none of their damned business!"

That hit a sore spot, Rhonwen thought. "Are you? From what your friends told me, I hope you are. You're the kind of man who needs a woman."

He laughed. "Most men need women."

"No," she said crisply, "in my experience – which is a lot more extensive than yours, I may add – what most men need is a convenient hole. You're at least as interested in the rest of the woman. You like to talk and laugh as much as to make love. You need a heart and mind to share as well as a body. And you found that with the doctor, didn't you?"

"It's very bad manners to discuss one woman while in bed with another," he said lightly.

"Oh, nonsense!" Rhonwen captured his hand. "And stop trying to distract me! Who else can you talk to sensibly about matters of the heart? It's not as if I want you for myself. If it embarrasses you we'll get dressed, though that seems a terrible waste of your last night. Now, then. Are you going back for her?"

He turned his face away. "I can't."

That was a response Rhonwen had not expected. "Why ever not?"

A pause and then, wretchedly, "She's married."

Oh, Blessed Lady Mary, Rhonwen thought, exasperated, *can't you do better than this?* Aloud, she said, "I thought her husband was missing, probably dead?"

"She insists he will come back."

"Well, she would, until she found someone else," Rhonwen said robustly. "As a wife she controls her husband's goods, as a widow she'd be living on the charity of either his family or hers. Not many women would accept that unless it was forced on them."

Eadwine recalled Severa's words. *My husband was not so complimentary – he had second thoughts, but I was well dowered – at Samhain a man who married for the dowry can seek out the woman he would rather have had.* There was nothing there to suggest her marriage had been a love match. And she had not been drunk on the night of the escape from the fort, and there had been no doubt of her feelings for him then. Except –

He said, in a small voice, "I asked her to come. When we parted. But she would not."

Rhonwen clicked her tongue impatiently. "Because you were rushing back to look for Aethelind, weren't you? And I bet you'd told her that, hadn't you? What were you planning to do with her when you found Aethelind? Keep her as a mistress? Drop one or other of them? Live in a delicious little threesome? No wonder she wouldn't come!"

Eadwine winced. "All right, Rhona, I'm a fool. I know it. You needn't rub it in."

"Ah, my dear. But you're free now. You have a second chance."

"What, ask her to leave her home and run off with a homeless exile?" He laughed bitterly. "No woman would do that, wife or widow."

"I did."

Eadwine raised himself on one elbow. "You never told me that."

"It wasn't any of your business." A dreamy note came into Rhonwen's voice. "Elphin, his name was. He was a horse breeder and trader and, to be honest, I think he was a horse thief too. I was a year married, to a pleasant enough man, a minor landowner, who didn't hit me or fart in bed, and I was content enough. Until we went to a horse fair and I saw Elphin. I couldn't take my eyes off him all day. He was so handsome, with the looks of a god and a laugh like sunshine on a spring morning. And two days later he came looking for me. He had seen me, and wanted me too, and I went with him. I could have asked my husband for a divorce in the Brittonic way and reclaimed my dowry, but Elphin would have had to pay him compensation and it would have taken time, and Elphin did not want to wait and neither did I. So I declared the marriage over, and abandoned my dowry to my husband, and married Elphin the next day, and left my comfortable house and my comfortable life for a tent at fairs and a lean-to shack against the city wall and never knowing where the next meal was coming from. And we were happy. I never knew joy like that before, nor ever hope to again. He was mine and I was his, and nothing else mattered in this world or the next."

Eadwine recognised that feeling. "What became of him?"

"He died," Rhonwen said simply. "There was an argument over the ownership of a horse, a brawl, someone had a knife and I was a widow –" She bit her lip to stifle a sob, and went on, more steadily, "His family would not take me in once it was clear I was not carrying his child and had no claim on them. My father said I had disgraced his name and wasted my dowry and turned me from his door. My first husband and his friends and kin scorned me for a scarlet woman, though one of them liked me well enough to take me in on condition I earned my keep in his bed. When he was tired of me he passed me on to a friend he owed a favour to, and he to another, and so I came to the house in Eboracum where I met you. No, he was not my uncle. I lied to you because I did not want you to think badly of me."

"Poor Rhona. I did not know."

"Poor?" She laughed. "I had fifteen months in Paradise while Elphin lived, whatever misery came after. Many people never know a love like that in a lifetime. I count myself a lucky woman. My dear, do you understand what I am telling you? A chance of happiness is a rare and precious thing in this life. Do not squander it."

"She said much the same thing once," Eadwine murmured.

"Did she? Then I think you have your answer."

***

Ashhere nudged Weasel and pointed up at the lowering cliffs above, silhouetted by the rising sun. "That's Kyndyr. I've been up there, you know."

"Oh, yes?" said Weasel, a city boy to his fingertips and profoundly unimpressed by scenery, however spectacular.

"That's where the witch – I mean, Severa – led us. Across to that waterfall up there. In the dark it was, and there were two trolls, and nothing but rocks and peat for miles and miles." He looked round to the south-east. "I suppose that means Navio valley is just two ridges that way – Oh." He beamed. "Now I know where Eadwine was going last night!"

Drust grinned at Lilla in triumph. "Come on, laddie, give me the sword. I havena forgot our bet."

"What are you three sniggering about?" Treowin grumbled, coming back from collecting water. "And where the hell has Eadwine got to? I don't want to hang about in this dump any longer than we have to."

"Hear, hear," agreed Weasel, with feeling. "They're savages up 'ere."

"You needn't worry, Weasel, nobody's going to eat you," Ashhere laughed. "You'd give anything a stomach-ache."

"Savages," echoed Treowin, crossly. "They burn witches alive in these hills."

The laughter died.

"What did you say?" Lilla demanded.

"They burn witches alive," Treowin repeated. "You heard me the first time."

"Who told you that?"

Treowin looked from one to the other, puzzled. "That fellow who was courting Lady Heledd. He was up somewhere in these hills in the early winter, hunting for Eadwine as it happens, and fell in with a mountain brigand who had some sort of grudge against a girl in the village he said was a witch. Well, some prisoners escaped from the brigand, and he blamed the witch and had her barred into a – what's the word? – a chapel, and burned it down with her in it. Pretty little thing apparently, black hair and green eyes. His standard-bearer wanted to buy her as a slave but the brigand wouldn't have it – What are you staring at me like that for?"

"By the Hammer!" muttered Ashhere, aghast, touching both his amulets in turn.

"Did you tell Eadwine this?" Lilla demanded.

Treowin shrugged. "Yes, it's not a secret, is it?"

"May the Great Mother care for her," Drust said gruffly. He handed the sword back to Lilla. "Go on, laddie, take it back. I dinna care to win a bet like this."

"Will someone tell me what the hell is going on?" Treowin exploded. Hurrying footsteps splashing across the stream made him turn. "Ah, Eadwine, there you are! About time. This lot have gone completely mad –"

He broke off. Eadwine was chalk-white, his face etched with lines of pain, his eyes glassy as though he was focussed on some inward vision. And his hands and face and clothes were smeared with wood ash and charcoal.

"And what have you been doing all night?" Treowin demanded. "By all the gods, you look as if you've been raking through a funeral pyre –"

"Shut up!" Drust hissed. "Just shut up!"

***

No-one spoke all day. No-one was surprised when Eadwine volunteered for the first watch of the night, or that he slipped off alone as soon as it was over. Lilla followed and found him sitting hunched against a tree, staring at something that gleamed dully silver in his palm.

"She might have escaped," he said. "You said yourself it's possible to escape a hall-burning."

"There was charred human bone among the ashes."

Lilla swallowed. "It might not have been her."

"Who else could it have been? And besides – there was this."

He held out the object in his palm and Lilla saw that it was a shapeless lump of silvery metal with a blue-veined stone pooled in it. It looked like Severa's betrothal pendant, discoloured and melted by some great heat.

"It isn't fair!" Lilla burst out. "She didn't deserve to die!"

"That could be said of many," Eadwine answered bitterly. "Since when do the Three Ladies care what you deserve? All they care for is what amuses them." He closed his hand over the melted pendant. "She had the choice of being a mistress, as she thought, or a slave, and she chose neither. A cruel choice, a false choice. If I had only known –!"

Lilla's throat closed up. "It – it – isn't your fault," he stammered, "it w-was us she rescued –"

"It was Navio's fault. May he be cursed by every god in the nine worlds!" Eadwine's knuckles showed white on his clenched hand. "And one day I will make him pay for it."

"When you do, remember I owe him vengeance for what he did to Luned. Even if it was a long while ago."

Eadwine did not answer.

"It wouldn't have worked," Lilla hurried on, too quickly. "Me and Luned, I mean. It's better like this." He found a smile. "The world is full of girls. I'll find another. So will you."

"Go away, Lilla," Eadwine said, sounding very tired. "And never mention her again, understand?"

Lilla turned back once, to see him sitting still and silent, turning the pendant over and over in his hand.

***

"Isn't it about time we turned south?" Treowin complained, as they were trussing packs and preparing to set off in the early morning, some days later. "We cleared the hills yesterday, but you're still heading west. This can't be the way to Lundencaster."

"I told you, we aren't going to Lundencaster," Eadwine answered.

"Where, then?"

The others looked up, wondering if they were going to get an answer at last.

"Gwynedd."

215

Ashhere looked at Lilla, who looked at Weasel, who shrugged. None of them had ever heard of it.

Treowin had, and reacted as if he had been told they were going to the Underworld. "A *Brittonic* kingdom? You're mad! Eadwine –"

"And don't use that name again." Eadwine included them all in a harsh look. "Not even between ourselves, understand? If it comes to Aethelferth's ears I'm dead, and most likely so are the rest of you."

"What should we call you?" Lilla asked. "Steeleye?"

A shadow crossed Eadwine's face. Severa had called him by that name. "No. I'll think of something else."

"But why Gwynedd?" Treowin protested.

"Because Iago Gwynedd is the strongest Brittonic king south of the Wall. Aethelferth will think at least twice before interfering in his lands. Besides, it's not an obvious place to look for an Anglian exile, is it?"

"No, it bloody isn't," said Treowin, with feeling. "Why can't you stay with your own kind?"

Eadwine regarded him with a level stare. "It was you that said I should go somewhere where other gods rule."

"Well, yes, but does it have to be Brittonic? They can't be trusted, you know."

The stare became cold. "My mother was Brittonic, in case you'd forgotten."

Treowin brightened. "Oh, I keep forgetting you're half-foreign. These kings of Gwynedd, are they family?"

"They're the hereditary enemies of my mother's house," Eadwine answered, with a straight face. "But that isn't going to matter, because Iago isn't going to know who I am."

"Then why should he give us refuge?"

"He isn't going to give us anything," Eadwine said coolly. "He's going to beg us to do him the favour of joining his warband." He got to his feet. "He doesn't know it yet, but he is."

Ashhere watched the tall, straight figure stride away up the track. Eadwine had lost everything except his life. His lands, his wealth, his position, his woman, his kingdom, his home, even his name, all were gone. And yet he was starting out on the long, hard, dangerous road to win them all back. Ashhere could not begin to imagine how it was to be done, but he knew it would never be dull.

He squared his shoulders, took a firmer grip on his spear, and followed his lord into exile.

The End

Historical Note

When I finish reading a historical novel, I always want to know what parts of the story are documented history, what the author made up to fill in gaps, and what (if anything) the author changed from documented facts. If anyone else shares this interest, this note is for you.

The novel is first and foremost a work of the imagination. My rule throughout has been that where I could find a solid fact, I would not change it. But solid facts are rare indeed in seventh-century Britain, and most of the story in *Paths of Exile* is my invention.

The primary source for seventh-century English history is the *Ecclesiastical History of the English People*, written in 731 AD by Bede, a monk at the monastery of Jarrow in modern Northumberland. I work from the modern English translation published by Penguin Classics. Other sources for the period include the *Historia Brittonum* believed to have been written (possibly by a monk called Nennius) in the ninth century, the Anglo-Saxon Chronicle, genealogies of medieval Welsh kings, Welsh poetry, the *Annales Cambriae*, the Welsh Triads, various medieval chroniclers, and a few stories in Geoffrey of Monmouth's *History of the Kings of Britain*. All of these were written down very much later than Bede's history, though they may well preserve kernels of older tradition. Where the sources conflict, I generally give Bede primacy because of the early date of his account.

***

Eadwine existed. Bede tells us he was the son of Aelle, and that he was driven out of Deira by Aethelferth. The later part of Eadwine's career is described by Bede (*Ecclesiastical History* Book 2, chapters 9–20), so anyone who wants to know how the story worked out in the end is welcome to look it up. Bede tells us very little of Eadwine's early life, saying only 'When Aethelferth was persecuting him, Eadwine wandered as an unknown fugitive for many years through many lands and kingdoms'. From Bede's information on the date of Eadwine's death and his age at death, it can be deduced that he was born some time around 585 AD. From information on Aethelferth's reign length in Deira and Bernicia given in Bede and *Historia Brittonum*, it can be deduced that Aethelferth annexed Deira around 605 AD, and therefore Eadwine was about twenty when he was driven into exile. Something of Eadwine's character can be gleaned from Bede's account, though Bede was a Northumbrian and may have given Eadwine an excessively good press out of patriotism. It is also fair to say that he was writing a century after the events and may have had an unduly rosy view of the 'good old days'. Medieval Welsh poems such as the *Moliant Cadwallon*, and the medieval Welsh Triads give a less favourable picture of Eadwine's character. It is my intention in this and subsequent novels to show both sides. There is some evidence from the Welsh Triads that Eadwine spent some time in Gwynedd (North Wales), and slight evidence from Bede that he knew of and admired Britain's Roman heritage. If the timber amphitheatre discovered in archaeological excavations at Yeavering is attributable to Eadwine's reign it would also be consistent with knowledge of and respect for Roman ways. Everything else in the story concerning Eadwine is my invention.

King Aelle of Deira existed, and ruled some time in the late sixth century as implied by Bede's account of Pope Gregory's encounter with Anglian slave boys in Rome some time before 597 AD. It is not known when Aelle became King of Deira or when and how he died.

King Aethelferth of Bernicia existed, and ruled Bernicia from 593 AD. Bede tells us that he was a very powerful and ambitious king who conquered large areas of British-controlled territory and who beat the King of Dal Riada (modern Argyll in West Scotland) in a decisive battle in 603 AD. Bede also tells us that he never gave up pursuing Eadwine, though the reason why is not known. He was indeed married to Eadwine's sister Acha, and from the dates given in Bede it is possible to work out that their son Oswald was born in 604 AD and therefore that Aethelferth and Acha must have been married at latest by early that year. *Historia Brittonum* says that Aethelferth was king of Bernicia for twelve years before he also became king of Deira, which places the date of the annexation around 605 AD. The method of Aethelferth's annexation of Deira is not known, but given Aethelferth's undoubted prowess as a warlord and the fact of his hostile relations with Eadwine, it seems very likely that it was by military force. Aethelferth's nickname 'Flesaurs', usually translated into modern English as 'The Artful' or 'The Twister', is recorded in *Historia Brittonum*.

Hereric existed and was Eadwine's nephew. It is not known whether Hereric was the son of a sister of Eadwine or of a brother, and his date of birth is not known. Bede tells us that Hereric fathered two daughters, one of whom was born in 614 AD, and therefore a minimum age can be conjectured. Bede also tells us that Hereric lived in Elmet during Aethelferth's reign in Deira. Everything else concerning Hereric is my invention.

King Ceretic of Elmet existed, and was king of Elmet during part or all of Aethelferth's reign in Deira, though the date of his accession is not known.

Osric of Deira, son of Eadwine's uncle Aelfric and therefore Eadwine's cousin, existed, though it is not known what happened to him during Aethelferth's reign in Deira.

Aethelric of Deira – there is confusion here. Bede does not mention him, but other sources preserve a tradition that there was a king called Aethelric in Deira who ruled briefly sometime between Aelle and Aethelferth, with a reign length of five years cited by some sources. If this Aethelric existed, his relationship to Aelle and Eadwine is not known. If he existed, he may have been confused with Aethelferth's father, Aethelric of Bernicia. Such a confusion could be the source of the assertion in some sources, often repeated in modern discussions, that Eadwine was driven into exile in 588 AD aged about three. I decided to make Aethelric of Deira a separate individual from Aethelferth's father, and to make him a cousin of Eadwine and a client king ruling as Aethelferth's puppet. This could account for his absence from Bede but also explain his appearance elsewhere.

Lilla existed, and Bede tells us that he was Eadwine's thane and best friend and describes the date and manner of his death. Nothing else is known.

A thane called Fordhere also existed and is mentioned in Bede, but all we are told is the date and manner of his death.

King Caedbaed of Lindsey is mentioned in the genealogy of the kings of Lindsey and his position in the list puts him in approximately the early seventh century. Nothing is known of him.

King Aethelbert of Kent, according to Bede, was overlord of all the English kingdoms of southern Britain in 604 AD and died in 616 AD.

King Iago of Gwynedd is mentioned in medieval Welsh genealogies and in the Welsh Triads and the traditions associated with him date him to the early seventh century.

All the other people and events in the story are my invention.

***

At the end of *Paths of Exile* we have reached early spring in 606 AD. There are still nearly eleven years to go before Bede takes up the story, so Eadwine and his friends will fight again.

***

I hope you enjoyed reading the novel. If you have any comments or questions, why not get in touch? I like to hear from readers, and can be contacted by email at: author@carlanayland.org.

Note on proper names

A small number of Old English personal names survived into later centuries and are still in use as Christian names (e.g. Edward, Edwin, Alfred). I have deliberately used archaic spellings for such names (e.g. Eadweard, Eadwine, Aelfred), for consistency with the many other Old English names that did not survive and do not have modern spellings.

The name Rhonwen is, as far as I know, a Welsh form of the English name Rowena and is not attested before Geoffrey of Monmouth. However, the man's name Rhun is recorded in 6th- and 7th-century contexts, and it seems not unreasonable to me that there might also have been an equivalent feminine form (Rhunwen, or Rhonwen) in use at the same time.

I have deliberately avoided using regional, ethnic or linguistic labels that still have meaning in a British context today. So I refer to the island as Britannia (not Britain), its Romano-British inhabitants and their language as Brittonic (not British or Welsh), and its Early English inhabitants and their language(s) as Anglian or Saxon (not English).

Where the place names of the period are recorded or can reasonably be conjectured, I have used them. Some of them, such as river and hill names, are still in use in the present day. Where multiple names are recorded for the same place (e.g. York was called Eboracum in Latin texts, Caer Ebrawg in medieval Welsh poetry, and Eoforwic by the early English), I have used the one which seemed most appropriate in the context. Where place names have been lost, for example in regions that would probably have spoken Brittonic languages at the time but now have English or Norse place names, I have invented place names that seem to me reasonable for the places described and have given them in modern English. For the most part these are topographical names (e.g. Black Hill, Stony Ford, Shivering Mountain), with a handful of mythological names (e.g. Portal of Annwn). This roughly reflects the form of modern place names in Welsh and Scots Gaelic, and therefore seems reasonable for an earlier relative of these cultures.

All the places described are real places. The glossary gives their modern equivalents, so the interested reader can identify them on a modern map such as a motoring atlas if so inclined. The major places are also plotted on the sketch map at the front of the book. Where I have been able to find out what the place looked like at the time (e.g. the Roman fortifications at York) I have described them faithfully. Otherwise I have made what seems to me to be a reasonable estimate, based where possible on evidence from similar sites elsewhere. I should admit here that the excavated Roman sewer at Church Street in York is only 1m high, and in the novel I describe a sewer (in a different part of the city) as about 2m high because otherwise it would have been a most unpleasant obstacle for Heledd to negotiate. Routes of Roman roads are derived from published sources, mostly from the Ordnance Survey map of Roman Britain.

219

Glossary of place names

Ardotalia	Melandra Castle Roman Fort, Glossop, Derbyshire. The English Place-Name Society is of the view that 'Melandra' is the invention of an 18th-century antiquarian, and that Ardotalia is the most likely Roman name of the fort
Beacon Bay	Whitby, Yorkshire (translation of Streanashalch)
Bebbanburgh	Bamburgh, Northumberland
Bernicia	Kingdom occupying roughly the area of modern Northumberland and parts of south-east Scotland
Bleak Hills*	Bleaklow Hill, Derbyshire
Boggle Bay*	Robin Hood's Bay, Yorkshire. Boggle Hole is still a local landmark at the southern edge of the bay, and the local name for the village is Bay Town. I have combined the two to invent a possible early name.
Britannia	The island of Britain
Caer Luel	Carlisle
Caerlegion	Chester
Calcacaster	Tadcaster, Yorkshire
Calchvynydd**	White Peak District, Derbyshire
Catraeth	Catterick Bridge Roman Fort, Yorkshire
Chilbage Brook	Ladybower Brook, Derbyshire. Chilbage Brook is recorded in a document of 1656. No meaning is known, nor are there earlier forms of the name recorded.
Combe*	Hope, Derbyshire
Dal Riada	Kingdom occupying roughly the area of modern Argyll
Deira	Kingdom occupying roughly the area of modern Yorkshire
Derwent Bridge*	Bamford, Derbyshire (from Bamford = beam ford = ford where there used to be a bridge built of beams)
Derwent Hafod*	Shieling at the confluence of Abbey Brook and River Derwent, beneath the present site of Howden Reservoir, Derbyshire
Derwent Stone*	Hope Cross, Derbyshire
Derwent Vale*	Valley of the River Derwent, Yorkshire, east of York city
Derwentcaster*	Malton Roman Fort, Yorkshire
Eboracum	York Roman Legionary Fortress. Also called Eoforcaster (Anglian) and Caer Ebrawg (Brittonic)
Eboracum Vale*	Vale of York, west of York city
Elmet	Kingdom occupying the area around modern Leeds
Eoforwic	Anglian settlement just south of York Roman Legionary Fortress, between the rivers Foss and Ouse
Fulla's cabins*	Fylingthorpe, North York Moors
Gododdin, kingdom of	Kingdom occupying roughly the area of modern Lothian and Edinburgh
Great Stone Edge*	Stanage Edge and Froggatt/Curbar/Baslow Edges, Derbyshire
Great Wall*	Hadrian's Wall

Guardian Howe*	Lilla Howe, North York Moors
Gwynedd	Kingdom occupying roughly modern North-west Wales
Heatherford*	Hathersage, Derbyshire
Home of the Gods*	Goodmanham, Yorkshire
Kyndyr	Kinder Scout, Derbyshire
Lindsey	Kingdom occupying roughly modern Lincolnshire
Loidis	Leeds
Lousy Hill Lane	Road linking Littlebeck with Red Gate, North York Moors. It's a modern name but too wonderfully descriptive to resist.
Lundencaster	London Roman Fort
Navio	Navio Roman Fort, Brough, Derbyshire
Picts, kingdom of	Kingdom occupying modern North and East Highlands of Scotland, north of the Forth valley and east of the main mountain spine. 'Picts' is a Latin name and their own name for themselves is not known.
Portal of Annwn*	Peak Cavern, Derbyshire
Rheged	Kingdom occupying modern Cumbria, southern Galloway and part of Lancashire
Shivering Mountain*	Mam Tor, Derbyshire. The hill is locally known as Shivering Mountain because of the frequent landslips on its southern face.
Strat Clut	Kingdom occupying the area of modern Strathclyde
Swine Hill	Lose Hill, Derbyshire (from hlose hyll = pigsty hill)
Water of Annwn*	Peakhole Water, Derbyshire
Wharfedale	Modern Wharfedale. Heledd's hall is imaginary, somewhere near modern Ilkley. I'm afraid 'dale' is an anachronism because it is derived from a Norse word that wouldn't have been in use in Britain for another two centuries, but it has the benefit of being recognisable.
Withy Hill	Win Hill, Derbyshire ('withy hill' recorded in late 13th century)

* Invented name

** Name documented but location uncertain. Various modern authorities place it in the Chilterns and in the area around Kelso; I have chosen to place it in the White Peak. As it is a descriptive topographical name (its elements mean 'chalk or limestone hills or uplands'), it is quite possible that several places with chalk or limestone uplands had this name in the seventh century, just as there are several hills called Ben More ('big hill') in modern Scotland.

***

It should be noted that the boundaries of the kingdoms are not known with any certainty and probably fluctuated considerably over time according to the relative military strength of their own and neighbouring kings.

LaVergne, TN USA
06 October 2009

160003LV00003B/163/P